'Though the damaged series detective is a familiar figure in crime fiction, Meyer is far too good a writer for this to matter. Griessel is very much his own man, juggling the demands of his career with those of his equally testing private life. The narrative is well-plotted, and the novel brings to live the rich and volatile diversity of contemporary South Africa. There's nothing flash here, just a good story, very well told. Would there were more like it.'
Spectator

'The reader is plunged into a maelstrom of murder investigation, political corruption, racial tension and the clock is ticking for that all-too-human cop Benny Griessel who is also fighting his battle with alcohol on an emotional second front this time . . . Deon Meyer is a top notch plotter and has created one of the best ensemble (and multi-racial) cast of any modern police procedural series.'
Shots

'There is no gainsaying the sheer momentum of the storytelling. And there is a key thing to praise in 7 DAYS: how does Meyer manage to make the hoariest cliché of crime fiction – the alcoholic copper – read as if we've never encountered this device?'
Independent

'7 DAYS is a clever blend of an Agatha Christie detective novel and a Frederick Forsyth thriller, with the carefully dropped clues (which I missed) and all the explicit detail of a gripping thriller . . . 7 DAYS is one of the best books I have read this year, because as well as the tension and thrills you learn so much about a very complex country.'
Crime Scraps

About the Author

Deon Meyer lives in Durbanville in South Africa with his wife and four children. Other than his family, Deon's big passions are motorcycling, music, reading, cooking and rugby. In January 2008 he retired from his day job as a consultant on brand strategy for BMW Motorrad, and is now a full-time author.

Deon Meyer's books have attracted worldwide critical acclaim and a growing international fanbase. Originally written in Afrikaans, they have now been translated into twenty-five languages.

Find out more about Deon Meyer and his books:
Visit his website at www.deonmeyer.com
Follow Deon on Twitter at @MeyerDeon

Also by Deon Meyer

Trackers

Thirteen Hours

Blood Safari

Devil's Peak

Heart of the Hunter

Dead at Daybreak

Dead Before Dying

DEON
MEYER

7DAYS

*Translated from Afrikaans
by K. L. Seegers*

HODDER

First published in Great Britain in 2012 by Hodder & Stoughton
An Hachette UK company

Originally published in Afrikaans in 2012 as *7 Dae* by Human & Rousseau

This paperback edition first published in 2013

1

A CIP catalogue record for this title is available from the British Library.

A Format ISBN 978 1 444 75176 5
B Format ISBN 978 1 444 72372 4

Typeset in Plantin Light by Hewer Text UK Ltd, Edinburgh

Printed and bound by Clays Ltd, St Ives plc

Hodder & Stoughton policy is to use papers that are natural, renewable
and recyclable products and made from wood grown in sustainable forests.
The logging and manufacturing processes are expected to conform to the
environmental regulations of the country of origin.

Hodder & Stoughton Ltd
338 Euston Road
London NW1 3BH

www.hodder.co.uk

For Anita

Day 1
Saturday

I

Whatever happened, he just didn't want to make a complete idiot of himself.

Detective Captain Benny Griessel was wearing a new suit of clothes that he could ill afford. There was a bouquet of flowers on the passenger seat, his hands gripping the steering wheel were clammy, and with all his being he yearned for the healing, calming powers of alcohol. Tonight he must just please not make a total idiot of himself. Not in front of Alexa Barnard, not in front of all the stars of the music world, not after all the past week's planning and preparation.

He'd started on Monday, with a haircut. Tuesday, Mat Joubert's wife, Margaret, had been his style consultant at Romens in Tyger Valley. 'It's smart casual, Benny, just a pair of chinos and a smart shirt,' she had said patiently in her charming English accent.

'No, I want a jacket too.' Griessel had dug in his heels, terrified of being caught between too 'casual' and not 'smart' enough. There would be some smart people there.

He had wanted a tie as well, but Margaret had put her foot down. 'Overdressed is worse than underdressed. No tie.' They had left with khaki chinos, a light blue cotton shirt, black belt, black shoes, a fashionable black jacket, and a credit card bill that made him shudder.

Since Wednesday he had been mentally preparing himself. He knew this thing, this event, had the potential to overwhelm him completely. His greatest fear was that he would swear, because that was what he always did when he got stressed. He would have to guard his tongue, all evening. No police-speak, no crude language, talk nice, stay calm. He had gone through it all in his imagination, visualised it, as Doc Barkhuizen, his sponsor at Alcoholics Anonymous, had prescribed.

To Anton L'Amour he would say: '*Kouevuur* is brilliant guitar.' That's all, no waxing lyrical and talking shit. To Theuns Jordaan: 'I like your work a lot.' That was a good thing to say, full of respect and appreciation, dignified. Lord, and if Schalk Joubert was there, he, Benny Griessel would take a deep breath, shake his hand and just say: 'Pleased to meet you, it's a great honour.' Then he had better walk away before the flood of words of hero worship, admiration of Joubert's mastery of bass guitar, spilled over all his careful defences.

Then, his biggest worry: Lize Beekman.

If he could just have one drink before he met her. To keep his nerves from getting out of control. He would have to dry his hand on his new trousers first, he couldn't greet Lize Beekman with his palm all sweaty. 'Miss Beekman, it's an exceptional honour. Your music gives me great pleasure.' And she would say 'thank you', and he would leave it at that and go and find Alexa, because that was the only way he would keep from making a total idiot of himself.

The white Chana panel van stopped under the trees in Second Avenue, between the Livingstone High School and the back yard of the South African Police Service's Claremont Station.

It was a nondescript vehicle, a 2009 model bearing the marks of hard labour – a dent in the front bumper, scrapes and scratches on the doors at the back. The windows in the middle and rear were blanked out with cheap white paint.

The side panels differed slightly in colour from the rest of the vehicle.

Behind the wheel, the sniper turned off the engine, put both hands on his knees and sat, for just a moment, dead still.

He wore a blue labourer's overall, slightly faded. Long blond hair hung down his back, a brown baseball cap was pulled down low over his eyes.

With deliberate focus he looked out of the passenger window at the deserted school grounds. Then right. He studied the high fence across the street, the double wire gate, and behind it, the SAPS yard, wrapped in the early-evening shadow of Table Mountain. It was quiet and deserted.

He made sure both doors in front were locked, clambered over the seat to the back. The storage space was untidy, boxes and trunks of metal, wood and cardboard. He sat down on a wooden box and loosened the home-made screen of faded yellow material from the carpet-lined roof. It separated him from the driver's cab, making him invisible to passers-by.

He took off the cap, laid it to one side, aware that he was breathing faster, his hands trembling slightly. He relaxed his shoulders with a forced sigh, bent down, opened a long, battered tool chest, and took out the removable tray. It was heavy, filled with well-worn tools – hammers, a collection of screwdrivers, cutters and pliers, metal saw blades. He put it gently down beside the chest, on the rubber matting covering the floor of the Chana.

There were two articles in the bottom of the red box – a firearm and a K-Way Kilimanjaro Trekking Pole.

He took out the hiking pole first, and propped it against his shoulder, picked up the rifle, pressed the silencer carefully through the black wrist strap on the end of the stick, so that the telescope of the rifle was not interfered with, and twisted the stick anti-clockwise until the loop was tight.

He pressed his cheek to the rifle butt, tested the height of the supporting hiking pole, and made an adjustment.

He slid the Chana's right side panel three centimetres to the right with the small handle he had attached. Then the magnetic panel outside, so he could aim the barrel and telescope outwards.

He pressed the rifle butt to his shoulder and looked at the SAPS car park through the scope. He adjusted the focus.

In front of the big Victorian house in Brownlow Street, Griessel picked up the bouquet, got out of the car and walked through the little garden gate to the front door.

Alexa Barnard was in the process of renovating the house. The ugly giant cactus against the front fence had been recently removed, the painters' scaffolding stood high against the walls.

It was all part of her recovery, he thought. Her new life.

He came to a halt at the front door, looked at his shoes. They gleamed.

He took a deep breath. What if he had misunderstood the whole thing, and it was a black-tie affair tonight, and Alexa opened the door in some exotic evening dress? Or it was totally informal, denims and open-neck shirts? He had never been to a music industry cocktail party before.

He rang the doorbell, heard her coming down the stairs.

The door opened. She stood in front of him.

'*Jissis*,' said Griessel.

Through the peephole the sniper saw the police van drive by close to the Chana. It slowed, ready for the turn in at the wide gate.

He waited for it to reappear in the car park in his field of vision. He kept his cheek pressed to the rifle butt, followed the van through the scope.

Only one occupant, in uniform.

The van drove over the tarred surface to the middle of the open area. It parked behind two other SAPS vehicles where he couldn't see it.

Between seventy and eighty metres, he guessed.

As he aimed the cross hairs on the front of one of the vehicles, waiting for the policeman to appear, he suddenly became aware of the beating of his heart.

He took a deep breath.

The uniform appeared in the telescope. A constable.

Difficult shot, moving target.

He aimed low, followed the movement, forced himself to stick to his procedure: keep the horizontal axis of the scope level, cross hairs on the target, breathe out, press the trigger gently, keep your eye open.

The rifle kicked softly against his shoulder, the muffled blurt of the shot was louder than he had expected, within the Chana's enclosed space.

A miss.

'You look . . .' Griessel wanted to say '*befok*', but he restrained himself, searched desperately for an acceptable word, one that would do her breathtaking appearance justice. '. . . fantastic.' She was standing there in a strapless black dress that draped to her ankles, a wide, tan leather belt just below her generous breasts, light brown platform sandals.

And her face – he had never seen her like this: carefully and skilfully made up, red, full lips, blonde hair cut and coloured, big silver hearts as earrings, her eyes a deep green behind long lashes.

For one fleeting moment he wondered, after everything, whether he would kiss her tonight for the first time.

She laughed and looked at him approvingly. 'You too, Benny.' Then, 'Are the flowers for me?'

'Oh. Yes . . .' He held them out to her awkwardly.

There was a blush on her cheeks, genuine appreciation for him, for this gesture.

'Thank you very much.' She stepped forward and kissed Griessel on the cheek.

He knew from experience the shot was barely audible outside, thanks to the silencer and the pieces of carpet glued to the Chana's interior. His palms perspired against the gun and his heart thumped. He worked the bolt, and the bullet casing sprang out, clinked against one of the toolboxes. He pushed another round into the chamber. He moved the weapon slightly, saw through the scope that the constable was unaware of the failed shot, his head turned away towards the mountain.

He aimed down, found the constable's legs in the cross hairs.

He led two, three centimetres ahead of moving legs, knee height, the panic blooming from the pit of his stomach, breathe, breathe, exhale slowly . . . He squeezed the trigger. Saw the constable fall.

Relief. Smell of cordite in his nostrils.

Then, urgency, knowing he must concentrate now, the next sixty seconds were make or break, do everything exactly according to the plan.

Unwind the strap of the support stick. Withdraw the rifle from the loop. Lay the weapon in the toolbox. Put the tray over it. Close the box. The pole can stay there.

Lift up the cloth drape.

The cap. Put on the cap.

He climbed through to the driver's seat.

Do not look at the target, do not, but the anxiety threatened to overwhelm him, so he quickly turned his head to see. The constable was eighty metres away, lying there. He was looking down, probably at his leg.

Look in front of you.

Turn the key, start the Chana, pull away slowly, only ten metres and you will be out of sight, seconds, not enough for the constable to see you, to notice, he will be in shock, confused. Don't attract attention, do everything calmly, normally.

He put the vehicle in gear. And drove away.

2

At the entrance to the Artscape Chandelier Foyer Griessel stared at the giant poster. In big letters it proclaimed *Anton Goosen Birthday Concert, Friday 4 March, Grand Arena*, with a photo below of all the stars who would be performing there in a week's time. Alexa Barnard was the focal point, right in the middle, just below the smaller announcement which used her stage name: *Xandra Barnard is back!*

And here he was with *that* legend on the arm of his new jacket. He swallowed hard, and held himself together.

Inside. Lots of people. He quickly surveyed the men, what they were wearing. Relief washed over him, because there were a lot of jackets. He relaxed a little, everything was going to be OK.

Heads turned towards Alexa, people called out her name, and suddenly they were surrounded. Alexa let go of his arm and began greeting people. Griessel stood back. He had suspected this would happen and was happy she was getting this reception. Last week she had been nervous and had told him: 'I've been out of it for so long, Benny. And that whole thing with Adam's death . . . I don't know what to expect.'

Adam had been her husband. Benny had investigated his murder; that was how he had met her.

'You're Paul Eilers, the actor,' someone said right beside

him. Then he realised the pretty young woman was talking to *him*.

'No,' he said. 'I'm Benny Griessel.'

'I could have sworn you were Paul Eilers,' she said, disappointed, and then she was gone.

He recognised some of the music stars. Laurika Rauch folding Alexa's hands in hers, saying something with great tenderness. Karen Zoid and Gian Groen in conversation. Emo Adams making Sonja Herholdt laugh out loud.

Where was Lize Beekman?

A waiter pushed through the mass of bodies, came past with a tray full of champagne glasses, offered him one. He stared at the golden liquid, the bubbles lazily drifting upwards, and felt the stirring inside, the desire. He came to his senses, shook his head. No, thank you.

Two hundred and twenty-seven days without a drink.

Maybe he ought to get himself a soft drink, something to hold in his hand, rather than just standing here, a dull island in a sea of glitterati. Look at Alexa, she was at home, in her element, she glowed.

Jissis. What was he doing here?

When he met Schalk Joubert the moment was almost too big for him.

'Schalk, this is Benny Griessel, he also plays bass,' Alexa introduced him, and he could feel his face turn red. With a trembling hand, 'Pleased to meet you, it's a helluva privilege.' His voice was hoarse and he was startled by the swear word that slipped out.

'Ah, a brother. Thank you very much, the privilege is all mine,' said Schalk Joubert easily and comfortably, his tone smoothing away Griessel's fears, making him relax. The enormous compliment of 'a brother' filled Griessel with gratitude, so that, in the light of Alexa's encouraging smile, he found the courage to strike up a conversation with Theuns Jordaan and Anton L'Amour. He asked them how *Kouevuur* had been put together. And then, emboldened by their generosity: 'So when are you going to record "Hexriviervallei" properly, a complete track? That song deserves it.'

He began to unwind, chatting here, laughing there, wondering what he had been so worried about. He felt almost proud of himself, and then Alexa tugged at his arm and he turned around and saw Anton Goosen *and* Lize Beekman, side by side, right in front of him, conspiratorial, a moment of silence that opened up in the hubbub and it was too sudden and too much and his brain shut down and his heart beat wildly and he grabbed for the tall, beautiful, blonde singer's hand, completely star-struck, and all that came out of his mouth, the word idiotically long and drawn-out and clear in the silence, was: '*Fok.*'

And then his cellphone began to ring in his jacket pocket. He just stood there. Frozen.

Somewhere in his head the impulse came: Do something.

He dropped Lize Beekman's hand. Shame and humiliation burning through him, he mumbled, 'Excuse me.' He fumbled for his phone, turned away, pressed the instrument to his ear.

'Hello.' Even his own voice sounded strange to him.

'Benny, I need you,' said Brigadier Musad Manie, commanding officer of the Hawks. 'Like *now*.'

He drove, too fast, angry with himself, angry with Alexa, how could she do that to him? Angry with the cellphone for ringing, he could definitely have recovered from his massive mistake, he could have added something, his practised sentence of 'this is a special privilege', it would have defused the whole mess. Angry with the brigadier making him come in on a Saturday night, his weekend off, angry because he couldn't get the damning chorus out of his head: he had made a complete and total arse of himself. That awful moment, the word uttered, hanging like a dead, black bird between him and Lize Beekman, everything frozen except the irritating ringing of his cellphone and the knowledge that sank down in him like lead: he had made a massive unforgivable arse of himself, in spite of all his resolutions and plans and preparations.

It was really Alexa's fault. She had wanted to know who he was keen to meet, two weeks ago already. From the beginning he had said nobody, he would just be around, available when she needed him. Because he knew he might lose it. But she had drawn the names out of him one by one, and she had said, 'I really want to do this for you,' and he had said, 'No, please,' but with ever diminishing conviction, because the prospect began to tempt him. Until he had agreed, for her sake, but the butterflies had been in his belly already, the faint terror, no, the premonition that he might not handle it well.

His fault. Just his own fucking fault.

He knew there was big trouble when he saw the three senior officers of the DPCI – the Directorate for Priority Crime Investigations – *and* General John Afrika, Western Cape head of Detective Services and Criminal Intelligence.

The burly Brigadier Musad Manie, commander of the Hawks, sat in the middle with a face of granite. On either side were Colonel Zola Nyathi, head of the Violent Crimes Group, and Griessel's immediate boss, and Colonel Werner du Preez, group head of Crimes Against the State (CATS). Afrika was on the opposite side of the table.

They greeted him, Manie invited him to sit down. Griessel saw there were files and documents in front of each of the senior officers.

'Sorry to interrupt your evening, Benny,' said the brigadier. 'But we've got a problem.'

'A nasty problem,' said Afrika.

Colonel Nyathi nodded.

The brigadier hesitated, holding his breath, as if there was a lot more to say. Then he reconsidered, pushed a sheet of paper across the table. 'Let's start with this.'

Griessel pulled the paper towards him, began to read, conscious of the four sets of eyes on him.

762a89z012@anonimail.com
Sent: Saturday 26 February. 06.51
To: j.afrika@saps.gov.za
Re: Hanneke Sloet – you were warned
Today it is precisely 40 days since Hanneke Sloet was murdered. That is 40 days of cover-up. You know why she was murdered.
This is my fifth message but you don't listen. Now you leave me no choice. Today I will shoot a policeman. In the leg. And every day I will shoot a policeman, until you charge the murderer.
If you don't have a report in the newspaper tomorrow that says you have reopened the Sloet case, the next bullet will not be in the leg.

No name. Griessel looked up.

'As you can see, this was sent this morning,' said the brigadier. 'And tonight Constable Brandon April was shot by a sniper in the leg in the parking lot of the Claremont Station. Just before seven.'

'Long distance shot,' said Afrika. 'They're still looking for the bastard's vantage point.'

'The knee is bad,' said Nyathi. 'Shattered.'

'A young man,' said Afrika. 'Won't ever walk normally again. This crazy bastard . . .' and he pointed at the email in

Griessel's hands, 'has written to me four times. Very confused emails, they don't make sense.' He tapped the file in front of him. 'You'll see.'

The brigadier leaned forward. 'We would like to announce that you will be leading the reopened investigation into the Sloet case, Benny.'

'I personally asked the brigadier if we could give it to you,' said Afrika.

'Cloete is currently working on the Sunday papers, he says there's a chance we can get something into the *Weekend Argus* and *Rapport*'s Cape section,' said Manie. Cloete was the liaison officer of SAPS who handled the press.

'We are going on radio as well, but I don't know if that will help,' said Afrika.

'It's a bit of a mess,' said Nyathi, his frown deepening. 'To say the least.'

'If you're willing, Benny. We will back you up. All of us.'

Griessel put the sheet of paper down on the table, straightened his new, fashionable black jacket and asked: 'Hanneke Sloet . . . she was the lawyer?'

3

'That's right,' said Manie and pushed the file across to Griessel. 'Mid-January. Green Point investigated the case . . .'

Griessel took the fat pack of documents and tried to remember what he had heard about the Sloet murder. There had been a small media storm about six weeks back, his colleagues had discussed the case constantly.

'Five blocks away from my office in her fancy apartment,' said Afrika. 'Nailed her.' And then half apologetically he added: 'With one helluva knife.'

The brigadier sighed. 'They found nothing. Nothing.

Look at the investigation diary, you'll see, they followed up everything.'

Griessel opened the dossier at the SAPS5 form in Section C, quickly paged through it, saw the extensive, detailed notes.'You know how it's been since the Steyn case,' said Afrika. 'Everyone makes doubly sure, nobody takes chances any more. The Sloet investigation was by the book. The forensics were good, the footwork was thorough, they talked to everyone who lived and breathed, there's no motive that stands up to scrutiny.'

'Except that she was a lawyer,' said Nyathi philosophically. 'Big clients. Big money.'

'True . . .' said Afrika.

'Crime of opportunity,' said Nyathi. 'Impossible case.'

Afrika sighed. 'Trouble is, she moved into the flat on the third of January, she was murdered on the eighteenth. She hadn't even finished unpacking. Nobody could tell the Green Point detectives if anything was stolen.'

'Let's not disclose everything,' said Manie carefully to the general. 'We want Benny to look at this with fresh eyes. Work through the file from the beginning, see what he can find.'

Afrika nodded in agreement.

Griessel picked up the email. 'Brigadier, what about this "cover-up . . . you know why she was murdered"?'

Before Manie could answer, Afrika said vigorously: 'It's rubbish, Benny, absolute rubbish. Take a look at his other emails. Dreadful insinuations.We are protecting the communists and the Antichrists and whatnot.'

'The guy's a loony,' said Nyathi. 'White supremacist, hates us, hates the government, hates gay people, hates everybody.'

'A terrorist, that's what he is, a terrorist hiding behind an anonymous email address. Untraceable.' Afrika slid the thin folder that lay in front of him over to Benny as well. 'Here are the other letters. You'll see.'

Was he supposed to investigate the sniper affair too?

The brigadier picked up on his uncertainty: 'You know how it is with these crazies, Benny – sometimes they fixate on a specific case. But if there is a connection between the gunman and Sloet, and we have missed it . . . CATS are going to hunt the gunman. Colonel du Preez is the JOC leader.'

'Mbali will be our official investigator, Brigadier,' said du Preez. 'She arrived back from Amsterdam yesterday . . .'

'Amsterdam, oh, Amsterdam,' said Afrika, shaking his head, but with good humour.

The unit had been abuzz the past week, over 'the incident in Amsterdam'. The stout Mbali Kaleni, a member of du Preez's CATS team for the past six months, had been one of a group of detectives taking a course in Holland. Something had happened to her – according to the bush telegraph it was a great embarrassment. But, despite pointed speculation in the corridors, nobody really knew what had happened. Except the top management, and they were as silent as the grave.

'You will have your hands full, Benny, but it's important that you know what progress CATS are making, what they are looking into. And if you find something that could help them . . .'

'You know how we work, Benny,' said Colonel du Preez. 'One big team . . .'

Griessel nodded again.

Nyathi folded his arms and sighed. 'Benny, if word gets out there's someone blackmailing us, shooting policemen . . . Feeding frenzy for the press, public panic.'

'Cloete will keep the constable's knee out of the papers. Just so you know, Benny,' said Manie. 'Please be careful with the press. In any case, Adjutant-Officer Nxesi is the Green Point detective who handled the Sloet case. You can call him, any time, he's ready to come in.'

'Our whole team is ready to support you,' said Nyathi.

'Not to put any extra pressure on you, Benny,' Afrika said seriously, 'but you must get moving. This mad bastard is going to keep on shooting policemen until you solve the case.'

At half past ten on a Saturday night Griessel walked to his office down the deathly silent, wide corridors of the DPCI – the Hawks – building. He was amazed at the effect that the Steyn affair, which Manie had referred to a few minutes ago, had had on the SAPS this past year.

Estelle Steyn, a newly qualified young chef, had been strangled eighteen months ago in her Pinelands town house – with a piece of material, probably a tie. No signs of breaking and entering, theft or sexual assault – it must have been someone whom she knew and trusted. Like her tie-wearing fiancé, the sombre, emotionless KPMG consultant with cold eyes and a key to her door. Within seventy-two hours he had been arrested and charged, and the media and fascinated public immediately declared him guilty. Because Estelle Steyn was a joyous, lively bundle of sunny energy, a brilliant cook with a bright future according to her colleagues. Alongside her blonde, smiling beauty on the front pages of the papers, her fiancé's photo looked brooding and forbidding, the taciturn stare turned away from the camera. Like a man burdened by his misdeeds.

Then came the court case.

Like a pack of wild dogs, the defence ripped apart the carcass of poor crime-scene management, the narrow focus of the investigation, and the creative assumptions of the forensic testimony.

After seven months of sensation, the fiancé walked away a free man.

The media scolded and squawked, the public were shocked and dumbstruck. Months later best-selling books by criminologists and forensics experts analysed and criticised every SAPS misstep. In parliament, time and again the opposition used the whole as a stick with which to beat the government – the damage and scandal would not go away.

The career of the investigating officer, Fanie Fick, was over. He was tucked away in the Information Management Centre (IMC) of the Hawks now, retrained and redeployed as a computer analyst, but everyone knew he would not be promoted again. Behind his back they talked about 'Fanie Fucked', the guy who relieved his pain after hours every day at the Drunken Duck in Stikland.

That was why the Sloet file that Griessel carried to his office was so painfully detailed and 'by the book'. The police service's wounds were still raw, their honour deeply dented, the fear of another detective scapegoat, of more punishment and criticism from top management, the press and Joe Public, loomed large.

That was why General John Afrika had sat in on the meeting at the DPCI tonight, and why he had asked for a specific investigator.

Fear. The Hawks did not usually accept orders or input from a provincial head of investigations. They were too protective of their independence, of their own structures.

Fear, he thought, was also the reason they were allowing the gunman to blackmail them. In the old days the SAPS would not have bowed to threats from a sharpshooter.

Griessel sighed, unlocked his office door. It was a recipe for trouble.

Life was never simple.

He arranged the files on his desk, first opening the slim one that John Afrika had given him. He began to read the emails in chronological order, initially struggling to focus, too many things had happened too fast tonight.

762a89z012@anonimail.com
Sent: Monday 24 January. 23.53
To: j.afrika@saps.gov.za
Re: Hanneke Sloet
You know very well who murdered Hanneke Sloet. Arrest
the communist, or I will hand everything to the press.

The second one was much longer:

762a89z012@anonimail.com
Sent: Monday 31 January. 23.13
To: j.afrika@saps.gov.za
Re: Hanneke Sloet, you're all going to hell!!!
You are ungodly and sinners (1 Timothy 1:9, Proverbs
17:23).
The truth will come out about the communist and about
the money he is paying you. You are all equally corrupt.
Your time is running out.
1 Timothy 1:9-10: Knowing this, that the law is not made
for a righteous man, but for the lawless and disobedient,
for the ungodly and for sinners, for unholy and profane,
for murderers of fathers and murderers of mothers, for
manslayers, for whoremongers, for them that defile
themselves with mankind, for menstealers, for liars, for
perjured persons, and if there be any other thing that is
contrary to sound doctrine.
Proverbs 17:23: A wicked man taketh a gift out of the
bosom to pervert the ways of judgement.
Proverbs 21:15: It is joy to the just to do judgement: but
destruction shall be to the workers of iniquity.

In the third he used a new tack:

762a89z012@anonimail.com
Sent: Sunday 6 February. 22.47
To: j.afrika@saps.gov.za

Re: Hanneke Sloet – on your conscience.
You have three weeks to arrest Hanneke Sloet's murderers.
The process to let justice prevail has begun.
I warned you twice, but you did nothing. What is to come
is on your and your communist bedfellows' consciences,
not mine. You leave me no choice.
Let justice be done.

And then, the second last one, sent on Sunday 13 February,
thirteen days ago:

Ecclesiastes 3: To every thing there is a time.
Verse 3: a time to kill, and a time to heal, a time to break
down, and a time to build up.
Verse 8: a time of war, and a time of peace.

Griessel put the email down and arranged all five in a row,
his eyes moving from one to the other.

Then he read them all over again.

4

When he was done, he propped his chin in his hands, and
thought.

The dates of the emails. The pace had increased systematically. The first two were a week apart. Then six days. Then
five. A fixed rhythm. Except for the last one.

Almost every one had been sent late at night.

In the first and second emails, the references to 'communist'. Singular. Then it became 'murderers'. And 'communist
bedfellows'. But back to the singular 'murderer' in the last
one.

The sudden jump to Bible verses, the religious justification, the building momentum of a crusade. But in the last one

there was a stronger style, more confidence. And purpose. Suddenly a man with a mission.

He could understand why John Afrika and Zola Nyathi thought these were the words of a disturbed man. All the signs were there: crazies did their things at night. And they became increasingly urgent with the passage of time, their communications more frequent. They phoned, breathless and anonymous, or wrote, disjointed, often full of racism or conspiracy theories or warning of the Day of Judgement, of the gods'-vengeance-on-a-land-of-sinners.

Like this one.

They were usually media parasites, studying every piece that appeared about a case, reacting to it, quoting it, embroidering on it.

This one didn't do that.

They almost always gave themselves a name when they wrote, some mythological or astrological or awe-inspiring pseudonym.

Not *this* one.

This one had a new tactic with every communication. This one went abruptly silent for two weeks before the final email. Which he had sent in daytime, a Saturday morning, twelve hours before he went out shooting.

This one referred to a motive in the last email: *You know why she was murdered.*

This one had carried out his threats, he had done the one thing that would ignite the wrath of the SAPS – he had shot a policeman. And he was threatening to do it again.

Something was not right here.

He put the emails back one by one in their file and drew the hefty Sloet folder closer. He opened it, he wanted to start at the beginning, take a look at the murder scene first, the photos, the forensic report, the pathologists . . .

Someone knocked on his door, softly and apologetically.

He was brought back from his reverie. 'Come in,' said Griessel.

Brigadier Musad Manie's nickname in the DPCI was 'the Camel'. Because 'Musad', one of the Hawk detectives had learned from a Muslim friend, meant 'loose camel' in Arabic. And when the tall, lean Colonel Zola Nyathi was appointed head of the Violent Crimes group – with his slow and stately, deliberate, slightly bent forward walk – he was swiftly dubbed 'the Kameelperd' or in the simpler English, 'the Giraffe'.

It was the Giraffe who ducked through the door now, his shaven head shining under the fluorescent lights of Griessel's office.

'No, please, Benny, don't get up . . .' He walked up to the desk, his slender fingers putting down a car key.

'You can use the BMW.'

'Thank you, sir.'

'Benny, you know we're a family here.'

'Yes, sir.'

'You know that we approach investigations as one big team.'

'Yes, sir. I just want to study the files first . . .'

'I understand that, Benny. But when you're ready, get the guys involved. I've already called Vaughn, he's on standby . . .'

'Yes, sir.'

Nyathi tapped a finger on the case files, his voice suddenly soft and confidential. 'Look,' he said. 'You're an old hand. I don't have to spell it out for you . . .' The colonel hesitated, lifted his head, looked Griessel right in the eyes. 'You come talk to me, Benny. Or to the Brig. You find any monkey business anywhere, you come to us . . .'

Griessel didn't know what to say.

'Are you with me, Benny?'

'Yes, sir,' he said in the hope that he would be able to decipher what the Giraffe meant later.

'Good.'

Nyathi turned and walked to the door. Just before he closed it, he said: 'Good luck.'

Griessel sat and looked at the door. Manie and Nyathi had also been taken by surprise over this affair, by Afrika's request and involvement. They were playing along, but cautiously.

He shook his head. Politics. Not his favourite game.

But he appreciated Nyathi's gesture. The problem was that he was not entirely convinced of this we-are-one-big-family-and-we-work-as-a-team strategy of the Hawks. He hadn't been part of the unit for even three weeks, he had only recently learned that JOC stood for Joint Operational Centre – group heads and detectives of the various DPCI units thrown together under one operational leader to investigate a case. Too many people – a recipe for chaos. He was accustomed to one shift partner, or to working alone, especially during the past year when he had been in Afrika's office.

He sighed. He still had no idea why Afrika had transferred him to the Hawks.

He reached for the case file, took out the crime-scene photographs one by one and arranged them in rows in front of him.

In full colour, Hanneke Sloet lay on the big, highly polished marble tiles beside a single round pillar. The red-black blood in stark contrast to her sleeveless white dress and the light grey floor. She lay on her back, right arm over her body, the right hand pressed to the wound in her belly. She had tried to stem the massive blood loss to the very end.

Her bare left arm was slightly outstretched, her hand open.

Her head on the floor, the back of the skull resting in blood, her dark hair fallen across her face, covering her eyes and nose, but the mouth was visible. A full mouth, dark red lipstick, almost the same colour as the blood.

She was barefoot, the dress with the skirt shifted up, her legs exposed to far above the knee.

It looked like a single wound, just below and to the right of her heart.

He wanted to get a feel for the scene, and studied the photos one by one. The apartment was new and modern, the walls and the single pillar were snow white, the floor grey and shiny, the windows large and without curtains – they looked out on a wide balcony outside, and over the multicoloured Bo-Kaap and Signal Hill.

Sloet lay in a spacious room. Behind her, in the centre, was a white couch and two chairs, square and stylish, on a loose white shagpile carpet. Against the long wall was one huge, unframed picture, the kind of modern art that Griessel did not understand – shapes and stripes in white and grey, like an aerial photo of waves in the sea. A single glass-and-chrome shelf housed a hi-fi system and two small speakers.

In the corner furthest from where Sloet lay, there was a spiral staircase that led to an upper level – gleaming light brown wood, with a narrow stainless steel rail.

At the window, a white telescope on a tripod pointed at the buildings of the city.

Behind the pillar there was a small open-plan kitchen – modern cupboards behind opaque olive-green glass, and an angular chrome-coloured fridge.

The front door was three metres to the left of the kitchen, and four metres from where Hanneke Sloet's lifeless body lay.

He looked at the last row of photos, of the two bedrooms in the apartment. The larger one was clearly where Sloet had slept. For the most part it was painfully neat. A wide double bed on a square white platform. The bed was made up with snow-white linen, with two dark brown pillows, matching the dark wood of the bedside cupboards.

The desk, a smooth white wooden top on two brown trestles, bore the only signs of activity: a laptop, a pair of folders, one of which was open, a fountain pen, uncapped. A glass of red wine, three-quarters empty, an Apple iPhone. The brown high-backed chair was pushed back, turned a little to the side. A brown standard lamp to the right was switched on.

The second bedroom was smaller. A single bed, without bedding, cardboard boxes on it, unopened. An empty white bookshelf, two rolled-up Persian carpets.

Griessel picked up the thick folder and placed it in front of him, on top of the photos. Like all SAPS case files it consisted of three parts: Section A contained the interviews, reports, statements and the photo album; in Section B the correspondence between SAPS departments, or other concerns such as banks or employers, was stored; Section C was the journal of the investigation on the SAPS5 form, this one comprised a detailed, chronological history of the case, with references to documents in Section A.

He paged to the pathologist's report in Section A, and was relieved to see that Prof Phil Pagel had done the autopsy. Pagel was the smartest man he knew, vastly experienced, extremely thorough. Above all, Pagel knew how to write a report so that detectives could both understand and use it. At the top there was always a summary that made the investigating officer's life easier – normal language, numbered points, short sentences and paragraphs, useful information.

Griessel read:

- *Time of death: Between 20.00 and 0.00 on Tuesday, 18 January. Probably around 22.00.*
- *Cause of death: radical loss of blood due to a single stab wound from the front, 8 mm above the fourth rib, 20 mm left of the breastbone (gladiolus), through the left lobe of the liver and the*

inferior vena cava (the large artery, carrying oxygen-poor blood from the lower body to the heart), to the T7 vertebra.

- *Wound pathology and weapon: the wound pathology indicates a stabbing object with, most likely, a sharp point (very even angle) and a double, asymmetrical cutting edge (diamond geometry?). The blade is apparently straight. The measurements of the blade are probably 6.5 to 7.5 cm wide, 1.5 cm thick, and longer than 20 cm (no bruising from a handle or hilt. The stabbing angle 85 to 105° relative to vertical torso.*

- *A single, fatal stab wound and the complete absence of defensive wounds to hands indicates significant violence of the stabbing action, or a very sharp blade, or a combination of the two. (Surprise attack?) (Home-made weapon? Assegai? Ornamental dagger? Sword?)*

- *Wound pathology and suspect: suspect is probably 200 to 400 mm taller than the victim (size of weapon, angle of stab wound, possibility of considerable violence). Single stab wound and unknown weapon prevents further speculation.*

- *Wound residue: none.*

- *No indication of sexual activity.*

With the new information in mind, Griessel examined the crime-scene photos again. Stabbed only once. She lay four metres from the front door, and there were no cuts on her hands to show that she had tried to defend herself.

No obvious signs of robbery, the brigadier had said. And according to Pagel, no signs of sex. That meant an absence of semen, of bruising on the victim.

He wondered who had found the victim. How did the building's security work?

He paged through Section A, looking for statements, found a white A4 envelope, loosely inserted behind the photograph album. Someone had written a single word on it in blue pen: *Sloet*.

He opened it, removed the contents.

Three large colour prints. Of a living Hanneke Sloet.

They excited him immediately, making him forget what he was looking for.

All three photos had been taken in a studio, under professional lighting. In the first, only her head, right shoulder and part of her arm were visible. She wore a thin white dress, etched against the smooth, tanned skin of her shoulder and arm. Her head was angled to the right, she was looking down, her eyes veiled, the right side of her face in dark shadow that accentuated the full lips and strong cheekbone. A single strand of hair draped across her face, down to her chin. The shoulder and arm were feminine, muscular. The grey background was an interesting texture, out of focus.

It was quite a sensual photo.

Lovely woman. And she knew it. She liked it, she was displaying it a little.

The second photo was of her upper body, her head slightly dipped so that her dark eyes looked up at the camera. She had an easy smile, showing a narrow gap between her front teeth. Her hair was tied back now. A thin, tight-fitting and collarless blouse with a low neckline displayed the full, prominent breasts, with a certain innocence.

The third was a nude study, dark and artistic. Tasteful. The background was pitch black, the lighting from the right and behind, her body turned, so that only a cheekbone, the tip of her nose, a large, round earring, the slim line of her neck, a shoulder, a single perfect breast and nipple, a hip and the outline of her leg were visible.

He suspected the photos had been taken recently, she seemed mature, close to her age of thirty-three, according to the file.

He arranged the photographs in a row. Looked over them again. What personality, what reason had motivated her to go to all this trouble? How many hours, to make the appointment with the photographer, choose the right clothes, complete the photo sessions? This woman, the corporate lawyer.

And the breasts. Unnaturally large and perfect, like someone who had had them surgically enhanced.

For whose benefit? he wondered. For whom had she had the photos taken?

He sat there staring, fascinated by this smouldering woman.

His cellphone rang, sudden and shrill.

He returned to the present with a vague feeling of guilt, had to look around for the phone first. He found it in the pocket of his jacket, hanging over the chair. He took it out: ALEXA, the screen read.

Fuck. He ought to have called her. He looked at his watch. It was nearly eleven.

He answered: 'Alexa, I'm so sorry . . .'

'No, this is not Alexa,' said a man's voice. Hostile. 'She asked me to call you to come and collect her.'

'Where is she?'

'She's drunk, sir. Falling down drunk.'

5

He jogged to the car with the files in his arms and the knowledge that it was *his* fault. He had embarrassed her, left her alone, kept her in the dark. She had been sober for a hundred and fifteen days and now he had driven her back to drink.

He opened the rear door of the BMW 130i, put the files on the back seat, slammed the door shut in frustration, got in the front and drove away.

He should have known that Alexa used to drink because she suffered from stage fright, and tonight was a sort of stage, her first interaction with the music people in years, her timid return to the limelight. He should have thought, should have controlled his language and his reactions. He should have told the brigadier he couldn't come right away, he should have taken Alexa home first. But no, all he could think of was his own humiliation. He was a dolt, a fucking idiot policeman.

What was wrong with him?

Doc Barkhuizen's warning flashed through his head: 'Careful, Benny, you haven't been dry a year yet. Two alcoholics . . . that's double the risk.'

He had protested and said they were only friends, he could support her, encourage her, they could attend AA gatherings together. And Doc had just shaken his head and said, 'Careful.'

How had he supported her tonight?

He should have listened to Doc. Doc knew the 'just friends' explanation was a smokescreen. Doc could see he *liked* Alexa. More and more.

And she liked him, he had thought.

And now? Now he'd fucked it all up.

Why did he always do that? Why was his life never simple? Never fucking ever. He was forty-five, the age at which you are supposed to reach inner calm and wisdom and resignation, the age at which you are supposed to have all your life shit sorted out. But not him. His life was constant chaos. An endless stream of trouble, a never-ending struggle to cope. But he just could not win, it was one thing on top of another. You could never get ahead.

He had only just, this past month, started to get used to the whole divorce thing, tried to make peace with the fact that he and Anna were over. Totally, irretrievably over. He still struggled with the fact that she was ever more seriously involved with a lawyer. A fucking lawyer. But he was working on that, fuck knows, he was trying.

He had cut back to pay the maintenance, and his contribution to Carla's studies, and he could almost live with that, though he felt he was being ripped off, he paid far more than Anna, and they earned about the same.

He'd worked hard the past weeks to fit in with the Hawks, the new relationship, the new structures, the new ranks. Everybody's rank had changed, back to the military hierarchy of the old days. Everybody's except his own, because a captain was still a captain. But he had accepted that too.

He had got back into a routine with his children. Carla, who was studying drama at Stellenbosch. Drama, as though she hadn't had enough drama in her life with an alcoholic policeman father and the whole divorce disaster. Drama. Where would the child find work? And his son, Fritz, who might or might not pass Matric, because he was playing guitar for Jack Parow's band. Jack Parow. Hip hop or rap or whatever you called it, swore worse than a policeman. But what could he do? Fritz had talent – Jack had approached him personally, come and play for me. Griessel had made peace with the fact that the world had changed, that children had choices today, that their approach to careers was different.

Peace with many things. On the brink of getting things straight.

And now in one night he had made a complete arse of himself in front of three people for whom he had immense respect: Anton Goosen, Lize Beekman, and Alexa Barnard. And driven the last one to drink.

He would just have to accept it. He was a fuck-up.

The words hung for a moment in his thoughts and he realised: it was the swearing. That was the problem, the thing that had caused all the trouble tonight. Here, now, it had to end. He was through with swearing. Finished. For the rest of his life. The same way he had stopped drinking, he would stop fucking swearing too.

And tomorrow, when she was sober, he would explain to Alexa about the Sloet case and ask her forgiveness, and get her to phone the other two, so she could tell them, it was all due to admiration and nerves, maybe it happened to other people too, maybe he wasn't the first.

And then he thought how beautiful Alexa had looked and his fleeting hope, at her house, that he would get lucky tonight, and he snorted in disgust at himself, at *this* world, in his Hawks BMW on the N1. And he thought, life is never fu— Damn. Life is never *flipping* simple.

He found no pleasure in his new word.

He stopped at the Artscape. His cellphone rang. It must be the centre manager again, about Alexa. He answered hastily, to say he had arrived.

'Griessel.'

'Captain, it's Tommy Nxesi from Green Point.' There was a wary note to his voice.

It took a moment to register – it was the warrant officer who had originally investigated the Sloet case.

'Yes, Tommy.'

'Captain, do I still have to come in?'

'No . . .' he realised the detective had been waiting for him to call, at the request of John Afrika. 'Sorry, Tommy, I should have let you know . . .' Griessel thought of what lay ahead, with Alexa. 'You don't need to . . . Can we talk tomorrow?'

'So, you don't need me tonight?'

'No, thanks a lot . . .'

'OK,' said Tommy, relieved.

'Thanks . . .' then he remembered, he wanted to have a look at the scene of the crime. 'Tommy, do you still have the keys to Sloet's apartment?'

'Not here with me.'

'No, I mean tomorrow morning – can we take a look

tomorrow morning?' And then he hurried to add – knowing how Nxesi would feel about it, he had been in the same position himself, 'You're the expert on this one. I want to hear what *you* think.'

'Sure, Captain. What time?'

'Nine o'clock?'

'See you there, thanks, Captain.'

Griessel put the phone back in his pocket.

He would have to keep his wits about him.

He was shocked when he saw her in the manager's office. Her make-up was smudged, her hair hung over her face, a mess, the neckline of her dress had slipped down too far, a sandal lay to one side, the other on her foot. She sat on a chair with her legs apart, elbows on her knees, swaying from side to side.

'Alexa . . .'

She looked up slowly. He could see she was very drunk. She battled to focus. Then slowly her face crumpled. She tried to straighten up, but it was hard. She began to cry.

He went to her, helped her up, tried to pull her dress higher, but she wrapped her arms around him. She smelled of liquor and perfume.

'I'm here,' he said. 'I'm sorry.' He put his arms around her, held her tightly.

Her face was in his neck and he felt the hot, wet tears trickling down him. 'I'm such . . .' she said, the sibilants coming out with difficulty. 'I'm such a loser, Benny.'

'You're not,' he said.

The manager stepped around them, bent and picked up her sandal and her little evening bag that was hanging over the arm of the chair. He held them out to Griessel, the shoe by one finger, as though it was contaminated, disgust on his face.

Benny took the shoe and the bag. Alexa sagged against him. 'Come,' he said gently. 'Let's go home.'

In the car she talked disjointedly, her head against the window.

'Intruder, Benny. That's all I am ... they know ...' She struggled to open her bag, took out her cigarettes, dropped the lighter.

He didn't want to see her like this, because it was his doing. He searched for words to repay, to console her, but all he could manage was: 'I'm so terribly sorry.'

It was as though she didn't hear him. She grabbed for the lighter on the floor, surrendered the battle, fell back in her seat and began a chorus: 'They saw *through* me.' Repeating it over and over, that maudlin tone of drunken self-pity.

His cellphone rang, *Jissis*, what *now*? He answered it.

'Benny, this is John Afrika. Cloete says a small article will appear on page fourteen of the *Weekend Argus*, and on the Internet, we were too late for anything else. It's a mess, Benny, I'm telling you. Anyway, I just wanted to let you know, you'll have to produce results. Pull out all the stops.'

'Yes, General.'

'OK, Benny.' Afrika concluded the call.

'They saw through me,' said Alexa.

He parked in front of her house, found her key in the evening bag. He got out.

'Don't leave me,' she pleaded, the voice of a child.

He got back in. 'I won't leave you. I just want to unlock the door.'

She looked at him uncomprehendingly. 'I'm an alcoholic, you know.'

He nodded, got out again, walked quickly to the front door, unlocked it. Jogged back to the car, opened the passenger door. 'Let's get you in the house.'

She didn't respond, just sat there, swaying again.

'Please, Alexa.'

She lifted her left arm slowly. He bent, pulled her arm over his back, pulled her up and out. She was unsteady. He shuffled through the gate with her, up onto the veranda. Inside he struggled to find the light switch, then he helped her slowly up the stairs. Her other sandal came off, rolled down two steps. They shuffled down the passage, into her room. He sat her down on the bed. She toppled sideways, her head on the bedspread. He switched on the bedside light, stood a moment undecided.

He had to fetch her bag, in the car. Had to lock the vehicle. Her lips moved, she murmured something.

'Alexa . . .'

He brought his head close, so he could hear what she said. But she didn't speak. She sang. The song that had made her famous. 'Soetwater', Sweet Water. Softly, nearly inaudible, but perfect, in tune, in her unique, rich voice.

> *A small glass of sunlight,*
> *A goblet of rain*
> *Pour sweet water*
> *A small sip of worship,*
> *A mouthful of pain*
> *Drink sweet water.*

'I'm just going to lock the car,' he said.

No response.

He walked fast. On the way down the stairs he remembered she had tried to commit suicide, the last time she had been drunk. When her husband had died.

He would have to stay here tonight.

He fetched the handbag, her cigarettes and lighter, then the stack of files, locked the car, and jogged back.

With her clumsy assistance he got both big earrings off and put them on the bedside cupboard. 'Try to sleep a little,' he said.

She looked at him with new focus and control. Her lips opened slightly. She put her hands behind his head and pulled him closer and kissed him, her mouth open and wet, he tasted alcohol on her. She pulled him down, to the bed.

He put his hands carefully on her shoulders, pushed her away gently.

She wept. 'You don't want me either.'

'I do,' he said. 'But not like this.'

Eventually she lay back against the cushions. He picked up her legs, put them on the bed. She turned her back to him. He walked around the bed, found the edge of the bedspread and folded it over her.

Then he stood there, for ten minutes, and listened as her breathing slowed. Until she slept.

He looked at his watch. It was ten past twelve. Sunday morning.

Day 2

Sunday

6

He worked on the case file until nearly half past three.

In the bedroom beside Alexa's he hung his jacket on a hook behind the door, unbuttoned his shirt and rolled up his shirtsleeves. He sat down on a stool at the dressing table, picked up the fat folder and began to work through it. For a long time he struggled to concentrate because his mind was on Alexa. *They saw through me.* How could she think that? He had seen her, tonight, at the cocktail party, her grace, her presence, how easy and at home she had been there.

The damage, he thought. Of self doubt, of a lifetime of insecurity and desire for success with music, the damage of a man who cheated on her, the damage of his death. But above all the damage of drink. If you gave in, if you threw four months of sobriety in the water, if you had to look your own weakness in the eye, realise once more you were not strong enough. To get up again . . .

She lay on the bed and sang 'Soetwater' and it burned through him, because there was a searching in her voice, a longing for a moment in her past when everything had been good and right. And he knew – you never get that back, no matter how hard you try. That was why he had felt like weeping with her at that moment.

You can never repair the damage.

And the taste of alcohol in her mouth. Lord, he could taste it still. When she had kissed him, he hadn't thought of love-making, he had had a sudden and violent longing for the bottle. And for the place where she was, that soft nebulous world of drunkenness where everything was round and harmless, no edges and corners to hurt you.

An alarm went off in the back of his mind: this was the road to trouble.

Careful, Benny, you haven't been dry a year yet. Two alcoholics ... that's double the risk.

Doc Barkhuizen was a clever man. But he would be able to tell Doc that tonight he had had another revelation, gained an insight. When he had pulled the bedspread over Alexa. A strong feeling of déjà vu, because he had been there before – on the bed, dead drunk, his ex, Anna, pulling the blanket over him with compassion and patience and love. How many times? How many evenings and nights? How had she put up with it for so long?

He felt the loathing for himself come and sit in his throat, and forced himself back to the case file.

Hanneke Sloet was born on 18 June 1977 in Ladybrand in the Free State. She graduated with an LLB from Stellenbosch University in 1999, and in 2001 she began work at the law firm Silberstein Lamarque, first as articled clerk, and then in 2002 as attorney in the corporate law department. In 2009 she was promoted to partner.

Up till December the previous year she lived alone in a town house in Stellenbosch, and commuted by car every day to Silberstein Lamarque House in Riebeek Street in Cape Town, where she had an office on the eighth floor. She bought the apartment in 36 on Rose for 3,850,000 rand ten months ago with a mortgage from Nedbank, but the development was only completed the previous December. On Monday 3 January she moved in on the fifth floor.

She wasn't in a serious or long-term relationship when she died.

On Tuesday 18 January she left the offices of Silberstein Lamarque at 19.46, according to the electronic time stamp on her access card. When she didn't arrive for a 09.00 meeting with her employer on 19 January, her personal assistant began to worry. *Because Hanneke was never late. Every workday she was in the gym at a quarter to six, and in the office at a quarter past seven,* according to the assistant's sworn statement.

I called her cellphone, because she didn't have a land line yet. She didn't answer. That is absolutely exceptional, it had never happened before. I went to talk to Mr Pruis, and at 09.40 left the office and drove to her apartment. The door was locked. I went down to the basement and saw her car was there. Only around 10.20 could I track down the caretaker. He refused to unlock the apartment. I phoned the office, and Mr Pruis called his contacts in the police. Two policemen arrived at the apartment around 11.00 and ordered the caretaker to open the door. We found her dead.

The two uniformed policemen simply established that Sloet was dead, left and alerted Green Point Station that they had a homicide. Warrant Officer Tommy Nxesi from Green Point and a colleague, Sergeant Vernon April, took over the crime scene officially at 11.35, and summoned Forensics and the pathologist.

The forensic report yielded only two small pieces of useful information: the handle of the front door seemed to have been wiped inside and outside; and apart from Sloet's own hair, a single, male, probably Caucasian, pubic hair was found in the shower of the en-suite bathroom. There was not enough of the hair follicle to get a DNA result.

Ten different sets of fingerprints were found in the apartment . . . *probably due to the removal company's workmen who handled practically all the furniture and cardboard cartons on 3*

January, the report read. Six sets were identified as those of Hanneke Sloet, the caretaker who had come to fix a leaking tap a week earlier, and four of the removal company's workers who could be traced. Only the victim's fingerprints were on the computer and the glass in her bedroom.

Blood spatter analysis showed that the victim was dealt the fatal wound probably 3.8 metres from the front door and 0.6 metres from where her body was found.

And that was all. No dust, soil samples or tracks. No lip prints, residue, strange chemicals or usable DNA.

Neither did Sloet's Facebook page, computer, or cellphone records produce much. Most of the emails, calls and SMSes on 18 January were work related. The exceptions were communications between two girlfriends, and a conversation with a telemarketer that was cut short. In the previous ten months there had been no contact with the last serious man in her life, one Egan Roch. Roch's statement confirmed that. *It's been nearly a year since we broke up. We had virtually no contact since.*

Griessel began to understand why the investigation had come up empty-handed. Everyone questioned sang the same tune: We can't think of anyone who would want to harm her.

He had to patch her working life together from the various statements of her colleagues. Hanneke Sloet at the time of her death was involved in the conclusion of a business transaction whereby Ingcebo Resources Limited would acquire a shareholding in Gariep Minerals Limited, a process that had been on the go for thirteen months. Six other employees of Silberstein Lamarque were part of the legal team, while a transaction consultant, four banks, a management consultation company, and two other law firms were also involved.

We are the law firm representing the interests of SA Merchant Bank, Griessel read in the statement of Mr Hannes Pruis, a director of Silberstein Lamarque. *They are one of the*

structuring advisors and underwriters. It is basically contract law,
a lot of drudgery. Administrative. Hanneke was one of six part-
ners on the team.

Apparently it was work without risk, without secrets or
sensation.

Her bank statements showed only a woman who made
good money and spent it well, but her financial affairs were
not out of control, there was nothing that drew his attention.

By twenty past two he could no longer concentrate. He
gathered all the documents together and put them back carefully in the file. He went and listened at Alexa's bedroom
door. She was sleeping.

He urinated in the second bathroom, washed his hands
and face. Walked back to the room, closed the door,
undressed. He set the alarm on his cellphone for seven
o'clock and climbed into the bed, his weariness a heavy
weight. Long day.

But Griessel's brain kept working.

There was something about the case that bothered him.
Not an obvious flaw, just a vague impression. Of an investigator who had looked in all the right places, asked all the
right questions. Thorough, complete, by the book. And
nothing more. No flair. No intuition. He knew how investigations worked, you went through your routine, starting
with the people closest to the victim, and, if that yielded
nothing, you spread your net wider and wider. Until somewhere you came across something that stuck in the back of
your mind, a suspicion, a false note, and then you dug there,
you focused, you applied pressure. And nine times out of
ten you were right.

Instinct.

He hadn't found that in the Sloet file. The trouble with
station detectives was partly the training, the strong em-
phasis on forensic aids and technology. Intuition didn't count

any more. And the lack of experience, because they were frequently young, often working in unfamiliar surroundings, other cultural and language groups, under a lot of pressure from all sides. They did their best, but . . .

It wasn't robbery. The laptop and the cellphone there on the work table . . . Even if no one could say whether anything was missing from the apartment, theft was most likely not the motive.

And she didn't die *at* the door. Her body lay nearly four metres inside the apartment, and the blood pattern said she was stabbed at least three metres from the door. From the front. She hadn't tried to turn around or run away – she had confronted her attacker, but not defended herself. Not fought for her life. From habit Griessel recreated the scene in his mind automatically, somewhat reluctantly. She opens the door. She sees who it is. She retreats . . .

But she doesn't defend herself?

The handle of the front door is wiped clean.

Hanneke Sloet was working upstairs in her bedroom. The glass of wine was there, the computer, the files.

It just wouldn't fit.

And the photographs. Sloet having them taken deliberately in a studio. Seductive. Naked.

Nonetheless she had not been in a serious relationship during the past year. It bothered him, *that* combination.

Maybe she didn't have time for relationships. In the gym at six in the morning, only home at eight at night. Last year she was still driving in from Stellenbosch, back in the evening.

Maybe. But why the photos then, the effort?

He must remember to ask Tommy Nxesi where they had found the photos. Where had she kept them?

He kept his thoughts deliberately on the case, because he didn't want to relive his great embarrassment. But somewhere on the edge of sleep he remembered with a degree of satisfaction that someone had mistaken him for Paul Eilers tonight.

So he couldn't be *that* ugly.

7

He dreamed of Lize Beekman. They were walking down a busy street and he was endlessly trying to explain why he had said such a ridiculous thing in front of her. But she wasn't paying attention to him. She disappeared, melted away in the crowd and people looked at him with great disdain on their faces.

The cellphone's alarm jerked him awake and he half sat up, not sure where he was.

He saw the file on the dressing table. The events of yesterday slowly penetrated through to him. He rubbed his palms over his face. He got up slowly, dressed and went to the bathroom to empty his bladder and wash his face. Then he took a cautious look in Alexa's bedroom.

She was still asleep.

He considered his options. He had to go home, shower, shave, brush his teeth and eat breakfast – he hadn't eaten a thing last night. And then meet Tommy Nxesi at Sloet's apartment. But he didn't want just to leave Alexa like this . . .

He made a decision, carried the files down to his car, found the notebook and pen in the glove compartment. The morning was bright and clear without a breath of wind, the mountain and cliffs glowing. He stood in the street for a moment taking it in, then he jogged back, sat down again at the dressing table in the second bedroom to write her a note.

Alexa
I am really sorry about last night. It was all my fault. Call
me when you wake up. I want to talk to you urgently.
Benny

He tore the page out, tiptoed into her room and put it on
the bedside cabinet where she would see it.

The sparkling new five-storey building at 36 on Rose was
designed to represent the Bo-Kaap architecture with a
modern twist. The lower levels were colourfully painted, just
like the little labourers' houses further down Rose Street.

Nxesi was waiting at the front door. He was the same
height as Griessel, but broader, slightly bow-legged. His
black-framed glasses and brown tweed jacket gave him a
professorial look. His greeting was friendly. 'I've got the keys,
but security will have to take us up to the floor.' He had a
township accent. He held the door open for Griessel.

'Sorry about this, Tommy,' Griessel said as he walked in.

'It's nothing, Captain. I expected you guys to take over the
case long ago.'

The entrance foyer was new and shiny. A man and a
woman in security uniforms sat behind a desk. Nxesi pointed
at the TV camera behind them, on the wall. 'The CCTV and
the card system in the lifts should have been operational by
the end of December, but at the end of January they were still
finishing up. On January eighteenth there was no security
except these people at reception. Trouble is, at the time, an
intruder could have entered via the parking garage.'

He showed his SAPS identification card to the female
guard, spoke to her in Xhosa. She made them sign a book
first, a precaution Griessel never could fathom, since you
could write absolutely anything there.

Then she led them to the lift. 'Nowadays you have to push

a card in if you want to go up.' Nxesi pointed to a slot just above the button panel of the lift. 'Then you press the right floor. If you press a number that is not programmed on your card, it won't work. Coming down, it works automatically.'

'But on January eighteenth it wasn't working?'

'No. Two days after the murder, then it was working.' He shook his head.

The security guard made a noise of protest. Nxesi adjusted his glasses. 'They're touchy about the murder, because half the flats are still for sale.'

At the door, while he unlocked, Nxesi said, 'Everything is just as it was, because the case is still open. But the lawyers have started to nag the SC, they want us to clean up, so they can wind up the estate. The parents inherit everything. They live in Jeffreys Bay. Retired.'

He pushed the door open, waited for Griessel to go ahead.

Griessel confirmed that there was a peephole in the front door, and a security chain and bolt, undamaged. Then he stopped, he wanted to get a feel for the room first.

It was smaller than the impression created by the photographs, but still spacious and attractive and modern. The morning light shining through the large windows made it look cheerful, and the view south included a part of Signal Hill. To his left was the single pillar, the kitchen behind it. He heard the quiet murmur of the fridge, an expensive double-door. The couch and chairs stood between the pillar and the windows, in the centre of the room. The painting hung on the wall to his right, above the stereo. The artwork looked more interesting than it did in the photographs. At the window stood the white telescope on a tripod.

He looked around, saw Nxesi watching him intently. 'Can I see the key, Tommy?'

The Xhosa detective held it out to him. 'This one is for the front door.' He showed the silver Yale key. 'This one is for her car, the other is for those cupboards up there.' The bunch was attached to a little metal ring.

'Were there any spare keys?'

'Just for the cupboards, and her car. She kept them in the drawer beside her bed.'

'In her office?'

Nxesi shook his head.

'And security? Do they have a key?'

'*Hayi*. Only the caretaker has a master key, but he doesn't have a lift card. Security has to bring him, but only if the owner has given permission.'

'Her car?'

'It's still here, down in the parking garage. Mini Cooper S Convertible. Forensics have been through it. Nothing.'

'Thanks.' Griessel handed the keys back.

He looked at the blood.

On the shiny, grey marble tiles, three paces from the entrance, was the first fan of fine brown dried blood spray, circled in black by Forensics. About a metre further on was the wide, hardened pool where she had lain.

Griessel reversed, as far as the threshold, took two steps forward, another shuffle. The murderer would have stood here. The mortal wound was inflicted right here. She had staggered backwards, probably from the violence of it. Then collapsed.

Griessel bent down, examined the first, delicate spatters. They had been perfectly preserved, no footprints, no smearing.

He walked past the pillar, to the kitchen. The sink was empty. The worktop was clean, just as it was in the photos.

'Tommy, was there nothing in the sink?'

Nxesi came and stood with him. 'Nothing. She ate at work. Ordered a Thai take-away, around about six-forty in the evening. The delivery service left it at reception at Silberstein House at five past seven. Then they phoned her and she went to collect it. The boxes were in her trash. That's why the pathologist was so certain about the time of death. He says that last meal had barely left the stomach, there was very little in the small intestine. If she ate just before seven, then the time of death was very close to ten o'clock.'

'You're a good detective, Tommy,' Griessel said pensively.

'I try . . .'

'When I . . . They did it to me too, Tommy. Gave my case to someone else. I know how it feels.'

'Captain, it's OK.' He fiddled with his glasses again.

'It's easier when you can read the whole case file first. All the footwork is done already.'

'It doesn't matter. Let's just catch the one who did this.'

Griessel noted Nxesi's earnest expression. 'Thanks, Tommy.' He pointed at the top floor. 'There was a wine glass, beside her computer. But no bottle . . .'

Nxesi opened a door of the free-standing kitchen counter, and pointed. 'The wine was here, Forensics took the bottle. Red wine, opened, the bottle was about half full.'

Sloet must have poured the wine, put the bottle away. 'She was tidy.'

'You should see the cupboards. It's like a shop.'

'Where is the drawer with the knives?'

Nxesi showed him a set of drawers. 'The cutlery is on top, the utensils in the third one,' he said.

Griessel pulled open the top drawer. Silver cutlery, forks, knives, spoons, teaspoons. Nothing that could remotely match the measurements of the murder weapon.

'There are three kitchen knives in the other one,' Nxesi said. 'But nothing that comes close.'

Benny opened the third drawer. It wasn't very full. A couple of serving and salad spoons, a modest collection of cooking utensils. And three knives with black handles, different sizes, the longest was a butcher's knife, but the dimensions were still too modest to have been the murder weapon.

'Even if there was a bigger one in that set, it would still be too narrow,' said Nxesi. 'I searched the flat, Captain. If she had a dagger or an assegai . . . No trace. I don't know . . .'

Griessel closed the drawer, walked over to the fridge, opened it. There wasn't much in there. Two containers of expensive flavoured yoghurt, and one of feta cheese. Two kinds of yellow cheese, each sealed in its own plastic cover, a two-litre bottle of orange juice, one third empty. A bottle of white wine, unopened, a container of margarine, a Tupperware tub with what looked like beetroot salad in it.

He opened the freezer compartment. A tub of ice cream, a few bags of frozen vegetables, a single bag of chicken thighs.

He closed the door again.

Upstairs he first looked into the spare bedroom, the one with the sealed cartons. The boxes were neatly stacked on the single bed, in line with the corners. Two rolled-up Persian carpets were pushed up against the empty white bookshelf, so you could walk to the bed easily.

Griessel went over to the bed and inspected the boxes. They were still sealed with the broad sticky tape that removals companies used.

Nxesi followed him as he went out, then down the short passage to the master bedroom. At the end of the passage, just before the bedroom door on the left, was a large window with a view over the city.

The bedroom was big. Built-in cupboards against a long wall. Sloet's desk opposite, between the two large windows, the cream-coloured curtains closed, just as they were in the photos. Against the door stood the wide, minimalistic double bed, left of that the entrance to the bathroom. On the floor was a big oriental carpet, also cream-coloured, with delicate brown patterning.

'The light was on,' Griessel said.

'It was.'

The desk top was clear now, the computer and files removed. He drew a breath to ask about the laptop, but his cellphone rang. He pulled it out of his shirt pocket. ALEXA, the screen read.

'Hello.'

'Benny, I can't do it.' There was utter terror in her voice.

He walked out into the passage before asking her, 'What do you mean?'

'I can't do the concert, Benny. I *can't.*'

8

'Alexa, no, don't worry about it, I'll soon be . . .'

'It's going to destroy me, Benny.'

He didn't know what to say to her, suddenly aware of his inability to find the right words, the right approach. 'It won't,' was the best he could do. 'You are Xandra Barnard.'

'I am nothing, Benny.' The tears were close in her voice.

'I . . . Alexa, just give me an hour. Have you had any coffee yet?'

'No,' she said in a small voice.

'Go and make yourself some coffee. Eat something. Bath . . . I'll come as soon as I can. I'm at work . . .'

Silence.

'Alexa . . . ?'

'I don't know what to do, Benny.'

'Will you go and make coffee?'

'I will.'

'I promise you I will come as soon as I can.'

'OK.'

'I'll call you back. Will you keep your cellphone with you?'

'OK.'

'I'll soon be there.'

'I'm sorry, Benny.'

'There's no need to be sorry, we'll talk about it . . .' He had to ring off, Nxesi was waiting. 'Just let me finish up here.'

'I shouldn't have bothered you, I'm sorry. Bye, Benny.' The line went dead.

He stood there and looked out of the window with the city view, but he could see nothing. He would have to wrap this up. There was no alcohol in Alexa's house, but he would have to stop her before she went to a hotel. That was what she did, because 'off-licences are such sad places'. He knew all the danger signs, he knew she would go looking for a drink at the Mount Nelson.

And it was all his fault.

Nxesi had the attitude of a man who had heard everything despite doing his best not to, but out of decency didn't want to show it.

'Sorry, Tommy . . .' was all Griessel said.

The warrant officer made a gesture that dismissed it as nothing.

Griessel stood there, trying to gather his thoughts. There was something important that he wanted to ask.

He remembered: 'The laptop. Was it on?'

'No. It was off. But her emails show she was sitting here working. At about half past nine she sent an email to Van Eeden. He's the . . . deal maker, the one who put the whole merger together. Official stuff, a sort of progress report.'

'He is the same one she sent an SMS to about ten to ten?'

Nxesi nodded. 'He said it was about that email – she let him know she had sent it.'

'And all the files that were lying here, were they about the transaction?'

'*Ewe.* They were.'

'She sat here working until just before ten.' The confirmation of the suspicion that he had gained from the photos, and the first inkling that he would find nothing new here.

He went into the bathroom. A shower, the entire width of the rear wall, with a glass panel in front. Where the single male pubic hair had been found. A large, white, modern bath. More grey marble tiles. Brown cabinets, brown towels. A brown cloth laundry basket hanging from a dark wood framework. He lifted the flap. It was empty.

'Forensics took it away,' Nxesi said.

'And found nothing.'

'*Shici.*'

They walked back to the bedroom. Griessel halted. 'Tommy, how do you see this thing? What happened?'

Nxesi adjusted his glasses with a thumb and two fingers. 'She brought work home, she sat here . . .'

Griessel's cellphone rang.

He sighed. 'Excuse me, Tommy,' he said, and took it out of his jacket pocket. MBALI.

'Hello, Mbali.'

'How are you, Benny?'

'I'm well, thanks. Welcome back.'

'Thank you,' she said without enthusiasm. 'You know I'm on the shooter team?'

'They told me last night.'

'I'm your liaison, Benny. You read the emails?'

'I did.'

'I want to know what you think. Could we meet?'

He would have to go to Alexa first, and he still had to finish here. He checked his watch.

Mbali interpreted his hesitation correctly. 'Any time, Benny, I'm at the scene at the moment, in Claremont.'

'Can I call you?'

'Of course, Benny. Bye.'

Nxesi looked at the ground with a grin. 'Mbali Kaleni?' he asked.

'Yes.'

'I hear things happened. In Holland.'

'That's what they say.'

'Must be *dagga*. She must have wanted to arrest someone for sitting and smoking dagga in the street.'

'Could be.'

'Mbali,' said Nxesi with a bemused smile.

'She's a good detective,' said Griessel.

Nxesi merely nodded.

'Tommy, how did this thing happen?'

The sniper sat in the Chana panel van. Beside him on the floor lay an electric lamp with an extension cord that snaked out of the window to a power point on the wall of the dark garage.

On his lap was the rifle. Beside him, on the tool chest, a set of cleaning materials was arranged in the aluminium case – the metal rods, brushes, mops, cloths and oil. He worked slowly and surely, not wanting to touch the telescope. He could not afford to take it back to a shooting range to calibrate it again.

Not any more.

It would be a long shot today. Perhaps the longest of all. That's why he wanted to get it over and done with.

And it had to happen before midday, before the streets turned into the quiet of a Sunday afternoon.

Today he would take his time. Stay calm. The first shot yesterday had missed because he hadn't handled the tension well. The ice was broken now. He would shoot better today.

He checked his watch. Twenty minutes, then he would have to leave.

'At the time, you could get inside this building easily,' said Warrant Officer Tommy Nxesi. 'Through the parking garage, up the stairs maybe, or in the lift. So he got in and then he knocked on the door. She had finished working, she might have been downstairs. She looked through the peephole. And she knew him. So she opened up. They talked there. Then they began to argue. He became very angry. He stabbed her. He saw she was dead. Then he left.'

'Could be.'

'There is nothing stolen, Captain. There is no motive. *Shici*. Nothing. No boyfriend, no social life aside from the two female friends, it was all work. They said she was nice. But ambitious, she worked so hard on this deal because she wanted to become a director at Silbersteins. And the promotion was in the pipeline, that's what Pruis told me. So I think it must have been something else. At first I thought it was drugs. These rich cats, they snort, I thought her dealer had come to make a delivery, and she didn't have enough cash, maybe she was high too, and he stabbed her. But then he would have stolen something too. And the post mortem showed no drugs. But it's something like that, Captain. Somebody came about something. Something that her work or friends don't know about. Something we can't put our finger on. One of those things that just happen, spur of the moment.'

9

Griessel asked him where he had found the photographs of Sloet, the ones in the white envelope.

Nxesi hesitated a second before walking over to the bedside

cupboard, on the right-hand side of the bed. There were two drawers, and a little door under them. He pulled open the second drawer. 'Come and see,' he said with barely disguised distaste. Then he stepped back, as though the contents of the drawer were toxic.

Griessel went and looked. On top was the vibrator, long and thick, a macabre, faithful imitation of a penis. And underneath, the box it came in. *Big Boy Vibrator*, in large letters.

'There's her boyfriend,' said Nxesi. 'The album is underneath.'

Giessel said nothing, pulled out the photo album and opened it.

In the front was the name of the photographer on a small silver sticker. *Anni de Waal*. And an address in De Waterkant Village.

More photos of Hanneke Sloet, in the same style as the ones he had seen, in a variety of poses, one A4 print per page. Her cleavage was frequently displayed, but there were no other nude pictures. And eight pages were empty.

'You only took three photos?'

'*Ewe*. Two for the file. And the nude one, because I didn't want her mother to see it.' Very earnest.

Griessel tried to push the album back under the vibrator and its packaging. He couldn't manage it, picked up the box, put the album away. He read on the carton: *Big Boy is a hugely satisfying multispeed vibrating realistic veined cock. It's a superhero love shaft for a meaty satisfaction designed to go deep and totally satisfy you with a greater girth for greater gratification. Real men just can't measure up to this wild toy. Free Eveready Gold batteries included!*

He looked up, saw the warrant officer waiting for his reaction.

'It's a strange world, Tommy.'

'*Hayi*,' he said, shaking his head before adjusting his glasses.

At his car Nxesi asked him to sign for receipt of the apartment keys. Once Griessel had done that, he saw the relief, fleeting, as if the warrant officer was shrugging a weight off his shoulders.

Just before he drove away, he asked: 'Tommy, I know it will sound strange, but during your investigation, was there any mention . . . anyone who talked about a "communist"?'

'A communist?'

His astonishment was Griessel's answer. 'Forget it, Tommy, just something the colonel said last night.'

Nxesi shook his head. 'All I found was a bunch of capitalists . . .'

Benny phoned Alexa while he was driving and told her he was on his way. She sounded absent and far away, as though it didn't matter, and his heart sank.

The trouble was that he didn't understand her, though he tried, even if he factored in the damage in her past. That enormous talent.

Three months ago she had come along for the first time and sung with Roes, an amateur rock-and-blues-band. Benny was their bass guitarist. They chose that name, Afrikaans for 'rust', because they were four middle-aged, middle-class, suburban men. It had taken them five months to shake off their considerable and collective rust, and slowly build up a repertoire of old classic songs, in the hope of performing at weddings and parties. He had invited her a few times. She turned up out of the blue and on her own at the old community hall in Woodstock where they rehearsed. She had sat and listened with a poker face while they gave of their best, dreadfully conscious of her musical status. And then, after the first set, she asked, 'Do you know "See See

Rider" by Ma Rainey?' And Vince Fortuin, their lead guitarist with the anchor tattoo on his sinewy shoulder and the little eyes that screwed shut with pleasure when they got going properly, said, 'That's a *lekker* one, but maybe a little bit more upbeat than Ma?' Alexa agreed with a slight smile and a nod. Vince and the drummer, Jaap, with his long grey hair and the cigarette clamped permanently between his lips, began, and Griessel and the heavily moustachioed rhythm guitarist, Jakes Jacobs, listened and joined in, beautifully strong and thumping, and Alexa took the microphone and turned her back to them.

And then she sang.

The thing was, he'd hoped, vaguely, though he should have known better, that she would consider performing with them. Not permanently, but maybe now and then. Special occasions. But that night, when she sang the first stanzas, he knew they were not in her class.

It was the first time in years that she had touched a microphone, but it was all there, immediate and overwhelming: the feeling, the intonation, the understanding of the music, of them, of Vince's tempo and style. And the rich, full voice, the charisma, the enchantment.

Instantly, she had raised their standard, their sound, their ability, suddenly she made them sound good.

When she finished, they clapped, and she said, 'No, don't.' And then she asked, self-conscious about her barely suppressed hunger: 'Tampa Red's "She's Love Crazy"?'

Vince nodded, impressed and keen, and played.

And Alexa sang.

For nearly an hour, one song after the other. Griessel saw the light in her eyes, and the metamorphosis. The homecoming, and the longing in her for what he guessed must be an audience, or real applause, the kind that thundered like the ocean, because that's what fed her talent, that was her right in those moments.

The same woman who said to him last night, 'They saw through me.'

Where was she coming from? Had she no idea how good she was?

How should he handle it, if he couldn't understand? What should he say to her?

And his other concern: he couldn't spend all day with her. He would have to call her Alcoholics Anonymous sponsor, Mrs Ellis, the school principal. Because he had to get a move on, he had to concentrate, his head should be full of the things he had seen in Sloet's apartment. He had asked Tommy, down at the cars, just before he signed for the keys, 'Who did *you* suspect for this?' And Nxesi said, 'The caretaker. Farock Klein. He had opportunity, and a master key. He carries tools, so maybe he had some big sharp thing to stab with in his box. His prints were in the flat. He knew how easy it was to get to her door. She would have opened up for him. He fancies himself as a handsome guy, I thought maybe he tried his luck with the woman with the big . . .' Nxesi motioned with his hands, too shy to call the breasts by their name, and quickly added, 'He has a record, Captain, assault with intent. The victim was a woman. He got a suspended sentence, nine years ago. So I liked him a lot for *this*. But he has an alibi – his new wife and her two teenagers said he was at home the whole evening. And I believe them, they look decent.'

'No one else?'

'I looked at the boyfriend for a long time. Roch. But it just wouldn't fit, he was overseas, in any case. There's no one, Captain, I looked at everyone. That's why I say, it's something that we can't put our finger on. A chance encounter, a spur of the moment argument.'

But he only partly agreed. There were a few things that bothered him. The total absence of defensive wounds. Where the blood pooled. And the third drawer in the kitchen.

If she had been stabbed right at the front door, if her hands had been cut or bruised, he might have accepted the chance visitor and the argument story. But she was an adult, a clever lawyer. If someone knocked on her door at ten o'clock at night, she would look through the peephole first. She would only open up if she knew the visitor. She would only unlock the bolt and unhook the security chain if she *trusted* him.

She had been stabbed from the front. She was face to face with the murderer. Three metres into the apartment. She hadn't fended it off.

And the contents of the third kitchen drawer showed someone who was not keen on cooking. He suspected that was the sum total of her kitchen utensils. Even if there had been a fourth, much bigger, broader, longer knife, he could not see how a murderer could waltz in, open the drawer and scrabble around until he found the right weapon, while Hanneke Sloet stood patiently waiting near the front door.

The murderer had to have brought the weapon along.

Deliberately. With single-minded purpose.

And all that meant that Nxesi was right to suspect the convenient, previously convicted caretaker, Faroek Klein. He would have to check his alibi again.

Alexa opened the front door for him. She was in her dressing gown, still unkempt. But she was sober.

Relief washed over him, and the guilt that he had carried inside since yesterday evening. 'I'm so terribly sorry, Alexa, I humiliated you and then I had to go off and work, I . . .' But by then she had turned away from him, with an odd expression on her face that he could not read.

She walked to the kitchen.

'Alexa . . .' he said. She shook her head, as though she didn't want to hear.

He followed.

Her mug was on the table, her chair pushed back. That was where she had been sitting when he arrived.

Without a word she poured him coffee and sat down at the table. She pushed the milk, sugar and teaspoon holder closer, wrapped her hands around her own coffee mug, her faced hidden behind the blonde hair.

He sat down, worried now. She had looked like this the first time he saw her, in the sitting room of this house. The morning after her husband's death.

'It wasn't your fault,' she said.

He wanted to disagree with her, but she lifted a hand and stopped him.

'I do that,' she said. 'With people.'

He put milk and sugar in his coffee.

'And I don't know how to stop, Benny.'

'You're fantastic, Alexa,' he said, and the word sounded pretentious and inadequate. 'You are . . . you have everything. You are the best singer in the country and every time you phone me, I wonder why, because *I'm* a cop.'

Her mouth distorted with emotion.

'It's the truth,' he said.

'Didn't occur to you that that is precisely the problem?'

'What do you mean?'

'Christ, Benny, this industry . . . You don't know what it's like. I'm not strong enough . . .'

'You are,' he said.

'You don't understand. It seduces you. The . . . *attention*. The focus, the intense, never-ending, unnatural attention. It's like . . . To sing . . . it's such a commonplace talent, it's no better or no different than any other talent. Like . . . the man who painted this house, who recommended the colours and textures, he's so creative, so competent, his talent is so . . . obvious. But people don't crowd around him, tell him how wonderful he is from morning to night, how magical he is and how he changed their lives and . . . You start believing it, Benny, even if you don't want to. It never stops, every day, every show, every time you stick your nose out the door. I had forgotten what it was like. Until last night. We're such egotistical creatures. We're so easily led astray. Addicted to it. Completely. It was . . . it is my drug. In those days I started collecting people around me who had to give it to me, say it to me, in the moments of doubt. Because sometimes reality and truth intervene, when you realise you and your talent are just ordinary, this following, this breathless worship and appreciation and applause is for the music, for the emotion it awakes in people. Not for you. And you get scared. That one day people will realise that.'

She sighed, as though it took a lot of energy to say all that, turned the mug between her fingers. 'So I collect people, Benny. Like Dave Burmeister, my first band leader. And Adam. And now I'm doing the same with you. People who can plaster over the moments of truth, you tell them you're a failure, and they say, no, Alexa, you're the best singer in the world. They feed you the drug when the crowds are not there. It's a vicious circle, a seductive process, not rational or normal or psychologically balanced. Because the world you live in is abnormal. False. Smoke and mirrors and sleight of hand. And if you realise that, if the truth suddenly penetrates through to you one day, then the fear is kindled. Of being caught out. And then you start to drink. Because when you're drunk, it's easier to believe it all—'

Then Griessel's cellphone rang and he wished he could ignore it, he didn't want to be interrupted, not now.

10

'Answer, please,' said Alexa with a wry smile.

He took out his phone.

CARLA.

He stood up and walked to the dining room to answer it. 'Hello, Carla.'

'Fritz wants to get a tatt, Pappa,' said his daughter in her accusatory I-am-the-older-smarter-sister voice.

'A what?'

'A tattoo. Over his whole arm.'

His mind wasn't wholly on this conversation: 'What sort of tattoo?'

'Pa! Does it matter? What will he look like when he's forty?' As though that were the age of damnation.

'Carla, I . . . Where did that come from?'

'Since he's been playing for Jack Parow, Pa. I'm worried about him.' The maternal Carla, a new phenomenon since the divorce – she worried about her father and brother.

'No, I mean, how do you know?'

'He just phoned me now. He said he's going to a tattoo parlour this week. It's so . . . suburban . . .'

'I'll talk to him, it's just awkward now . . .'

'Shame, Pappa, are you working?'

'Yes. Quite an urgent case.'

'Ay. Don't work too hard, anyway, I just thought I'd tell you, Pappa.' Back in her normal, fizzy, exuberant mode. 'Will I see you next week?'

'You must let me know where you want to go and eat.'

'I will. But not with a kid with a tattoo. Love you, Pappa.'

'Love you too,' he said, and then she was gone with a cheerful 'bye', and he stood there for a while to get his thoughts together. He went back to the kitchen, stood in the doorway, a foot in two different worlds.

Lost in thought he said, 'Fritz wants to get a tattoo.'

Alexa Barnard swept the blonde hair out of her face with one hand, and then suddenly she began to laugh. Her head thrown back, the sound deep and surprising, and, so it sounded to Griessel, with a great deal of relief.

The Chana panel van drove into the parking lot of the Sea Point library, just to the right of the Town Hall. Right to the back, up against the M6 Western Boulevard, reversed it into the last parking spot, so that it could exit quickly and easily.

The sharpshooter switched off the engine, relieved about the windfalls: the car park was completely empty on a Sunday morning. In the two side mirrors outside he could see the grey, open terrain behind the vehicle, and then the long tarred bowls club lot where a bunch of cars was parked more than sixty metres away. And right beside the Chana, the screen of milkwood trees between him and the M6. The leaves and branches were still. There was practically no wind.

Through the gap between the two trees he inspected the Green Point Police Station on the other side of the double highway. A hundred and thirty metres, according to his Google Earth calculations. A long shot for this calibre, for his level of skill. But a greater problem was the high fence around the SAPS building. His only unhindered view of the entrance was through the wide front gate. It narrowed his sights dramatically; gave him very little time to track a target. He would have to wait until a policeman walked towards the door, that instant when he paused to pull it open . . .

Then there was the traffic on the M6. The trajectory was above normal cars, but a bus or a lorry could divert the shot. And through the tiny opening in the side panel of the Chana his field of vision was too small to refine his timing.

But this position was his only safe option.

He inspected the area one last time. He was aware of the quickening of his pulse, of his knuckles white on the steering wheel. He was disappointed. He had thought he would be calmer the second time.

Alexa told Griessel she had heard, through his conversation with Carla, that he had an urgent case.

With the self-mocking smile of the relapsed alcoholic, she said she had already called Mrs Ellis, her AA sponsor. There was no need to worry, she wouldn't drink again today. He must go to work, he could come around tonight or tomorrow or whenever he had a little time, and tell her all about it. And, please, he mustn't blame himself.

Would she please phone Lize Beekman and Anton Goosen and apologise on his behalf?

It wasn't necessary, she said. They were used to overwrought fans.

Please, he asked.

She would. But only if he went back to work now.

He phoned Mbali, and drove off to meet her at a street café in Greenmarket Square.

He arrived there before her, and watched the Zulu detective coming towards him through the crowds of tourists. The short, stout body with her 'don't-mess-with-me' attitude. She was, as always, dressed in a black trouser suit. The big black handbag over her shoulder, Beretta 92FS on her hip, the SAPS identity card slung on a tape around her neck for all the world to see. The over-the-top dark glasses. And nowadays a white scarf, to hide the scars.

He felt compassion for this woman. Perhaps because she had a kind of hero worship for him. She firmly believed he had saved her life, months ago, when she had been shot and he had staunched the awful wound in her neck until the ambulance arrived. But also because there were many SAPS members in the Cape who disliked her, since she was outspoken and a feminist, not afraid to criticise, pedantic, and painstakingly methodical. She did not hold her tongue for anyone, and her self-confidence sometimes bordered on the unacceptable. He felt it had something to do with the almost exclusive man's world of detectives, and her appearance. If *that* personality had come in a slim, attractive package, they would have queued up to work with her. They would have said she deserved her promotion to the Hawks. Maybe it was because he was an alcoholic and a fuck-up that he could identify with her. Because he knew what it was like to have people laugh behind your back. Or maybe it was his experience – after twenty-six years in the Force you knew that good, reliable detectives were scarce, it made no difference what shape they came in.

'Hi, Benny.'

He stood up, greeted her, and waited for her to be seated.

She did so with a sigh, putting her handbag down on the chair beside her. She fiddled inside it, pulled out a thin file, took one sheet of paper out of it, and placed it in front of him.

'This is for you.' Then she pushed her dark glasses up above her forehead and, frowning, looked around for a waiter.

The Green Point Police Station was quieter than the sniper had expected. It made the spring of tension wind slowly tighter inside him: how long could he sit here with the shooting hole open, rifle in hand, before someone noticed – someone walking past, a car pulling off the M6 right in front of him? It was the unpredictable, chance, the things no one could plan for, that presented the greatest risk. He knew that. In his preparation, his research, thinking through his plan over and over, he kept coming back to that truth. The solution was to limit the influence of chance at all costs. Don't become over-keen or over-confident. Don't underestimate them. Don't hesitate. Don't take risks.

He wished for the euphoria of yesterday afternoon, that light-headed jumble of relief and satisfaction and content-ment – he had outmanoeuvred them, he had got away, he had hit back. He had known then that his strategy was masterful, infallible. But now doubts were eating away at him. And the fear of being caught.

A white SAPS sedan drove through the gate opposite.

More adrenaline.

He pressed his cheek against the rifle, looked through the scope.

762a89z012@anonimail.com
Sent: Sunday 27 February. 06.57
To: j.afrika@saps.gov.za
Re: To Kaptein Bennie Griessel
I saw the article in the Weekend Argus. Can you do right (Proverbs 21:15)? Are you also hand in glove with the communists? I hope not, because then I would have to escalate things.
I shot the policeman in Claremont yesterday. Today there will be another one. Every day, until you charge the murderer.
You know who it is.

Griessel looked up. Mbali told him General Afrika had forwarded it to both of them that morning, and asked her to take it to him.

He thanked her, and asked her if she had found anything in Claremont.

She counted off the problems one by one, slow and measured, on her podgy fingers, her face filled with frustra-tion. One: there were no eye witnesses. Nobody heard the shot, nobody saw anything strange. Two: the bullet that shattered Constable Brandon April's knee had disintegrated entirely. Three: the nature of the wound made determination of the trajectory difficult – they still did not know where the shot had been fired. 'If you take into account the parking area's possible field of vision, it could have been from the school, or from a block of flats, but he would have had to be inside, or on the roof. All access was locked, and there is no sign of forced entry anywhere. It doesn't make sense.' The waiter came and stood beside her, and she said sternly, 'Coca Cola, but bring the ice separately, no half a glass monkey business.'

The man raised his eyebrows, glanced at Griessel, who indicated he didn't want anything. Then he left.

'So we have no real crime scene,' said Mbali. 'And today he is going to shoot again.'

Lieutenant Colonel Bevan Dlodlo pulled on the aluminium handle to open the door of the Green Point Police Station.

At that instant, with a thunderous clap, the glass directly in front of him exploded.

His whole body jerked in fright, a glass shard stung his forehead. Shouts from inside, the tinkle of glass raining down and shattering on the concrete. His instinct was to duck, to move to the wall, away from the door. His hand reached for the service pistol on his hip.

With his back to the wall, the pistol in his hand, on his haunches, head turned to the door, he wanted to shout to those inside to find out what was going on. He felt the warm trickle of blood running down his forehead. Then something jerked at his ankle, with so much violence that he fell over onto his left side.

He looked down in astonishment at his lower leg. He saw his blue police boot in tatters, the blood seeping through it and slowly spreading in a growing pool on the concrete.

He looked across the parking lot. There was no one.
He looked at the street outside. There was nothing.
Only then did he feel the incredible pain.

I I

With the file open in front of her Mbali tapped her finger on
the emails and said, 'I don't get this guy. Am I missing something, is it the culture gap?'

'No,' said Griessel. 'I don't understand him either. Last
night I thought . . . it's like he's trying to sound like a crazy. I
think . . . if you read the emails, he comes across a lot like a
wacko. But then he actually goes and shoots someone . . . I've
never seen that before. If you look at that one email, he said:
You have two weeks to catch the killer. He was planning back
then. He was preparing. He's . . . different. And he's not . . .
your everyday crazy.'

She nodded in agreement. 'You think he knew Sloet?'

That was a good question, one that he had wondered
about last night. He shook his head slowly. 'I don't know.
Maybe. If he was part of her life, he must have known
that it could lead us to him, eventually. So I have my
doubts.'

'Unless he *is* crazy.'

'Yes.'

'No candidates,' said Mbali, a statement.

'No.'

'No communists?'

'I don't think he means a real communist. It's a . . .' His
English let him down.

'A metaphor?'

He wasn't sure what that meant. She saw that. 'Like he's
using a figure of speech. Maybe he means black people?'

'Something like that. As if he doesn't want to sound like a racist.'

'But he doesn't mind sounding like a religious nut.'

'Yes.'

'So, any black suspects?'

'Maybe a coloured guy. The caretaker . . .'

Mbali closed the file in front of her, pushed it into her handbag. 'I'm going to send the emails to Ilse Brody at Investigative Psychology . . . but what else, Benny? What am I missing? Where would *you* look?'

'There's not much to look at . . .'

From the expectation on her face he could see she was hoping for more. He thought it over, then asked, 'Nobody heard the shot? Not even the constable?'

'Nobody.'

'Then it's probably a long-range weapon. A rifle, probably a scope. And a silencer. I'll look at silencers, they're scarce, I don't think you can buy them from a shop . . . Do you know Giel de Villiers? From the armoury?'

'No.'

'He's the one I go to if I have questions about weapons. He's very quiet, but he knows everything. That's what I would do. Talk to Giel.' Realising it was Sunday, Griessel added, 'He lives out in Bothasig. He'll probably be in the book.'

'Thank you, Benny.' She got up and picked up her handbag. 'Why do you think they gave me the case?'

That caught him off guard. 'How do you mean?'

'I'm new at CATS, I only got back on Friday. I was still unpacking . . .'

'You know how it is, everybody's got too much work . . .'

He wanted to add that she was a good methodical investigator, but with a look of suspicion she said, 'Doesn't make sense.' Then her cellphone started to ring, and she had to scrabble in her big handbag to find it before she could answer.

The conversation was brief. She made only a few affirmative grunts, then said, 'I'm coming.' Then to Griessel, resigned, 'He's shot another one. The SC, at Green Point.'

He drove to the Bo-Kaap, only four blocks away, to the home of the caretaker, Faroek Klein, in Bryant Street. His mind was in too many places at once, he wanted to think about how to approach the man, about Mbali's parting words, but the new email haunted him. *You know who it is.* This one addressed to him personally now.

In the very first one it was, *You know very well who murdered Hanneke Sloet.* In one of the others, *You know why she was murdered.* Between all the variation in singulars and plurals and Bible verses, this repetitive theme.

He had read the case file, he had been to the scene, he knew enough to be able to say that it was nonsense. There was no obvious suspect.

Mbali had said, 'Unless he *is* crazy.' What he could add was, 'Maybe he's even crazier than we think.' In normal circumstances he would have ignored the emails – just another lunatic.

The rifle, the scope and the silencer were the problem. You couldn't be too crazy if you could put all that together with a long-distance shot and get away with it. And the latest email, there was a new tone to it, self-satisfied, a certain awareness of power. *I hope not, because then I would have to escalate things.* This was a man who could force the SAPS to reopen a case, a blackmailer who had to be taken seriously.

This was trouble. It fuelled his frustration. He still knew too little. About everything.

He struggled to find parking, had to cross Bloem Street for a bay in front of the St Paul Primary School. Griessel got out and walked back, between the brightly-painted little houses.

Coloured people sat on their porches, their eyes following his progress with a certain wariness. He thought of Mbali back at the street café. Just before she walked away, she'd said, 'Thanks, Benny, for not asking about Amsterdam.' She had a vulnerability about her he had never seen before. And she was subdued this morning, not her old, obstreperous self.

Now he too was curious about what had happened in Holland.

Klein's home was a yellow terraced house with white pillars, and a tree that dominated the small front garden. Griessel reached to open the red garden gate. His cellphone rang.

He paused, saw an unfamiliar number, and answered simply, 'Yes.'

'Hey, Benny, it's Vaughn, where are you?' Captain Vaughn Cupido.

'I'm still in the city, Vaughn.'

'I thought you were going to call me?'

'Call you?'

'*Jis*. The Giraffe said you would phone me. About the Sloet case.'

Griessel tried to remember what Colonel Nyathi had said the night before. 'As far as I know, you are just on standby, Vaughn, nobody said I had to phone you.'

'*Jissis*, the brass . . . always mixed messages. Anyway, I'm keen to help, Benny. Can I come and get the files, get myself up to speed?'

'I'm still busy with it myself. Listen, I'm standing in front of a . . .' If he said 'suspect', Cupido would definitely broadcast the news that Griessel had made great progress. '. . . witness's house, I'll call you as soon as I have something. Thanks, Vaughn, I appreciate your offer.'

Silence over the line. Then, 'Cool,' his tone unenthusiastic.

Griessel ended the call. Cupido was not his favourite

detective. He was one of those men who knew everything, and was extremely pleased with the fact that he was a Hawk. Vaughn was with the former Organised Crime Unit, which had been directly incorporated in the DPCI. Cowboys.

He put his phone away and opened the garden gate.

She was as slim and sleek as a cat, with long black hair and big dark brown eyes, beautiful, and not much older than sixteen. She looked Griessel up and down critically and then called over her shoulder into the house: 'Dadda, the Boere are here again.'

She tossed the cascade of straight hair over her shoulder with a gesture of disdain, turned and stalked off, as if he didn't exist.

Heavier footsteps on the wooden floor, as a man walked into the small hallway. 'Can I help?' Surly.

'Mr Klein?'

'That's right.'

Griessel held up his SAPS identity card. Klein glanced at it. He was taller than Griessel, with manicured stubble on his upper lip and chin, the thick black hair combed, a strong face. Early forties. He said, 'What do you want this time?'

'Is there a place we can talk?'

'Here is good.'

A woman appeared behind Klein, middle-aged, with the same enchanting heritage of Malay genes as her daughter, the same antipathy on her face. 'Invite him in,' she said, turned and walked away.

Griessel could see Klein was not in the mood. He stood patiently waiting.

'Come in.'

They were a united front on the sofa, Klein in the middle, the wife and two teenage daughters beside him.

Griessel sat opposite, in an easy chair, his notebook in hand. He didn't get the chance to ask a question, before the wife began, 'I am Noor, this is Laila, and this is Asmida. I am Faroek's second wife, he is the stepfather of my children. You can ask them, he is a good stepfather. Faroek's first wife was a bad apple. He caught her sleeping around, and not only once. When he couldn't stand it any more, he smacked her, and she laid a complaint and they made a case. He pleaded guilty, he got a suspended sentence, he divorced her. Last year she got married for the fourth time.' Everything said with a factual tone, without judgement.

The two daughters glared. Klein sat there with a hidden, satisfied smile, encircled by three pretty women.

Griessel nodded, drew a breath to say something, but she didn't give him a chance.

'The evening the Sloet woman was murdered, Faroek was here at home. With all three of us. We ate at seven o'clock, like we do every night, and then the girls sat in the kitchen doing homework, and Faroek and I watched TV. These two went to bed around ten, and Faroek and I at about half past ten, because we are both gainfully employed and we take our responsibilities seriously. We love each other very much. We aren't white, we aren't rich, but we have our values. And they do not include lying if any one of us commits murder. Is there anything else you would like to know?'

He closed his notebook. There was one question remaining, but he suspected the answer would not come without more chastisement. 'Mr Klein, are you . . . communist in your politics?'

They laughed at him, all four of them.

'No,' said Klein. And they laughed again.

The tall, beautiful woman stood up. 'We are about to have Sunday lunch, would you like to join us?'

12

He drove home, wanting to get rid of the pressure inside, the urge to curse and beat the steering wheel. There were times he didn't want to be a policeman – to go knocking on the door of a house on a Sunday morning, to disturb the peace, to carry trouble across the threshold with him. The Klein family, standing united against him, had upset him in a peculiar way. And the undisguised reprimand, *We aren't white, we aren't rich, but we have our values.* He wanted to protest, wanted to say it had nothing to do with colour, it was about who had keys and a criminal record. They wouldn't have believed him – that's what frustrated him. Only in this country . . . Colour, everything revolved around colour, all the time, every which way you looked, it was there. *Jissis*. He just wanted to do his job.

We have our values. They were actually implying that he didn't, that his very presence proved it. And when he left with his tail between his legs, he wondered fleetingly, if Anna married the lawyer, would they sit on a couch like that with his children, such a new, happy family, so communally pious, free of the struggling alcoholic policeman? Anna who would sit and explain, 'My first husband was a bad apple, a drinker and a wife-beater.' Would he ever get away from the consequences of his weakness?

He pulled in at the Engen garage near his flat to buy lunch at the Woolies Food. Without any appetite he looked at the sandwiches and the microwave meals, angry all over again at Steers, for discontinuing their Dagwood burger. 'It takes too much time, sir, the clients don't want to wait that long, sir.' What was happening to the world – people didn't want to wait for decent food any more. Everything had to be fast: tasteless, ugly, but fast.

Nothing was ever simple.

He remembered the dream he had had repeatedly a month or so ago, four nights in a row. He was playing with Roes, he couldn't get the notes of the bass guitar to keep to the tempo, he buggered into the wrong key, and the band members gave him sidelong glances with questioning, worried faces.

That's how he'd felt, since yesterday. Out of rhythm with the world. Out of tune.

On the other hand, in the last ten years had he ever felt any other way?

In his kitchen he shoved the chicken and broccoli in cheese sauce into the microwave and phoned Mbali.

'It's chaos, Benny, they brought in Forensics before I could call the PCSI task team. The whole station trampled my crime scene to help the SC. I had to interview him in the ambulance.

'He's not sure where the shot came from, maybe from the tennis courts. But we are talking to the players, and they didn't see or hear anything.'

'He was shot in the leg?'

'In the ankle. But there was another shot, Benny. He hit the door first, the entrance door, we have two bullets to search for. It might help.'

'So he missed.'

'Yes. The first shot was a miss.'

At his breakfast counter he ate the chicken straight out of the container, without pleasure. He sat and stared at his mountain bike – it hadn't moved in two weeks. There wasn't enough time in the morning to ride – he had to get up earlier to handle the traffic all the way to the DPCI offices in Bellville. If they would only finish building the damn flyovers on the

N5. But the World Cup was over now, everything was at a standstill again.

The solution was to move, to find himself a flat in the northern suburbs. He didn't want to. He liked living under the mountain, near the city and the Gardens Centre. And the distance from Anna, from his old problems and trouble. Bellville was full of temptation, all his old drinking spots, his old drinking buddies . . .

But he wasn't getting to ride his bike now.

Life was never simple.

He got up, went and lay down on the couch, hands on his chest. He felt the fatigue of too little sleep, maybe he should take a nap, half an hour, to clear his head.

You must get moving. This mad bastard is going to shoot policemen until you solve the case. Afrika's winged words.

He tried to focus. Premeditated murder. Someone she knew.

Not the caretaker.

No other suspect. No motive.

The trouble was, he actually knew nothing about Sloet.

He sighed, got up, fetched the file, sat down again at the breakfast counter. He read the statements of Mr Hannes Pruis, director of Silberstein Lamarque, and Gabriélle (Gabby) Villette, Sloet's personal assistant, over again. There was detail about the morning the body was found, there was broad information about her work, but basically they said nothing about *her*.

He pulled his notebook closer, found the telephone numbers and wrote them down.

Gabriélle Villette lived alone in a town house, in the back of the Avenues complex in Sea Point, away from the noise of High Level Road. She was barefoot, her body as small and skinny as a child. Her face was narrow beneath her short blonde hair. He guessed she was just under thirty. Her mouth was a stingy line, so her warmth surprised him. Griessel apologised for the hour and the short notice. She said, 'I don't sleep during the day, please come in,' with a smile that revealed two prominent eye teeth, reminding him vaguely of a vampire. 'I saw the piece in the newspaper this morning.'

The sitting room was a cheerful blue and yellow. There was a series of framed colour photos of fruit on the wall, very close-up shots of a glowing green bunch of grapes, a red apple, a yellow pear, an enamel bucket full of bright orange apricots. She saw him looking. 'It's my hobby,' she said, nothing more, and he wondered if she meant the fruit or the photography. 'Please sit,' she encouraged him, and made herself comfortable on the light blue-grey sofa. Her eyes were almost the same shade.

He sat in a pale yellow chair, took out his notebook. He saw her cross her legs and look at him expectantly.

'I'm trying to find out who Hanneke Sloet was,' he said.

She nodded slowly and thoughtfully, looked at the nest of books, magazines and newspapers on the coffee table. 'I tried for three years. And I'm not sure if I made much progress,' she said almost formally, every word pronounced clearly. And then, as though coming to her senses: 'No disrespect to her memory.'

'Anything will help,' he said.

Again the nod, as though she was considering the words and consenting, the eyes cast down. He guessed it was a usual mannerism of hers.

'Hanneke was . . . My first boss at Silberstein was Barry Brink. I had to do everything for him. Open his post and email, answer his cellphone, make his hair appointments, call his wife when he was going to be late. And I helped his daughter with her school projects, on the Internet. They invited me along to their beach house at Jongensfontein, or

Sunday dinners in Blouberg. Barry was an open book. You get two kinds of bosses, Captain. Barry was an includer. Hanneke was the other kind. An excluder. I prefer them, because they are much easier to work for. The boundaries are clear: handle the diary, liaise, find the references and court cases and articles, answer the office phone, and my cell only if I'm in a meeting. Personal stuff is completely excluded. Only after her death did I realise how little I knew about her. Because you wonder, after the worst shock is over. You can't help it.'

'How long did you work for her?'

'Nearly two years.'

'And how was she? As your boss?'

'I liked her,' she said, this time more quickly, without the nod and the thoughtful pause.

He didn't react, waited for her to say more.

The silence stretched, she folded her hands together. He knew this reaction, piety for the dead. He waited.

'I admired her,' the voice was a bit quieter, eyes on the floor. 'She was pretty and clever. And hard working. So focused. She put in a lot of hours. She was precise, in everything. Organised. Always on time. Always well groomed. And fair.' Gabby Villette looked up at him, as if she were grateful that it occurred to her, 'She treated me very fairly.'

Not much more than was in the file. He asked what Hanneke Sloet's typical day looked like. Before Villette answered, the hesitation was back, the thorough consideration, the slow nod. Then she said you must differentiate between last year, and January. Sloet probably moved to the city because she knew her pace was going to burn her out. While she lived in Stellenbosch, she must have got up at half past four to get to the gym by a quarter to six, the Virgin Active in Jetty Street. She exercised until a quarter to seven, and she was at the office every weekday at a quarter past.

'How do you know she was at the gym?'

'That was where she did her dictation. On the exercise bike. I could hear it, on the recorder.'

He asked about the rest of the day. She said Sloet would prepare until half past eight, planned the day with Villette until nine, when the meetings began. There were a lot of meetings in the team environment at Silbersteins. In the afternoon, between one and three, she answered calls and emails, then worked on contracts and reports, mostly until eight o'clock at night. Villette knew because she never went home before her boss. Sometimes there were business lunches and evening cocktail parties, there were short business trips especially to Gauteng, there were two days in winter that Villette could remember when Hanneke Sloet phoned in with a hoarse, nasal voice to say she was as sick as a dog, in bed with flu and a lot of medicine. And the operation, last year, she was off for a week . . .

The subtle intonation of 'the operation' made him ask, 'What operation?'

'The boob job,' she said, glancing quickly at her own small bosom, the tone of her voice slightly *too* neutral.

'When last year?'

'April.'

He knew it was the right time for the question. 'Did everyone like her?'

Villette's gaze flitted down to the coffee table. She shook her head slowly before quietly saying: 'No.'

13

Mbali had to push through the bystanders to walk out of the gate of Green Point Station. They stood just outside the circle of yellow crime-scene tape that was stretched around the front door, complainants who wanted to enter, the curious, everyone was watching Thick and Thin of Forensics as they sifted through the glass shards.

She went and stood in the gateway, drew an imaginary bead for the shot, and walked along it. Every now and then she would stop, look back, see how the opening narrowed as the distance increased.

She walked across the grey, open space beside the tennis courts, up to the Western Boulevard. To stop here, to aim, shoot. Two shots? Unlikely.

She waited for an opening in the traffic, trotted across the tar to the island, then over to the other side. Her handbag swung from the shoulder strap so that she had to steady it with her hand.

A little out of breath she looked back at the gate, now seeming impossibly small.

Then she looked at the possibilities on this side of the double highway – the open space to the left, the bowls club behind it. Then to the right, the brick and rail fence of the Town Hall. On top of it was an electrified wire. Nobody could climb over that.

She stood there for a long time, looking and thinking. And eventually made her deductions.

Griessel sat and waited until Gabby Villette filled the silence. 'You have to understand the context,' she said. 'Silbersteins is . . . All the directors are men, ninety per cent of the associates too. And all the PAs are women. Hanneke was somewhere in the middle . . .' She looked up, the eye teeth suddenly displayed in an apologetic grin. 'I'm not used to talking about my work with outsiders. That's the problem with Silbersteins, it becomes your world, your whole life . . .'

He could see she wanted to talk about it.

She folded her arms. 'It's such an . . . intense place, the hours, the pace, the pressure, money drives everyone, chargeable hours . . .'

The arms opened slowly. 'So, in this atmosphere, it's hard to explain. We . . . the PAs, it's like a subculture, a network, we *have* to know everything for the place to function. Know everyone's quirks. Hanneke distanced herself from us so deliberately, I think it was so that everyone would know she was a woman, but not one of us, she was one of *them*. Am I making sense? I believe she had to, to make her mark. Not everyone liked that. Sometimes they were nasty. Not from jealousy, but a feeling of "she needn't make it so obvious", like she was insulting them. So there was always gossip. Stories . . .'

She looked up at Griessel for encouragement.

He supplied it, 'What stories?'

The slow nod. 'Most of them weren't true.'

He showed he understood.

'They said she would do anything for promotion.'

She folded her arms again and looked at the window.

'She *was* ambitious. That was where the gossip began. But then . . . If she went to lunch with a director, then they would talk. You know . . . And after the boob job last year, then it was "yes, now she's aiming higher" . . .'

'Did she have an affair with anyone at work?'

The 'no' came too quickly, and Villette knew it. 'I don't know. I really don't.'

'What do you think?'

'Definitely not since I started working for her.'

He knew she was leading him, wanting him to ask more. 'And before that?'

'Maybe.'

He nodded encouragingly.

'That was when she was still an articled clerk. A long time

ago. 2002? She worked in Corporate and Commercial Litigation. The director was Werner Gelderbloem. He was her sort of mentor, he was over fifty by then. A good-looking man. And he's married . . . in any case, there was talk of . . . You know . . .'

'Talk?'

'Apparently they would still be talking in his office when his PA went home in the evening. And he took her along for a case in Pretoria, and when his PA phoned the hotel one morning, she heard Hanneke's voice in the room . . . Or she thought it was Hanneke's voice.'

Griessel had hoped for more. Something recent.

Villette said, 'Gossip . . .'

He nodded, trying to hide his disappointment. 'Did you know her former friend . . .' he referred to his notes, 'Egan Roch?'

'I met him. Twice. He came to the office one day, just after I started with Hanneke. And then at the Christmas party, year before last.' As an afterthought, 'They suited each other.'

'In what way?'

'Two good-looking people. And the way he had with her . . . I think he understood her. He is . . . very comfortable with himself.'

'Do you know why they broke up?'

She shook her head.

In his car he called Hannes Pruis, Silberstein Director. The cellphone switched over to voicemail. He left a message, then typed in Egan Roch's number. The man answered, the signal was poor, he could hear the hum of a moving vehicle. Griessel explained the situation. Roch said he was on the other side of Citrusdal, he would only be home after seven, could they meet tomorrow?

Benny agreed, made an appointment for ten o'clock, time

for him to get to where Roch worked, on a wine farm outside Stellenbosch. Then he rang off and drove to the SAPS station in Green Point, which was nearby. He had to park in front of the small supermarket, because the gate was cordoned off. He got out and went in search of Mbali.

Thick and Thin of Forensics were packing up.

'Hey, Benny,' Arnold, the short, fat one, greeted him.

'Now we can relax,' said Jimmy, tall and skinny.

'The Hawks have landed,' said Arnold.

'Hi,' said Griessel.

'Hi?' said Arnold. 'So it's "hi" now?'

'What happened to *fokkof*? Is it a Hawks' thing? No swearing?'

'No sense of tradition. That's the trouble with these elite units.'

Griessel sighed. 'Have you seen Mbali?'

'The Hefty Hawk,' Arnold giggled.

'Falcus Giganticus,' smirked Jimmy.

'Benny is the Chanting Goshawk,' said Arnold. 'I hear you've got a band . . .'

'*Fokkof*,' said Griessel against his will.

'That's better,' said Arnold.

'Sorry, another band already has that name. *Fokkofpoliesiekar.* But Hawk Off could work . . .'

'Mbali,' said Griessel, because it was no use getting angry with them.

'Flew off,' said Jimmy. 'Back to the Claremont crime scene.'

'Has she told you yet, Benny?'

'What?'

'What happened in Amsterdam?'

'I'm telling you, someone tried to pick her up in Walletjie Street, so she *moered* him . . .' said Jimmy.

'Did she, Benny?'

'I'm a hawk, not a rat,' said Griessel, and walked towards the gate.

At seven minutes to four the sniper sent the email, but the pressure and uncertainty deprived him of any sense of pleasure. His nerves drove him up from the computer. He tugged open the drawer, took out the Chana's keys, walked anxiously to the kitchen and opened the access door to the garage. Then he stopped, conscious of his feverish haste.

Exactly what he couldn't afford.

One mistake. That's all it would take. He would have to calm down. He would have to think hard about what he wanted to do next. Every minute on the road in the Chana was a risk.

He paused, reaching for calm, for reason.

He had no choice. He would have to drive. Go run the test.

He closed the door slowly behind him, climbed into the vehicle. Looked in the back. Everything in its place.

He turned on the engine. Pressed the button of the remote to open the door of the garage.

He drove, out on the R7, towards Melkbosstrand, then along the M19 east, to where the old Atlantis road turned off. He looked for a place, found one five kilometres further – a gravel road to the left, across a railway line. He turned off, saw a possible target, more or less a hundred metres away. A blue gum tree, thick trunk, the bark peeling off in strips.

He parked, switched off the engine. He felt the prickle of nerves in his neck, the tension in his guts, the bottled-up worry. Why couldn't he get rid of it?

Because he had missed twice already. That was what was ratcheting up the pressure, and what took away the pleasure. All his perfect planning, but *this* he could not have foreseen.

Calm down. Solve the problem.

He waited. Looked. Listened. Eventually he got in the

back, unhooked the fabric curtain, got the gun, and slid open the side panel.

He aimed for the tree.

So much easier if the target was not alive.

He shot.

Looked through the telescope.

Perfect.

So much easier if the target did not move.

It wasn't the rifle. The problem lay with him.

14

The urge to do something, to build up momentum, to utilise the time, took Griessel back to Sloet's apartment. He had no other immediate options, he would have to search the place anyway, thoroughly and meticulously, sooner or later. And there was the undefined question about the place, which since his visit to Gabby Villette, was lurking in the back of his mind.

In the lift, the security woman asked, 'When will you be finished?'

'Soon,' he said.

She didn't respond.

In the apartment he shut the front door behind him, then pulled at it. It had locked automatically. He leaned back against the door.

There was one problem with his theory that Sloet knew the murderer: the missing spare key for this door. The bunch he held in his hand now only had four; one for the front door, one for her Mini, two for the cupboards in the bedroom. And Nxesi said there were extra cupboard keys in a drawer upstairs, but that was all.

Before he left Villette, he had asked her who Sloet would

trust with her spare key. She nodded and thought it over and shook her head. 'I don't know ... I'll think about it,' she promised.

He turned around, studied the security chain. There was absolutely no damage to it.

Had someone stolen the spare keys? Someone she didn't know? Maybe she sometimes forgot to hook the chain or close the bolt, because she could use the peephole?

Why then a murder without robbery or sexual assault?

The big question: who had motive?

He began his search upstairs, in the second bedroom, already used to the way it felt, the odd mix of vague voyeurism and excitement. Using a knife he fetched from the kitchen, he carefully slit open every cardboard box, unpacked the contents one by one, and then back again.

Textbooks, probably from her student days. African Customary Law, Private Law, Roman Law, Criminal Law, Public Law, Interpretation of Law, Law of Criminal Procedure, Competition Law, Insurance Law, Intellectual Property Law, Internet Law.

So much Law. No wonder the courts and the jails were chock-full. No wonder the police couldn't keep up.

A stack of coffee-table books about wine and art and interior decorating, a couple of Afrikaans novels by Marita van der Vyver, Etienne van Heerden and André P. Brink, a diverse collection of English paperbacks by, among others, Jodi Picoult, Anne Tyler and John Grisham.

Nineteen DVDs. Most looked like European art films, the sort with subtitles. Two were pornographic, but the covers were tasteful. *Five Hot Stories for Her* and *Urban Friction*.

A whole box full of music CDs. Vanilla Ice, Mariah Carey, Nirvana, Paula Abdul, Whitney Houston, Duran Duran, Pearl Jam, Alanis Morissette, Laurika Rauch, Boyz II Men, Nine Inch Nails, Al Jarreau, Koos Kombuis, Madonna, Riku

Latti, Red Hot Chili Peppers, Radiohead. Six classical music collections with titles such as *The Best Classical Album Ever* and *Chill with Mozart*.

Memorabilia. Old programmes and tickets to concerts and plays, postcards, greetings cards of congratulations for birthdays, graduation, promotion. Used plane tickets and brochures for trips to Europe and the USA, cheap jewellery, a chunky old cellphone. Decorative hair combs and grips, two scratched pairs of sunglasses, iPod cables, loose photos of groups of people.

Six photograph albums and a smaller box of letters. He put them to one side. The other boxes were filled with clothes and shoes. Lots of shoes.

He carried the letters and photo albums down to the sitting room, sat down on the couch, lifted the lid of the box of letters. Foreknowledge made him hesitate: he knew he would be crossing a boundary now. Sloet would become flesh and blood, a person with a life, with emotions and regrets and few secrets. It would rob him of his distance, his objectivity, it would all become that bit more personal. That was where the trouble lay, the root of the evil. Because he knew what came next. This case had been easier from the start. He hadn't been at the scene of the murder. He hadn't stood beside her, and seen the terrible fragility of the female body, her expression caught at the moment of death. He hadn't smelled the blood and perfume and decomposition. He hadn't lived her last moments with her in his mind, felt her acute fear of the darkness of death, or heard the silent scream they all uttered when they lost that final grip on life.

Doc Barkhuizen said over and over again: 'Don't internalise it, Benny.' Doc knew that was his reason for drinking. Until, at last, about a month ago, Griessel had confessed: 'I don't know how, Doc.'

'Go and talk to a shrink, Benny.'

And he asked, 'What for, Doc?' because he already knew where it had begun, he could remember the first time, crystal-clear, although it was fourteen years ago. The sunny Saturday morning, the five-year-old child in the middle of the park at Rylands, her white socks and white sandals, the blue ribbons in her ponytails, the heart-rending beauty of her delicate features. The red and purple bruises of the rape and strangulation, the dried semen, the tender little hand gripping a Wilson's toffee wrapping like a last treasure.

It was his fourth murder that week, an impossible time. Too few people, too little sleep, too much work. They all suffered from post-traumatic stress, but nobody knew. That morning, he saw her expression at her moment of death and he heard the primitive scream, and he knew, everyone screams when they die, everyone holds on to life terribly tightly, and when someone loosens their fingers, they fall and cry out in terror. Of the end.

Of course he drank before that – controllably, four, five times a week, in the afternoon with the guys. But after that it got out of control. Alcohol was the only thing that could keep all the noises and images out of his head, the all-consuming fear that it could happen to his family too, to Anna and Carla and Fritz.

Tell all that to a shrink and all he would say was: 'Here's a bunch of pills.' And then he, Griessel would be addicted to something else. Or even worse: 'Get another job.' At forty-five. White. With the maintenance payments after the divorce and university fees and not a fucking cent saved in the bank.

Life was never simple.

Eventually he reached into the box.

Systematically, he built up the jigsaw puzzle of her life. The phantom pieces from the albums and letters were not enough to form a clear image, so he had to fill the gaps with his imagination. The story was ordinary, mostly typical Afrikaner middle class. It began in Ladybrand in the Free State in the mid-seventies. Willem Sloet, co-op clerk, tall and thin and slightly stooped; the hairline already beginning to recede in the face of more than thirty summers, the little moustache uncertain, like an experiment – on some of the photos he had the intimidated expression of a man who had married above his station and had, slowly, begun to realise the consequences. His wife, Marna, with her pleasant face, her smile frequently determined and brave. And the only child, Hanneke, lucky to have inherited from the start the best combination of her parents' features.

In the early eighties there was a move to Paarl, apparently a better position for Willem, because the old reddish-brown Ford Escort in the holiday photos is replaced by a white Volkswagen Passat station wagon. Hanneke grows into a lanky schoolgirl, her thick hair in a plait, the slight gap between her front teeth displayed without embarrassment in every smile, cute, plucky and carefree.

Willem Sloet becomes a marginal character, presumably behind the camera most of the time. Where he does appear in the photos, the space between him and Marna has subtly widened, a deliberate distancing by one of them perhaps. Marna's grace increases, her attractiveness becomes more interesting with the years, and their offspring blossoms, in a single album page, somewhere around her fifteenth year. In the photo on the top left she was still a child, skinny, crouching before the unpredictable leap into puberty; bottom right the metamorphosis is nearly complete, and the chips have fallen in her favour. Suddenly a head taller than her mother, athletic, but with feminine, elegant lines, the eyes wider apart, the mouth full, the curve of her neck and shoulder enchanting. And, along with that, another apparent awakening: at the Paarl Girls High School, she was chairperson of debating, hockey captain, member of the student council, and winner of the academic prize for accountancy.

He looked through the letters. There were two from boys, raw and clumsy declarations of teenage love and desire, warm letters of friendship from other girls, their admiration shining through. And a series written by mother Marna, initially just best wishes for her daughter's achievements in school – the encouragement and aspiration delicately camouflaged. Later, at university and during Hanneke Sloet's backpacking year in Europe, her mother's wistfulness over her own lost opportunities, her disappointment in her husband, and her ambitions for her daughter glimmered through ever more strongly.

The letters ended there, at the end of 2000, just before Hanneke Sloet started at Silberstein Lamarque. The glued and captioned snapshots too. In the back of the last album was a sheaf of loose photographs of Sloet and someone whom Griessel assumed must be Egan Roch. The man was tall, with powerful shoulders and arms, and abundant self-confidence. They were, in the words of Gabriélle Villette, 'two good-looking people'. The photographs showed they had frequently walked in the mountains, had visited a wine farm, sailed in Table Bay, socialised, and been to New York together at least once.

Loose photographs, thought Captain Benny Griessel. As though Hanneke Sloet didn't want to commit this relationship to permanent record.

He thought it all over while he searched the master bedroom meticulously. He tried all the parts of Villette's revelations for fit and what he could glean from the albums and letters.

Hanneke Sloet the Ambitious.

Should he be concerned with this?

The thing was, he had often seen the dangers of extreme ambition. In women, the consuming desire to rise in social stature, to keep up with neighbours and colleagues, sometimes led to fraud and theft from the employer, or the smuggling of drugs on planes.

But Sloet had followed another route, honourable and acceptable. Hard, disciplined work at school and university, later at Silbersteins. The alleged affair with the older, married man early in her career could as easily be attributed to compensation for a weak father figure as to the desire for advancement.

This was the territory that roused his instincts: the forbidden affair, the sensual photos, the breast enlargement, the pornographic movies, the bizarre vibrator. Therein lay a pattern, and he believed absolutely in patterns of behaviour – you always find one if you look long and acutely enough. Add to that the fact that eight out of ten women were murdered by the husband, the fiancé, the lover, the hopeful suitor, the sex partner . . .

15

He could find nothing. No spare key, no new insights or clues.

In the sitting room, out of desperation, he examined the telescope and decided it was ornamental, the magnification unimpressive, the interesting peeping tom possibilities outside the window just too far away.

Griessel walked to the door, stopping in frustration and indecision beside the pool of dry blood. He understood why Nxesi's investigation had yielded nothing, because there were only shadows of possibilities, vague spectres that evaporated when you looked more closely. Communists? The shooter had the wrong end of the stick – there were no communists in her life, just a Big Boy vibrator in the bedside cupboard. A whole day wasted and he had made no progress, and tomorrow the bastard would blow another policeman's leg away.

He bit off the F-word with considerable effort.

He would phone Cupido and tell him he was leaving the case files at the DPCI office, see if *you* can find something. He reached out to turn off the light and suddenly came to a realisation, the thing that had been in his subconscious since his visit to Villette: the contrast between the two apartments. Villette's was personal, with obvious signs of life – the framed photographs of fruit on the wall, the coffee table in the sitting room strewn with books and magazines and newspapers . . . But Sloet's was too bare, too neat, too impersonal.

Before he could consider the meaning of this, his cellphone rang – the DPCI office number.

He answered.

'Benny, can you come down here?' asked Brigadier Manie, and Griessel knew this spelled trouble.

He said he was in the city, he could be there in fifteen minutes. He hastily locked the apartment, waited impatiently for the lift, jogged to the BMW and drove with sirens and lights flashing through the sparse Sunday traffic. It took him twenty minutes anyway, because Durban Road was, as usual, a traffic light mess.

He found them in the brigadier's office. Manie, Nyathi, du Preez, Mbali Kaleni, and Cloete, the liaison officer. No John Afrika.

'The bastard sent emails to the papers,' said Manie.

'The sniper?' Griessel asked, and sat down in a vacant chair.

'Yes. And now there are two stories. One about how he is going to shoot policemen until the Sloet case is solved, the other about how the SAPS tried to keep it quiet.'

'Three,' said Cloete. 'They are asking if we only reopened the Sloet case because someone was shooting at us.'

'It's a mess,' said Nyathi.

Manie shoved the email towards Griessel. 'How are you getting on, Benny?'

'Badly, Brigadier,' he answered, because he had learned to stick to the truth. It didn't help to say what your boss wanted to hear.

Manie's granite face revealed nothing. He merely nodded, as if it was what he had expected.

Griessel read.

762a89z012@anonimail.com
Sent: Sunday 27 February. 16.07
To: jannie.erlank@dieburger.com
Re: Why haven't SAPS told the media about wounded policemen?
Yesterday at 18.45 I shot a policeman yetserday at Claremont police station. This morning at 11.50 I shot a policeman at Green Point police station. Why haven't the SASP told the media about that?
Becuase they are hiding something. They know who the murderers of Hanneke Sloet are. Why has no one been arrested yet? I will keep on shooting policemen in the leg until they charge the murderers of Hanneke Sloet.

'He doesn't say anything about a communist,' Griessel said.

'Thank God,' said Manie.

'He was in a hurry. Or he's feeling the pressure.'

'How do you mean?' Mbali asked.

'The spelling. He made a lot of mistakes this time,' said Griessel.

The brigadier's phone rang on his desk. 'The pressure,' said Manie, 'is on us. That is the general. Calling from Pretoria.'

*   *   *

From where he sat, Griessel could hear the lieutenant general from Pretoria's agitation, his shrill, angry tone, tinny, like an enraged electronic insect.

He listened to Brigadier Manie's stoic 'Yes, General,' and 'No, General, we will formulate and release a statement, General.' He looked at Nyathi, sitting with his chin in his hands, deeply worried, and Colonel Werner du Preez of CATS, twirling his cigarette lighter around and around in his fingers. At Cloete, always so astonishingly patient, but the nicotine stains on his fingers and dark rings under his eyes testified that it came at a price. He was the one between the devil of the media and the deep blue sea of the SAPS. And Mbali Kaleni, with her scowl and body language, which said she had no time for this tripe, they had work to do. He felt anger stirring inside. Why were the press and the top management always at it? Why the extra pressure, as if this job wasn't hard enough already.

Griessel's phone rang loudly in the room, which had been quiet for a second. He quickly rejected the call, turned it off.

When Manie eventually returned to the table, and he and Cloete and Nyathi planned the press release word for word, Griessel thought it was a good thing he had drunk away his career prospects. He wouldn't want to be a boss, he couldn't play this game. He would tell the press, you sit and wait like vultures for us to mess up, so you can make a hysterical fuss about it. But where are you when we do something right? When a murderer or a robber or a rapist is found guilty, where's the piece about 'thanks to the good work of the SAPS'? Why do you think the jails are full? Because the bastards turn themselves in? So fuck you all, write what you want.

It took half an hour to finish the release:

A decision to transfer the Sloet case to the Hawks for further investigation was already taken at high level two weeks ago, and was subject to standard evaluation and transfer procedures. On

Saturday 26 February it was placed on a fast track, due to a possible link between the case and sniper attacks on members of the SAPS.

Any allegations that the guilty parties are already known to investigating officers is devoid of any truth. DPCI task teams to investigate the Hanneke Sloet murder and the sniper case have recently been set up, and the SAPS will spare no effort to bring the guilty parties to justice.

The possible link between email threats that have been sent to the SAPS and a sniper, were only finally confirmed on Sunday 27 February. That, together with considerations about the safety of the public, and priorities in the investigation of the sniper, prevented the SAPS from issuing a statement earlier.

In the course of high profile criminal investigations, the SAPS receives many telephonic, postal and email messages. While some useful information from responsible members of the public is often acquired this way, unfortunately there are also many communications that are of no value. Due to the incoherent, seemingly religious extremist, homophobic (Mbali's word contribution) and racist nature of the sniper's earlier correspondence about the Sloet investigation, the SAPS view its credibility as suspect.

When they at last began to discuss the case, Mbali said firmly and confidently, 'He is shooting from a car.'

She could see the men were sceptical. 'There is no other explanation. At Green Point the only secluded vantage point is from the Civic Centre across the road, where everything is locked. I went back to Claremont to look at the scene again, and it is the only thing that makes sense. That parking area, it faces a quiet little street.'

'A car is very visible,' said Colonel Nyathi, still not convinced.

'I know. But do you remember the Beltway Sniper in America, in 2002? Two men who shot people from a car?'

Those were Griessel's drunken years, he didn't remember that.

'Yes,' said Manie, with growing understanding. 'In Washington DC. Didn't they take out the back seat so they could lie flat? Made a hole in the boot . . . ?'

'Exactly.'

'A mobile crime scene,' said Werner du Preez. 'You take all the evidence with you.'

'Yes. That's how they shot thirteen people before they were caught. I Googled the case just now. One of the big problems for law enforcement was that nobody notices a car. There are so many of them, all the time. And they thought it was a van, they ended up looking at the wrong sort of car.'

'You think our shooter isn't working alone?' asked Nyathi.

'It is a possibility. One to watch the road, while the other one does the shooting.'

'I don't know,' said Griessel, and pointed at the email. 'This fellow . . . All his letters, it's just, "I, I, I".'

'You know how the Yanks caught the buggers, in the end?' Manie asked, gloomily, and then answered his own question, 'By accident.'

'Yes, sir,' said Mbali, 'and there are a lot of similarities. The Beltway Sniper was a religious nut, he sent letters to the police and the media. But it's how my case is different that is important. The Beltway Sniper shot members of the public at random, no real motive, despite the theories. His letters were weird, really crazy. Our guy specifically shoots policemen at police stations. It narrows things down in a geographical sense. His letters are much more specific and coherent. And he's got a thing about the Sloet murder. There must be motive in there somewhere.'

'Why has he dropped the issue about the communists?' asked Griessel. 'In the emails to the papers?'

Everyone looked at him.

'Brigadier, this man is not a moron. He must have known the media would be interested in communists. But he said nothing.'

'Why do you think?' Mbali asked Griessel.

'Because the "communists" are a crock of ... rubbish. Like Nxesi says, in Sloet's world there are only capitalists. I think it's a smokescreen. I just don't know why.'

'The big question is, did he know Sloet?' said Nyathi.

Nobody wanted to venture an answer. With fanatics you never knew.

'We'll keep our options open,' said du Preez.

'I think we have to deploy people around police stations,' said Mbali. 'They must start looking for a car.'

16

Griessel listened to his cellphone messages in his office. The first one was from Hannes Pruis, the director of Silberstein Lamarque. 'Captain, I only received your message now. Can we talk tomorrow? I will be at the office from seven.'

The second was from Alexa. Just a tentative, 'Hello,' a short moment of silence, and then the click of a call cut short.

Griessel felt unease stirring. He called her number. It rang for a long time. She didn't answer.

Bad sign.

'I won't drink again today,' she had said when he had left, in the late morning.

Maybe she was in the shower or something.

He should have phoned this afternoon.

He had better go and check.

Hastily he looked up Cupido's number and called, because Brigadier Manie had said to him emphatically, 'Benny, people are queueing up to help. Use them.'

'Thought you would never call,' Cupido answered with barely concealed reproach, like a sulky teenager. Which reminded Griessel of Fritz's tattooing plans.

'Vaughn, I've just come out of a meeting with Manie.'

'I'm just saying, partner.'

'I'll leave the files on your desk. See if you can spot anything. Tomorrow at ten we are talking to her former boyfriend, Roch. I'll come by around half past nine tomorrow, if you want to come along.'

'Cool.'

He said goodbye and rang off, then took out the white envelope with the risqué photographs. Tomorrow morning he wanted to talk to Anni de Waal, the photographer in De Waterkant Village, before they drove to Stellenbosch. He knew Cupido would have something clever to say about the photos, and he wasn't in the mood for that at all.

It was nearly half past nine when he drove back to the city. First he prepared for his conversation with Fritz, making sure not to step into traps like, 'Where are you?' or, 'What are you doing?', because what came next would be, 'Don't you trust me, Pa?'

His relationship with Fritz had become complicated since the divorce. In contrast to the motherly, forgiving Carla, his son blamed him for everything. He had cautiously pointed out to Fritz that, in accordance with Anna's ultimatum at that time, he had not drunk for one hundred and fifty-seven days. And *then* she told him, 'There is someone else.' The little lawyer with the BMW and the shiny suits and his fringe combed oh-so neatly. And Fritz had said, 'But, Pa, you were drunk for thirteen years.'

It was the truth.

He phoned.

'OK, so Carla told you,' were Fritz's opening words.

'Told me what?'

'About the tatt, *jissis*, she is such a sneak.'

'How are you, Fritz?'

'Pa, I'm eighteen, I can get a tatt if I want to. It's a free country.'

'How was your weekend?'

'That's not what you want to talk about. You never phone on a Sunday night at this time.'

Griessel gave up. 'What does your mother say about the tatt?'

'Carla hasn't told Ma about it yet, but it's only a matter of time. Supposed to be a varsity student, but she's still so childish.'

'It's a big step, Fritz. To get a tattoo.'

'Pa, it's a small tattoo on my arm. My shoulder.'

'Carla says you want to tattoo your whole arm.'

'She's talking shit, Pa, she exaggerates so much . . .'

'Fritz, you can't talk to me like that.'

'I learned it from you, Pa.'

Touché. 'What kind of tattoo do you want?'

'What does it matter, Pa?'

'I'm just curious.'

'Pa, you won't like it anyway.'

'So you might as well tell me.'

A long pause. 'Parow Arrow.'

'Parow Arrow?'

'With an arrow through it.' Very defensive.

'Because you play in Jack Parow's band.'

'No, Pa. Parow is in my roots.'

'You were born in Panorama Medi-Clinic and you grew up in Brackenfell.'

'Parow is where you grew up, Pa. It's part of my working-class heritage.'

Griessel sighed. He suspected 'Brackenfell Brak' was a tad

too long for a skinny teenage shoulder, which was why Fritz was suddenly taking his 'heritage' from his father's origins – and the contrived name of Jack Parow. And the 'working class' was pure hip hop. 'Just do me one favour,' he said.

'What, Pa?'

'Just wait a week.'

'So Pa can tell Ma.'

'I won't say a word.' He and Anna couldn't talk about anything without arguing anyway. She would blame him for this too.

'You swear, Pa?'

'I swear.'

Long silence. 'OK.'

When he turned the handle of Alexa's front door and found it unlocked, he knew.

He found her in the sitting room. She was slumped in the big easy chair, snoring softly. An empty glass lay on the carpet, a bottle of gin stood on the table, three-quarters empty. The ashtray was overflowing.

'Fuck,' he said quietly. He couldn't help it.

He picked up the bottle first and emptied it down the kitchen sink. That smell in his nostrils . . . Gin had never been his poison, but the desire for what it could do moved like a paralysing wave through him, so that he just stood there. His brain said, Fetch a glass, just pour a little one.

He shook himself. *Jissis.* He threw the bottle in the rubbish. Where had she got it?

He went up to her room. The bed was unmade. He pulled the sheets straight, readied it for her. Went back down to the sitting room. Woke her up, with a great deal of difficulty. She was very drunk, mumbling incoherent words, her body as limp as a rag doll when he tried to get her to stand. She smelled of drink, sweat and cigarettes. They struggled up the stairs for the second night in a row. At last he laid her on the bed.

'Where were . . . ?' she said, forming the words with effort, her eyes already closed.

He sat down beside her.

'. . . were you?'

'At work,' he said quietly.

Her eyes slowly opened. 'You . . . stay . . . please,' she said, still struggling with the 's' sounds.

'I'll stay,' he said.

Her eyes closed again, followed by a lazy nod.

Day 3
Monday

17

At a quarter to six in the morning he put the coffee cup on her bedside table, sat down next to her and said her name, over and over, louder and louder, until she began to stir, and eventually opened her eyes.

She looked terrible, her skin pale and sallow, with red blotches, eyes bloodshot. There was a white trail of dried saliva down her chin. She was disorientated at first, said, 'What?' and struggled to sit up.

'I brought you some coffee.'

She shifted upright against the pillows, as the present slowly penetrated.

'You can't see me like this,' she said, and covered her face with her hands.

But she hadn't cared about him seeing her dead drunk in the sitting room the night before. Those words were on the tip of his tongue, along with the déjà vu: Anna's reaction to his drunken state, Anna's reproaches during so many hung over, morning talks and his own denial and self-justification back then, all this came back to him now and he struggled to shake the memories off. He realised he was tired – two nights with little sleep, tossing around, worrying about the case and Alexa, waking every now and again in the strange bed. It was going to be a long day.

'Two hundred and seventy days ago my boss pulled me out from behind my desk,' he said, 'because I was drunk at work.' His tone was firm, unsympathetic: any sympathy he'd felt had evaporated some time during the course of the night. 'Mat Joubert was my commanding officer at the time. He drove me to Danie Uys Park in Bellville, and showed me Swart Piet. Swart Piet was once a health inspector in Milnerton. Wife, children, house, he had the lot. And he drank it all away, became a *bergie*, a hobo, with a Checkers shopping trolley in Danie Uys Park. I was furious with Mat that day, how could he possibly compare me to Swart Piet? But the thing is, I was going that way too.'

'I don't want you to see me like this,' she said.

'I don't want you to throw it all away, Alexa. Not now.'

She didn't reply, still hid her face behind her hands.

'Where's the other bottle?'

She didn't answer.

'Alexa.'

She raised her knees, put her arms around them, and dropped her head behind them.

'Where did you hide it?'

One hand moved away from her knees, a finger pointed at the dressing table.

'Which drawer?'

'The third one.'

He got up, pulled open the drawer. Underwear. He put his hand in, felt around, found it. More gin.

'Is this the only one?'

She nodded, her face still hidden.

He sat down with her again, the bottle in his hands. 'You bought it at a hotel.' The seal was broken.

Nodded.

'The Mount Nelson?'

Nod.

That was the place she went to drink, in the past. She had told him.

'I'm going to my flat now to wash and eat. I'll pick you up at seven.'

'Where are we going?' she asked, with fear in her voice.

'I have to go to work. you'll have to come along until I can make another plan.'

'No, Benny . . .'

He knew it wouldn't help to argue. He stood up. 'Please, Alexa. Just be ready at seven.' Then he walked out.

At three minutes past seven he knocked on the front door of her house. She opened. She had repaired the damage reasonably well. She was wearing a grey skirt and jacket, with a white blouse. Her face was made up, her hair clean and neat. Only her eyes betrayed the drinking.

'Come, we have to go.'

She stood still. 'You're angry with me.'

'I'm the last one who could be angry with you. Come on, please.'

'Benny, you can't look after me. I won't drink. Not today. I'm rehearsing this afternoon.'

'I'm going to be late. Come on, please.'

'You *are* angry.' But she came out reluctantly, locked the door behind her, and walked with him to his car.

When they were on the road she said again, 'You can't look after me.'

'Your face is on the poster, Alexa.'

Her head drooped. 'Yes. My face is on the poster.'

Griessel reached over to the back seat, picked up the white envelope and handed it to her. 'Look at that, please.'

She unfolded the flap, took out the photographs.

'Her name is Hanneke Sloet. She was murdered in her flat on the eighteenth of January. Just over there.' He pointed down at the city.

'She was beautiful.'

More sexy than beautiful, but he didn't say that. He knew men and women didn't think the same about beauty. 'She was a corporate lawyer, and she hadn't been in a steady relationship for over a year. Last year in April she had her breasts enlarged. These photos were taken then. Why do you think she did it?'

'Why did she have the pictures taken?'

'Yes.'

She studied each photo carefully while he drove through the heavy traffic in Buitengracht. Eventually she said, 'It's a celebration of her beauty. Her new assets. Her sexuality.'

'Why was she celebrating it?'

Alexa looked at him enquiringly.

He explained, 'Did you ever celebrate your beauty like *that*? I'm not talking about photos for your work . . .'

'You can't compare me to her.'

'Why not? You're lovely . . .' Griessel couldn't help it, he dropped his eyes fleetingly to her bosom, '. . . and all.'

'I am forty-six. I'm a lush.' But by her curt laugh he could tell that she liked it.

'She was thirty-three,' he said. 'Why didn't you do that in your thirties?'

'I didn't have the self-confidence.'

'Is that the only reason?'

'I suppose not . . . It takes a certain kind of personality.'

'What kind?'

She grasped it at last. 'Aha. You're consulting me.'

He nodded.

'I'll have to think about it,' she said, pleased.

Alexa waited for him in a coffee shop on the corner of Long and Riebeeck Street while he asked at the reception in Silberstein Lamarque House to see Hannes Pruis.

His office was on the twelfth floor, spacious and quietly

luxurious, like the building. Pruis was short and strong, the thick black hair expensively cut. He was maybe fifty, full of bubbling joviality. There was a little diamond in each of the cufflinks in his snow-white shirtsleeves. The small, rectangular glasses were the same shade as his silver temples.

And he was a talker.

'Captain, have a seat,' he said in a melodious courtroom voice. 'Coffee? Sugar and milk?'

Griessel said, 'Please', and Pruis ordered over the intercom. Then he continued, 'I see you are in the media firing line again, somewhat undeserved. I must say I was most impressed with the first investigation. The man ... can't remember his name ... Nxesi, thank you, Nxesi, thorough fellow, very thorough. I assume you studied my statement? It was an enormous shock to us all, enormous. Hanneke, what a fantastic person, such a terribly huge loss. And so senseless. We still can't explain it. And now the man who is shooting your people over her case, have you any idea ... ?' The door opened, a pretty woman with long black hair brought in the tray, put it down in front of them.

'Please, help yourself,' said Pruis. 'Thank you, Natalie.' She nodded and smiled, went out again. Pruis remained standing, one hand on the desk. 'Have you any idea who is shooting at you?'

'I hoped you would be able to help us,' said Benny and took out his notebook.

'No, dear God, Captain, not the faintest idea. I mean, the whole thing was inexplicable from the start, there is nobody who would want to harm Hanneke.'

Griessel nodded. 'Mr Pruis, someone *did* harm her. And the scene indicates that it was someone she knew one way or another. There are two possibilities. Work or personal life. Or both. There are sources who say Miss Sloet had an affair in 2002 with a married colleague.'

'Now, you have to be careful . . .' Pruis raised a warning finger.

He didn't have the desire or the energy for a pissing contest. 'Mr Pruis, the only thing I *have* to do is my job,' said Griessel. 'If a source makes an allegation, I have to investigate it.'

'It's a very vague allegation.'

'The source says it was Werner Gelderbloem. Did you know about it?'

That stopped Pruis for a second. Then he sat down in the high leather chair and folded his arms across his chest. 'Yes, I knew about it,' he said stiffly, 'but it's old news. It was a long time ago. Eight, nine years ago.'

'Are you sure?'

The jovial mood had evaporated. The lawyer leaned forward, pointed his finger at Griessel. 'You're poking your nose into this because you have nothing else, that's the problem. Let me tell you now, it's old potatoes, it only went on for a month or two. These things happen. I'm sure you've also had a bit on the side.'

'Are you sure the relationship was completely over?'

Pruis leaned back in his chair. 'Yes, I'm sure.' He sighed, reconsidered his attitude. 'Listen, I'm probably a little sensitive about this, but Werner Gelderbloem . . . he's retiring in two years . . . I mean, Captain, Hanneke was a desirable woman. At a certain age . . . You realise you're getting old, you've been with the same woman for thirty years, call it a mid-life crisis, here is this smart, pretty young thing who admires you . . . I mean, which of us wouldn't be tempted? He made a mistake. Nearly nine years ago. He ended it. We transferred her from Corporate Litigation to Commercial Law, and it died a silent death. If there was the slightest chance that it had anything to do with her murder . . .'

He was protesting too much, thought Griessel. 'Mr Pruis,

we all have behaviour patterns. We do the same thing over
and over. If she had an affair at work once, the chances are
good . . .'

'No.' Angry. 'Why do you think she only became an asso-
ciate two years ago? She was brilliant, one of the sharpest
here. The thing with Werner . . . We called her in at the time,
we told her, you're young and inexperienced in this sort of
thing, you get one chance. One. It stays on your record for
five years, one more time and you're out. It gave her a fright.
A big, big fright.' And the finger was back: 'I won't allow
Silberstein's name to be dragged through the media mud, let
me tell you.'

Is that why he was so defensive? Griessel nodded, opened
his notebook on a new page. 'I will have to ask about the deal
she was working on . . .'

He saw Pruis raise his eyes heavenwards.

'Were there any communists involved?' he asked.

The gear changes were visible on Pruis's face.
'Communists?'

'Yes.'

The lawyer pondered, and then to Griessel's astonishment
said, 'Maybe one or two. Why?'

18

'There *were* communists involved?'

'Captain, it's a BEE transaction, and I can't tell you the
political affiliation of all the parties involved. There surely are
some who are members of the South African Communist
Party. Or were. You know, the cadres, the alliances . . .'

'A BEE transaction?'

'Black Economic Empowerment.'

Realisation came to him slowly, all the connotations, the

implications, the link to the sniper's emails. Griessel's heart
sank. 'Mr Pruis, can you explain the whole transaction to me.
In layman's terms.'

'Captain, there are no layman's terms for this sort of transaction. It's complicated. But it remains a typical BEE
transaction, there is one every month or two. Where is the
connection to Hanneke Sloet's death?'

'Please try to explain it to me,' Griessel said.

Pruis looked at his watch and shook his head in irritation.
'Ingcebo Resources Limited is the BEE company. Majority
of black shareholders, seven black people on the board of
directors, some of them were formerly in government.
Ingcebo is borrowing a fraction over four billion rand and
using it to buy a fifteen per cent share in Gariep Minerals
Limited. Because it's very risky to buy a single share with
borrowed money, Ingcebo's financiers have to reduce their
risk by structuring it as a five-year convertible loan.'

Griessel raised his hand. 'Mr Pruis, I need to understand
that.'

'I told you, it's complicated – that's why there are so many
legal professionals involved.' He sighed heavily. 'Basically it
comes down to Gariep Minerals selling a fifteen per cent
shareholding to Ingcebo, risk free. Ingcebo still has to finance
the amount through banks and other investors, but Gariep's
support makes it possible. The whole thing is structured in
such a way that . . . Are you sure you want to know all this?'

'Please.'

Pruis pulled open a drawer, took out an expensive leather-
bound writing pad. He opened it, pushed it closer to Griessel
and drew a circle with a fountain pen on the paper. 'Here is
Ingcebo Resources Limited, the BEE mother company. OK?'

Griessel nodded.

Pruis drew another circle beside it. 'This is Gariep
Minerals. It's a mining company, nearly a hundred years old,

in white ownership. They are mostly in gold, platinum, aluminium. They are a local entity, but operate internationally. They have mines here, in Canada, Australia.'

Griessel nodded. He was keeping up.

Pruis drew a line from Ingcebo Resources Limited, connected it to a smaller circle. 'This is Ingcebo Bauxite. It belongs to Ingcebo Resources Limited. A full subsidiary. In other words, Ingcebo Resources Limited owns Ingcebo Bauxite. You understand?'

'Yes.'

'Now, Ingcebo Bauxite, the subsidiary, lends four billion rand to Gariep Minerals, the white company, for five years. If Gariep's share price falls over the period, they have to repay the loan with interest, or simply issue the shares to Ingcebo. Because the shares are worth more than the bank loan, Ingcebo can repay the banks in full and retain the balance as profit or an unencumbered share in Gariep.'

'*Jissis*,' said Griessel.

'I told you this is complicated.

'So where does Silbersteins come in?'

'We are only one of four legal firms involved. SA Merchant Bank is our client. They are underwriting a part of the loan to Ingcebo Bauxite. There are four banks involved: two from America, one from England, and the local SA Merchant Bank. We have to see that SA Merchant Bank's contracts are watertight.'

Griessel realised he wasn't going to get his head around everything. 'The communists are with Ingcebo?'

'I'm not saying they are communists. I said they *might have* been.'

'Did Hanneke Sloet have any contact with them?'

'With the directors of Ingcebo?'

'With the possible communists.'

'No. I mean, she must have met them briefly, somewhere

at one of the meetings. But there was no contact other than that. Remember, we work for SA Merchant Bank, not for Ingcebo.'

'What about telephone conversations? Letters? Email?'

'I doubt it. I . . . don't know. Maybe.'

Griessel put his notebook down on the table. 'Mr Pruis, can you please give me the names of the Ingcebo people?'

'You haven't even drunk your coffee yet.'

Alexa was sitting reading the newspaper. Griessel went up to her table and said, 'We must go.'

She tapped a finger on the newspaper and looked up at him. 'Is it this Sloet case you're investigating?'

'It is.'

'And you also have to try and keep an alky singer sober . . .'

'It's the least I can do after Saturday night . . .'

'Benny!' she said loudly, so that a couple of coffee shop clients turned their heads. She lowered her voice. 'It is *not* your fault . . .'

'I'm late,' he said.

She gave him a penetrating look with bloodshot eyes. Then she took money from her purse, put it in the saucer with the bill, folded up the newspaper and stood. 'In any case, when I read the article . . . I can't do that to you. I organised a sitter . . .'

'A sitter?' he asked as they walked to the door, his head still full of complicated BEE transactions.

'Ella. From the promoters.'

'The promoters?'

'Benny, you're repeating everything I say. The concert promoters. Ella is my temporary assistant. She . . . You can drop me off at Grand West. She'll look after me.'

He stopped outside on the pavement. 'What did you tell her?'

'That I'm not allowed to drink.'

He began to walk to the car again, unlocked the door for her, got in the other side. Switched on the ignition. Switched it off again. He turned to her. 'Does she know you are an alcoholic?'

'No,' she said, and looked out of the window.

'Does she know how an alcoholic's mind works?'

'No.'

'You'll have to tell her.'

Alexa just sat there.

'I can only drop you off there,' Griessel said, 'if she knows everything.'

Now she turned on him, angry. 'Who do you think you are?'

'I am nothing,' he said quietly. 'But you are not. You are Xandra Barnard.'

'Is it necessary for all the world to know, Benny? Is that what you want? Why don't you just have it printed on the bottom of the posters. *Xandra Barnard, alcoholic, is back. And drunk again.* Is that what you want?'

He stared at her, searching for some other way to handle this, but he could think of nothing, his brain was fuzzy.

Abruptly she jerked open her handbag, pulled out her cell-phone. She tapped a number crossly while glaring at him aggressively. She pressed another key on the phone, so that it rang and Ella's voice was audible over the tiny speaker.

'This is Ella,' the woman answered.

'Ella, it's Alexa. Do you have a moment?'

'Yes.'

'Are you sitting down?'

'Yes?'

'Listen carefully. There are a few things you must know. Number one: I am an alcoholic. Number two: I was sober for one hundred and fifteen days, but on Saturday I started drinking again. Last night as well. Number three: If you don't watch me very carefully, I am going to drink again today. Number four: Alcoholics lie and cheat. Don't believe anything I say. You mustn't let me out of your sight. Especially late afternoon and evening. Do you understand?' Her eyes were on Griessel with an expression that said: Are you satisfied now?

Ella sounded shocked. 'I think so.'

'And you must know, if you tell anyone about this conversation, anyone under the sun, I will . . . destroy you. Do you understand?'

'I understand . . .' the reply came back hesitantly.

'Ella,' said Griessel quickly, 'can you hear me?'

'Yes?'

'My name is Benny Griessel. I'm going to give you my number now. If you feel you can't cope with Alexa, phone me. At any time.'

'OK.' But he could hear she was intimidated.

'I will come and relieve you tonight. You have to know, Alexa will try to manipulate you. She is going to be angry, she will cry, she will ask nicely, she will use all her charm. She is going to have withdrawal symptoms this afternoon, she will shout at you, she will try to blackmail you emotionally.' He saw Alexa's eyes flashing. 'That is not Alexa, that is the booze. You must understand that. If you can't deal with it, say so now.'

'I . . . I'll try.' The fear coming through.

'Call me. Any time. Here is my number.'

19

Her arms were firmly crossed and she stared out of the window.

'I'll be grateful if you would come with me to the photographer first,' he said. 'The one who took the photos of her.'

She just stared fixedly outside. He could see Alexa's mouth was drawn. He knew how her mind was working right now. The denial, the I-can-stop-drinking-if-I-want-to argument, the memory of how sly drink made you. And she would have the thirst now, after two nights of drunkenness, the fever would be in her blood. But he also knew that it helped, exposure, the recognition of the first of the Twelve Steps: We are powerless against drink, our lives have become uncontrollable. And Step Five: To confess our sins to ourselves and other people.

She did not reply, so he started the car and drove away. She would have to give him directions if she wanted him to drop her off at the promoters, in the meantime he was going to the photographer.

In Somerset Street his phone rang. MBALI, the screen read.

He answered.

'He's a part-time shooter, Benny,' said Mbali with a degree of excitement. 'He's a working man, a weekend warrior.'

'How do you know?'

'I looked at the time stamp on the emails. On weekdays, he sends them late at night. Always on a Monday. On weekends, it's early morning on a Saturday, and middle of the day on Sundays. The fact is, all his emails were sent on those three days. Saturday, Sunday, Monday. And the first two shootings were on the weekend. That can't be a coincidence. So I'm thinking he must be busy in the week. He is employed, and he probably works with other people, he has to wait for the evenings or the weekends to write the emails.'

'Yes,' he said, 'that sounds right.'

'And you know what that means, Benny? If he is going to shoot someone today, it won't be until after hours. So we have to make sure the stations are alert. I'm going to be very unpopular . . . And I might be wrong.'

He knew what she meant. The day shift at the stations would have to work a few hours longer. 'Talk to Colonel du Preez. Because if you're right . . .'

'Then we might just catch him. I'm on my way to the armoury. I'll talk to Nyathi when I get back. Good luck, Benny.'

In Loader Street, high up the flank of Signal Hill, he parked in front of the small restored house. The hanging sign, in slim, elegant lettering, said *Anni de Waal. Photographer.* With three half-moon brush strokes representing a camera lens.

He turned off the engine. Before he got out, Alexa broke the silence. 'Simóne. Do you remember Simóne, the singer?' she whispered.

'No,' he said apologetically.

'Long red hair, big white smile?'

He shook his head.

'Well endowed, always a bit of a low neckline, in the mid nineties she sang a lot of commercial pop? One or two hits, then she sort of disappeared?'

'No.' There had been so many of them who had come and gone.

'One night, back then, before a concert, she showed me her photos. They were almost like Hanneke Sloet's, the same soft lighting. Flattering angles. Not as naked as these photos, but specially taken. For herself. Simóne was a real little diva, very narcissistic. Very aware of her appearance, always near a mirror. And concerned about her status, because she wanted recognition so badly. Appreciation. Ambitious, she never stopped talking about what she wanted to achieve. If she considered you her inferior, she would ignore you. Envious, if you were more successful than she was. And she was manipulative. Like an alcoholic . . .' Alexa smiled at him, small and hurt and forgiving.

He touched her arm gently.

'I think . . . That night I thought she had the photos taken . . . because that was how she wanted to see herself. As desirable and smouldering . . . and mysterious. It was . . . I don't know if I will express it correctly . . . As though the stage personality, the public image, wasn't quite sexy enough. If you sing for Afrikaners, you can't be too sexy. And those photos were to set that right for *her*, they had to serve as the truth. A monument? Or . . . No, let me stick with that.'

He looked at her, saw the ravages of drink, now somewhat camouflaged, and thought of the demons that were consuming her. But behind everything was this glittering intelligence that he had discovered little by little in the past months. Sometimes it filled him with despair – what would she see in him – and sometimes with total admiration. Like now.

Why would someone like that drink?

'Thank you,' said Griessel.

Anni de Waal and an assistant were in the studio busy setting up lighting. She looked up and a curious frown changed into a beaming smile.

'Alexa!' she said, and approached them with wide welcoming arms.

De Waal was middle-aged, with intense eyes behind small round glasses. Her long grey hair was gathered up in two ponytails. A light blue scarf was knotted around her neck above the collar of the white T-shirt. For a woman of her age, thought Griessel, her bottom looked surprisingly good in the faded denim.

He stood and watched the women greet, a ritual that he had only recently learned, at Alexa's side: lower bodies far apart, a light hug, and the air kisses, one beside each cheek. The manner of the rich and famous. Usually it secretly annoyed him; what was wrong with the old way? A kiss on the mouth if you wanted to kiss, shake hands if you didn't. And he could never remember which cheek the air kisses began, left or right. But this morning he didn't have enough energy for irritation.

He stood and waited until the 'Phenomenal surprise!' and 'You look so *good*!' and 'I hear you're back!' and '*So* fantastic to see you, what is it, seven, eight years?' were over.

'Anni did the cover of my second album,' said Alexa to Griessel. She introduced him: 'This is my friend, Captain Benny Griessel.' And added with a touch of drama, 'Of the Hawks.'

De Waal glanced back at Alexa fleetingly, as though trying to work out the connection. She was quick. 'Hanneke Sloet,' she said.

'That's right,' said Griessel.

'You'd better sit down, my darling.'

They sat around a white painted coffee table in the corner of the studio, on deep blue easy chairs, Anni de Waal consulted her iPad with practised fingers. 'Saturday fourteenth of August. Last year. She must have booked ahead in June, because my diary stays full.'

'Did she say why she wanted the photos taken?'

'Personal use. That's what I wrote down. I have to ask, because it influences the whole approach.'

'Is that . . . what you do?'

De Waal shook her head. The ponytails bobbed. Her hands talked along. 'I do fashion shoots, mostly for overseas magazines. It's much more . . . Let's just say they pay in Euros. Personal portraits are time consuming, and to be frank, there are always complications. The sort of people who have them done . . . they are usually not as photogenic as they like to think. So I am expensive. To discourage them.'

'May I ask *how* expensive?'

'For you, my darling, a special price,' she said with a vague flirtation in her voice. 'Ten thousand. Rand, of course. You have an interesting face. Are you of Slavic origin?'

'Parow,' he said.

'Wonderful,' said Anni de Waal, and clapped her hands together, laughing.

'Is that what Hanneke Sloet paid?'

'I will have to look it up in my books, but it would have been more. Twelve thousand, thereabouts.' Somewhat defensively she added, 'It *was* a whole Saturday morning, my darling.'

Jissis, he thought. But he merely nodded. 'What can you remember about her?'

'A lot. She was impressive. Photogenic. Strong woman. Pretty. And because I do so few personal portfolios . . . Naturally, when I saw her in the papers, in January . . . then it all comes back to you again.'

'Tell me, please.'

'She made the appointment, she arrived here with a small suitcase of clothes, and she knew exactly what she wanted. She articulated her requirements intelligently, which helps a great deal, of course. It was a cold rainy morning, and I had the heaters on, it takes a while, it's a big room. So we did the outfits first, before the nude studies . . .'

'Were there complications with her?'

'Not really. Before we began shooting . . . She wanted to know who would see the pictures, how exactly that worked. Then I told her we could do the prints ourselves, it would cost a little more. She was satisfied with that. And the shoot itself . . . The way I work – the photos go straight to Adobe Lightroom, so the client can assess them immediately. She was easy. We adjusted the exposure slightly, she wanted it to be darker. More mysterious. When we were finished, she chose her prints, the rest I put on a DVD. She collected them a week or so later. It takes time, my darling, I shoot in RAW, my assistant converts them to jpeg for the DVD.'

'She just said the photos were personal? Nothing more?'

'Not that I can remember.'

'Why do you think she wanted the photos?'

'My darling,' she said with an expansive gesture. 'Who knows the secrets of the human heart? And let me tell you, the human heart is a wonderful, perverse thing. I get people begging me to photograph their dogs. And they are prepared to *pay*. There was a man and woman who wanted me to shoot them in bed. Stark naked. And they were ... somewhat weighty. Some do it for fun, others do it for ... But that's not what you want to hear, so let me tell you what I think. This child had a boob job. And I think she had been waiting a long time for it, and was very pleased with it. About how it made her feel and look. She wanted to *show* it. No, she wanted to *see* it. Not in a mirror. Something more tangible. That's what I think.'

'It's a woman thing,' said Alexa.

'Precisely,' said Anni de Waal. 'With all due respect, my darling, men just don't understand.'

20

Mbali was immediately offended by the way the constable sat behind the weathered desk at the SAPS armoury. He was leaning back in the chair, his long legs stretched out in front of him, his nose buried in the *Soccer-Laduma*.

'*Molo*, Mama,' he said after a swift glance.

'*Hayi*,' said Mbali, and her tongue clicked through the room. 'Mama? Is that how you address an officer?'

He focused on her, astonished, saw the identity card around her neck, screwed up his eyes to decipher it. Only

then did he spring to his feet, still holding the magazine.
'*Uxolo*, Captain,' he said, and saluted.

'Do not speak Xhosa to me.'

'Sorry, so sorry, Captain, how can I help you?'

'I am looking for Giel de Villiers.'

'Ah. *Icilikishe*. He is in the back.'

'*Icilikishe*?'

'You will see, Captain. Come with me, I will take you to
him.'

He was very keen now.

She walked after him crossly. That was the trouble with the
young ones. No work ethic, no respect for women, senior
officers or colleagues.

Giel de Villiers, in a blue oil-stained police overall, was
stooped over a lathe with a can of lubricant in his hand. He
didn't hear them come in, and the constable had to tap him
on the shoulder. He looked up, saw Mbali, and gave a slow
double blink. For a moment it confused her, she thought the
look was critical, superior. But then she saw the strange
eyelids that blinked from below, like a lizard. She immediately understood his nickname.

'Good day, Sergeant,' she called above the noise of the
lathe.

He raised his hand in greeting, turned the lathe off carefully, put down the can, and wiped his hands on a cloth. His
bald head gleamed in the sunlight that shone through the
window. His eyes blink-blinked again.

'Sarge, this is Captain Mbali Kaleni, from the Hawks,' the
constable said.

'I'm sorry, Captain, my English is not good,' said de
Villiers.

'Captain Benny Griessel said you could help me,' she said
slowly, so he could follow.

'OK. I hear he is a Hawk now.'

'I would really appreciate your help. We need information on silencers. For a rifle.'

'Suppressors,' he said.

'Excuse me?'

'A firearm, you cannot silence it,' he said slowly and carefully, the Afrikaans accent heavy on the 'r' sounds. 'It can only be suppressed. That is why it is called a sound suppressor.'

'I see . . .' She realised the constable was standing behind her, wide-eyed and fascinated. 'You can go and man your post,' she said.

He drew himself to attention, saluted smartly. 'Yes, Captain!' Clicked his heels, turned, and walked out briskly.

She turned her attention to de Villiers. 'We have reason to believe that the man shooting members of the SAPS is using a rifle with a telescope and a suppressor. Where can people buy a suppressor?'

'You mean like in a shop?'

'Yes.'

'There's a gun shop in Jo'burg . . . But they don't sold many.'

'So they're not illegal?'

'No. A lot of hunters use them.'

Mbali's scowl deepened. 'So, if a lot of hunters use them, but this shop does not sell many . . . I don't understand.'

'This gun shop . . . how you say . . . imports the suppressors from Vaime in Finland. They are too . . .'

He shut his eyes while trying to find the English words. '. . . expensive. So people have them made by . . . gunsmiths.'

'In South Africa?'

'Yes.'

'Where do I find these gunsmiths?'

'In *Wild en Jag*. Game and Hunting. It is a magazine. They advertise.'

'All of them?'

'I don't know. But I think all of them.'

Mbali opened her massive handbag, took out her note-book and pen, and wrote in it. 'So I just go to these people and ask them to build me a suppressor?'

'Yes.'

'Is it expensive?'

'Not very.'

'How much?'

'Depends on the type of suppressor. About one thousand eight hundred, or two thousand rand. For the . . . how you say . . . screw-on.'

'How many types are there?'

'*Basies*, uh, basically two. The screw-on, that's the one for hunters. And the sleeved, the one that sleeves back halfway over the rifle. It is the type military snipers use. Because it does not make the rifle that much longer. It is easier to . . . how you say . . . manoeuvre it.'

'And these gunsmiths build both types?'

'You will have to ask them. Some do both.'

'Why would a hunter want a suppressor?'

De Villiers' peculiar eyes never stopped blinking.

'Game farms. They have tourists, and they have hunters at the same time. So they don't want to have noise from the hunters' shots. And the hunters want to shoot more bucks. If you hunt springbuck in the Karoo, and they hear the shoot, they all ran away. If you use a suppressor, they stand longer. And you can shoot more.'

'I don't like the killing of animals,' said Mbali dubiously.

Giel de Villiers shrugged.

'Are there any of these gunsmiths in Cape Town?'

'No. There is one in Villiersdorp.'

'Do you have his contact details?'

'It is in *Wild en Jag*.'

'Do you have it?'

'Yes, in my office. I will give you all the numbers.'

'Thank you. You said suppressors can be imported from Finland?'

'Yes.'

'And some hunters do that?'

'Maybe.'

'Will there be some sort of record?'

'Yes. At Customs. Anything . . . *geklassifiseer* . . . how you say . . . classified as firearm things must be inspected. That is why it is too much trouble.'

'Do you need a permit to have a suppressor built over here?'

'No.'

She wrote, then asked, 'Just how much of the noise is suppressed?'

'Depends on the rifle.'

'How quiet? If I shoot a rifle from a car in a street, how far can the shot be heard?'

'A good suppressor can make it very quiet.' He unfolded his arms, clapped his hands together, hard. 'About like that. Eighty-five per cent more quiet.'

Mbali nodded. 'OK,' she said. 'Can you get me the contact details?'

De Villiers began walking to the door. Then he stopped and looked at her. His eyes closed as if he was having deep thoughts. 'You can also build your own suppressor.'

'Oh?'

'You just need to make a space for the gasses to . . . How you say?' He gave up: 'You need a pipe, some rubber . . . disks, and washers. And other things. You can buy it all from a hardware store. There are plans on the Internet . . . You can even just use a PVC pipe and a sponge, if you want to . . .'

'*Hayi*,' sighed Mbali.

De Villiers opened his eyes.

Alexa and he drove in silence to the Grand West Casino in Goodwood.

Griessel thought he understood Sloet better now. Gabby Villette had described her as an 'excluder' who deliberately distanced herself from the personal assistants. Then Alexa's story of the narcissistic singer who ignored people if she felt they were her inferior.

Both of them had talked about ambition, of a woman who would do anything for prestige and promotion.

And Anni de Waal, '*This* child had a boob job, and was very pleased with it. With the way it made her feel and look.'

It all meant that the photos were meaningless, they weren't relevant to her murder. She was just a self-satisfied woman who wanted to show off her assets. 'A monument,' Alexa had called it. De Waal had referred to 'something tangible'.

It meant the communist thing was all they had.

And that was a mess.

Nothing was ever simple.

He pulled the cellphone out of his pocket, called Cupido. 'Vaughn, I'm going to be late. And I will have to see the colonel first. Can you let Roch know we will be there closer to half past ten?'

'Did you find something?'

'Trouble,' he said. 'Only trouble.'

He ended the call.

'You have never talked about your work,' said Alexa.

He didn't know what to say. She wouldn't understand, that was how he kept the evil away from the people close to him. Doc Barkhuizen was always on his case: 'Don't keep internalising it, Benny, talk about it.' He didn't want to. He needed to keep the two worlds separate – he needed a place that was unspoiled.

'I won't drink today,' she said. 'But you must come and tell me tonight. About . . . how you're getting on.'

'Alexa, it's hard. It's . . .'

'Harder than not drinking?'

'No,' he said.

When they drove through the gate of the Grand West Casino, Alexa phoned Ella. 'We're here. It's best if you come and fetch me from the car, otherwise my detective will think I'm going to escape.'

Griessel saw her hand shaking. Her battle of the day was intensifying.

She indicated where he should go, where he should stop.

A young woman came jogging out of the building. He recognised her. It was the pretty one who had confused him with Paul Eilers on Saturday evening. Before he made a complete fool of himself.

She came around to his side, and he wound the window down. 'Oh,' she said, 'so *you're* the detective.'

He shook her hand. 'I am.'

'No need to worry, Paul Eilers, I'll handle this,' she said with great self-confidence.

'You've got my number?'

I'm a tough cookie,' she said. 'It won't be necessary.'

'Hey, I'm here too, you know,' said Alexa.

21

Colonel Zola 'Giraffe' Nyathi looked at the seven names on the list of directors of Ingcebo Resources Limited. His face grew sombre, then he rose and said, 'I think we should talk to the brig.'

Griessel followed him to the office of Musad Manie. The

brigadier was in a meeting with four group heads. Nyathi said, 'Apologies, but we need to talk to you.'

'Gentlemen, if you don't mind,' said Manie to the senior officers. They stood up, walked to the door, looking curiously at Griessel.

Nyathi and Griessel sat down. The colonel waited until the door closed and slid Benny's notebook over to Manie. 'The deal Hanneke Sloet was working on. It's BEE.'

'I see,' said Manie, the foreboding of trouble in his voice.

'This is the list of company directors. There is a former ANC cabinet minister, and two were provincial premiers. These three I'm not sure about . . . But director number seven could be our problem.'

'A. T. Masondo,' Manie read. 'I don't know him.'

'He was on the Central Committee of the Communist Party, late nineties.'

A shadow crossed Manie's granite face when he put two and two together. 'Our communist.'

'Yes. He was also in Mbeki's second cabinet. Deputy Minister of Mining, I think.'

Griessel saw the look the two senior officers exchanged. He had a strong suspicion why. 'Brigadier,' he said, 'the problem is that Sloet's boss said there was nothing funny about the transaction. It was all in the newspapers, there is nothing to hide. And Sloet hardly knew *these* people at all.'

'Hardly at all?'

'She met them briefly. Her boss said he doubts she had any further contact with them.'

'We will have to make sure.'

Griessel nodded. 'Brigadier, the whole transaction . . . It's people borrowing money to buy fifteen per cent of a company, but without risk . . . I don't really understand it . . . I will have to get Bones in.'

'Yes,' said Manie. 'All right.' He looked at the colonel. 'Will you talk to Bones?'

'Shall I get him in now?'

'I have to go to Stellenbosch first, Brigadier,' said Griessel. 'To talk to Sloet's ex . . .'

'I'll get Bones on standby.'

'Zola, please, you know Bones. Make absolutely sure he understands: this is completely confidential.'

'I will.'

'Let him read the file,' said Manie. 'I swear, I will fire his butt if he talks. This thing is a minefield.'

'I'll make sure he understands,' said Nyathi patiently.

'Benny, please. Only the four of us know. Let's keep it that way.' Very earnest.

'Yes, Brigadier. But there is something else . . .'

'Yes?'

'The gunman not mentioning the communist to the media. It doesn't make sense. He's looking for attention, he's looking for publicity. He wants the papers to go after us. The whole time he's been saying: "You're taking money from the communist, you are in cahoots with the communist." But when he writes to the press, there's nothing about communists, just "the SAPS know who it is".'

'You think it's political, Benny? Is that it?'

'Sir, I don't know what it is. It's just . . . strange.'

'The whole damned thing is strange,' said Manie. He tapped the list in Griessel's notebook. 'But we can't afford to ignore it.'

'No, Brigadier.'

'And we don't have anything else.'

'No, Brigadier. We don't have anything else.'

'I'll brief Bones,' said Colonel Nyathi, the tension in him obvious now. He stood up.

★ ★ ★

They drove to Stellenbosch. Griessel was at the wheel. Cupido sat with the photos of Hanneke Sloet in his hands. '*Jissis*,' he said. 'What a fucking waste. Bloody majestic jugs.'

Griessel was angry with himself for forgetting the envelope on the back seat of the car. Cupido spotted the word *Sloet* in blue ink and homed in on it.

'Where did you get this?' Cupido asked.

'In her bedroom. Bedside cupboard.'

'*Fokkit*. Little porn star. How come she didn't have a boyfriend, at the time of death? I mean, a chick like *this*, body to die for, and she flaunts it. I'm telling you, Tommy Nxesi missed something. That's the problem with the new *mannetjies*, they don't do footwork any more.'

'Her cellphone records don't show anything. There were no other men.'

'That's the problem. Cellphone is yesterday's technology. I mean, did they check her Facebook account?'

'Nxesi said he did . . .'

'Did she have Gmail? Was she on Twitter?'

'Twitter?'

'*Jissis*, Benny, you're so *fokken* old school, it's scary . . .' Cupido, ten years younger than Griessel, pulled out his cellphone. 'This, my friend, is the HTC Desire HD, runs on Android. TweetDeck at the tap of an icon . . .' He showed Benny. 'That's Twitter. You have to motor, Pops, to keep up, there's a new tweet every second.'

Griessel was driving, he stole a quick glance at the screen of the smartphone. 'A *twiet*?'

'Tweeeet,' Cupido stretched the vowel to correct the pronunciation. 'It's social media, Pops. You broadcast yourself.'

'What for?'

'It's the new way. You tell the world what you're doing.'

'But why?'

'For the fun of it, Benny. To say: Check me out, I am here.'

'That's what Sloet did. With the photos.'

'What do you mean?'

'It was her way of saying: Check me out.'

'But for who?'

'For herself. That's what the photographer said. It's a woman thing.'

'And you believe that shit?' Cupido worked his phone again. 'Let us see if Sloet had a Twitter account . . .'

'Forensics report says Lithpel checked the computer.'

Reginald 'Lithpel' Davids was Forensics' lisping computer whizz, small and frail, with the face of a boy, two missing front teeth and a big Afro hairstyle.

'OK. Lithpel doesn't miss much. Canny coloured, that bro' . . . Nope. No account, not under her own name anyway. Big tits, no tweets . . . So what were you and the Giraffe and the Camel doing just now?'

The Hawks' bush telegraph, lightning fast as usual. 'Politics,' said Griessel. 'You don't want to know.'

'*Fokken* politics.' Cupido picked up the photos again and stared at them. 'What a waste. Majestic jugs . . .'

The Bonne Espérance estate was on the R310, just beyond the Helshoogte Pass. They drove through the white, gabled gate and the avenue of oaks to the visitor's centre.

'Tourist trap,' said Cupido when they got out and he looked at the advertising signs. 'Wine tasting, five-star dining, spa . . . Don't they make enough money from the wine?'

Griessel went to ask reception where Egan Roch could be found. The young woman gave them directions: behind the cellar, in the cooper's shop.

'Another shop,' said Cupido. 'What do you sell there?'

She giggled. 'Nothing. That's where Egan and the guys make the barrels, sir.'

That shut Cupido up as they walked, past the gracious old homestead and the cellar, to the back, where crates were stacked beside tidy rows of viticulture implements. A farm labourer had to direct them again, until they found the entrance, a nondescript wooden door.

Griessel pushed it open, smelled the smoke and the fire. It was a large space, with yellow lime-washed walls. It was hot inside. In one corner a big man stood with his back to them. He was working on a small vat. He was tap-tapping a metal hoop down over the pieces of wood, with smoke coiling through the opening of the barrel. His white T-shirt was wet with sweat.

'Hello,' said Cupido.

The man did not respond. Griessel noticed the earphones behind the thick black hair, the little wire down to an iPod on his belt. He went closer.

'Benny,' said Cupido and pointed at the wall.

Rows of tools hung there, odd hammers and axes, wood planes, files, and a series of long, thin metal staves. The points were very sharp.

22

Cupido tapped the broad shoulder. Roch looked around, smiled apologetically, put the adze down on a wooden work-bench and took out the earphones. 'Sorry,' he said.

'Egan Roch?'

'That's right, excuse the dirty hand,' he said, and held it out to Cupido, his voice deep, his smile full of self-confidence.

Griessel recognised him from the photos in Sloet's album. Roch in real life looked even more like a man who should be on TV, his face strong and symmetrical. Powerful arms, big hands, he was a head taller than Cupido.

'Captain Vaughn Cupido, Hawks. And this is Captain Benny Griessel.'

'Oh . . . OK, pleased to meet you. Do you . . . I have a little office . . .'

'No, this is fine,' said Cupido. 'Tell me, where did Tommy Nxesi interview you?'

'Who?'

'The investigating officer. The one who took your statement.'

'I went to see *him*. In Green Point. He asked . . . Why?'

'Just routine. So, you make barrels.'

'Vats.'

'How does a guy learn to do that?'

'You do an apprenticeship. Overseas. Are you sure you don't want to sit down. Coffee? Tea?'

'No thanks. What do you learn when you make barrels?'

'Phew. It's a long list. You first have to learn to select the right wood. French oak, the best comes from the forests of Tronçais and Jupilles . . .'

'No, I mean what sort of manual work. Woodwork? Metalwork?'

'Oh, yes, of course, a bit of both, it's very specialised . . .'

Griessel knew Cupido was also thinking of Prof Pagel's pathology report, the 'considerable force of the stabbing action', the possibility of a home-made weapon. He knew his colleague would take over the interview, it was his way. But he was in too much of a hurry, his approach was too aggressive.

'I wouldn't mind a cup of coffee,' said Benny.

'Great, I could do with a cup myself. Please come through.' Roch gestured at an interior door.

The 'little office' was a work of art. The desk was raw oak, the same fine grain as the vats, the chairs were antique ball-and-claw, upholstered in red, the floor was grey cement, polished to a shine, with a single Persian carpet over it. Against the wall was a painting of a cooper's workshop from a bygone era, against the other a huge oil painting of a vineyard landscape in a foreign country.

Roch made a phone call to order the coffee, and came and sat down with the detectives in one of the old chairs, stretching his legs out in front of him in a relaxed way.

'I heard on the radio that you have taken over the case. It's rough, the guy shooting . . .'

'We have to interview everyone again,' said Griessel quickly, before Cupido could get going again.

'Of course . . .'

'According to your statement you and Hanneke broke up a year before her death.'

'It wasn't a whole year. Eleven months. February last year.'

'She ended the relationship?'

'Yes.'

'Why?'

Roch made a gesture with his hand that said: Who knows? 'It was . . . You know how it is . . .'

'How did you meet?'

'At Moyo, the restaurant at Spier. One Sunday evening, December 2007.'

'You remember well,' Cupido said.

Roch smiled with nostalgia. 'It was a night to remember. Hanneke was . . . There were five or six women at the table, and she stood out. In every way . . .'

'So you introduced yourself?'

'That's right. I couldn't resist the temptation. We . . . myself and two friends, we went and sat with them. And . . . the rest is history.'

'Why did she end the relationship?' Griessel asked again.

'Relationships cool off, I suppose that's life . . . We'd been together for two years, her hours kept getting longer. And those last two, three months, we barely saw each other. Now and then on a Saturday night, a Sunday morning. We would have gone skiing together that December, but she had to cancel. And then, in February last year, she arrived here one evening . . .'

'Here at the workshop?' Cupido asked.

'No, I live in a cottage up against the mountain. She phoned from her office, about five, to ask if she could come over. She was late, she only arrived after nine. She came to tell me we should take a breather.'

'A breather?'

'Those were her words. She said . . . she was very sorry, very sad, she said it was unfair to both of us, the fact that we never saw each other any more. And she didn't want to prevent me from finding anyone else.'

'And what did you say?'

'I said I didn't want anyone else, and I understood that she was working hard. It didn't worry me, it was temporary, she wouldn't be that busy for ever.'

'So you didn't want to break up?'

'Of course not. I . . . Hanneke . . . I thought she would be my wife.'

'But then she told you it was over?'

'Yes.'

'And you were angry?'

'Not angry. Disappointed. No, more than that . . . Hang on, surely you're not insinuating . . .' The outstretched legs were pulled back and he sat up straight in the chair.

'I'm not insinuating anything. I'm asking,' said Cupido.

Roch put his forearms on his knees, leaned forward. He shook his head in disbelief. 'You actually think that I . . . It's one helluva insult. About everything,' he said, controlled but hurt.

'I think that you *what*, Mr Roch?'

'You think that I could . . . do anything to Hanneke. A year after we broke up? A year? What sort of person do you think I am?'

'I don't know you.'

'Did you read my statement? I wasn't even in the country when Hanneke died. How do you do your work?' he asked with more astonishment than rage.

Griessel said soothingly, 'Mr Roch, we need your help. We have to investigate everything over again. We have to make sure . . .'

He looked from one to the other. 'Good cop, bad cop. I see.'

'What do you see?' Cupido asked.

'I see what you're trying to do. But hell, it's insulting . . .'

'Why? Because we think a guy gets angry when his future wife drops him? That's insulting?' Cupido asked.

Griessel wanted to calm things. 'Mr Roch . . .'

'Wait, please.' A polite request, with his big hand in the air. 'I can understand . . . I was probably angry too.'

'With her?'

'With the bunch of lawyers who made her work so late. With myself, for not seeing it coming, for not doing something about it earlier. I could have made more time, been more supportive. But with her . . . I was very disappointed. Because she didn't love me enough, because she was so stubborn, because she didn't want to wait, because she wouldn't give us a chance.'

'But not angry with her.'

Roch looked reproachfully at Cupido. 'Hurt, Captain. The hurt was worse. I loved her. Genuinely loved her. She was an amazing person. We were great together. In every way. The same interests, the same sort of friends . . . it's a great loss, when you lose something like that. But what can you do? You take it like a man and you get through it. Even if it takes six months, nine months, you come out on the other side. You don't look back. And you respect her decision, that's what you do, because that is what love means, you respect her decision.'

A soft knock on the door. The coffee had arrived.

23

Once the coffee was poured and handed around, Roch sat down again, still with a long-suffering, wounded expression on his face.

'You were overseas in January?' Griessel asked.

Roch nodded, sipped his coffee.

'Where were you?'

'Aime la Plagne, in the Alps, for a week. Then Bordeaux. In France.'

'When did you return?'

'The nineteenth. The day *after* she died.'

'The day her body was found?'

'That's right.'

'What time on the nineteenth?'

'I landed in Johannesburg in the morning. I was back in the Cape around two o'clock in the afternoon, if I remember correctly. I can go and check . . .'

'Do you still have the documentation for the flight?'

'I faxed it to the other detective.'

'To Nxesi?'

'Yes. It must be on record.'

'The tickets?'

'No, the reservation, the proof of payment.'

'But you still have it?'

'Yes.'

'The trip – was it a holiday?'

'For the most part. Aime was for skiing. Then I went to Bordeaux to visit my mentor, at Château Haut Lafitte. So it was sort of work too . . .'

'Were you alone on the plane?'

'Do you mean . . . ? Yes, I was alone.'

'I would be grateful if you could find the documentation for us.'

'It's not in your records?'

'We haven't seen it.'

'OK.'

'Did you see Sloet again after you broke up?' Cupido asked.

'Yes. Once or twice.'

'Which is it? Once or twice?'

'It's an expression, Captain. I saw her twice. If you are together for two years, you leave stuff in each other's places. About two weeks after . . . sometime in March last year, I took two boxes of her stuff to her.'

'When she still lived in Stellenbosch?'

'That's right.'

'How did it go?'

'Not well.'

'Why?'

'I said things I shouldn't have said.'

'What things?'

'I said she'd lied to me.'

'What about?'

'About why we broke up.'

'Go on.'

'I had . . . I couldn't understand it, the whole thing. But it was that time, I was hurt, I just couldn't figure out how she could just turn her back on everything, out of the blue.'

'Hurt, but not angry,' said Cupido sarcastically.

'What did you say to her?' Griessel asked.

'I thought there was someone else.'

'And what did she say then?'

'She asked me if I really thought she wouldn't have the guts to admit it if it was so.'

'And then?'

'Then I said, no, that's true. She had always had guts. For anything.'

'And then?'

'Then I left.'

'And the second time?'

'That was in December. She called me . . .'

'When in December?'

'The first week. Tuesday night? She had started packing up, for the move to Cape Town. She found more of my stuff. Jerseys, socks, stuff like that. She brought them to me one evening.'

'How did that go?'

'Well.'

'What happened?'

'She brought the stuff. We talked . . .' For the first time the body language was less comfortable, the eyes glanced once quickly at the door.

Cupido homed in on that. 'What about?'

'Well . . . it was the first time I had seen her with the new . . .' He cupped his hands in front of his chest.

'Her boob job?'

'That's right.'

'And you talked about it?'

'Yes. I asked her why.'

'And what did she say?'

'She said she had wanted to do it for a long time. And she asked me if I liked it.'

'And?'

'I said "yes".'

'The operation – was it a surprise for you?' Griessel asked.

'Yes. She never talked about it while we were together. And it wasn't as if she was small . . .'

'Wait, wait,' said Cupido. 'She asked you if you liked the boobs?'

'Yes.'

'And you said "yes"?'

'That's right.'

'And then?'

Roch's eyes drifted to the door.

'Mr Roch . . .' Cupido prodded him.

'Then she showed them to me,' he said at last, as if he was relieved to get it off his chest.

'Her boobs?'

'Yes.'

'Just undressed and showed you?'

'She didn't undress. She was just wearing a T-shirt, she . . . you know, loosened her bra, lifted her shirt . . .'

'Just like that?'

'We were together for two years, Captain, it's not like we had never been naked together.'

'But you'd broken up what . . . ten months before? And she comes in and shows you her boobs?'

'You make it sound so cheap. I never said she just walked in and showed me her breasts. We sat talking for ages. Drank wine. Later I asked her why she had had it done.'

'And then she flashed her headlights. And you just looked?'

'I . . .'

'Yes?'

Roch got up in a flowing movement, walked behind the chair. 'I'm not sure it's . . .' He went to the desk, turned around, came and sat down again. The detective's eyes followed him.

'What does it matter?'

'You told Warrant Officer Nxesi that you had practically no contact any more, Mr Roch,' Griessel said.

'Twice. In more than a year. What would you call it?'

'What happened that night?' Griessel asked.

Roch moved his hands in frustration, he gripped the arms of the chair, and said, 'If you really must know, we had sex.'

'Oh yes,' said Cupido, 'that's practically no contact.'

'What difference does it make?' Roch asked, for the first time truly angry. 'Tell me, what difference does it make? We didn't plan it, we had been together two years, we were . . . both very physical, we had already had a few glasses, we were two consenting adults. Tell me, what difference does it make?'

'Let me tell you,' Cupido leaned forward in his chair, his index finger pointed at Roch, 'you lied to Nxesi.'

'I didn't lie. Never.'

'Why didn't you tell him you *njapsed* her? What are you hiding?'

'What have I got to hide? I was on a fucking plane when somebody killed Hanneke. What have I got to hide?'

'You say you were on a plane. Alone. You are going to show us your reservation, but not the actual tickets. But you made that reservation long before the time. Then you took another flight, say a day earlier, paid cash for your ticket, came home. And you took one of the big iron stakes in your shop and went knocking on her door. She knows you, so she lets you in. And you stab her. Because she wouldn't let you *njaps* her again.'

Roch looked intently at Cupido. If this man jumped up now, Griessel thought, they were in trouble. He shifted in his chair to make his service pistol accessible.

But Egan Roch sank slowly back. He shook his head as if he couldn't believe what he was hearing. 'That is such an insult,' he said finally. 'Do me a favour. Call the office of Air

France. Ask them if they have an air hostess by the name of Danielle Fournier who was on the flight from Charles de Gaulle to O.R. Tambo on the nineteenth of January. And then go and talk to her. Ask her if she remembers me. And then come back to me with your shit.'

24

'He's lying,' Cupido said when they got back in the car. 'Egan. What kind of name is Egan? How do you come by a name like that? Do you look at this baby, your *laaitie*, and say, "*nooit*, this is an Egan"? Sounds like the name of an alien in a Spielberg movie. Fucking Egan. Egan the Vegan. I'm telling you, that whitey is lying. *Jissis*, that attitude . . . I'm a handsome bugger, I work on a wine estate, I make oak barrels, actually I'm fucking cool. Pisses me off. But what pisses me off most, is that he thinks we are fucking fools. He saw those tits, he felt those tits, he *njapsed* her, and he wanted it again. And she said to him, sorry, mister, it's all over, you had your chance, you blew it. And then he thinks, if I can't have it, nobody will. Those jugs must have kept him awake at night, middle of the night. So he lay there and schemed, he was anyway going to Oo-la-laa, so the *man makes a plan*. Thinks we are fucking fools, I'm telling you, the air hostess story is a lot of *kak*, she's going to say "who?". I scheme he got hold of the name, must have chatted her up when he was flying over, heard she was on the same aeroplane on the nineteenth, one of those short blanket alibis, don't cover the feet, now he thinks because he can cover his head . . . But I'm gonna nail him, pappie, I'm telling you. *Fokken* barrel maker. Egan. What kind of name is Egan anyway?'

Griessel did not entirely share Cupido's assurance. There was too much quiet bravado in Roch's 'Call the office of Air France'. And Home Affairs would be able to confirm when his passport was registered again on his return. But they would have to follow up, because Cupido was right, the man hadn't told Nxesi the whole truth.

'We will have to get a two-oh-five,' said Griessel. The SAPS could only request cellphone records if they had a two-zero-five subpoena. 'See if he phoned her at work.'

'IMC handles that whole process. And we get a search warrant. We've got enough. He lied to Nxesi, a month before her death he fucked her, he's got these *moerse* big irons in his barrel shop. And I'm telling you now, *fokken* "shop", my arse, where do they get off on that?'

'Vaughn, you'll have to handle it.'

'Right. Captain Cupido will nail him.' And after a moment to reflect. 'Because you have other fish to fry?'

Griessel nodded. 'Politics.'

'Is that why you asked him about the communists?'

'Yes.'

'So? What's the story?'

'Can't talk about it yet.'

'Fuckin' politics. Which reminds me: have you found out what the Flower got up to in Amsterdam?' Cupido asked, because Mbali's name meant 'flower' in Zulu.

'No,' said Griessel. And in that instant, inexplicably, he knew what was bothering him about the sniper's last email.

He would have to go and tell the Flower.

Major Benedict Boshigo, member of the Statutory Crimes Group of the Hawks' Commercial Crimes Branch in the Cape, was sitting behind his chaotic desk when Griessel entered. Boshigo's nose was almost pressed to the printouts that covered the whole surface of the desk.

'Hi, Bones.'

'Hey, Benny. You got something here, *nè*,' said Bones as he looked up. His eyes had always made Griessel feel somewhat uncomfortable, prominent and vulnerable in the very thin face, like a famine victim.

Boshigo was something of a legend, a long distance athlete, a man who had finished the Comrades seventeen times, and the Boston and New York marathons once each. Thanks to those events and a frightening training regime, he was a walking skeleton, literally skin and bone, And that was why his friends called him 'Bones'. .

'Did you find anything?'

Bones grinned. 'BEE deals are always full of tricks, *nè*. Always full of tricks. What we have to ask, is whether this one has any illegal tricks. So far, not, everything above board, it's not Kebble style corporate raiding, it's just run-of-the-mill stuff. I think it's too early, Benny, BEE companies only start flirting with the limits of the Companies Act and the Broad-Based Socio-Economic Empowerment Charter when the contracts are signed . . .'

'Bones . . .'

'I know, I know, when I worked with Vusi, he used to tell me all the time: "Speak English, Bones".'

Griessel had already heard that one of Boshigo's favourite sayings was 'when I worked with Vusi'. With the Scorpions, then part of the national prosecuting authority, Bones had worked with the legendary Advocate Vusi Pikoli. The other saying that his colleagues good-naturedly teased him over was: 'When I was studying in the States . . .' Boshigo was very proud of the Bachelor's degree in economics he had earned at Boston University's Metropolitan College.

'Bottom line, Benny, I looked at the detailed joint cautionary announcement of Ingcebo and Gariep. That's the announcement they made about the whole deal, November 2009, that's the blueprint for the transaction, how they plan to do the whole thing. A road map. I looked at where they are now, how they adhered to the plan. There's no motive for murder. I looked at Ingcebo, at the registration documents, at the company charter, at the appointment of directors, it's all clean. There's nothing.'

'And the communist?'

Again the cynical smile. 'Benny, Benny, there are no communists in Azania any more, *nè*. Only lip service. A. T. Masondo is Ambrose Thenjiwe Masondo. In exile till ninety-three, he was a member of the Central Committee of the Communist Party, Treasurer of the National Union of Mineworkers, and on the National Congress of COSATU. Mbeki made him Deputy Minister of Mining, he retired along with his boss in 2007, he became a director of Ingcebo in 2009, and managing director of Ingcebo Bauxite. Only interesting thing is . . .'

Boshigo shuffled through the documents until he found the right one, and held it out to Griessel.

A printout of the corporate web page. The caption read *Minister Masondo at AGM*. Underneath was a photograph of four white men, and a black man in the middle, smiling at the camera. All in suits and ties.

'That's Masondo, along with the directors of Gariep Minerals. Taken in 2006, when he was minister. He was the guest speaker at their AGM.'

'What does it mean, Bones?'

'It looks like he's the one who brought in the Gariep deal for Ingcebo. It was his ticket for a seat on the gravy train. Problem is, that's no crime. It's all in the public domain.'

Griessel sighed. 'What do we do now?'

'We dig a little deeper, *nè*. Maybe it's an iceberg.'

At 13.05 the sniper sat in front of his computer. The Bible website was on the screen, the one where you can type in any word, like *law* and *right* and *bribe* and *war*, and in seconds it gives the complete references, even the verses themselves.

He copied and pasted what he needed.

The insecurity of the previous night, the all-consuming fear, was gone. He was aware of the excitement inside him, the quiet satisfaction. But not complacency. He would guard against complacency, *that's* where the danger lay, the risk of underestimating and making mistakes. But he could enjoy this morning, the euphoria that he was experiencing since he had seen the newspapers.

SAPS say sniper is religious extremist, the headlines broadcast this morning.

Extremist. He had aimed lower. He had hoped they would think he was a serious Bible Basher, but *extremist* was better. It fitted with: *According to Captain John Cloete, the SAPS media spokesman, the communication between the sniper and Hawks was 'incoherent'* . . .

An incoherent extremist. A disturbed, unpredictable person who would make a stupid blunder sooner or later. That's what they thought, and it suited him very well.

He must confirm that perception. He must lead them further from the truth.

He directed the web browser to anonimail.com and logged in. Then he copied and pasted the folder, the first of two emails that he had formulated, in controlled, suppressed self-satisfaction.

Just as Griessel stood up from his desk to go to Cupido, his cellphone rang.

FRITZ.

He sat down again and answered.

'Hello, Fritz.'

'Pa, Carla is so hypocritical.'

'Fritz, I'm . . .'

'Did you see her Facebook yet, Pa?' He reconsidered: 'OK, OK, let me rephrase that, Pa, she's got a photo on Facebook of her new boyfriend.'

'New boyfriend?' He hadn't even known she had an old boyfriend.

'Some or other rugby dude. Muscleman.' The last word pronounced as though it was something unmentionable. 'Calla Etzebeth.'

'Fritz, I . . .'

'He's got a tattoo, Pa. A *moerse* Maori type of thing on his arm. And she tells me I mustn't get a tatt. What sort of hypocrite is that? Height of hypocrity.'

'Hypocrisy,' Griessel corrected him. 'Fritz, it doesn't matter. Just because *he* has one doesn't mean *you* must too . . .'

'I know, Pa, I'm not stupid. But it's hypocrisy. That's what I say.'

'Since when is this guy her boyfriend?'

'Seems like they met during Rag. During the Windows festival. And now Rag is history. A year before I can go and study.'

Griessel couldn't keep up. 'Now you want to study? I thought you just wanted to play music . . .'

'Pa, it's an option. A guy has to keep his options open. How could Maties do away with Rag?'

The telephone on his desk rang. 'Fritz, hold on . . .' He picked up. 'Griessel.'

Brigadier Manie's deep voice: 'CATS are doing a briefing, Benny. Can you and your team attend?'

25

Cupido was busy on the phone. 'Lady, I understand that. But I am a captain in the Directorate for Priority Crime Investigation. The *Hawks. And I'm investigating a murder . . .*'

Griessel sat down, his mind on Carla. And Calla, the muscle-bound rugby player with the Maori tattoo.

He had a good relationship with his daughter. They talked about a lot of things. Why hadn't she told him about Calla Etzebeth, new boyfriend? There must be a reason. Was she afraid of the muscle man? Was he on steroids, one of those that produced outbursts of rage and pimples? What had he said to her, complain to your father and I'll smack you?

He would *bliksem* the fucker, muscles or no muscles.

'Do you want me to call the press, lady?' Cupido asked over the phone. 'Tell them Air France isn't interested in aiding the police in apprehending the cold-blooded killer of an innocent young woman?'

Did Anna know about the relationship? What did a Maori tattoo look like? What sort of young man would let that be done to him? He would have to take a look on Facebook. First have to find out how. Facebook. Twitter. Cupido calling him 'old school'. Maybe it was true, but where did people find the time for all this stuff?

'When will you get back to me? Every minute this killer is loose . . .' said Cupido, and cast his eyes up to the heavens.

'You broadcast yourself,' Cupido had said. All that he could broadcast was: I am Benny Griessel. I am an alcoholic. A man who makes a fool of himself. Often. An old-school policeman who doesn't get enough sleep.

'Thank you,' said Cupido, and slammed the phone down. 'Fucking Frenchies,' he said. 'Won't give me mademoiselle Danielle Fornicate's telephone number. Eet ees not cahm-pahnee poleecee,' he put on his French accent, but to Griessel it sounded more like Spanish.

'Have you got the Facebook, Vaughn?'

'You don't ask: "Have you got *the* Facebook?" You ask: "Are you *on* Facebook?" And of course I am. Why?'

Griessel sighed. 'I have to look at something on it. Later. We have to go and listen to Mbali first.'

In the parade room, Colonel du Preez, commanding officer of CATS, and Mbali stood in front of a substantial team. There were four senior uniforms, CATS detectives, and Captain Philip van Wyk of IMC, the Hawks' Information Management Centre.

Mbali was already busy: '. . . stress that this is only a preliminary ballistics report.' She looked up, saw Griessel and Cupido. She motioned them to come and sit down. 'A preliminary report, because the bullets were very fragmented, but they recovered enough from the boot and the ankle of Lieutenant Colonel Dlodlo to tell me the calibre is either triple-two or two-two-three. The reason why the bullets were fragmented is because they are most likely Remington Premier Accutip cartridges. These bullets have a polymer tip, and when they hit, the tip is driven to the back so that the soft lead core explodes. They use this ammunition to kill problem animals like jackals and crows on farms – it's not very popular for other hunting, because it damages the meat.'

Small calibre, Griessel thought. Strange. He had expected something more impressive.

'This helps us a lot,' said Mbali. 'I am going to ask you four guys to help Captain van Wyk and the IMC. We need to get the names of everyone who owns a triple-two or a two-two-three rifle from National Firearms Registry, and those who bought Remington Premier Accutip cartridges. IMC will create a database to crosscheck them. I know it's a big job, it's a tedious job, but we have to remember, we have this madman who's shooting our colleagues. So, as the data comes in, we also have to check it against a list of people who had suppressors made. I've spoken to two gunsmiths who build suppressors, and they say they all keep invoices with names and addresses. I need you to be forceful and assertive in getting the data from the gun shops and the gunsmiths. Time isn't on our side. We'll start with the Western Cape, and broaden the search from there if we don't have any luck.'

Mbali delegated the work, explained the latest theories, that it was one or two working men, who had to keep to office hours, Afrikaans-speaking, most probably white. She was still waiting for the forensic psychologist's report, so there was as yet no official profile of age and race. She said the uniformed officers must please instruct the stations to keep their eyes open for a parked sedan car, for a blanket or tarp that might hide the back seat, because there was a suspicion he was shooting through the boot. The silencer made the rifle longer, therefore it was unlikely to be a small vehicle. A minibus was also a possibility, maybe with curtains over the windows, anything that could hide the sniper from curious eyes while he took aim and shot. The possibility that it might be another type of vehicle could not be excluded, so therefore to be on alert in *all* cases.

Griessel watched how the men sat and listened to her. They were focused, as always when members of the Force were in the firing line.

Mbali gave a description of the silencer. She clapped her hands to illustrate the sound. She said it could be masked by street noise, therefore police stations in the busier parts of the Peninsula should be especially alert. The task team was ready, she gave them the number again. If any patrol spotted a suspicious vehicle, please, just write down the particulars, the make and colour and registration number, let her and the task team know.

When the detectives and the uniformed officers stood up and filed out, Griessel approached her. Cupido followed him.

'Benny, did I do all right?' Mbali asked.

'Yes,' he said, 'of course. Mbali, the sniper . . . I've been thinking all morning. There must be a reason he didn't tell the media about the communists . . .'

'Yes.'

'And all I can think of is that he is worried someone will then be able to identify him.'

'Hang on,' said Cupido. 'The sniper is talking about communists? Is that why you . . .'

'Vaughn, the brigadier will fire us both if you talk about this.'

'My lips are zipped.'

'In his emails . . . the sniper says a communist is behind Sloet's murder. And he says we know who it is.'

'But that's bullshit.'

'Captain,' said Mbali. 'Please. When a man uses profanity to support an argument, either the man or the argument is weak.'

'Don't you lecture me,' said Cupido aggressively.

Mbali ignored him. 'Benny, you think he's worried someone can identify him?'

'Maybe the shooter knew her. Maybe . . . he's worried that someone will make the connection if it gets into the media that he's talking about communists. And he knows we can't afford to go public with the information . . . I don't know. There must be a reason.'

He nursed his dull head, he just couldn't formulate the thing right.

'Why can't we go public?' asked Cupido.

'Vaughn, I can't talk about it. Politics.'

The light went on for Cupido. 'So you're saying, there's a commie . . . Part of the big transaction?'

'No comment,' Griessel said. He looked at Mbali. 'All I'm saying is that we should look at all her friends' and colleagues' firearm licences, do another crosscheck . . .'

'That's a good idea, Benny. Will you give me the names?'

'Wait a bit,' said Cupido. 'Egan Roch works on a farm.'

'What do you mean?'

'Mbali said those bullets, they use them on farms for vermin. They must have vermin on a wine farm? That they shoot?'

'You think Roch is the gunman?'

'You just said friends and colleagues. Egan is a friend. With benefits. He *njapsed* her in December. Is *njaps* also a profanity, Mbali?'

'Don't be childish. Who is this Egan?'

'Egan Roch. Sloet's ex-boyfriend. Vaughn and I went to see him this morning. He lied to Nxesi, so he's now officially a suspect.'

'But if Roch killed her, why would he shoot policemen? Why would he write about communists?'

'Because he's panicking,' said Cupido.

'Two months after he killed her?'

Her tone was very sceptical.

'Hell, Mbali, he has no idea how the investigation is going. He sits in his barrel shop and worries, why is everything so quiet? What are the cops up to? Are they going to take another look at me if they don't find anything else? So he pulls a communist out of the hat quickly. Come on, don't look so sceptical. Sloet opened that door for somebody she knew. A month before her death, he was *njapsing* her. And afterwards, while they were lying there she says: Egan, darling, I must tell you the one about the communist and the big deal . . . So he could have known.'

Griessel considered the possibility. He thought of the missing spare key to Sloet's front door, which she could have given to someone she trusted. Someone who might now and then bonk her. 'It's possible,' he said, 'because the more we look for a communist and a motive, the less likely it is—'

Mbali's cellphone rang inside her giant handbag. She took it out, answered.

They listened to her say, 'Yes, sir', and, 'Thank you, sir', then ring off.

'There's another email,' she said.

'Interesting timing,' said Cupido. 'Right after we were at the barrel maker.'

'No,' said Mbali. 'Bad timing. There goes my whole theory about the weekend warrior.'

26

762a89z012@anonimail.com
Sent: Monday 28 February. 13.29
To: j.afrika@saps.gov.za
Re: To the Liar Captain Benny Griessel
Am I a religious extremist because I am glad when justice prevails? (Proverbs 21:15)
I pray that you are shocked at the injustice done since 18 January. Why do you say I am incoherent? I said the same thing from the begining. You know who Hanneke Sloet's murderer is. You have all been in this together with the communist for years. I have to do something to force you to break your old loyalties. I take my strength from Ecclesiastes 3. It is not extremism, it is The Truth.
Is it more important to you to protect the communist than protecting policemen?
You have to decide.

'Crazy mother—' said Cupido, and swallowed the last part of the word.

Mbali barely heard him. 'He sent it during lunch time,' she said, relieved.

'This is new,' said Griessel. '*For years . . . old loyalties.*'

'And the singular again,' said Mbali. 'Yesterday it was plural, in his email to the media.'

'Only one spelling mistake.'

'He's right, you know. He has been saying the same thing.'

'But only to us. Why not to the media?'

'Maybe that will change . . .'

Griessel shook his head. 'I don't think so.'

'I'm going to get a search warrant,' said Cupido. 'Maybe there is an underlined Bible in the barrel maker's house.'

'I want the case file back from you first,' said Griessel.

He closed his office door, put the thick folder on his desk, and sat down, elbows on the desktop. He rubbed his eyes.

He would have to pull himself together. He had to focus. He just couldn't tell one end from the other right now.

He opened the file, took out the latest email.

You have all been in this together with the communist for years.

Why did the gunman only say this now? Why hadn't he said from the beginning that there was an old connection between the communist and the SAPS? If it wasn't for the Bible verses, he would say the fucker was playing them.

He took out the older emails, read them in order.

This guy was jumping around, from the first powerful, punchy threats, to the hyper-religious, self-justifying quotes, and the misspelled hysteria of yesterday. And now the new one. With exactly the same verses. The same message: It is the communist. You know who it is.

But they didn't know.

The same verses. Over and over.

A new possibility occurred to him. Maybe the man was very religious. Not an extremist, just a happy-clappy, belonging to one of those charismatic churches where they healed with the laying on of hands and spoke in tongues. Did Hanneke Sloet belong to a church? Could it be someone

she had got to know that way? Did she have seriously religious friends or colleagues? He would have to find out, and
he would have to go and show Bones the *in this together for
years* quote.

But first he should make the call he had been putting off
for two days now. He dialled the Jeffreys Bay code, then the
number. It rang for a long time. Then a woman's voice, 'This
is Marna.'

'Ma'am, this is Captain Benny Griessel of the Hawks in
Cape Town. I am working on the—'

'I have to read in the papers that you've reopened the case.'
A statement, without recrimination, just calm and strong.

'Ma'am, I'm truly—'

'It's a disgrace, Captain. The papers are calling us non-
stop. I don't want to portray the police in a bad light, but you
make it very difficult for me.'

'I am very sorry, ma'am. It . . . There is no excuse, I should
have phoned you.'

'Very well. Apology accepted. Do you have any news?'

'Ma'am, it is too early—'

'What is going on with this man who keeps shooting
policemen? Does he have a connection with my daughter?
He is bringing her name into disrepute.'

This was something he didn't want to discuss now. 'Ma'am,
there are many more questions that we cannot answer. That
is one of the reasons I am phoning.'

'So how may I help you?'

'Ma'am, let me say I am sorry for your loss. I can understand that this is a difficult time.'

'Thank you. We have to persevere, Captain. We have no
choice. What do you want to ask me?'

'According to your statement, Miss Sloet spent Christmas
with you . . .'

'That's right.'

'How long was she there?'

'Just three days. She arrived on the twenty-fourth, and she went back on the twenty-seventh. There was some uncertainty about the new apartment, whether it would be ready on time. She couldn't stay longer.'

'What was her state of mind?'

'Captain, you know officer Nxesi asked us all this back in January?'

'Yes, ma'am, and I am sorry. I know it is difficult to go through all this again ... the trouble is, only your official statement is on record, along with the investigating officer's notes. And I am trying to see it all with fresh eyes.'

'I told Nxesi I had never seen Hanneke like that before. She was ...' Her voice deepened with emotion, as though the wound had reopened. She was quiet a moment, and when she spoke again, Griessel could hear the effort in her voice. 'She was happy. She was never very demonstrative. Just like her mother. But I could see my child was happy. That is why her death ...' Again she had to stop to gather her strength. 'It was such a loss, Captain.'

'I understand, ma'am.'

'Do you have children?'

'Two.'

'Yes. Then you will understand.'

'Did she say why she was so happy?'

'Not precisely. And I didn't ask. She was such a private person, ever since she was small. I gathered things were going well at work, and she was excited about her new apartment.' As an afterthought: 'I think she was enjoying her freedom.'

'Because she was no longer in a relationship?'

'I think so.'

'Ma'am, Egan Roch said they had a good relationship.'

'They did! She just wasn't ready for the big step. She worked so hard, she had so little time for herself. What you need to know about Hanneke, Captain, is that she set very high standards for herself. She had goals. Dreams. And I think she wanted to attain them before she thought about marriage.'

'Did she say anything about Egan Roch? When she was with you at Christmas?'

'She just said she was glad they had parted as friends. She saw him a few weeks before, took him some of his things. And she said it was good to say goodbye like that. On good terms.'

'Nothing else?'

'No, nothing else . . . Why do you ask?' Sudden concern in her voice.

'Ma'am, we have to make sure we look at every angle.'

'Egan is a wonderful man. We liked him so much.'

'Did she talk about her work?'

'Her work was her life. Sometimes it was all she could talk about.'

'Did she say anything about the big transaction she was working on?'

'She did. Not that I could understand everything. But she said she was enjoying it very much. And she was meeting the most interesting people. She said she would very much like to specialise in that area. Or she would . . . I wish I had paid more attention . . . It was very complex, she tried to explain, but what do I know? In any case, she said there was so much potential in the black transactions. She was very excited about a proposal she wanted to make. To her bosses, when these contracts were finalised. And then she said she might go on her own – I remember that well, because I said she mustn't bite off more than she could chew, she had such a good job. Then she said she would approach her bosses first.'

'You don't know what the proposal was?'

'I can't remember the detail. It sounded to me as though

she wanted . . . She said, "Ma, the sums are astronomical. We can do so much better."'

'And the interesting people that were involved . . . ?'

'That is all that she said. "There are such interesting people involved." I noticed, because Hanneke didn't say things like that lightly. She was . . . quite critical of people. Because she was so sharp. She didn't suffer fools gladly . . .'

He waited for her to say more, but nothing came. 'Ma'am, was she very religious?'

She hesitated only for a moment. 'Is this about the religious extremist?'

'Yes, ma'am.'

'No, Hanneke was not religious at all.'

'So she didn't belong to a church?'

Marna Sloet was quiet for a while. Then in a muted voice, 'No. Her father had a habit of blaming his professional and personal failures on the Higher Power, Captain. Hanneke hated that. Her motto was that you were responsible for your own fate.'

27

He needed time to absorb it all. That was how his head worked. Anna always used to say it was like a washing machine: he would put all the dirty laundry in and let it tumble and turn, and when the time was right, when his instinct kicked in, he would open it up and take out a fresh, clean theory.

Hanneke Sloet wanted to take a proposal to her bosses. She had thought of going it alone. Because there were large sums involved, and they could do so much better. And the 'interesting people'? What did she mean? Politicians? Communists? Something else? This fucking deal, he'd best just get up and hand the whole thing over to Bones, because he couldn't make head or tail of it.

His door burst open and Cupido leaned half-way in. 'Barrel maker is a no-go for the murder. The air hostess just phoned. Egan the Vegan chatted her up on the flight of the eighteenth. They would have had dinner here in the Cape on the twentieth, but he phoned her and said he'd just lost someone near and dear.'

Griessel was surprised that Cupido showed so little disappointment. Until his colleague said, '*Jissis*, Benny, those French chicks. You gotta hear that accent, pappie, sensuality dripping from every word. That mouth is begging for a French kiss, Danielle Fournier . . .' Her name was pronounced in his best French accent, as though it was the most captivating thing he had ever heard.

'Thank you, Vaughn,' said Griessel.

'He could still be the gunman. And Captain Cupido will check it out. *Voilà.*' He turned and nearly bumped into Mbali, who bustled in with a sheet of paper in her hand.

'*Voilà* is French, Mbali,' said Cupido to her. 'Not profanity.'

'Get a life,' she said to him. Then she closed Griessel's office door behind her, sat down and passed the document over to him. 'His new email to the newspapers . . .'

He read.

762a89z012@anonimail.com
Sent: Monday 28 February. 13.30
To: jannie.erlank@dieburger.com
Re: Proverbs 21:15
The police call me an extremist.
Am I?
Proverbs 17:23: A wicked man taketh a gift out of the
bosom to pervert the ways of judgement.

Proverbs 21:15: It is joy to the just to do judgement: but destruction shall be to the workers of iniquity.

Our country has descended into corruption. Murderers walk free. It is the just who are destroyed. The motto is Extremis malis extrema remedia.

You will see, only an extremist will let justice be done. The SAPS knows who the murderers of Hanneke Sloet are. I know that for a fact. Now, destruction shall be to them, unless they do their work.

'You were right,' said Mbali. 'He is still not saying a word about the communist. Just the hints about corruption . . .'

'That's Latin,' said Griessel.

'Yes. He's educated. And he's grandstanding, he's playing politics. The public will love this.'

A polite knock on the closed door.

'Come in,' Benny called.

Bones Boshigo opened it, his eyes bigger than usual. 'Good afternoon, Captain Kaleni. Benny, that iceberg, *nè*. I think you should come with me . . .'

On their way out, Boshigo walked quickly down the corridor, and Griessel had to scurry to keep up. The Hawks' unwritten dress code was jacket and tie. Bones was in his usual T-shirt, jeans, and running shoes. This rebel streak made him popular with his colleagues, and made top management shake their heads. But the reason Griessel had so much respect for him was because the skinny man never touched a drop of alcohol. 'Don't see the use,' was all he would say about it.

'I talked to Len de Beer, Benny. He's a genius, *nè*. Runs a subscription blog on share trading and investment, a thousand rand a month to read it. He's very weird, you'll see. Anyway, I couldn't get anywhere, so I phoned Len – he's been my source ever since I worked with Vusi. And Len said he would take a look. He phoned back just now and he said, "There's smoke, Bones." But Len is like that, he won't talk on the phone, you have to sit down with him. Which is an experience in itself. Eccentric, *nè*. But clever, very clever.'

While Bones drove to the city, Griessel phoned Alexa.

He heard the young sitter's whispered answer, 'This is Ella.'

'This is Benny Griessel. Is everything OK?'

'Sort of. She's onstage, she's going to rehearse now.'

'Why do you say "sort of"?'

'She's having a hard time, Benny. She took a handful of pain pills. She's perspiring and shaking, and she's very irritable. But she says she made a deal with you. She's very brave.' Still whispering.

'OK,' he said, relieved. 'Thanks. You know you can call me.'

'I know, Paul Eilers. Relax. I can handle it. Have to go. Bye.'

He put the phone away. One less thing to worry about.

'Bones, are you *on* Facebook?' Griessel made certain he had the right preposition.

'I was, Benny. Been there, done that. Facebook is yesterday's news. I'm on LinkedIn.'

'Is that like Twitter?'

Boshigo laughed. 'No. Let me put it to you this way. Facebook is for people you went to school with. Twitter is for people you wish you went to school with. And LinkedIn is for people who don't think about school any more, they want to do business.'

'But you know Facebook?'

'I do.'

'If I want to find a photo of someone, how do I go about it?'

'You become a friend.'

'But it's family.'

Boshigo's chortle was so infectious that Griessel had to laugh along. 'Vaughn says I am old school, Bones.'

'From now on I'm calling you Noah, *nè*. First you have to register with Facebook. Then you can see everyone's public photos. But if a photo is private, then you send a friend request to the one whose photos you want to see. Then, if they accept you, you can see them.'

Griessel shook his head. It seemed too complicated. 'But I don't want to register with Facebook.'

'Then you have to get someone who is on Facebook, and you ask them to email you the photo.'

'OK,' said Griessel, taking out his phone and calling his son.

Len de Beer lived in Bertram Street in Sea Point, where the pitched-roof houses were small and squeezed together. There was an unkempt garden the size of a blanket, a white picket fence, and a slightly rusted iron gate that protested on opening.

He was a big man in a blue short-sleeved checked shirt, old grey tracksuit pants and slippers, considerably overweight, his voice surprisingly high as he said, 'Come in, come in'. The thick bushy hair and beard were dark red, and he reminded Griessel of Hagar the Horrible. Behind a pair of cheap black-rimmed glasses mended with tape his eyes were clear and bright blue. He greeted Bones with a practised township handshake of grip and re-grip, shook Griessel's hand briefly, and walked with a heavy tread to his study.

It smelled of smoke. There were bookshelves from floor to ceiling, a massive desk with a green lamp, a keyboard, mouse, four computer screens, and two television screens that apparently provided share prices and financial news.

De Beer waved them to chairs, sank down in his own with a sigh, tapped a Gauloise out of a blue pack, lit it with a match, and inhaled the smoke deeply. While his eyes flitted from one computer screen to the next, he asked, 'Clever then, are you?' His mouth was barely visible behind the beard that he combed lovingly with his fingers.

Griessel realised the question was aimed at him. He shrugged, unsure how to answer. 'I don't understand this transaction at all.'

'Doesn't make you dumb. Bones says you aren't with corporate crime.'

'That's right.'

'Layman's language,' de Beer said, like a memo to self.

Griessel looked at Bones, who winked at him.

'Pension funds,' said de Beer in his high voice, the hand in the beard again. 'Milk cows of South Africa. Large scale fraud. A thousand ways. One works like this: trade union has its own pension fund. Pension funds are run by trustees. You with me?' His eyes remained fixed on the screens in front of him.

'I'm with you.' Griessel began to understand the 'eccentric' tag.

'Lovely. Trustees decide about the investment of pension funds. Trustees are chosen from the membership of trade unions, election of trustees is manipulated. Not all trade unions. Some of them. Get the right people on the board. Simple people. Labourers. Uninformed. Grateful for the good fortune. Easy to manipulate. You with me?'

'Yes.'

'Lovely. Financial Services Board has to regulate and monitor everything. They are hopeless. Fertile ground for monkey business. Example: You establish an investment company. Get your tame trustees to invest two hundred million with you. Take the money, finance your lifestyle. Or buy another company with it. Or set one up. You with me?'

'Yes.' But Griessel wasn't all that sure any more.

'Lovely. You're clever.' And de Beer's fingers danced over the keyboard first, then he leaned forward and focused on one of the screens. Typed some more. Used the mouse, clicking repeatedly, eyes dancing from one screen to the next. Eventually he looked up, stroked his beard, and for the first time focused all his attention on Benny. 'Very well. Finished multi-tasking.'

'Excuse me?'

'Now we can discuss this, unimpeded and with full attention. Comrade Ambrose Thenjiwe Masondo, the communist that Bones asked me about, is a man who, in 2007, was elected to the board of trustees of the NASWU pension fund. The National Aluminium Smelter Workers Union. And afterwards he made work of getting the "right" people on the board with him, so that he could persuade them to entrust money to his brand new investment company. Which they duly did, to the tune of one hundred and ninety million rand.'

De Beer scanned the screens quickly, nodded in satisfaction, and lit another cigarette. 'I will try to keep it simple. A. T., as our comrade is known, invested the money in a new mining company, in which he coincidentally held the majority share. And he began to spend it just as fast on a very large salary for himself, and on an attempt to win a concession for the exploitation of a rich deposit of bauxite ore near Ponta do Ouro in Mozambique. Bauxite, just so you know, is the ore you get aluminium from. But as is often the case, decision-making is slow in Mozambique. And because A. T.'s attention was divided between all his many irons in the fire, he realised too late that advocate Victor Dlamini was elected to the NASWU pension fund board of trustees in 2009. This advocate is a firebrand, an activist, a right-or-wrong kind of man, with a very good head for figures. When Dlamini looked at the books, he began asking questions about the hundred and ninety million rand, the poor investment, the self-enrichment, and the fact that NASWU was yet to receive one cent in dividends. Captain Benny, am I still making sense?'

He was struggling to get it all into his head, but he said, 'Yes.' He could hear from de Beer's tone of voice that they were nearing a conclusion.

'Excellent. As you probably suspected, our A. T. began to get seriously concerned. He had to get himself out of a tight spot. His solution was to court Ingcebo Resources Limited – with Gariep as bait.'

'Court?' asked Griessel.

'A. T. told Ingcebo: Buy my faltering mining company, and I will bring you fifteen per cent of Gariep as a BEE deal.'

'The photo, Benny, *nè*,' Bones helped. 'A. T. knew the people of Gariep.'

'Exactly. That was the heart of the whole transaction that Hanneke Sloet was working on. In short: A. T.'s mining company was bought by Ingcebo, and the NASWU money was more or less paid back. Without a cent in interest. That mining company is now known as Ingcebo Bauxite.'

'The company that is lending billions of rands to Gariep,' said Griessel, with huge relief that he could keep up.

'He's a genius,' said de Beer to Bones Boshigo, who shook his head laughing.

'But how does that help me?' Griessel asked. 'Where's the motive for murder?'

'Aha,' said de Beer. 'The four-billion-dollar question. I suspect not one of the banks that are involved would be completely comfortable underwriting and financing four billion if they knew of A. T.'s capers. And Hanneke Sloet and Silberstein Lamarque were looking after the interests of one of those banks.'

'How can the banks not know? *You* know,' said Griessel.

'Oh, Captain, my Captain.' Len de Beer made an expansive gesture towards the monitors in front of him. 'I know everything. And I can read between the lines as well. A. T. was managing director of Ingcebo Bauxite. But suddenly, just before the BEE deal kicked off, they redeployed him. He is still director of the mother- and sister-companies, because they needed him. But they drastically reduced his profile. They wanted to conceal his sins from the banks.'

28

'You will have to find out,' said Hagar the Horrible, 'whether Hanneke Sloet knew of A. T.'s misdemeanours.'

'How?' asked Griessel.

'If you want to know the way a river flows, you need to find the source.'

'What source?'

'BEE deals begin with the big player, the initiator, the so-called deal maker. That is the man who watches the business world, spots opportunities, tests the water, brings the different companies together. Great work if you can get it, because it's big money for relatively little work. You kickstart the deal, and then you just massage until everything is complete. The deal maker in the instance of Gariep–Ingcebo is the legendary Henry van Eeden.'

The name sounded familiar to him. 'He sounds white.'

'Indeed, white and Afrikaans. He was in-house legal advisor to ConProp, the chaps who develop and own forty per cent of our shopping centres. ConProp was one of the first companies to apply black economic empowerment, around about 1997. Henry managed that transaction just about single-handed. It was pioneering work, basically, a steep learning curve, and very valuable experience. Then he took his experience and did his own thing. Right time at the right place, he must have brokered ten or twelve BEE deals. I believe he is starting to work with Chinese companies that want to invest here. I think one can describe him as "extraordinarily wealthy". Lives in Constantia.'

'And he would know if the banks knew about A. T. Masondo's shenanigans?'

'If anyone knew, it would be *him*. And Henry van Eeden would also be able to tell you whether Hanneke Sloet had access to that information.'

That was when Griessel remembered where he had heard van Eeden's name for the first time. According to Tommy Nxesi, the last email Hanneke Sloet had sent before her death, was to van Eeden. 'Official stuff, a sort of progress report,' was how Tommy had described it.

In the car Griessel phoned Cupido and asked him to get van Eeden's contact details from the case file.

'OK,' said Cupido. 'And by the way, the barrel maker has a licence for a Taurus pistol. The PT92. But nothing else. I'm checking the people at the wine estate now. Call you back.'

Griessel rang off. He wondered about Cupido's fervour for Egan Roch – first as Sloet's murderer, now as the shooter. There was something about Roch that made Cupido smell a rat. He understood that, he was like that too, an intuitive detective – get a scent, follow it like a bloodhound. But Cupido was too erratic, he didn't always think everything through properly. And after the fiasco of the Steyn case they had to be careful, they couldn't afford to focus exclusively on a single suspect again.

Besides, he didn't share Cupido's suspicion of the vat maker. Roch hadn't shared the whole truth with Nxesi because, Griessel believed, he wanted to protect Hanneke Sloet's reputation. And because he had a watertight alibi in any case.

The problem with this case was that he had no feel for it,

no intuition about it. He was hanging by the tips of his fingers over a cliff of ignorance, of too many complex things that he only understood in the broadest terms. And he wasn't even completely sure of those.

He would have to give the case to Bones. Before he made a fool of himself again. Before he was responsible for more policemen being shot. Brigadier Manie wasn't going to like that. Yesterday the Hawks had announced with a fanfare that he, Benny Griessel, would be taking over the case. And the media would crow all over again if the investigative officer changed within twenty-four hours.

Let them talk to Henry van Eeden, the big deal maker first. Then he would bring up the subject.

'Big money,' said Bones Boshigo when they stopped in front of the big wrought-iron gate in Hohenhort Avenue, Constantia. 'Very big money.'

A high, white plastered wall, but through the gate they could see the paved driveway that wound between expansive green lawns and dense trees. The house was not visible from here.

Boshigo pressed a button on the intercom beside the driver's door. A tinny voice answered after a while. 'Yes?'

'Major Benedict Boshigo and Captain Benny Griessel for Mr van Eeden.'

'He is expecting you. Drive straight on to the house, please.' The big decorative gates swung slowly and silently open.

They drove in. The estate opened up, the view of Constantia Mountain beyond to the right, and False Bay to the left. The house appeared on the rise behind oak trees, Cape Dutch and massive.

'*Eish*,' said Boshigo. Griessel just stared.

The driveway flowed into an oval parking area. A white

sports car was parked outside one of the four garages, crouched like a predator, glittering in the sun. A black man in neat overalls was polishing it. 'Lamborghini Gallardo,' said Bones. 'Two million, Benny. Eight years' salary.'

They got out. Griessel looked at the swimming pool that sparkled one level down, at the rose bushes in full white bloom, the borders spilling over with multicoloured summer flowers, at the rolling lawns, the perfect neatness. How did you mow all that? How many people did it take to look after this garden? How big was their water bill? He followed Bones towards the front door. Suddenly, just to the left of the path, someone stood up from behind the roses – a woman in a light blue sun hat, wearing gardening gloves and holding pruning shears in her hand.

For a second Griessel froze, because he thought it was Alexa Barnard – the same long blonde hair, green eyes, tall, full figure. But then he saw this woman was more beautiful, perhaps younger than Alexa. The elegant sweep of cheek-bone and mouth and chin was so lovely to him that he suddenly felt guilty. Her nose was delicate, the skin unlined and flawless, without the damage of drink. And the smile was warm, serene, a woman without demons, content with her world.

'Good afternoon,' she said.

He realised he was staring. 'Afternoon, ma'am,' he said, and introduced himself and Bones. She shook their hands with her gloves on. 'Annemarie van Eeden,' she said, and pointed the pruning shears at the house. 'You must be looking for Henry. Just knock, the door is open.'

'Thank you, ma'am.' They walked on, and all he could think of was that that was how Alexa could have looked if she hadn't been a drinker. Again the feeling of guilt – it was wrong to make comparisons.

Up the broad sandstone steps. Elegant garden furniture

arranged under umbrellas on the long veranda, the front door was wide and beautiful. Bones walked ahead, and raised a hand to knock, but someone was already approaching from the cool interior. A man in his forties, athletic, energetic, in a yellow golf shirt and dark blue trousers, running shoes. His black hair was short and neat, he wore a large watch on his arm. 'Major Boshigo,' he said. 'I am Henry van Eeden.'

They sat on the veranda and drank Earl Grey tea from fine porcelain. Bones and van Eeden talked economics. 'Our future lies in the hands of the Greeks, of all nations,' said van Eeden.

'Go figure,' said Boshigo.

Griessel was listening with half an ear. He looked over False Bay, sparkling in the distance, and he wished he were clever. Being clever made you rich. This man who talked so easily with them was clever enough to study law. Clever enough to set up a black empowerment transaction on his own. Clever enough to see there was big money in it. Being clever made it possible for him and his beautiful wife to live here on Constantia's lovely slopes. While he, Griessel, had to make do with a bachelor flat in Gardens, with furniture from a pawn shop, and no wife. Because he was barely smart enough to scrape through matric. With an E for maths. And woodwork. Carla had inherited her mother's brains, the first Griessel in this branch of the family tree to go to university. And what does she choose? Drama. On the strength of one inspirational conversation with the step-daughter of his friend and former colleague Matt Joubert, who was already studying it. They had money, Matt's wife Margaret restored houses and sold them, they would be able to help if Michele couldn't find work. But what was he going to do? He could barely manage Carla's university fees. And now Fritz was talking about going to university too. God knows what he wanted to study. Music? Maybe he and Anna should have followed Marna Sloet's example, taught their children from when they were little to be ambitious. Hungry, for success and riches.

'How can I be of assistance to you?' Henry van Eeden asked, putting down his empty cup and leaning back comfortably in the upholstered veranda chair.

'We are on the horns of a dilemma, *nè*,' Boshigo said. 'The investigation is at a sensitive stage, we can't tell you everything. But there are questions about A. T. Masondo. Trouble with a pension fund.'

'You are well informed,' said van Eeden smoothly.

'We think if the banks knew about Masondo and the pension money, they would have asked Ingcebo to kick him out.'

The smile broadened. 'Major, in a perfect world that could surely happen. But not here.'

'Are you saying they knew?'

'Gariep knew. From the beginning. That is why they insisted that Masondo was replaced as managing director of Ingcebo Bauxite.'

'And the underwriters? SA Merchant Bank? HSBC? Did *they* know?'

'I suspect they did. They are very thorough when it comes to four billion.'

Griessel's heart began to sink. If this communist was not their man, where would they find another one?

'But you're not sure?' Bones asked.

'The banks' due diligence is exhaustive. And their evaluation reports are confidential. They don't even share them with each other. Silberstein Lamarque would know whether SA Merchant Bank knew of it. I would be very surprised if they didn't. But no, I don't know for sure.'

'Oh,' said Boshigo, disappointed.

'Major, I gather you suspect Hanneke Sloet's murder had something to do with the transaction.'

'That is one possibility.'

'I would very much like to help,' said van Eeden in earnest.

Bones looked at Benny. Griessel nodded, because he couldn't see what harm it could do.

'You'll have to keep it confidential,' said Boshigo.

'Confidentiality is my bread and butter, Major.'

'We received information that there was a communist involved with the murder of Sloet.'

'A communist,' said van Eeden. Then he smiled carefully, as though he thought Boshigo was pulling his leg. 'You're not serious.'

'I am.'

Van Eeden nodded, suddenly sober. 'Hence A. T. Masondo.'

'We thought Hanneke Sloet might have heard of his trade union tricks. Maybe she wanted to stop the loan. Or go to the press. And Masondo wanted to silence her, to stay on the gravy train.'

Van Eeden pondered it all, and then he said. 'I understand your theory. But there is just one problem: if Hanneke wanted to interfere with the deal – or with Masondo – it would have exploded in her and Silberstein Lamarque's faces. *They* would have been fired.'

29

'The competition,' said Henry van Eeden, 'is phenomenal. Every big legal firm in the country would give an arm and a leg to be players in the BEE world. And once you're allowed into the inner circle, you want to stay there. Silberstein Lamarque would have fired Hanneke like a shot . . . And I'm sure that's the last thing Hanneke would have wanted. The other question is, the banks' due diligence was completed fourteen months ago. Why would she want to do something with that information only in January this year?'

'I don't know,' said Boshigo.

'Mr van Eeden . . .' said Griessel.

'Henry, please.'

'You say you are sure that is the last thing Hanneke would have wanted.'

'Yes.'

'Why?'

Van Eeden opened his hands as if he was sharing a secret. He sat up straight, searching for a moment for the right place to start. 'I've been involved with BEE for nearly fifteen years. I've worked with literally hundreds of people. Businessmen, politicians and former politicians, bankers, auditors, legal people. I have seen it all. The honest, the greedy, the chancers, the professionals and the inept, the lazy and the dedicated. Hanneke was a first. Unique. So much unyielding focus, so much hard work, so much desire to learn about every detail. She didn't just want to know how she could do her work with the merchant bank contracts as well as possible, she wanted to know *everything*. About the whole transaction. In January last year she asked me if I would mind sharing my knowledge with her. She made an appointment, and for four hours she grilled me. In the minutest detail. In April and September she did it again, shorter sessions, but with the same intensity. Later I said to her it looked like she wanted my job.' His smile at the recollection held a hint of tenderness. 'And then she asked me what I thought was the biggest gap in her arsenal, what could possibly keep her from doing my work. Just like that. And then I said, the building and maintenance of a relationship of trust with the right people.'

'And then.'

'She wrote it down. My point is, A. T. Masondo, despite his past, has influence. A network. He is one of the "right people". Hanneke knew that. She would have her priorities right.'

Before they left, Griessel asked some half-hearted questions, his heart in his boots. He wanted to know from van Eeden if he had been worried that Sloet's ambitions could have negatively influenced his own business.

A roguish laugh, then van Eeden said, 'Captain, this is probably my last BEE transaction. The Chinese potential is massive, so many of them want to invest here. Fallow earth, ready for the plough. That is where I want to focus now.'

'Did Hanneke Sloet have any contact with Masondo?'

'Not really. Maybe briefly at a meeting or a cocktail party.'

'What about email? Telephone?'

'I seriously doubt that,' said van Eeden. 'She simply had no need to communicate with him.'

'Are there any other communists involved with this whole deal?' Griessel wanted to know.

'Masondo was the only member of the SA Communist Party. The others showed no sign that they had any ideological leaning in that direction.'

They thanked van Eeden and drove away, in silence.

Griessel had two voice messages on his cellphone. The first was from Cupido. He said there were two firearms registered to the Bonne Espérance Estate. A two-seven-oh and a thirty-oh-six. They hunted occasionally, especially up in Limpopo. Apart from that, nothing. Egan the Vegan was most likely not the shooter.

The second was from Cloete, the media liaison officer. 'Benny, call me, please.'

Griessel called him back.

'They are calling him the Solomon Shooter, Benny,' said

Cloete, with the guilty tone of a parent explaining the behaviour of a naughty child.

'Because of the Bible verses.'

'Yes. Because of the verses. Benny, they like the guy. They like his references to corruption, they like his Latin even more. They are asking for comment from the National Commissioner and the cabinet, stuff like, "Is this not another sign that the SAPS are failing at their job?" And, of course, about the assertion that we actually know who the murderer is.'

'It's not true,' said Griessel wearily.

'Are we one hundred per cent sure, Benny? God knows, it will come back to haunt us . . .'

'It's not true, John.'

'OK. Have you anything I can clear with the Camel?'

'Nothing.'

Griessel could hear Cloete slowly blowing out cigarette smoke. 'OK,' said the liaison officer, ever-patient. 'We'll talk again.'

Griessel put the phone away, leaned back against the headrest and said, '*Jissis.*'

'I'm sorry, Benny,' said Boshigo. 'I tried.'

'No, Bones, I don't know what I would have done without you. It's just . . . It's five o'clock. And this mad bastard is going to shoot one of our people any moment now, and we have nothing. Absolutely nothing. I'm beginning to think he's playing us, Bones. There is no communist. Or he wants us to suspect Masondo, to waste our time. And I can't think of a single reason why he would want to play us. Except that he likes shooting policemen. And that means he is mad and cunning, and you know how difficult it is to catch *those* ones.'

'They always make mistakes.'

'Sooner or later. But we don't have time. We don't even have a suspect. Nothing. I look at this whole thing and I see nothing. That apartment of hers, the block was not even finished when she moved in. There were plumbers, electricians, labourers . . . There are the men who carried in her boxes. One of them could have stolen her spare key . . . Or sold her some story. Practically impossible to catch a guy like that, there's nothing forensic, just a ball hair in the bathroom, and old fingerprints on the boxes – which helps us not one bit.'

'Shit, *nè.*'

Griessel thought long and hard. Then he said, 'Footwork. Footwork and a big stroke of luck. That's all that's going to save us.'

In Otto du Plessis Drive, trapped in the snail's pace of rush-hour traffic, the sniper watched the IRT bus passing him in the fast lane. He felt envious.

On the radio of his Audi A4 he heard the five o'clock time signal, and he turned the sound up a bit to listen to the news.

In another email to the media the Cape Shooter, who has already wounded two policemen, justified his actions with the statement that extreme diseases required extreme cures. This quote was made famous by the Roman Catholic political extremist, Guy Fawkes, who tried to blow up the British Parliament with gunpowder in 1605.

The sniper, whom some in the media are referring to as the Solomon Shooter, due to his quotes from the biblical book of Proverbs, alleged in the email that the South African Police Services know who murdered the late corporate lawyer Hanneke Sloet.

A spokesperson for the Directorate of Priority Crime Investigations said a statement about the situation would be released later today.

The Solomon Shooter.

He liked it. The wisdom of Solomon. The opposite of this morning's accusations of incoherence and religious extremism, homophobia and racism.

The Solomon Shooter. Who was wise enough to know that the SAPS would have ramped up its guard on police stations significantly. In two hours he would have a new surprise for them.

Before he went to tell Manie and Nyathi that there were no communists with any motive for taking Hanneke Sloet's life, Griessel sat down in his office and phoned Hannes Pruis, the director of Silberstein Lamarque.

Pruis didn't answer his cellphone. Griessel phoned the office number. Eventually his PA answered. 'I am sorry, sir, Mr Pruis is in a meeting.'

'Go and get him out of it,' said Griessel.

'I'm sorry, Captain, I can't do that.'

'Miss, we have two options. Either you go and get him out of that meeting, or I drive all the way to the city and haul him out myself.'

'Hold on.'

While he waited, he checked his laptop to see whether Fritz had sent him an email yet.

It was right at the top, the only one that wasn't a Hawks bulletin. The subject was *Your new son-in-law*.

He clicked on it.

The Hypocrite and the Tatoo Dude, Fritz had typed at the top, spelling mistake and all. In the photo, Carla was laughing, happy. She looked directly into the camera. And beside her, with a huge arm possessively around her shoulders, towered the muscle man, his eyes fixed on her with an expression of complete enchantment. Griessel could see the black flames of a tattoo curling out from under the tight, short-sleeved shirt and down the bulging biceps.

'Fuck,' said Griessel.

'What?' said Hannes Pruis over the phone.

'Mr Pruis . . .'

'This better be good, Captain, I'm in a meeting.'

'You knew about Masondo,' said Griessel.

'Excuse me?'

'You knew that Masondo has misused trade union funds. You knew he is a communist. And you said nothing.'

'It had absolutely nothing to do with Hanneke's death,' Pruis said, curt and angry.

Not enough sleep, the frustration of not getting anywhere with the investigation, the man's attitude, and the muscle man photograph all conspired together. Griessel lost his temper. 'But I asked you specifically about communists. And then you were very vague and said maybe. And you gave me seven names. While you knew very well that there was only one communist, and he had already made trouble. As far as I know, that is called obstructing the course of justice.'

'And now you're threatening me?'

'Why didn't you say anything?'

'Now listen carefully. I will not be threatened by a mere captain. If you want to make accusations, make them in court, then we will see.'

'I'm going to do more than that. Because this is not a threat. I am going to get a search warrant, and I'm going to get your people to bring every last document about the whole transaction over here, and we are going to go through them piece by piece, until I have evidence that you lied to me. And I am going to tell the press about your lack of cooperation with us in solving the murder of one of your own people. And let me tell you now, if there is the slightest connection between Masondo and Sloet's death, I am going to arrest *you*. Goodbye, Mr Pruis . . .'

'Captain, wait . . .'

'I'm listening,' Griessel said.

'You must try to understand . . .' The attitude was still there, but somewhat tempered now, a man clinging to his patch of high ground. 'We . . . Silbersteins signed a confidentiality agreement. If we violate that . . . I can't gossip about the parties involved in the transaction. And Masondo . . . That was long ago. It's been dealt with, he's been moved out. Hanneke had no contact with him. None.'

'Did Hanneke know all about it?'

'We all knew about it. *We* did the due diligence for SA Merchant Bank, a year ago already. We were satisfied that it posed no risk to our client. I can't understand how you could believe there's a connection between that matter and her death.'

'Did she ever talk about him?'

'As a team we talked about him once, early last year. When we weighed up the risk. Since then, never. He is a nonentity in the scheme of things. He draws a salary as director but has no influence. That is why I said nothing to you. Because there is nothing. Absolutely nothing.'

'You're dead certain that I'm not going to find something tomorrow, or the day after tomorrow that shows that . . .'

'Captain, let me say now, I would not put my firm and my own professional reputation on the line if I thought there was the slightest possibility. If I thought Masondo were involved, I would go and arrest the bastard right now myself.'

30

'Benny, are you sure?' Manie asked.

'I am sure, Brigadier.'

Griessel could see the relief on his commanding officer's face, the great weight of a political mess falling away. But then Manie frowned, 'Then why does the shooter keep going on about the communist?'

'He's playing us, Brigadier. I think he knows there's a communist somewhere. He wants us to waste our time. So he can shoot more policemen.'

'You think he was part of the transaction?'

'I think he knew her, Brigadier. And she said something.'

'Or he's taking a shot in the dark . . . in a manner of speaking. There are just too many different possibilities, Benny.' Then, pensively, 'Why does he want to shoot our people?'

Griessel shook his head, then said in resignation, 'I will understand if you want to give the Sloet case to someone else, Brigadier.'

'No, Benny,' he said decidedly. 'This is your case. What I will do is show you how the Hawks operate.'

They gathered in the parade room of the Violent Crimes unit. The room was full, with the entire Information Management team, all the detectives of Violent Crimes, a bunch of CATS, Bones Boshigo of Corporate Crime, the warrant officer of the TOMS group – the Tactical Operational Management Service that did searches – Nyathi, and Manie all sitting in front of him. It took Griessel twenty minutes to sketch the broad outlines of the Sloet case, and the state of the investigation. With the greatest concentration – he did not want to look like a clown in front of all *these* people. He put all his cards on the table. He said they had nothing, except that the victim knew her attacker somehow or other. That could mean anything, from a worker who carried or fixed something for her, to a friend or colleague. He explained about the missing front door key, the removal company that had helped Sloet with the move, the security personnel of the apartment block, builders and tradesmen, the set-up at Silberstein Lamarque, and the little they knew of her private life.

Then he said any suggestions would be welcome.

Musad Manie spoke first. 'Benny, you're the JOC leader on this one.'

'*Jissie*, Brigadier . . .' He didn't know how to manage a joint operational command centre, it was usually the work of a colonel. And there was a lot he still wanted to do himself.

'We're behind you, Benny. Philip, tell him what you can do.'

'We make connections, Benny,' said Captain van Wyk of the IMC in his quiet voice. 'We take all her contacts – phone, Internet, everything, and we start to draw lines. As the information comes in, we can give you a graph of everyone she has been in contact with. And who they are. Criminal records, credit black-listings, traffic fines . . . Just give us her cellphone and office numbers, her email addresses, her Facebook ID . . . Oh, and her banking details. We can do a full analysis, look at tendencies and patterns, anything out of the ordinary.'

'We'll have to get all the names and ID numbers of the law firm people, her friends, the builders, and the removal company,' said Nyathi. 'The Violent Crimes group will have to do the legwork. Benny can divide you into groups and allocate responsibilities.'

'As the info comes in, we capture it,' said van Wyk.

'Benny, would you consider bringing in PCSI? Let them go over the crime scene again?' asked Nyathi.

The PCSI were the elite forensic people, the Provincial Crime Scene Investigation unit, who worked almost exclusively for the Hawks. Griessel had never seen them in action, only heard of the advanced technological toys they used.

'There has been contamination, sir . . .'

'These guys are really good.'

'Can't do any harm,' Manie encouraged him.

'Let's bring them in,' said Griessel. He tried to think what else was needed. 'We must look at similar crimes as well,' he said. 'The past five years. Murder and assaults on women who live alone, especially where robbery is not the motive. Large stab wounds. We will have to talk to the pathologists, we will have to get bulletins out to the detective branches.'

'Don't be too specific,' said Manie. 'We spread the net wide in the beginning. Pull the parole records too, see if anyone with a similar modus operandi has been released in the past year.'

'There is the possibility that the shooter knew her . . .' said Griessel.

'We will connect the databases of the two JOCs,' said Philip van Wyk. 'See what jumps out.'

'OK,' said Nyathi, 'we'll manage this thing as it develops. Let's get cracking.'

He tried to muster some self-confidence from his earlier sense of satisfaction, but it deserted him when he put on the overall, the wig and the cap and climbed into the Chana.

Then the tension came, from deep inside him, spreading slowly through him like a fever. He began to perspire, his hands clammy on the steering wheel, with nausea in his guts and his thoughts flitting and leaping from one risk to the other. Doubt. He wasn't made of the right stuff. They were going to catch him.

Only sheer willpower stopped him from dropping it all.

He drove south down Koeberg Road, past the police station in Milnerton. He didn't look, he knew they would be on their guard, people on the lookout. He was too scared to make a U-turn, and used Mansfield Road and Masson Road to change direction legally, then come back down Koeberg with his van pointing north.

Milnerton was busy, just before seven. Busier than he had expected. It was vehicle traffic, he consoled himself, people hurrying home, very few pedestrians.

He parked just beyond Loxton Road, so that he had an unimpeded view of the entrance to the supermarket. He scanned the area first, made very sure that no one was paying him or his panel van any attention. He climbed over the seat, pulled the curtain down quickly. Sat still for a while. His breathing was rapid. Sweat ran down his cheek – it was the wig, and the closed windows in the Cape summer heat. He wiped his hands on the overall, took the old Nokia out of his pocket. He had memorised the number. He typed it in, and phoned.

It rang six, seven times. 'SAPS Milnerton, can I help you?'

He let his anxiety show. 'There is a robbery, at the Spar, Milnerton Mall, you have to come quickly!'

'Sir, I need your name and address, please.'

'No, no, they will shoot me, please come quickly, it's a robbery, four men! The Spar in the Milnerton Mall, Millvale Road!' Then he cut the call, turning the cellphone off imme- diately. His hands shook, so that he struggled to open the battery cover. His fingers slipped. He swore softly, and then it came off. He ripped out the battery, shoved it all back in his pocket.

Then he bent down and opened the toolbox.

It was the support of his colleagues that caught Griessel offside, that made him gulp back the emotion. He knew it was the fatigue, lack of sleep, the intense day, and the stress of the unexpected new responsibility that dragged him down. He must disguise his gratitude. He gave IMC section A of the case file so they could copy all the information, he divided the detectives into teams and allocated tasks. He noticed their zeal, their focus and willingness. He heard their encouragement ('We will get him, Benny') and saw Brigadier Manie sitting off to the side and watching it all with satisfaction.

Once everyone was busy, he walked over to the commanding officer of the Hawks. 'Brigadier, there are some of the interviews I want to do myself . . .'

'Carry on, Benny, JOC leader is a mobile position, we are all only a call away. They must just keep you informed, and you keep me and Zola . . .'

Griessel's cellphone rang. He answered. 'This is Faber from the PCSI. We are at the apartment, can you come and unlock for us?'

Before he could reply, he heard Mbali's voice from the doorway. 'Brigadier, he's just shot another one. And this time it's serious.'

31

His mouth gaped in panic, he panted for air. His first instinct was to stamp on the accelerator, to flee, to hide away in the safety of the dark garage, but he had to suppress that desperate wish. He bellowed in frustration and fear. Everything had changed.

It wasn't his fault.

After an eternity, they had come, three patrol vehicles with sirens and lights had raced past, tyres squealing around the corner of Loxton Road. One had screeched to a halt there, the others had raced past, turned up Millvale, right to the front of the supermarket. Less than a hundred metres from him.

Five uniforms had jumped out, weapons in hand.

He had the rifle ready, followed the nearest one through the scope. He knew he must wait, the shot was too difficult while they were running.

Then the policeman stopped, to his surprise and relief, and he hastily positioned the cross hairs on the leg. This was his chance, he squeezed the trigger. At that instant the man crouched down on his haunches, the rifle bucked, and he knew, immediately, he could see through the lens, it was through the belly, a gut shot. A cry erupted from his throat, Christ, and the panic exploded inside him. No time to unscrew the hiking pole, he lost all self-control, throwing the rifle down on the carpet, tearing the screen up, clambering about in feverish haste. The overall hooked on something, he tugged, it ripped, he leaped over into the seat, switched the Chana on and drove, without looking. The shrill blare of a hooter just beside him, his head jerked. 'Christ,' aloud this time. A woman in a Toyota, her face twisted with rage, he just looked straight ahead, and drove. He knew he had made a big mistake. Two. Three.

He had killed a policeman. The Chana had attracted attention. And now the rifle lay in the back, out in the open.

In the CATS parade room Griessel listened as a visibly upset Mbali, phone to her ear, asked again and again, 'Is the ambulance there yet?' Then, on her way to the door, she said to Manie, 'I'm going, Brig, I have to be there.'

Detectives on their cellphones asking stations in Bothasig, Table View and Maitland to set up roadblocks, their voices loud and urgent. Someone spoke angrily to Telkom, giving information about the telephone call that Milnerton Station had received. 'You don't understand. I can't wait until tomorrow . . .'

He realised he could do something himself. He used the

call-back function, got Faber of PCSI Forensics team on the line. 'You will have to go to Milnerton first. There's been another officer shot.'

'Solomon?'

'We think so.'

'Do you have an address?'

He gave it. Faber said they were on their way, and rang off.

Griessel stood a little longer, looking and listening, with a vague desire to be part of *this* team right now. The adrenaline of the chase, the terrible urgency, the tangibility of a prey with a name.

And then the realisation came back, of the increased pressure on his investigation. He was the one who had to get his arse in gear. To stop Solomon from shooting again.

He only got away at a quarter past ten. When the news came that Constable Errol Matthys had died of his wounds in the Milnerton Medi-Clinic; the internal bleeding and organ damage were just too severe. When they were sure the roadblocks were too late, the shooter had slipped through the net. When there was nothing more for him to do.

He phoned Alexa while he was driving. She answered herself. She asked, 'How's the case going?' He could hear she was sober, and relief flooded over him.

'Not too well. I'm on my way.'

'I'll tell Ella she can go to bed then.'

'I'll be there soon.'

When he stopped in front of her house twenty minutes later, the veranda light went on, she opened the door and stood waiting for him. 'You're tired,' she said, and kissed him on the cheek. 'I kept a pizza warm for you. Ella ordered them.'

He saw the deep lines, her sallow skin tone and the sheen of perspiration on her face. She was having a hard time. Momentarily, he recalled her doppelgänger, the unblemished

Annemarie van Eeden, and he felt an immense compassion for Alexa.

'I am very proud of you,' he said, and closed the door behind him.

Her shoulders sagged, as if her strength had reached its limit, and she wept. He put his arms around her. She leaned into him.

For a long time they simply stood like that, until she was calm.

He kept to his agreement dutifully. In the kitchen, while he ate the pizza and drank a glass of orange juice, he told her about his day.

She laughed at Griessel's description of Bones Boshigo and the eccentric Len de Beer, and she shook her head with a little smile over the wealth of Henry van Eeden. When he told her about Egan Roch, she leaned forward with greater concentration and nodded as though it all made sense to her.

She carried his plate and cutlery to the sink, and sat down again. They lit cigarettes together. 'I've been doing a lot of thinking,' she said. 'I don't know if it will help.'

'Anything will help,' he said, grateful for her effort.

'Simóne, the singer with the photos . . . It seems to me there have been more of them in the past few years. Especially in Afrikaans music. It's an interesting phenomenon. Odd, surely, because I think most of them are women. It's as if . . . they are moths, Benny, in the bright light of musical lime-light. They're not attracted because they're addicted to singing, they're attracted because they're drawn to the spotlight. They want to be famous. That's all.'

He heard the seriousness, the sincerity, behind her words, and realised she was giving him a gift, a kind of apology. She had clung on to this today, her refuge in the midst of the flood.

He wanted to touch her.

'I don't get the feeling that it's about wealth,' she said. 'Men . . . to them, fame means money. And sex. But to these women it's just the concept of being known. Of being special. I struggle to understand it. I have wondered whether it's something to do with the Afrikaner and where we are now, in this South Africa? Afrikaner men have lost their power, their dramatic image. There's so much indifference about their lot now, there's only compassion for the new nation, that greater whole. Is it a woman's way of restoring some balance? A kind of rebellion, an instinctive way of filling the vacuum? Perhaps it's a universal phenomenon, too many people, there are no individuals or characters any more, we are all just . . . conduits.'

Her eyes came back to him, as though she guessed she was going off on a tangent. 'I don't know, Benny, these women, so terribly hungry for fame. They go to endless trouble, singing and elocution lessons, diets . . . Their parents spend thousands on stylists and photographers and musicians and recording studios. The girls who wait at the doors of the music promoters with a CD in their hands . . . They market themselves unashamedly. They have no loyalty, they are like butterflies that flit from flower to flower, in search of the strongest nectar to make the dream come true. And they all have the narcissistic streak, envy, jealousy, the big hair, the hours spent in front of the mirror, the promotional photos taken over and over again. There are the tight clothes and the cleavage, everything that screams: "Look at me, look at me, please just notice me." What I'm trying to say is that Hanneke Sloet might have had the same desire, the same personality. The legal world was her stage, her spotlight. That is where she would have wanted to make her mark.'

He remembered his conversations today. 'Sloet told her mother about the big money in BEE deals,' he told Alexa.

'She thought about starting up on her own. She told the big brain behind it all that she wanted his job.'

'That terrible hunger,' she said.

'Nine years ago she had an affair with one of the senior partners. Married man, in his fifties.'

'She probably thought he would help her get on in her career. And I think that's the reason she broke up with her boyfriend . . . I don't think he was useful to her any more.'

'That makes sense,' he said.

She smiled, in self-mockery. 'You don't need an amateur detective, do you?'

'I need someone who understands women like her.'

'Do you want to hear my theory?'

'I do.'

'Her hunger. Who did her hunger put at greatest risk?'

That was a good question. 'Not van Eeden. He's already rich . . . Do you think Egan Roch? Do you think he still had hopes?'

'No,' she said. 'The air hostess . . . he's moved on. I think her colleagues. *One* of her colleagues.'

Day 4

Tuesday

32

At a quarter to seven he was in the parade room for the JOC
meeting, fresh, having slept fairly well. And Alexa had
looked so much better, the worst withdrawal symptoms
behind her. She didn't have to rehearse today. Ella was
coming to her house, and they were planning on going
shopping – their specific purpose disguised in a vague and
all-encompassing 'girls' stuff' brush-off that he was happy
not to pursue.

The burden of guilt felt lighter this morning.

The team leaders didn't have much to report – most of the
information about the builders and security personnel of the
apartment block would only be available during office hours.
Griessel asked Cupido to unlock the crime scene for PCSI,
and said that he would be in discussions with Sloet's friends
and colleagues, and that his cellphone would be on at all times.

When the meeting was over, Griessel walked with van Wyk
to the IMC office.

It was a large room, seven people sat at laptops in the
gloom of muted lighting. A video projector displayed a graph
on the wall.

'That is Hanneke Sloet's provisional contact graph for
January,' said van Wyk. In the centre of the screen was a small
square, marked with the initials HS. From there a delicate
network of thin lines stretched to top and bottom like the
facets of a diamond. 'Up here are the numbers of people who
phoned her cellphone in January – the dotted lines are SMSs

– and here are those she contacted. In the course of the day we will add names to the numbers. And we will get data from the service providers of calls made from July to December last year. We put each number through the RICA database for IDs, and then again through criminal records. By tonight we should have a more complete picture. And of course we will include the latest shooter developments.'

'There are developments?'

'The cellphone, and the vehicle.'

'We have a vehicle?'

'Woman read the story in the paper this morning, said she was driving past the scene last night, at practically the exact time, when a hippy in a white delivery van cut in front of her. Mbali is busy with her now in Milnerton.'

'A hippy,' said Griessel sceptically. Women were usually better eye witnesses than men, he didn't know why, but a hippy?

'Yes, we'll see about that. There's the cellphone too, at least. The shooter used it last night to phone the Milnerton station. It's not RICAed, he made no other calls during the past month with it, and he turned it off. But the phone is pay-as-you-go, he regularly bought a top-up, the last was on Saturday February fifth, airtime of R49 bought at Clicks in Canal Walk. We're following that up. Naturally we'll cross reference the number with all the gun owners . . . At the moment we have one hundred and forty-seven people with licences for a triple-two and two-two-three rifles in the Western Cape, who also bought Remington Accutips in the past year. Three of the rifles have been stolen in the interim, so CATS have to follow up each of those cases as well. It's going to take a long time. We haven't linked that database with Sloet's yet, we just haven't got enough manpower. This afternoon perhaps . . . when we know more about the panel van too.'

★ ★ ★

Mbali stood with the woman on the pavement beside Koeberg Road. She had to talk loudly to make herself heard over the noise of heavy traffic.

'How can you be sure about the time?'

'Because I left the office at exactly ten past seven,' the woman said. She was in her late forties, her hair heavily sprayed, a severe face.

'Down in Rugby.'

'Yes. It's five minutes from here. No more than that.'

'OK. Where was he parked?'

'Right here.'

Mbali looked around her. It made sense. He would have had a perfect view from here, a clean shot. Eighty metres, maybe. 'And then you came past.'

'I was in the left lane. I'm always in the left lane, because a lot of traffic turns right at the Bosmansdam intersection. And then he shot out of the parking area, right here, he just swerved right into my lane.'

'But he was in front of you?'

'I wanted to give him the finger. So I came past.'

'And then you saw him.'

'Clear as day. I hooted at him, and he looked at me. He had this little baseball cap, like faded red, and the long hair. Blond. Real hippy type, and he had these really crazy eyes, like he was going to kill me. Creepy, really, really creepy.'

'Did you see what clothes he was wearing?'

'Not really. I was too furious, the asshole. If I didn't look where I was going . . .'

'And you said it was a delivery vehicle?'

The woman nodded with great certainty. 'Light beige, or faded white, and it wasn't new. A Kia.'

'A Kia? On the telephone you said you weren't sure.'

'Well, after I called, I remembered that it was the same as the vans used by the people who deliver our spares. So I called them. They use Kias. The K2700, they say,' she said with enormous satisfaction, as though she had just solved the whole case.

It took him fifteen minutes to phone back and forth between Sloet's two friends – Aldri de Koker and Samantha Grobler – before he got a joint appointment for half past two. He phoned Prof Phil Pagel, the pathologist, and Hannes Pruis of Silberstein Lamarque. The lawyer was none too pleased to hear from him, giving a deep and heavy sigh when Griessel asked if he could see all the colleagues who had worked with Sloet, at five o'clock.

Then he drove to Roch.

On the way through Stellenbosch he thought of his daughter. How should he manage the situation with the muscle man? Why hadn't Carla told him about it?

He stopped himself. He mustn't let his detective's imagination run away with him. He had a good relationship with his daughter. She would have told him if there was something. And Fritz was desperate, about the tattoo. Ten to one it was just a photo taken at random, during Rag. Carla would never fall for a man with a face like that anyway – the brow so heavy, the eyes too close together. And that tattoo . . .

He would phone her later. Just to make sure. If he could think of what to say.

Over Helshoogte Pass he saw the dark green vineyards on either side of the road, the beauty of the mountains behind them. He came here too seldom. He too seldom went anywhere, it was just work and sleep and a bit of music with Roes, and now and then dropping by at Alexa's. Maybe he could bring her here to one of these guesthouses one day.

Maybe. If he ever got back on his feet financially.

The Bonne Espérance Estate was much quieter on a Tuesday morning. He parked in front of the wine tasting centre again and walked straight over to the coopers shop, because he didn't want his arrival to be announced.

As he pushed open the door, he smelled the wood smoke, felt the heat. Roch was standing at one of the work-benches, a water bottle to his mouth, raised high. He saw Griessel and lowered it slowly. Not too overjoyed at the repeat visit.

'Captain,' he said tersely, and put the bottle down on the workbench.

'Mr Roch.'

'I hear you got hold of Danielle after all. Or don't you believe her either?'

'We believe her.'

'Hallelujah.'

'Can we talk?'

'Do you have some new accusations?'

'It depends whether you're going to withhold information again.'

Roch raised his eyes to the roof. 'I didn't . . .' He sighed. 'Come through.'

This time he didn't offer coffee. He sat down in his chair, his body language irritable. Griessel ignored it. 'You must have wondered who murdered Hanneke,' he said evenly.

'Of course.'

'Any ideas?'

'You're asking *me*?'

'That's right.'

He looked at Griessel with dislike. 'No wonder the crooks are taking over the country.'

'I'm here because I need your help,' Griessel said.

'After you insulted me.'

'Mr Roch, in more than eighty per cent of cases like this, the murderer is known to the victim, or in a relationship with her. You have metal tools on your wall that are similar to the murder weapon. And you didn't disclose the whole truth . . .'

Roch made a gesture of barely suppressed frustration. 'I wasn't even here.'

'Will you help?'

Roch looked down at his hands for a long time, and then up again. 'OK.'

'It seems as though there are two possibilities. She opened the door to someone she knew, or the murderer had her spare key. Have you any idea who she might have given it to?'

'When she was still living in Stellenbosch . . . she gave her spare key to me. She said then it was no good her keeping it inside . . .' The negative attitude lifted as he slowly sat up straight.

'And the key of the new apartment?'

'I don't know . . . Definitely not to me. But . . . it was important to her that someone should keep her spare key. I used to tease her about it, she was so organised, I told her there was no chance of her losing her keys. Then she said that was not what she was afraid of. She was afraid she would fall in the shower, or something . . .'

'So you think there is a good chance she gave it to someone?'

'Yes . . .'

'Who?'

'I don't know. Maybe one of her girl friends. Or . . . Did you ask at her work?'

'Her assistant says she doesn't know either.'

Roch merely nodded.

'You believed there was a new man in her life,' Griessel said.

'I was wrong.'

'But you did think that at first.'

'I suppose it's the way a guy reacts . . .'

'Is that all?'

'Why? Did you find something?' With the same subtle reaction as yesterday, the movement of the eyes that showed there was something that made him uncomfortable.

'Mr Roch, I will treat everything as confidential as far as I can. I understand it's difficult, in the circumstances, to talk about personal things. But I would be glad if you would tell me why that was your first reaction.'

Roch put his elbows on the arms of the chair, intertwined his fingers, peered thoughtfully over them at Griessel. 'It *is* difficult. I always believed you don't talk out of . . . you know . . .'

'I understand.'

'It's just that Hanneke . . . She was . . . Hell, Captain, this is . . . This doesn't feel right.'

'It might help us, Mr Roch.'

'I wonder. Let's just say . . . She was very . . . physical. From the start. I mean, before Hanneke, it's not as though I had many girlfriends, but at least, you know . . .' He blushed bright red, and looked down. 'A guy has a certain experience, especially with Afrikaans women. They are . . . reserved, if you know what I mean. Hell, I've never talked like this with a strange man . . . Hanneke . . . As I said, from the start, she was . . . *physical*. And she wasn't embarrassed about it. She said she *liked* sex. It was because . . . She was a late starter, right through to the end of her studies she was still . . . you know, a virgin. And then she went to Europe for a year and she met this guy, an Aussie . . .' The jealousy obvious in his voice. 'And they travelled together for about a month, and apparently he had it bad. He kept on at her until she gave in, and then she discovered the whole sex thing. As you can imagine, I didn't want to hear about it. But she said they . . . you know, were wild, and she couldn't understand why she'd waited so long. And that she would never deprive herself that way again . . .' He gave Griessel a look, one that said that was that, he wasn't prepared to expand any further.

33

'And that's why you thought there was someone else?'

'That's right.'

'Did you tell her why you thought that?'

'I did. And I'm sorry for it. I said things . . . But then she said it wasn't such a priority for her any more. *Now* was her chance at work. To make her mark.'

'Did you believe her?'

'I only believed her when we saw each other again last year. Here . . .' He pointed towards the mountain.

'Why?'

'Because she was . . . so intense. As though it was a long time . . . you know.'

'Since she had had sex?'

Roch dropped his eyes, and nodded.

'So you don't think there was another man in her life?'

'Not since that last time. No. I don't believe it.' Roch shifted in his chair, leaned forward. 'Hanneke was . . . This was something that I realised from the beginning. She was so different. It was as though she had this very specific, power-ful image of herself. A kind of vision. *This* was who she was, *that* was what she wanted to be. I'm not like that. I . . . sort of follow my heart, I let life happen, see where it takes me. But Hanneke . . . To her it wasn't about the journey. It was about the destination. That was all that counted.'

'What was her destination?'

He waved his hands to show he didn't really know. 'I never asked her outright. Maybe because . . . I don't know if she could have explained it. At first I thought it was professional success. Boss of the company. Money. Then I thought it was a moving target, once she had one thing, it led to another. But later I thought she had father issues. The old man sort of disappeared, in her teens. He struggled . . . She didn't really want to talk about it, but that's the idea I got. She had this rage, at his weakness. So, I think her goal was to get him out of her system. His genes, in a way.'

Griessel digested that before he asked, 'Who would she have opened the door for?'

'For very few people. Her parents, her girl friends. For me. A few from work . . .'

'Were there any of her colleagues who didn't like her?'

'One never knows, with that bunch of lawyers. They are so obsessed with money, as long as she was valuable to them, they would like her.'

'You didn't like them?'

'I didn't really know them. I was at a Christmas party, and we were invited to dinner with some of the directors once or twice, but then it was ten or twenty people. They are not really my sort.'

'Do you have a theory? About who killed her?'

'I just assumed, you know . . . I mean, this is the country we live in. I just assumed it was some black man who was stalking her, from the street, who waited until she opened the door. Murdered her because he could. That's what I thought.'

At nine o'clock the sniper bought ten cans of red spray paint and two rolls of masking tape at Melkbos Hardware. He was nervous when he got out of the Audi A4, tormented by the vague fear that someone would suddenly point an accusing finger at him, and shout, 'That's him!'

After that he bought another ten spray cans and two rolls of masking tape at Makro in Montague Gardens, and at a café in Blaauwberg Road he bought all the morning papers.

In the twilight of the garage, two things dominated his thoughts as he covered the windows, chrome and lights of the Chana with the newspaper and masking tape: How was he going to explain that the last shot was an accident? That he was not a murderer. And were the twenty cans enough to paint the whole vehicle?

In his mind he composed emails to the police and the press over and over, but he couldn't find the right approach.

It would be twelve o'clock before he realised the paint was not enough.

Griessel drove out through Bonne Espérance's avenue of oaks, marvelling at a world where a big, strong, handsome and apparently intelligent man could blush blood red one minute when discussing intimate matters with a policeman. And the next minute, without blinking an eye, calmly admit to a racist prejudice.

People were never simple.

Just like life.

And where did Roch get that nonsense about 'no wonder the crooks are taking over the country'? He heard and saw that more and more, the public idea that crime was out of control. It was simply not true, the statistics showed that, the SAPS was slowly winning. But that was just one more thing he blamed the media for, that misconception. Because it sold more papers.

Roch was well-read and well-travelled, he ought to know better. It was something Griessel learned time and time again: with people you never knew what you would get.

Which brought him back to Carla. She didn't have the life experience to understand these things. She could easily get mixed up with the wrong sort.

And the thing about Hanneke Sloet's 'father issues' had disturbed him. *The old man sort of disappeared, in her teens.*

Griessel himself had disappeared in a haze of booze when Carla was a teenager. What effect would that have had on his daughter, on her choice of men?

Did it help that he was rehabilitated now?

As he drove through Stellenbosch, he couldn't contain it any more. He called her number.

'Hi, Pappa!' Surprise and joy in her voice.

'I'm driving through your town, so I thought I would call you.' Which was more or less the truth.

'Let's go and have coffee!'

'I can't, I have to get back to Bellville.'

'I've been telling everyone it's my pa who's doing the Sloet case.'

'How did you know?'

'Drama queens read newspapers too, Pappa.'

'So, what's new?' One of Fritz's phrases, one he had never used with his daughter. He was certain she would smell a rat now.

'*Ag*, not much. Just very busy. But it's *such* fun, Pappa, I've just had Theatre Studies, it's *so* interesting . . .'

'You mustn't work too hard.' He wanted to fish with, 'You should go out too,' but he knew that was one step too far. 'You should relax as well,' he said.

'Oh, don't worry, Pa, we do that a lot.'

The sentence came out before he could stop it, 'You and the girls . . . ?' The query disguised as much as possible.

'Not *always* . . .' she said with a teasing tone.

That was not what he wanted to hear. 'Just tell those student guys your father carries a Z88 and there are a lot of shotguns in the police magazine . . .'

Carla laughed, and he imagined he heard the tiniest hint of hysteria in her voice. '*Ag*, there are very nice guys out there too . . .'

★   ★   ★

The Directorate of Priority Crime Investigations' offices were in the old Revenue Services building in AJ West Street in Bellville. Griessel parked the BMW in the basement, between the other Hawks vehicles – the Golf GTIs, Isuzus, Nissan 4x4s, Tiidas, Ford Focuses, and the two large unmarked Ford Everests. He jogged up the stairs to the second floor. The SARS desks and cubicles were all still there. There were rumours that Public Works were going to redo the whole place for the Hawks within weeks. But if you were 'old school', you knew all about the promises of Public Works.

His JOC parade room was deserted, but IMC was a hive of activity. All the computer stations were busy, nine CATS detectives stood in a semicircle and studied the screen where Mbali was sitting beside a researcher. Griessel walked up and had a look. There was a progress bar on the screen. *Search 67% complete.*

'Any news?' Griessel asked.

'We have a vehicle description,' the detective beside him said. 'Kia van. Looking for a match on the database, Kia owners and triple-two rifles.'

'It's definitely a triple-two?'

Mbali looked up, saw Benny. 'They recovered enough fragments from the body of Constable Matthys last night. It's definitely triple-two. Problem is, most of the Kias are registered to companies. But we're hoping our vehicle is privately owned. You can't cut holes in your boss's van . . .'

'What sort of person shoots policemen with a triple-two?' one of the detectives asked.

'Stolen, it's all he's got,' said another.

A chorus of agreement.

'Because he's a cunt,' whispered the one beside Griessel, but very quietly, so Mbali wouldn't hear.

Griessel wanted to agree, but his cellphone rang in his

jacket pocket and he said, 'Sorry,' and walked out. He could see it was Cupido's number.

'Vaughn?'

'Benna, you had better come. PCSI have found something weird. Very weird, pappie.'

34

The PCSI minibuses were parked in front of the 36 on Rose apartment block in the Bo Kaap. The woman at security was grumpy when Griessel asked for access. He suspected she must have been up and down many times already today.

In the lift she said, 'The wireless people need to test that flat. When will you be done?'

'Very soon,' he said.

Before he went inside Sloet's apartment he saw the yellow crime-scene tape was strung up to just inside the door. The technicians stood with Cupido on the other side, near the couch and chairs. They saw him and came closer. 'Benny, it's just here,' said Cupido, and pointed at a series of damp spots on the floor. Inside one was a marker with the figure five. 'Just walk *there*.'

He looked, recognised the spots. Griessel ducked under the tape and stepped carefully. 'Luminol,' he said.

'Damn straight, pappie. Seems like Thick and Thin never thought to test – they saw the visible blood and thought that was all. But it wasn't.' Cupido addressed himself to a technician with a camera slung around his neck and said, 'Show him the photos.'

The PCSI Forensics team gathered around. Griessel knew some of them. Others were new, and introduced themselves.

The one with the camera was Rabinowitz, young, crew cut, in a light blue overall. He turned the Canon 7D so that

Griessel could see the little screen. He knew what to expect. The Luminol solution reacted with blood, and emitted a blue glow for thirty seconds only, which had to be captured on camera. What he saw was an underexposed photo, with a few dimly glowing blue smears.

'The blood was there at marker five,' said Rabinowitz.

'But someone wiped it up,' said Cupido.

'With soap and water,' said the technician. 'That is why we could still find the trace elements.'

Griessel looked from the photo to the floor and back. The marker was less than a metre from where Hanneke Sloet's body had lain.

'The same thing happened in the kitchen. At the basin . . .' Cupido pointed at the kitchen sink. Griessel noticed that the little door below it had been unscrewed. It was leaning against the cupboards, wrapped in a plastic bag. 'But there are more trace elements, so there was more blood in the basin,' said Cupido.

'Look,' said the technician, and displayed another photo. The kitchen sink, with the same ghostly glow, but much more of it.

'Is there enough for DNA?' Griessel asked.

'Perhaps in the sink,' said the technician.

'It's her blood. Must be,' said Cupido. 'I mean, there's nothing else. Nowhere.'

'Why would he wipe the floor just *there*?' Griessel asked, and pointed at marker five.

'Wollie is our spatter expert,' the technician said, pointing at one of his colleagues, slightly older, with a goatee. Wollie came and stood beside them. 'The visible blood is caused by the stab wound, and is very typical.' He indicated the reddish brown fan of fine blood spatters. 'That was from the stabbing action itself, the drops are between one point three and two millimetres large, that means a relatively fast attack speed of between two and five metres per second, which you would expect from sharp trauma of this kind. The shape and tails of the drops give us the angle and height of the stabbing, and the place the victim was standing.'

Griessel nodded. He had heard the technique described many times in court.

Wollie pointed at the big pool of dried blood. 'This one shows no spatters, this is where she was lying, with the blood running from the wound through her clothes and onto the floor. The combination of the big pool and the spatters tells the whole story, that is precisely what you expect with a single stab wound. That is why the Luminol results are so strange.'

'So what do you think he was cleaning up?'

'The first possibility would be his own blood. She might have wounded him. The main problem with that is the place we found it. It doesn't completely fit the scene. Vaughn says there were no defensive wounds or foreign blood on her clothes or hands. The other problem is the amount and concentration. It was relatively little to begin with. He spread it over a larger area while wiping it up, but I think it was relatively localised. A patch, not spatter. And because there is more blood rinsed off in the sink, that doesn't make sense either.'

'OK,' said Griessel.

'Which means it may have been a bloody print. But there is no indication that he stepped in this blood. Both visible samples are uncontaminated. I don't think it could be a piece of clothing either. Let's say a jacket that had been spattered with blood that he put down. Clothes absorb blood. And our visible spatters show a complete pattern of the attack – no obstruction. All I can think of is that he put down the weapon itself. Because there would have been blood on it.'

'Remember, he has this huge iron thing, and he wanted to bend down to feel for a pulse,' said Cupido.

'The other possibility is that he wanted to search her, or take something from her. So he put the weapon down to use both hands.'

Griessel tried to envisage it. 'Did her dress have pockets?'

'No. But her hand. Remember the crime-scene photos, her hand that was open like that?' asked Cupido.

'We think,' said Wollie the spatter man, 'he either wanted to make sure she was dead, or she might have been clutching something in her hand. And he must have put the weapon down, or maybe rested the point on the floor. And when he picked it up again, he saw the localised blood where it had rested on the floor. So he fetched a cloth to wipe it up, and rinsed the cloth in the kitchen. And then the weapon too. That would explain why there was more blood residue in the sink than on the floor.'

'*Voilà*,' said Cupido.

'Wait,' said Griessel, still battling to visualise it all. 'After he stabbed her, he put the weapon down . . .'

'*Yebo*, yes,' said Cupido.

'And he did something else, and when he picked the weapon up again, he saw there was blood on the floor.'

'Like an outline,' said Cupido. 'And he thought, no, that's a dead give-away.'

'So he went to look for a cloth. Here. In the kitchen . . .'

'In the cupboard under the sink,' said Rabinowitz. 'That's where her cleaning products are. We're taking the door to the lab. And the plastic bag that her cloths were in.'

'Super Glue fumes, pappie. For latent prints, these *manne* are hi-tec.'

'He wiped the handle of the front door clean,' said Griessel sceptically. 'But maybe we'll get lucky.' He thought about the possibilities again. He said, 'When he was finished, he took the cloth with him. And the weapon.'

'Must be.'

'But what would he have taken from her?' He stared at the damp Luminol spot.

'The question is,' said Cupido, 'what did she have?'

He went to buy a sandwich and a cool drink at Woolies Food in Mill Street, then fled to the peace of his flat, so he could think.

He sat at the small breakfast counter and ate, letting his thoughts loose, all the stuff that had been bottled up.

Last night, his conversation with Alexa. When she had talked about Afrikaner men who had lost their power, and women rebelling against it, there had been a lot of things running through his mind. Too rapidly, because he had had to concentrate on what she was saying. Then he had become afraid again that he would become too attached to her, because *this* thing between them could not work. The trouble was that he didn't know about all this philosophical stuff. He didn't want to either. He didn't want to worry about people's dramatic image or whether they were conduits, because frankly, he thought it was a crock of shit. He had been in the police for twenty-six years, and as far as he could tell, people were exactly the same as when he had begun. They stole and murdered for the same reasons. Afrikaans, English. White, black, brown. And he suspected it had always been like that, for hundreds of years. He thought there had always been women who wanted more attention than others. His instincts told him that life, people's actions, came down to the old criminal rule of tendency, background and opportunity. The New South Africa didn't change that. Nor did Facebook and Twitter and Linked Up or In or whatever the latest craze might be.

He didn't mind that Alexa wondered about such things; he understood she lived in another world – she was an artist, they thought differently. But he would be totally honest with her, tell her such things went right over his head, sooner or later. He couldn't embarrass her in front of her friends *and* lie about who he was.

And when he told her, he would lose her.

But rather that. Because when he recalled the photos of Hanneke Sloet's father, Willem, that expression of . . . defeat, of a man who had lost the battle in his attempt to be the person his wife wanted him to be. He wasn't prepared to go through that, he had enough trouble as it was. He had to protect and preserve what little dignity he still had – the thing that made Carla say, 'My father is handling the Sloet case.' Being a detective. Even though much of this world would look down on that. People like Roch, and Hannes Pruis who would 'not be threatened by a mere captain'. And surely someone like Hanneke Sloet too. He saw women like her in the Gardens Centre, pretty and well-off and sophisticated, all dolled up, all dressed up to the nines . . . When he walked past in his Mr Price clothes, with his cheap haircut and his booze-ravaged face, he simply did not exist for them. The only reason Alexa was involved with him was because of her damage, her weakness, she had no idea how much better she could do.

The world was a place of hierarchies and groupings and classes. The haves and the have-nots. Sloet had lived in the former, and, like all of them, she had wanted more. More money, more power, more status, more security against the danger of being dragged back to the struggling classes. Anni de Waal and Alexa could say what they liked, the boob job was part of *that* desire: to create more distance. He didn't know how to explain it properly, it was just a sense, a know-ledge, she wanted to make herself more exclusive, she wanted to say she belonged in a certain league, and only men of that league could look at her. Because that is what people with money did. They separated themselves more and more, like

Henry van Eeden with his high walls, and his two-million-rand Lamborghini.

Sloet had worked so hard on the deal because it would open doors to new opportunities for making the gap wider. She had had an idea, a plan. For more power at the law firm, or, if they would not accede, to go it alone. To be a player, a deal maker. He couldn't say that to Alexa last night, but Sloet's hunger, in general, did not really pose a threat to anyone, if you thought about it. Silberstein Lamarque could just have said to her, 'Pack your bags, we're not interested'. And more likely they would have had the opposite reaction.

Which brought him to what Cupido had said, 'The question is, what did she have?'

That changed everything. Up till now they had looked at 'what had she *done*', not at 'what did she *have*'.

And this was the first time that anything began to make sense to him. It took away the randomness, it provided a reason for the attacker to come to her door, a motive to bring a large stabbing weapon along. A tangible motive: robbery. Not in the conventional sense of steal-her-cellphone-and-laptop. Something specific that she possessed. Something of great value to someone. Someone she knew, and whom she allowed to come in. Someone with whom she may have wanted to negotiate.

And the who and the what were somewhere in Hanneke Sloet's tendency, background and opportunity. That was what had instinctively led him back to Roch this morning, to ask more questions. That was why it was on his schedule to talk to her two best friends this afternoon. And with each of her colleagues who had worked with her on the big deal.

35

At ten past one he knocked on Prof Pagel's office door at the University of Stellenbosch's Health Sciences faculty next to the Tygerberg Hospital.

'Come in,' called the well-modulated voice.

Prof Pagel, with his long, aristocratic face, sat behind the desk. As usual he was flamboyantly dressed. He was tanned and fit for his close to sixty years.

'Nikita,' said the pathologist as if he were genuinely happy to see Griessel. Pagel had been calling him 'Nikita' for thirteen years. He had given Griessel one look back then and said, 'I am sure that's what the young Khrushchev looked like.'

'Afternoon, Prof.'

'Come in, take a seat. And how was your evening with the rich and famous?'

He had forgotten he had asked Pagel's advice about the cocktail party. '*Ai*, Prof,' he said now. 'Not too good.'

'Whatever happened?'

Griessel told him. The whole truth.

Pagel threw back his big head and laughed. And Benny, burning with shame, could only smile weakly, because he knew it would have been funny, if it weren't about himself.

'Let me tell you,' said Pagel once he had calmed down, 'about my great faux pas, Nikita. You know who Luciano Pavarotti was?'

'That fat guy, Prof? With the handkerchief?'

'The very one, Nikita, in my opinion the best tenor in history. Phenomenal voice. I'm not talking about his later years, the more popular work, I am talking about his prime. Perfect pitch. He sang so unselfconsciously, so effortlessly. Incredible. In any case, to say I was a fan was an understatement. I had every recording, I listened to them over and over, it was my dream to hear him in real life, just once. And then, in 1987, he and Joan Sutherland held a concert at the Met in New York. Sutherland, Nikita. La Stupenda. The soprano of sopranos. And my good friend James Cabot of Johns Hopkins let me know he hadn't just got tickets, he could get us into the dressing room afterwards. I could meet Pavarotti. To cut a long story short, Nikita, for the first time in my life I had the money and the time, and we went over, to New York. Sat and listened to the concert. Overwhelming, indescribable. The quartet from *Rigoletto*, magnificent, I shall remember it all my life. Anyway, afterwards we went backstage. Now you must know, I had been practising my little bit of opera Italian for two weeks, I wanted to express my admiration for the man in his own language. I wanted to say: "*Voi siete magnifici. Sono un grande fan.*" You are wonderful, I am a huge fan. But I went blank, Nikita, just like you did with the lovely Miss Beekman. Totally star-struck, overwhelmed by the moment, I told the man I admired so much: "*Sono magnifici.*" I am wonderful.' And Phil Pagel laughed heartily again.

'Genuine, Prof?' asked Griessel in amazement.

'Genuine, Nikita. The man gave me an astonished look, turned away and began to talk to someone else. By the time I realised the extent of my faux pas, it was too late. For months afterwards I still blushed and regretted it and reproached myself. But all you can really do is laugh. And know your intention was true. And still enjoy the delight of his voice.'

Griessel felt the relief slowly spread through him. If something like that could happen to Phil Pagel, this man for whom he had such admiration . . .

'A *vopah*, prof?'

'Faux pas,' Pagel spelled the word. 'French. For making an idiot of yourself. It takes the sting out of the concept somewhat.'

'Faux pas,' Griessel tested it. He liked it.

'Happens to all of us. But you're not here to listen to embarrassing stories, Nikita . . .' He pulled a thick file closer. 'As a consequence of your call I took another look at my Sloet notes. Reminds me of our assegai case a few years back. Do you remember, Artemis, the vigilante murderer?'

'I remember it well, Prof.'

'That was the last time I saw similar wound pathology, Nikita. Not identical. Similar. The single stab wound in Sloet is problematic, it offers much less data. So, any conclusion by definition must be speculative. But you're here because you want me to speculate.'

'Please, Prof.'

'This murder weapon has characteristics in common with an assegai blade. The diamond geometry – hence the shape, if you examine the blade from the front, it is created in the manufacture of the blade. The length: there is no bruising from a hilt or hand guard. The even angle of the stabbing point. But there are a few crucial differences. And I must reiterate, Nikita, it's speculation, since we only have a single stab wound, directly from the front. Nevertheless: the diamond geometry seems more prominent here, the central ridge about five millimetres thicker. Width of the blade is again about a centimetre narrower than the cross section of the assegai. These are measurements that might fit a sword, but the cutting edges are too unequal, it seems as though the workmanship is hasty and amateurish. He wanted to sharpen it, but not necessarily neatly. That is why I wrote down "home-made" first. The more I looked and measured, the more I got the idea that it was a blade made in a backyard. A metal stave that was filed and honed, from inside to outside, to get the diamond form, and the razor-sharp blades. The spectroscope analysis was not conclusive, there was too little residue, but that was my feeling, Nikita.'

'Prof, he brought this thing along with him. So it couldn't have been too big or too heavy.'

'I can tell you the blade was definitely longer than twenty centimetres. But let's look at the wound location and the stab angle. A short weapon typically produces an angle of 130 degrees or more in the chest – the up- or downward stabbing action of a knife or a dagger, for maximum momentum. The Sloet stab angle is just less than a hundred degrees. Thus from slightly above. If you take the standard deviation for human height into account, it looks like a horizontal action. Again, like a sword. Which tells me it was a longer weapon. Forty centimetres or more. Even if the weapon were sixty or seventy centimetres long, according to the breadth and width and average weight of steel, it need not have weighed more than a kilogram . . .'

Griessel shook his head. 'But why, Prof? Why make such a long thing and bring it along? It's a lot of trouble. Except if you want to frighten someone. But this *ou* didn't want to scare. He wanted to kill.'

'Forensically speaking it's safe, Nikita. Clever. No ballistic trail, no physical contact with the victim . . .'

Griessel thought about it. Then he told Pagel about PCSI's latest discovery this morning, and the theory that she had been holding something in her hand.

'Mmm,' said Pagel, and picked up his reading glasses. He opened the file, talking while he looked for something. 'I doubt it. One of the strange things – the lack of defensive wounds, or bruises,' he said deep in thought. 'It was like a surprise attack. From the front. But there was one small anomaly . . . Ah, here it is . . .' He glanced up at Griessel. 'Pathologically there is no evidence that anything was taken out of her hand. The other possibility, something I noticed during the autopsy: she wasn't wearing panties, Nikita. In itself that is not significant. It was a hot summer evening, the temperature in the high twenties. As I am led to understand, women sometimes find underwear uncomfortable in the heat. After all she was alone at home, slip out of the panties, the bra maybe just too much trouble to get rid of? Now, following on from your new forensic evidence one wonders: did he perhaps remove the panties, post mortem? Or cut them off? Not unheard of, as you know.'

'A keepsake, Prof,' said Griessel reluctantly, because it opened up a hornets' nest, the world of the serial killer, someone who liked to keep something from every victim.

'Indeed, Nikita. The memento. To take off the panties, he would have to put the weapon down.'

He didn't want to be late for his half past two appointment with the two girl friends, so he phoned the DPCI office while he drove and asked to talk to Captain Philip van Wyk of IMC. He must get the possibility of a serial killer into the system, even though the evidence was slim. But the clean crime scene and the single wound could point to an organised, experienced serial killer. As far as he knew, they weren't investigating a similar modus operandi in the Cape.

He got van Wyk on the line at last. He could hear the Information Centre was busy, and explained hastily what he wanted.

'We will have to ask IPS in Pretoria to look nationally,' said van Wyk, referring to the Investigative Psychology Section. 'We don't believe there are locally related cases. It could take a while, but I will set the wheels in motion immediately. Listen, the people doing your graphs have come across something.'

'Oh?'

'I'll give the phone to Fanie Fick . . .'

'Philip, just a second . . .'

'Yes?'

'You do have Sloet's banking details?'

'Yes.'

'Can you see who did her insurance?'

'Short or long term?'

'Short term.'

'That's an easy one.'

'I want to know if she insured any very valuable stuff. Jewels . . . I don't know, anything relatively small and worth a lot of money.'

'Will do.'

'Did you find anything about the Kia?'

'A couple of possibles so far. CATS are following up now.'

'Thanks. Philip, you can hand over to Fick now.'

'Here he is . . .'

'Benny?' Fanie 'Fucked' Fick asked after a moment, his voice quiet and apologetic. His habitual tone ever since the humiliation of the Steyn case.

'You found something?'

'Maybe. You know about the SMS Sloet sent the night of her death, around 21.52?'

He had to think about that first. 'Yes . . . To Henry van Eeden, I think.'

'That's right. We plotted van Eeden's number along with all the rest. And we found two calls from him to Sloet, later that night. The first was at 22.48, the second around 23.01. She didn't answer either of them, but I see the pathologist says the time of death was around 22.00, with two hours of play either side. So she could have been dead already . . .'

'Van Eeden phoned *her* . . .'

'That's right. But now I must add, his first call registered on the Vodacom tower at Somerset West, the one at 22.48. And thirteen minutes later, at 23.01, the second call registered on the towers at Nyanga and Gugulethu. Seems he was on the N2, on the way to the city.'

'OK,' said Griessel, while he tried to understand it.

'So you knew about that?'

'No, I didn't.'

'That's the only funny thing we've picked up so far.'

He stopped in front of the offices of Blue Oceans Productions in Prestwich Street where he was going to interview Sloet's two friends. He was a few minutes late, but he looked up Henry van Eeden's number on his cellphone first, and pressed call.

It rang only three times before the man answered. Griessel identified himself, van Eeden's voice was just as warm as it had been the day before. 'Afternoon, Captain. I'm glad you're phoning . . .'

'How so?'

'Yesterday . . . After you left here yesterday, something kept bothering me. Something that Hanneke had said, I just couldn't place it, it is two months ago after all. It's relevant to what you said about a communist who might be involved.'

'Yes?'

'Late last night, I remembered what it was. On the twenty-second of December we had a short meeting, with representatives of all the big role players, just before Christmas. Just after we adjourned, Hanneke took a call on her phone. She seemed a little upset, so I asked her if everything was OK, and she said, yes, just an annoying Russian.'

'An annoying Russian?'

'That's right. But the Russians haven't been communists for a long time, that's why I didn't immediately make the connection. It might be irrelevant, but I thought I would mention it to you.'

'You don't know who the Russian is?'

'No, sorry . . .'

'Thank you, Mr van Eeden, we will see if we can find

anything. I wonder if you could help me to understand something else.'

'Naturally, if I can—'

'Our records say you phoned Hanneke Sloet twice, the night of her murder.'

'That's right. I informed Sergeant Nxesi about it.' Van Eeden's tongue-clicking pronunciation of the Xhosa surname was perfect.

'I don't see a reference in the file. Can you tell me why you phoned her?'

'Of course. About her SMS.'

'But she sent the SMS before ten. You only phoned just before eleven . . .'

'I only received it at about a quarter to eleven. I was a speaker at the BEE conference at the Lord Charles . . .'

'In Somerset West.'

'That's right. You know how it is, you turn your phone off when you're talking. I finished about half past ten, and switched my phone back on when I walked to my car. That's when I got her SMS. And so I phoned her back.'

'What did the SMS say?'

'I can't remember the exact words, but it was about the report she had sent. She wanted me to look at it urgently.'

'Why did you phone her?'

'I wanted to tell her I would only be able to look at it the following day.'

'And she didn't answer?'

'That's right. I thought she might be in the bath. So I phoned again, on the way home.'

'You didn't leave a message.'

'I didn't think it was necessary. She would have seen the missed calls.'

36

Aldri de Koker was plump and soft, with a maternal air about her. 'Hanneke and I were roomies at varsity,' she said.

'We did Private Law together in second year,' said Samantha ('call me Sam') Grobler, the film producer. They sat in the reception room of Blue Ocean Productions, all black leather and glass, framed film posters against the wall. Grobler was tall and very slim, with high, prominent cheekbones. The tightly fitting blouse showed a breast measurement completely out of keeping with her slimness. Griessel wondered whether she had also had a boob job.

'It feels as though we always knew each other,' said de Koker.

'We miss her every day.'

'I can't believe she's gone.'

'She's in a better place . . . '

'I know . . .'

'You both talked to Hanneke on the eighteenth?' Griessel asked.

'We talked every day,' said Grobler.

'Even if it was just for a minute or two,' said de Koker.

'What sort of work do you do?' Griessel asked her.

'PR. I have my own boutique agency.'

'And she makes money like it's going out of fashion,' said Grobler. Through the glass of the big coffee table Griessel could see her long slender legs in tight, bleached denim. And the high-heeled sandals. He struggled to reconcile these two – the plump de Koker in her wide red skirt, loose white blouse and flat shoes, and her girl friend with the accentuated, sexy slimness.

'What did you talk about that day?'

'Boo Radley's,' they said in unison, looked at each other and shared an empathetic smile.

'Boo Radley's?'

'It's a pub and bistro,' said Grobler. 'In Hout Street.'

'We went there every Wednesday night,' said de Koker.

'Girls' night out. Live music.'

'Sam and I still go.'

'We still order a Corona for Hanneke . . .' They talked rapidly, without pauses between each other's sentences, as though each knew what the other was going to say. Griessel had to concentrate to keep up.

'With a slice of lemon . . .'

'In memory . . .'

'But it was a Tuesday,' said Griessel.

'Planning,' said Grobler.

'It was what we did, on a Tuesday,' said de Koker. 'Confirm Wednesday evening.'

'You saw her the previous Wednesday?'

'We did.'

'It was big. Hanneke's first Boo evening since she moved.'

'And her last,' said de Koker quietly.

'She wouldn't want us to think about it like that,' said Grobler.

'I know . . .'

'Did she say anything about the apartment? About the move, or the builders . . . ?'

'She just said she didn't know why she'd waited so long before moving to the city.'

'She loved it in the city . . .'

'And she said the apartment was fabulous . . .'

'We were still discussing who she was going to invite to the house-warming . . .'

'She wanted to have that this month . . .'

'If her work allowed it . . .'

'She put in an incredible number of hours . . .'

'Nothing about problems with the builders?' Griessel asked.

'No.'

'Anyone who made her angry?'

'Only the agents.'

'What agents?'

'The estate agents. They promised her she would have wireless when she moved in, but it still wasn't up and running.'

'She gave them hell.'

'Is that all?'

'Yes.'

'Nobody bothering her?'

'No.'

'The people who did the moving?'

'No.'

'The security people?'

'No.'

'Problems at work?'

'Just the long hours . . .'

'No disagreements?'

'No.'

'How security conscious was she?'

'Very.'

'Her door always bolted?'

'Of course.'

'Did she have any very valuable possessions in the apartment? Jewels, that sort of thing . . . ?'

'Not really.'

'What about the Aalbers?' de Koker asked.

'It could be. She paid fifteen thousand . . .' said Grobler.

'The what?' Griessel asked.

'The painting. In her sitting room. It's an Aalbers.'

'The one with the stripes?' he asked.

'It is supposed to represent the folds of the brain. The title is *Memory*.'

'She paid fifteen thousand for that?'

'It's an Aalbers,' said de Koker again, as if that explained everything.

'Nothing else?'

'No,' they said in unison.

'Did she mention anything about keys going missing?'

'No . . .'

'Something about her spare key? About who she gave it to?'

'The spare key of her apartment?' asked de Koker.

'That's right.'

'To me.'

'She told you who—'

'No, she gave the key to me.'

'The spare key?'

'Yes.'

'For the *new* apartment?'

'Yes . . .'

'What did you do with it?'

De Koker lifted a large raffia handbag off the floor, put it on her lap, put in her hand and almost immediately brought out a key holder – a small pink bear, on a ring with a single key. 'Here it is.'

A heartfelt 'Fuck' hovered at the tip of his tongue. Just in time, he found a replacement: 'Faux pas,' he said.

'What?' asked de Koker. 'Nobody asked me anything about it.'

'When did she give it to you?'

'On the fourth. The day after she moved in. She phoned me and asked if I wanted to come around. Sam was still on location . . .'

'In Mozambique,' said Grobler. 'Awfully hot . . .'

'She asked me if I would keep the key. She always used to give it to Mister Big . . .'

'But they had broken up,' said Grobler.

'Except for December's quickie . . .' said de Koker.

'That's true,' said Grobler.

'Wait, please,' said Griessel, hands in the air. 'Mister Big?'

'Egan,' said Grobler.

'Roch,' said de Koker.

'Why Mister Big?' he asked.

'*Sex and the City*?' said Grobler.

'The TV show?' said de Koker.

'I don't know it,' said Griessel.

He saw the women exchange a meaningful glance, as though he had failed a test. 'We called Egan Mister Big,' said de Koker.

'And apparently not without reason,' said Grobler suggestively. He suspected she generally flirted a little with men.

'And she told you about her and Roch, in December?'

'Of course,' said Grobler. 'We didn't have any secrets from each other.'

'What did she say?'

'A girl has to do what a girl has to do.'

'If you have a new pair of puppies, you have to take them out for a walk,' said de Koker, and put a hand over her mouth, as if she couldn't believe what she had just said. '*You* started it,' she pointed an accusing finger at Grobler.

Griessel's cellphone rang. He wanted to explain to them that he was JOC leader, he had to take the call, but then he realised how big-headed that would sound, so he just said, 'Excuse me,' stood up, took the phone, and walked towards the door.

'Griessel,' he said as he went out into the passage and closed the door behind him, though his thoughts were still inside.

'Hannes Pruis told me to email you Sloet's diary,' said a man's voice, hurried, hoarse and somewhat fuzzy. 'But we don't have your address.'

'I'll see you in an hour,' said Griessel. He couldn't remember asking Pruis to send her diary . . .

'It's too much to print out, we would rather send it.'

'OK,' he said, and spelled out his email address.

'Thanks.' And the line went dead.

Griessel shook his head, put the phone away, and went back in. 'Excuse me,' he said to the two women. 'Where were we?'

'Mister Big,' said Grobler.

'Oh. Yes. So she told you about her and Egan. In December?'

'Everything,' said Grobler.

'And as far as she was concerned it was just a one-off . . .'

'Quickie,' said Grobler.

'. . . occurrence?' said Griessel.

'Yes,' said de Koker.

'And there were no other men in her life?'

'There were,' said de Koker.

'Hannes Pruis,' said Grobler.

'The pig,' said de Koker.

'Hannes Pr—' His phone rang again.

He managed to change the instinctive fricative to 'faux pas' again, took the phone out of his pocket, and stood up.

'You don't need to go outside, we understand,' said Grobler.

'About the investigation and all,' said de Koker.

He could see on the screen it was the DPCI. He didn't want to take a call now, he wanted to hear about Hannes Pruis, his lifebuoy after their flood of words had washed away his spare key theory. But he would have to answer. 'Excuse me,' he told the women. 'Griessel,' he said into the instrument, halfway between his chair and the door.

'Benny, this is Fanie Fick of IMC. Did you just receive a phone call?'

'Yes,' said Griessel.

'It was the shooter,' said Fick.

'Excuse me?'

'Solomon. The shooter. It's the same phone he used to call Milnerton station yesterday.

'Fuck,' said Griessel before he could stop himself.

And then he looked guiltily into the eyes of the plump, motherly Aldri de Koker.

37

'He called the provincial office switchboard first, fifteen minutes ago,' said Fick. 'They can't tell us who he spoke to. No logs, too many calls. We were caught napping, it was so unexpected, but then we knew he was on the air again. What did he say to you?'

'He wanted my email address. He said Hannes Pruis wanted to send Hanneke Sloet's diary.' So the shooter knew about Pruis, Griessel realised.

'Do you want us to look at your emails?'

'Yes, pl—' He remembered the photo of Carla and the muscle man that Fritz had sent. 'No, wait,' he said, 'I'm coming.'

'He phoned from the city, Benny. The call was too short to triangulate. If he phones again, try to keep him on the line.'

'His phone is off now?'

'Totally.'

'OK. I'm coming. Give me . . .' He still wanted to hear the story of Hannes Pruis and Hanneke Sloet. '. . . forty minutes.'

He put the phone away. Both women were sitting and watching him intently. It took a moment to gather his thoughts. 'Hannes Pruis?' he said to Grobler and de Koker. 'He and Hanneke had an affair?'

'An affair?' asked de Koker, a bit shocked.

'Never!' said Grobler. 'Mister Small.'

'But just now you said they had . . .'

'You asked if there was a man in her life,' said de Koker.

'Hannes Pruis made sure that he was the only man in her life,' said Grobler.

'Slave driver,' said de Koker. 'Little man. Jealous of Mister Big, he made sure they didn't have any time together.'

'So Pruis had a thing for Hanneke?'

'All men had a thing for Hanneke.'

'But he was jealous of Roch?'

'Wouldn't you have been too?'

'But did he do anything? I mean, did he harass her?'

'He made her *work* late.'

'She wore herself out for him.'

'So you are talking about a professional relationship?'

'An understanding,' said Grobler. 'Hanneke had the understanding . . .'

'And Pruis just had the standing,' said de Koker.

'You should have heard him at the memorial service.'

'As if he really knew her at all.'

'Used her, yes. He used her.'

'Worked her butt off.'

'Even weekends . . .'

'We had to put up with that. And Mister Big. That's why they broke up.'

'Apart from the quickie.'

'We barely saw her, those last months.'

'Please,' said Griessel. 'Just a minute.'

They looked at him expectantly.

'She never had an affair with Hannes Pruis.'

'Not in the Mister Big sense of the word,' said Grobler.

'That means "no, absolutely not",' de Koker explained. 'Except that he made her work too hard.'

'There was no other man in her life?'

'No,' said Grobler. 'Where would she find the time?'

Griessel breathed out, as if he had survived a sprint. 'Thank you,' he said.

'Faux pas?' Grobler asked. 'Is that some sort of police code?'

He knew everything was happening too fast, he had to keep his wits about him. In the BMW he first phoned Cupido and asked if he would go to the law firm straight away and supervise the questioning of personnel.

'Sure, Benna.'

'I found the spare key, Vaughn. She gave it to one of her friends. Aldri de Koker.'

'Knock me down with a *vrot* fish . . . Aldri? What kind of name is Aldri? Look, we coloureds have our peculiarities, but fuck knows, you whiteys can think up *kak* names. What is our approach with the lawyers now?'

He thought of the shooter knowing about Pruis. 'Alibis, Vaughn. For the eighteenth of January, *and* for the shooter.'

'You think?'

'Let's make sure. Ask about fights, jealousy, office politics, affairs . . . Who would be angry if she set up on her own? Oh, and, did she have anything valuable in her apartment, something that might have belonged to the lawyers? Anything. Documents . . . I don't know, Vaughn, something that might have had great value.'

'OK. The whole shebang,' said Cupido. 'I'm on my way.'

Griessel put on the BMW's lights and siren and drove to Bellville.

The fucker had phoned him. *Jissis*, and he wasn't on the ball. He replayed the conversation with Solomon. The hoarse voice, half dulled, he must have been holding something over the mouthpiece. The hurried words. He wanted to be quick, he knew he could be traced.

But he was calm. Shot a policeman dead yesterday, today he was calm. And cheeky.

For the first time he felt rage against this insane bastard. But also the knowledge: this was not your usual mad hatter.

What did he want to send? Why now? He had only used John Afrika's email address up till now.

There was something else, a note that he felt he should write down. And now he couldn't recall it, those women had talked a hole in his head.

Was it something he had forgotten to ask them?

His cellphone rang again. It was Colonel Nyathi. 'Benny, we're having a meeting in half an hour, in the brig's office.'

There were no new emails.

He deleted the one from Fritz after one last look at the picture of Carla and Etzebeth. Then he carried his laptop down to IMC.

There was no longer the frenetic activity of this morning, only the IMS personnel at their work stations, concentrating. He put his laptop down on Fanie Fick's table. 'He hasn't sent anything yet,' said Griessel.

'I know. We're watching the mail server. Put your laptop here and log in. I'll keep an eye on it.' With his apologetic attitude and sad eyes, like a bloodhound.

'Thanks,' said Griessel, and looked for a wall socket. It was hard for him to look at Fanie Fucked. As if he saw how he'd end up.

'We have more or less all the names and numbers of the builders of 36 on Rose,' Fick said. 'Plus the removals, and security. Her Vodacom records for the last six months of last year are coming soon.' He looked at his watch. 'I should be able to start running the match at about eight o'clock.'

'You'll call me . . .'

'I will.'

'Anything on the shooter's panel van?'

Fick shook his head. 'Chances are good that he stole the Kia. They can't find anything.'

'He's clever,' said Griessel.

'We'll get him,' said Fick.

Griessel opened his email, and turned the screen so that Fick could see. 'We still don't have Sloet's cellphone records for December?'

'They should be here any moment now.'

'Can you see if there is anyone with a Russian surname who phoned her on the twenty-second?'

'Sure.'

'I have to go to a meeting . . .' He took out his notebook and pen. 'If you get a chance – I just want to check someone's criminal record . . .'

'Sure,' said Fick. Eager to help. To be part of a case again.

'There's no rush . . .' Griessel wrote down the name and surname, tore out the page.

Fick read. 'Calla Etzebeth. Where does he fit in?'

'I don't know yet.'

'OK.'

'Thanks, Fanie.' It was an effort to keep the pity from his voice.

There was a moment that morning, with the sickening smell of the red spray paint in his nose and the uncertainty gnawing at him like a slow cancer, that the sniper was ready to pack it all in.

There was huge relief in the idea. Just walk away. Drive the Chana and take the rifle and the cellphone and the wig and the clothes and go and pour petrol over them. Set it all on fire and just walk away.

He put down the spray can, untied the rag from over his mouth, pulled off the gloves, and sat down on the garage floor, his head between his knees.

After a while he pictured himself like that, defeated and dejected, and it was too much to bear. He could not let it end here, because then they would have won.

It was the turning point, that knowledge: His life depended on it.

Slowly he crawled back up the slope of despair, warmed his hands over the glowing embers of old fires. And then the plan came to him, the strategy, the knowledge that the best defence was attack. That he held the trump cards. He just had to play them right.

He got up, turned on his computer and searched on Google for 'Benny Griessel, SAPS'. In the news databases of Media24 and iol.co.za he found enough about the detective's career to work with: for the previous two years Griessel had been attached to the office of General John Afrika, Western Cape head of Detective Services and Criminal Intelligence, before he was transferred to the Hawks, probably quite recently.

It brought him new insight.

He used the Peninsula telephone directory, and wrote down the possible numbers.

He considered his timing and the fact that the origin of cellphone calls could be determined. He drove the Audi into the city, to the big parking lot at the Waterfront. There he took a deep breath, steadied pen and paper on his knee, and called the SAPS Provincial Office. He asked for the Administrative Department. A woman with a coloured accent answered.

'Who am I talking to now?' he asked in an irritable voice.

'Sergeant April.'

'This is Colonel Botha, Directorate of Priority Crimes.' A deliberately intimidating high rank. He went on, obvious frustration and irritation in his tone: 'Did you send us the correct home address of Captain Benny Griessel? Because his post keeps being sent back.'

'Colonel knows I can't give that out over the phone.'

'Sergeant, what do you want me to do? If I don't have the correct information, the Captain will not be paid at the end of the month. Is that what you want?'

'No, Colonel.'

'And it's *your* fault. I feel like phoning John Afrika, it can't go on like this.'

'Couldn't Colonel ask the Captain himself?' she tried to divert him.

'What's your name?'

'Veronica . . .' Very intimidated.

'Benny is busy with the Sloet case, Veronica. Do you really want me to bother him with such nonsense?'

'No, Colonel.'

'Let me give you the address I have, and then you tell me if it is the one you have.'

He held his breath, unsure whether his gamble would work, aware of the ticking of the clock, that the length of this call must be limited. She hesitated, and he tried another approach.

'Sergeant, I understand it's not your fault. But please help me – you know how it is if someone doesn't get their pay cheque.'

She sighed at last, then asked, resigned, 'What is his personnel number, Colonel?'

His brain froze and he mentally kicked himself, he should have thought. Then an inspiration: 'That's not here either.'

'Benny Griessel?'

'That's right.'

'Hold on,' she said apologetically.

Then he heard her typing on a keyboard. And she said, 'There is only one Benjamin Griessel. Number 128, Nelson's Mansions, Vriende Street, Gardens?'

'That's not what we have.' He scribbled it down hastily,

delighted with the success of his little ploy. Then he made another mistake. 'And his email?'

'Colonel, he will have a DPCI email . . .'

He scrabbled for an answer. 'We have to remove the old one.'

'Oh. Yes.'

Relief. But he had to get the email address.

How?

A possibility formed in his mind, another gamble, but with an irresistible pay-off: he could talk to Griessel himself. He could taunt his hunter.

'Is this the correct cell number?' He gave her a fictitious one.

'No,' she said, and slowly read out the correct one.

He ended the call, switched off his phone, and, with the warm glow of success, drove to Sea Point, to change his location. He parked on the other side of the swimming pool, in the area that looked out over the flat, windless summer sea. He phoned the detective. In that moment, when the man answered, there was a separation from reality, and he was curious to hear his own voice. Would it tremble, would it hesitate?

It didn't.

The detective, the Benny Griessel he had seen in the news photos, sounded unsettled. Absent. And that gave him pleasure – it was the result of the pressure he brought to bear, his actions, his campaign. He wrote down the email address, put the cellphone down, took out the battery. He put everything in the glove compartment and drove home before the rush hour could detain him. To write the email. And he knew this tranquillity he had found would stay with him.

Tonight, in the dark, he would go and reconnoitre the area around Vriende Street and Nelson's Mansions. In the Audi, and on foot.

Because that was where he wanted to fire his next shot.

38

They were all sitting around the big table in Musad Manie's office – the brigadier himself, Zola Nyathi, Werner du Preez of CATS, Philip van Wyk of IMC, Cloete of Public Relations, Mbali and Griessel.

The voice of Captain Ilse Brody, criminal behaviour analyst of the Investigative Psychology Section in Pretoria, came clearly over the conference phone in the centre of the table. 'You all know a profile is a moving target,' she said. 'But this is what I have: male, white, and Afrikaans. His terminology and ideology betray that, and his age. He is fond of the word "communist". He also uses "communist bedfellows". That strongly indicates to me someone who grew up under the previous dispensation. He could be anything between forty and seventy years old. But it takes a certain amount of physical ability to do what he is doing, so he would most likely fall in the age bracket between forty and mid-fifties. If I take everything into account, my best guess is that he is in his mid to late forties.

'He has a hunting rifle at his disposal, scope and ammunition, and therefore most likely a gun licence. He has the means and space to adapt to his specific purpose. He has access to the Internet, knowledge of anonymous email servers, quotes in Latin, and has relatively good language skills. All that, along with the timing of the police attacks, indicates to me a white collar worker who is not unemployed.

'I'll come back to timing later, because it has more interesting implications. But let's look at the religious and political references first. There is a degree of self-justification in those, but my instinct tells me we are working with someone who is on the right of the political spectrum. Probably not far right,

he isn't fanatical enough for the Boeremag, but he would
have sympathy with them. And if I may interject here: the
long hair that the eye witness saw, does not fit *this* picture.
The anti-communist, the religious right would have short
hair, probably a moustache, beard, or both. The chances are
good that he was wearing a wig.

'He is religious, but I don't think he belongs to an extremist or charismatic group. To tell the truth, I don't think he is
in any way a community or group person. He sees himself as
the white knight, the lone wolf, the solitary protector of moral
values and justice. There are no psychoses, but most likely a
personality disorder – perhaps a kind of Messiah complex.'

They could hear the rustle of paper over the line. Then she
went on: 'This offers us some possibilities. He is on the social
and professional fringes, not the sort of come-and-braai-at-
my-place-tonight kind of guy. An introvert, living just a little
secretively, very serious about himself and life. He might be
married, but will not be loving towards or involved in his
wife's life, rather cold and aloof. The kind who believes he is
head of the house, he makes the decisions.

'The most interesting thing for me is the temporary regres-
sion of his correspondence. His first emails are short and
powerful, careful and full of confidence, and without spelling
or grammatical errors. It seems he spent time on them, went
to some trouble. He knew he had the upper hand, he was
writing from a position of strength. He is busy positioning
and justifying himself, as though he is preparing the stage for
the media attention to come. That brings me back to the
megalomania and the Messiah complex. Make no mistake,
that is how he sees himself: he occupies the moral high
ground, the SAPS does not. But then, in the email of February
twenty-seventh to the press, it changes. Not spelling mistakes,
but typos. Suddenly he's in a hurry and nervous, as though
the moment is greater than he anticipated.

'I think the email of February twenty-seventh is important, because it tells us he experienced pressure and tension. I can speculate and say it was because he was announcing himself to the media with that message, but things didn't play out exactly as he expected. He missed, but it may have been because he was nearly discovered, that he had some kind of narrow escape. You might well look into that. A speeding fine? Ran a red light? Or perhaps it was merely a case of his initial motivation decreasing, so that he began to wonder about the moral justification behind it all. He clearly knows the difference between right and wrong – the Bible verses are good evidence – but to shoot someone in reality is a traumatic experience. What I am trying to say, is that he is not a hundred per cent stable. But highly motivated – it takes an enormous amount of faith in your cause to prepare a vehicle and weapon, to wait in ambush and shoot a policeman. And that combination makes him dangerous. The dilemma is, the more policemen he shoots, the less he has to lose. Mbali, you asked me this morning to take the calibre and the missed shot into account . . .'

'Yes, please,' said Mbali.

'If you consider the calibre along with the missed shot and the stress of the email, you can deduce that he has not had specialised military training. I know men of the apartheid era all did military service, but this man was most likely in a support unit, and did not have combat experience.'

'Thank you,' said Mbali, taking notes.

'For what it's worth,' the psychologist said. 'Now, I promised to say something more about the timing: the conclusion that he is a white collar nine-to-fiver, is naturally easy. But it could also mean that he has to work among other people, that he's not alone in an office, with a door that he can lock. Given the fringe personality profile, I believe he is not popular at work, at most in a middle management job, but more likely in a lowlier position. For a man of his age and intellectual ability it must be a frustration and an insult, and might form part of his motivation to regain power and self-respect in this way.

'But there is another alternative. We know that a crime committed after five o'clock in the afternoon usually results in less accurate eye-witness accounts. People are tired, they are hurrying home, they are reluctant to become involved. Now, the question is: does Solomon know that?'

'What are you saying?'

'You know it's all conjecture, Mbali, but it could mean that he has knowledge of the nature of police investigations. He may have worked for, or with the SAPS. There is also the fact that he is specifically shooting members of the Service. It could be that he has a grudge. Probably not a policeman, if we look at the calibre and the bad shooting, but you never know. I would look at dishonourable discharges of administrative personnel or reservists, people who were arrested or investigated for misconduct.'

'In the past year or so?'

'In the past ten years.'

Colonel Werner du Preez of CATS sighed audibly.

'I'm sorry, but that's the reality,' the forensic psychologist said. 'If he has a grudge, it could have taken years to progress this far.'

'Ilse, this is Musad Manie. The shooter phoned Captain Benny Griessel directly to get his email address . . .'

'At what time, Brigadier?' asked Captain Brody.

Manie looked at Griessel. 'About half past three,' he said. 'From somewhere in the city.'

'Interesting. Has he sent anything yet?'

'Not yet.'

'The question I have,' said Manie, 'is whether we should try to start a conversation with him through Benny?'

There was a long silence over the line before she answered.

'That is a very difficult one, brigadier. All the usual rules of interrogation apply. You want him to do all the talking, so your communication must be very short and cryptic. It's almost like hostage negotiation, you want to keep rephrasing what he says in order to draw him out. But in this case he's sitting safely behind his anonymity, he has time to think everything through before he answers an email.'

'So you don't recommend it?'

'It's thin ice. Perhaps too thin.'

'Ilse, Werner du Preez of CATS. It doesn't seem as though our search for the Kia is going to produce anything. We have to assume it is one of the three that were stolen in the past few months and not recovered . . .'

'Colonel, with respect, I would be most surprised. Middle-aged white collar workers are practically never car thieves. They just don't have the skills . . .'

'But there is a very good chance that the rifle was also stolen,' said Mbali. 'We have eliminated almost all the legal owners.'

'Let me think a minute . . .' said Ilse Brody. Silence in the room while they waited for her response. Then she said, 'As we all know, nothing is impossible. But it really does not fit with anything else. My best guess would be someone close to law enforcement. Perhaps a rifle that was handed in to the police? An impounded van? I don't know . . .'

'What will he do if we go to the media with the description of the vehicle?' du Preez asked.

'Colonel, does he know we know about the Kia?'

'He might suspect.'

'I wouldn't recommend it. He will just change vehicles. And naturally, every Kia on the road would panic the public . . .'

'That's what I thought. And then there is the possibility of copycats . . .'

'I don't think copycats are very likely in this case. As you know, Colonel, it happens mostly with economic crime in this country.'

'Any advice, Ilse?' Manie asked.

'Brigadier, the key lies in that email of February twenty-seventh. Since last night he has become a murderer. He will feel the pressure, and I think he struggles under pressure. In his next communication he will try to justify it, he will offer more Bible verses. I am specially thinking of "A time to kill" and "a time for war". He will try to blame everyone but himself, a case of "the police made me do it". Our message to the media must remain consistent: He is psychologically unstable, he is an extremist and a murderer. We must continue to attack his moral high ground, the Messiah thing. That is how we increase the pressure on him. So that he makes more mistakes. That is the only way we'll catch him.'

After the meeting was over, Griessel walked to his office and phoned Cupido.

'How does it look, Vaughn?'

'Nearly finished, but it's the three wise monkeys, Benna. Hear and speak and see no evil, they were this happy band of lawyer brothers and sisters all working together in paradise.'

That was the way it usually went. He told Cupido of his brief phone conversation with the shooter, and Captain Ilse Brody's theory of a professional fringe figure. 'He knew her, Vaughn, and he knew Pruis. More and more I think he's in a corner at Silbersteins. Ask them if they know about such a man, in his late forties. Loner. A lurker, bad tempered and quiet and arrogant, with a superior attitude, that he's better than them.'

'These are lawyers, Benna, they all think they are better than the rest. But I get the picture. I'll ask.'

'I want to hold a JOC meeting at six o'clock. Will you be able to make it?'

'Make it quarter past and I'll be there.'

He phoned Alexa. She answered immediately, a little anxiously. 'Don't tell me you're on your way already.'

'No,' he said. 'Why?'

'I'm not allowed to say.' There was a mischievous note in her voice. 'Will you phone before you come?'

'I will, but it could get late tonight.'

'That doesn't matter, as long as you phone.'

'I will. Is Ella still there?'

'She is, and she will stay until just before you come.'

He heard Ella say something in the background, and then both women laughed conspiratorially. But before he could ask what it was about, Fick appeared in the door, his blood-hound face excited for the first time in months.

'Benny, you better come. The shooter has sent you an email . . .'

39

762a89z012@anonimail.com
Sent: Tuesday 1 March. 16.57
To: jannie.erlank@dieburger.com
CC: j.afrika@saps.gov.za; b.griessel@dpmo.saps.gov.za
Re: Collateral damage
I want to convey my sincere sympathy to the next of kin of Constable Errol Matthys. His death was never my intention and I wish to apologise for this tragic incident. If the SAPS had not protected the murderers of Hanneke Sloet, it would not have been necessary for me to use extrema remedia. Unfortunately Errol Matthys is part of the SAPS and part

of the government of this country, and they do not do what is just: Deuteronomy 16:20: 'That which is altogether just shalt thou follow, that thou mayest live, and inherit the land which the Lord thy God giveth thee'.

After this tragic incident I will give the SAPS one day's grace to tell the truth: 1 Kings 22:16: 'How many times shall I adjure thee that thou tell me nothing but that which is true in the name of the Lord?'

Today I will not shoot a policeman. Proverbs 3:8: a time for peace.

If the SAPS still has not made an announcement regarding the arrest of Hanneke Sloet's murderers, it will be a time for war again. If there is more collateral damage I will not be the one to blame.

I have no other choice. I warned them forty days ago.

Solomon

They crowded around the screen to read it. Griessel noted their attention and focus. He thought, the shooter bastard had them just where he wanted.

'He is pretty desperate to regain the moral high ground,' said Mbali.

'New verses,' said Brigadier Manie. 'Now he wants to inherit the land.'

'And a few old ones,' said Nyathi.

'And the same Latin,' said Manie. 'That's all he knows. But Ilse was right. He blames everyone but himself.'

'And he likes his nickname,' said Mbali.

'Benny, haven't you anything to say?' asked Manie.

The rage at the shooter grew inside him. But if he let himself say what he wanted to say, he would disappoint Mbali deeply. 'Brigadier, why did he go to all that trouble to get my email address? For *this* load of tripe? It doesn't make sense.'

* * *

There were thirty-seven people in the big parade room on the ground floor.

Griessel stood in front at the table and began a summary of the new information he had gained: Roch and Sloet's two girl friends who said she spent practically all her time at work. The newly discovered blood smears, apparently made by the weapon, which had been put down on the floor. Prof Phil Pagel's theory about a home-made weapon, the size and length of it, and the outside chance of a well-organised serial killer who might have taken her underwear as a memento. The strongest likelihood was that it was pure robbery, something small and valuable that Sloet had in her possession.

One of the Violent Crimes detectives stood up. 'Benny, robbery is our best chance. We have found four *okes* who worked at the block of flats and who have previous convictions.'

'Good work,' said Nyathi, as the room buzzed.

'An *oke* who worked for the removals company has done time for robbery,' said the detective. 'Three of the builders' and plumbers' people have records too. Breaking and entering, assault and robbery. They're being brought in now. But we have to know what was stolen from her flat.'

'Do we have news, Philip?' Griessel asked Captain van Wyk of IMC.

Van Wyk shook his head. 'We looked at Sloet's short-term insurance policy. There were no valuable items specified. Just the usual. Household contents and car.'

'Her friends said the same thing,' said Griessel. 'And Sloet left the spare key of her apartment with one of them. That leaves us with two possibilities: she forgot to lock her door and bolt it, put on the safety chain. Or she knew the suspect.'

'And drugs?' asked the Violent Crimes detective.

'Nothing in her apartment, nothing in her blood,' said Griessel.

'People neglect to specify valuables,' said Nyathi. 'Grill the four with criminal records, really turn up the heat. If an alibi looks just a little shaky, you come to me right away, and we'll get a search warrant. Are we posting people at their homes, to make sure they don't get their buddies to offload evidence?'

'We're working with the uniform branches, sir,' said the Violent Crimes detective. 'All the premises are secure.'

'OK,' said Nyathi. 'What else?'

Captain Philip van Wyk stood up again. 'Sloet's cellphone records from July to December last year have come, we are busy putting them into the system. There's a lot of new data, along with the apartment building's people. We are going to work through the night, so we should have plotted everything by early tomorrow morning. Then we looked at serial murders with a similar modus operandi, and there is nothing. Not locally or nationally. And only one other matter, it might not mean anything: I asked one of my people to put Sloet's financial affairs through our analysis program. It seems as though she has been spending less and less each month, especially on her credit card since January last year. The decrease was relatively small at first, between three and five per cent in January and February, but then it got bigger. By December it was a twelve per cent decrease on a year-to-year basis, while her disposable income increased in this period.'

'It could be the work,' said Griessel. 'Her friends said in the last year she had much less free time.'

He thanked van Wyk, and asked Cupido whether the interrogations at Silbersteins had produced anything. Vaughn stole the limelight with his usual witticisms about the character, pomp and circumstance of lawyers. He said they had looked at everything – even Sloet's access card and keys to the office building – and there was nothing valuable missing. 'And the shrink's profile of an obnoxious recluse didn't pan out. Pruis the Ace told me they don't appoint people like that.'

When he emerged from the meeting and switched his phone back on, there was a voicemail. He listened. It was General Afrika. 'Benny, I see the scoundrel now has your email too. Just wanted to know whether he has sent you anything else.'

Before he called back, the Violent Crimes group brought in the first of four suspects with criminal records – the plumber's assistant. Shortly after that the packer from the removals company and the two construction workers arrived.

A duet of experienced detectives questioned each one separately in a DPCI office, while another two stood by to take calls and check alibis in cooperation with the SAPS stations. Nyathi himself drove to KFC to buy cold drinks and a few buckets of chicken. They ate and worked without stopping.

Griessel walked from room to room listening. His heart sank, little by little, as the innocence of one suspect after the other was confirmed.

At a quarter to eleven he walked to Manie's office. The commanding officer was on the phone, but beckoned Griessel to enter. Benny sat and listened to Manie soothingly bring the Lieutenant General in Pretoria up to date.

'I know the media are having a field day, General . . . No, I didn't watch the TV news . . . I understand, General. The whole unit is involved, but . . . No, General, we have no excuses . . . I assure you, we are doing our absolute best . . .' All said with stoic patience, until he at last put the receiver softly and carefully down on its cradle.

'I'm sorry, Brigadier,' said Griessel.

'You have nothing to be sorry about, Benny.' Manie wearily wiped his forehead, the first sign Griessel had seen that the pressure was getting to him.

'The men with records, Brigadier ... We couldn't find anything. They're all clean.'

'You were expecting that, Benny.'

'Yes, Brigadier. She wouldn't have opened the door to any of them.'

'And she would have locked the door. In that half empty building.'

'Yes, Brigadier.'

Manie stood up and picked up his jacket. 'In other words, IMC is our last hope,' he said.

'Yes, Brigadier.'

Again the hand wiping the brow, eyebrows to crown. 'I want you to know I think you have done excellent work so far, Benny. It makes no difference what the general says.'

'Not excellent enough, Brigadier.'

Manie gripped his arm. 'Come on, let's go home. Tomorrow is another day.'

Griessel fetched the case file and his jacket from his office, walked down the silent passage to the lift. He heard hurried footsteps from the stairwell side.

'Captain!'

He turned. Fick trotted towards him. 'There's another email, Benny. From the shooter.'

'Did you read it?'

'That's the thing. He didn't write anything. It's just a photo.'

'Of what?'

'Of a man.'

'Who?'

'I haven't the faintest idea.'

It was a black-and-white photograph, just the head and shoulders of a white man in a black jacket of perfect cut, white shirt and tie. His face was slightly angled to the right, his eyes turned away from the camera. He grinned with small, sharp teeth, like a shark. There were lines around his mouth and eyes, he looked about fifty-something. The hair was combed straight back, with the help of gel or hair oil maybe, so that his forehead stretched high above the dark eyebrows. He was clean-shaven.

'Do you know him, Captain?'

'Never seen him before,' said Griessel. 'Didn't he write anything with this?'

'Nothing. He sent it to you, Captain, and General Afrika. And he saved the photo as "MK".'

'What do you mean?'

'It looks like it is scanned out of a newspaper or something, and then he saved it as a jpeg file with the name "MK".'

'MK,' said Griessel.

'It couldn't be Umkhonto we Sizwe, *this* guy is white.'

'There were white people in Umkhonto,' said Griessel.

'Where do we begin, Captain? It could be anyone.'

He thought about it. Could it be a banker or a businessman in this suit? Maybe Boshigo knew him. 'Let's email the photo to Bones.'

'I can MMS it,' said Fick, sat down and tapped at the mouse and keyboard.

'I'll phone him now,' said Griessel, and called Boshigo's number.

'The man who never sleeps,' said Bones when he answered, the sound of a television programme in the background.

'Sorry, Bones . . .'

'Don't worry, Benny. What can I do?'

Griessel explained about the photo.

'He's playing games, *nè*,' said Bones. 'Wait, it's coming through now . . .' After a few seconds: 'Sorry, Benny, I don't know him.'

'Thanks, Bones. I just wanted to be sure.'

'Looks like a conman from the fifties,' said Bones. 'Or a loan shark . . .'

40

He looked closely at the photo again. Bones was right. There was something reminiscent of a bygone era. Was it the hairstyle?

It had been sent to him and John Afrika. Maybe the general knew who it was. He called Afrika's number. It went straight to voicemail. He didn't leave a message, he would try again tomorrow. Then he called Nyathi and Manie, to inform them of the latest developments.

When he had finished, he asked Fanie Fick, 'Will you let me know if anything else comes in?'

'I will. Oh, and that name you gave me: I found three possible Calla Etzebeths on the NPR . . .'

'Oh. Yes . . . the one I am looking at is around twenty,' said Griessel.

'OK. That would be Carel Ignatius Etzebeth. And he's clean. No record.'

'Thank you very much,' said Griessel, and he had to hide his relief.

'His cellphone number has been RICAed. Do you want me to plot it?'

That was the only way he could find out how seriously involved Carla was with the Neanderthal. But it would be misuse of the Hawks' time and manpower. 'You are busy, it's probably not worth the effort,' he said.

'It's no trouble, Captain. I have to wait for the other data to be processed anyway.'

* * *

In the basement, beside the BMW, he checked his watch. It was half past eleven. He phoned Alexa to tell her he was on his way.

'Hello, Benny . . .' Ella answered in a whisper.

'Is everything OK?'

'Yes, Alexa is fine. But she's fallen asleep. Don't worry about it, she was quite tired after the day's shopping and all. I don't think we should wake her.'

'I'm sorry, it was . . .'

'It's OK. We watched the news, we know you're having a hard time. Just between you and me, she bought this very sexy dress, and then we prepared a dinner for you, with candles and everything. And Alexa really can't cook – the duck is so tough, you can barely chew it. But she wanted to do that for you, to say thank you. I think she hoped tonight . . . you know . . .' A conspiratorial suggestion in her voice.

He didn't know. 'What do you mean?'

'Use your imagination, Benny. Anyway, I am going to sleep here at her place tonight, we'll talk again tomorrow . . . Good luck, Benny.'

'I'm . . .' he said, but the line was already dead.

He stood there and said, very quietly and with extreme frustration: 'Faux pas.'

He lay on his back in the darkness, the sheets and blankets kicked off in the heat. He knew he was going to battle to sleep, even though he was back in his flat, even though the sounds were familiar and soothing – his pawnshop fridge downstairs, the TV of the woman next door, and the hum of traffic in Annandale Street. Now that the crazy day was over, his rage at the shooter overwhelmed him, slowly, like a tide coming in.

It was only during the reading of the last email, in the company of his colleagues in front of the screen, that he really began to hate the fucker. The cunt who phoned him, who sat on the other end of the line and lied to him while he struggled and fought and scrambled and ran from one false hope to the next. Not just him. Mbali Kaleni had looked lost tonight, dead tired and despairing, because nothing was working out. And Musad Manie's voice when he spoke to the general in Pretoria . . . There was a hopelessness there for the first time, as though he knew they were worn out. And this thing had scarcely begun.

And then he sent that meaningless, self-glorifying, apologetic email giving the SAPS 'grace'. Like a fucking lord.

What kind of person was that?

What kind of person phoned the police to stop a robbery, and then shot one of them dead? It was the lowest form of cowardice.

If he truly believed the SAPS were protecting someone, why didn't he tell the press? Why didn't he reveal his information and suspicions and accusations to the media? He must know they would descend on it like vultures and try to rip up the carcass of the SAPS.

Jissis.

He knew it wasn't just the shooter, it was the whole Sloet case. The frustration, the pressure, trying everything, getting nowhere. Running in circles, powerless. He hated this kind of case where there was just nothing – working like a blind man in the dark.

And then the shooter came and made everything even more difficult. The screaming injustice of it all seared through him, stoking his hatred.

If it was up to him, he would ignore the advice of the forensic psychologist and he would write back to that little shit. 'You coward, you play your games, you lie, you hide behind anonymous emails and mystery photos, you sneak around in a fucking Kia and shoot policemen who are trying to do their thankless jobs. Because you have some hangup about communists and Hanneke Sloet's death. You think you are this *moerse* hero, but you don't have the guts to stand in front of us and say this is who I think murdered Sloet. Why not? Because you are a sick fuck and you think you are the Messiah, because you know the fucking media is loving every minute of it. Let me tell you, you are nothing. You're a lame duck, spineless, you're complete and utter shit and I'm going to put you away so deep and for so long, among people who will fuck you up so bad that you will wish you'd taken your fucking little triple-two *moffie* gun and blown your brains out all over your little wig.'

So strong was the feeling of rage that he wanted to get up and get out the old laptop that he'd bought on a police auction a while back, and pound away on the keyboard until he'd sent the email off, and he wondered suddenly, where did it come from, all this fury?

But he knew.

He sighed, shifted the pillow, turned on his side.

It came from yesterday evening. When he had sat and told Alexa about his day.

The first time in his life. He had never done that when he was married to Anna. He had wanted to keep the death and killing away from her and the children, had wanted one place that was normal and unspoiled.

And last night, he realised – fleetingly and reluctantly – it was a kind of relief, the offloading of experiences and frustrations. A sort of release, to tell someone. For the first time he truly understood what Doc Barkhuizen meant by 'don't internalise your work'.

And the idea that had come to burden him, in that moment during his conversation with Alexa, was how different his life could have been if he hadn't been so blindly stupid. He had avoided it the whole day, but now he had to admit it: Anna would have listened. Anna would have sympathised, Anna would have understood if he came home at night and told her everything: death, and how scared it made him. The blood and the smell and the lifeless, helpless bodies of children and women and old people, and the knowledge that that was what people could do to people. The pressure. The tension about everything – not enough money, the long hours, the expectations of the next of kin of the victims, and bosses. And the derision of the public and the press.

If he had shared all that with Anna, ten to one he would never have started drinking, and ten to one Anna would not have left him, and he would be sleeping curled around her back in their marriage bed tonight, without the frustration and hatred that he was feeling.

And he'd thought he was over the whole divorce thing.

Life was never simple. It didn't help at all to reason like that. Especially not today, because he had had enough.

Today, in Manie's office, after the conference call with Ilse Brody, the psychologist, Cloete had read them some things off the Internet. People reacting to the shooter news reports, tweeting and Facebooking, and they all sat there feeling the crying injustice of it all, because there was only scorn for them.

And he, Griessel, had sat and thought, that is how it was going to be with the Hawks: big cases, big publicity, big pressure. And fuck-all appreciation. The SAPS could do what they liked, they could solve one case after the other, they could force the crime statistics down slowly but surely, but, in his lifetime they were never going to get either thanks or respect.

And he had no option, he had to put up with it. Because that was all he was. A policeman. He couldn't do anything else. And he didn't want to. But fuck knows, if you looked ahead and only saw trouble, then you wondered, was it all worth it?

And he had thought maybe he could talk to Alexa about it tonight. Maybe it would help to get some of the stuff out of his head.

Alexa, who had bought a sexy dress and cooked him dinner and lit candles.

And then fallen asleep, because the shooter had fucked up his whole evening.

I think she hoped tonight . . . you know . . .

If Ella meant what he thought she meant . . .

Jissis. It was nearly a year since he had had a bit, two weeks ago he had woken up on this very bed from a dream where he and Alexa were lying naked, his hands everywhere on her, and everything felt just right.

Tonight that dream might have become reality. If it wasn't for the shooter.

The bastard.

Day 5

Wednesday

41

The first turning point came at half past five in the morning, when they phoned Griessel.

He woke up suddenly from a deep sleep, fumbled and fumbled again for the cellphone on his bedside cupboard, knocked it to the floor. He eventually got hold of it, kneeling on all fours on the carpet. 'Hello?' His mouth was dry and his voice hoarse.

'Benny, I'm so sorry to wake—' said van Wyk of IMC.

Griessel straightened up, sat down on the bed. 'Have you found something?'

'The guy in the photo. He's a Russian. And he knew Sloet.'

'A Russian.' Henry van Eeden had been right. 'Who is he?'

'Makar Kotko. As in "MK".'

'Makar Kotko,' he savoured the foreign name. 'Where does he fit in?'

'Benny, the brigadier and Nyathi are on their way too. The situation is a bit sensitive. I don't want to say too much over the phone . . .'

He wasn't in the mood for 'sensitive'. Not at this time of the morning. He suppressed a sigh and said: 'I'm on my way.'

'*Uyesu*,' said Nyathi.

They stared at the photograph in disbelief, printed out on plain A4 paper. The resolution was not very good. Makar Kotko, just as he appeared in the shooter's photo, but now in the wider context of three other people. Kotko was in the middle, shaking the hand of the man beside him. Two others, on either end, looking on smiling.

Manie just wiped his hand over his brow.

'That's why I called you so early,' said van Wyk.

'It was the right thing,' said Manie. He looked old, the lines on his face cut deep this morning.

'That's the Youth League *ou*?' Griessel asked, and pointed at the man shaking hands with Kotko, because he wasn't entirely sure.

'That's right,' said van Wyk.

'Edwin Baloyi,' said Manie reproachfully.

'Secretary General of the ANC Youth League,' said Nyathi dumbfounded. 'The motor-mouth . . .'

'So who is Kotko?' Manie asked, and then held up his hand. 'No, first explain to me how you got hold of this photo.'

Griessel knew what he meant. It was preparation, so that Manie had an answer ready for his superiors when the circus began.

'Last night we put Sloet's cellphone records from last year into the system,' said van Wyk. 'We began with December, and worked backwards from there, because we reckoned that the months closer to her death were more important. And so they were. In December there were sixteen numbers that did not fit with those we had on record of her family, colleagues, her friends, or her work responsibilities. So we went through them, and compared them to her bank statements and credit card account to clarify matters. Fifteen of them made sense. Estate agents, transfer attorneys, her bank manager, the removals company, the municipal offices, et cetera. But one number, a cellphone, didn't fit in anywhere. Someone who phoned her, on Saturday the eighteenth of December, Monday the twentieth of December, and Wednesday the twenty-second. Benny told us to look specifically at the twenty-second, possibly some Russian person phoning her. This *ou* phoned her three times on the twenty-second. At a quarter to six in the afternoon, the conversation lasted seventeen seconds. Then he phoned again at eight thirty, she did not answer and he left a voice message, and the last one was at ten forty-one, again unanswered, again to voicemail. And when we saw the name, we began to wonder, because it did sound Russian and the initials were MK. And when we Googled him, we came across this photo.' Van Wyk pointed at the printout lying in front of them. 'It's the same one that the shooter sent, except that he cropped it to show only Kotko.'

'Who is he?' Manie asked.

'Brigadier, we only began researching him just after five this morning, so we haven't got much. His full name is Makar Vladovich Kotko. He is a Russian citizen, and a director of ZIC. Zoloto Investment Corporation. It is a South African company – they have very little information on their website, they seem to be consultants. But ZIC is a full affiliate of MZ. That stands for Magadan Zoloto, or Magadan Gold, a Russian mining company.'

'What is he doing in this photo with Baloyi?' Manie asked in a tone of voice that sounded as though he didn't really want to know the answer.

'The photo appeared in August last year in *Hlomelang*, the official Internet newsletter of the Youth League. Kotko visited their offices to make a donation. On behalf of ZIC. Five hundred thousand rand.'

'*Uyesu*,' said Nyathi again.

'That's not all, Brigadier,' said van Wyk. He put another printout down between them – a news report. The headline read *Russian interest in SA mining?* 'This is from *Mining Weekly* of November last year. Apparently Kotko's ZIC is looking into investing in some of our mining companies. And Gariep Minerals is one of them.'

Manie looked at Griessel. 'Gariep is part of the whole BEE set-up?'

'He could have met Sloet through that, Brigadier.'

Brigadier Manie read the news report, then looked at the photo again, for a long time, and poker-faced. 'How do we know the shooter isn't messing around with us again?' he asked at last.

'We don't know. But it looks like Kotko is around fifty years old. He is definitely out of the Russian communist era,' said van Wyk.

'And he knew Sloet well enough to have her cellphone number,' said Griessel. 'She wasn't the sort of woman who would just hand it out.'

'Is Kotko in the Cape?'

'ZIC's offices are in Sandton. According to their website. We have requested Kotko's cellphone records. We will have to see if he was in the Cape at the time of Sloet's death.'

'What worries me,' said Nyathi, 'is why the shooter says the SAPS is protecting Kotko. And then sends us a photo cropped from a Youth League meeting.'

Manie sighed. 'It's a minefield, and we will have to tread extremely carefully. Benny, get hold of Bones. He'll have to come and help.'

'We will have to tell Mbali as well, Brigadier. Because somewhere between the Russian and Sloet, is the shooter.'

The second turning point came at half past six, when van Wyk walked into Griessel's office. His eyes were red from lack of sleep. He put a few sheets of paper on the desk and said, 'Kotko may have connections with the Russian Mafia.'

'Faux pas,' said Griessel and scribbled frantic notes in his book.

'It's in here,' said van Wyk, and tapped the printouts. 'Magadan Gold belongs to Arseny Egorov. Egorov is what

they call an oligarch, a billionaire who made his money after
the fall of communism. No one really knows how he got his
start, but later he bought a media company, and then mining
and oil. Last year he left Russia, as Putin's people were investigating him for "irregularities". He lives in England now, but
there are quite a few stories in the *Wall Street Journal* and
Fortune about his connections with the Solntsevo Brotherhood.
And that is organised crime. Dangerous *okes* . . .'

Griessel said, 'We must take it to Oom Skip.' 'Uncle' or
rather, Colonel Skip Scheepers of the Hawks' Organised
Crime Group was past his retirement age, but the DPCI had
asked him to stay on because of his encyclopaedic knowledge
of international gangs.

'I've phoned Oom Skip already. He and Bones are going
to look at all this.'

The third turning point was eleven minutes later.

Colonel Zola Nyathi, with a severe expression and a curt,
'Please come with me', fetched Griessel and walked to
Brigadier Manie's office.

When they walked in, General Afrika looked up from
where he was sitting. Griessel could see the aversion and
disappointment, as though Afrika did not want him there.
The first thought that came to mind, considering Nyathi and
Afrika's attitudes, was that they had found out that he had
misused the IMC system to spy on the Neanderthal. His
heart sank.

'Benny,' Afrika greeted him dourly.

Nyathi closed the door behind them. Brigadier Manie
said: 'Take a seat.'

Griessel greeted them, and tried to think up some excuses.
He and Nyathi took their seats, on either side of Afrika.

'General, please repeat what you told me and Colonel
Nyathi,' said Manie.

It was a while before Afrika responded. With his eyes on the floor he said, 'I know Kotko.'

Those words were not what he had expected. Griessel nearly blurted out, 'Excuse me?'

Afrika made a small gesture with his hand. 'I want it on record that I had no idea that Kotko had any contact with Sloet. I want it on record that I did not know he is the communist that the shooter was referring to. And I want it on record that I shared this information voluntarily.'

'Very well, General. Please tell us how you came to know Kotko.'

Emotions came and went across John Afrika's face. 'People make mistakes, Musad,' he said. 'We all make mistakes . . .'

42

Afrika put a hand in his jacket and took out a folded sheet of paper. He unfolded it, looked at it, took a deep breath, and said seriously, as though he were testifying in court, 'On the morning of Thursday twenty-third September last year I received a call from a member of the Ministerial Committee. That person—'

'The Ministerial Committee for Police?'

'Yes. That person asked me to be of assistance with a request from a Mr Kotko—'

'Who is this person, General?'

'Musad, I am not going to tell you now.'

Manie just sat there, frozen and without emotion.

'The person asked me to help with a request from this Kotko, who was entirely unknown to me at the time. Shortly thereafter I received a call from Kotko, who invited me to lunch with him that afternoon. I did so. Kotko told me how many of the people in government he knew from the struggle days. And that he was a businessman now living in Johannesburg, and investing in the economy. Then he asked me to help two of his friends. These two . . .' Afrika consulted the paper in his hand ' . . . were Fedor Vazov and Lev Grigoryev, who had been arrested the previous night, September twenty-second, by the Table View station after a complaint of assault in a nightclub. They were still being detained. Kotko said he believed the whole affair was a misunderstanding, one of those things where everyone involved has had a little too much to drink. And he and the member of the Ministerial Committee would appreciate it very much if I could solve the problem. After the meal I phoned the station. The SC confirmed that it was a bar brawl, and that it would be difficult to make a case against the suspects. I asked him to release them, and drop the charges. It was done.'

'That's all, General?' Nyathi asked, with relief audible in his voice.

Afrika shook his head slowly. 'No, Zola, that is not all.' He consulted his notes again. 'On the twenty-ninth of September last year I drew money from an ATM in Long Street. I noticed that the balance in my cheque account was larger than I expected. I went into the bank and requested a statement. I saw that on the twenty-seventh there had been a deposit of twenty-five thousand rand. I enquired about the origin of the money, and the bank informed me it came from the Isando Friendship Trust. I said that must be a mistake, and told the bank I have to contact the Trust. But I could not track them down.'

Afrika slowly folded up the paper. 'I phoned Kotko, because I suspected he might be behind the money. He said it was just to say thank you. For my help. So I said, I can't accept it, he must please arrange to reverse the payment, or he must give me the bank account number of the Trust so I

could pay it back. He just laughed and said he didn't know if
that could be done, he would have to find out. He never came
back to me.'

Silence descended. Outside, a pigeon fluttered at the
window, and then perched on the windowsill.

Nyathi sighed deeply. 'Do you know what *isando* means,
General?'

'No, Zola.'

'It means "hammer" in Xhosa. And Zulu.'

'I see.'

'General, you had no idea that Kotko was the communist
to whom the shooter was referring?'

'No. Not at all.'

'I have to ask, when you brought the Sloet case to us, and
the emails, why did you specifically ask for Benny and Mbali
to work on the investigations?'

'Because I know how brilliant they are.'

'It's not because you recommended Benny to us in
December? And you thought he owed you?'

'Look, Zola, I understand that you have to ask these questions, but I'm telling you that it is not true.'

'And you are the only one who knows what happened to
Mbali in Amsterdam? You got her on the Dutch training
programme when she was still working at Bellville, and the
Dutch reported back to you.'

Afrika threw his hands in the air. 'I know what it looks like.
But I am telling you now, that is not how it is.' For the first
time he looked at Griessel. 'Benny, you know me . . . Musad,
you and I have come a long way together. You know I wouldn't
do something like that. Tell them.'

Manie folded his large hands. 'General, how does a white
conservative Afrikaner know about your connection to
Kotko?'

'I don't have a connection to Kotko.'

'General, how does he know?'

'*I* don't know. I mean, we ate together at Balduccis. The world walks past that restaurant. And I wouldn't know who the SC at Table View spoke to.'

Manie nodded thoughtfully. 'Has there been any contact between you and Kotko since the shooter began sending emails?'

'Since September, I never had any contact with him again.' In a heavy tone.

'Does the person on the Ministerial Committee know about the shooter's emails?'

'No.'

'What will happen if we arrest Kotko?'

Afrika looked at the pigeon on the windowsill, and shook his head. 'God, Musad, it will be a mess. He's got connections . . .'

'Think for a moment about the mess we're in now, General. If we arrest him, it will be a sea of politics and drama. And another media circus, because the whole world will be able to see that photo of him and Baloyi. If we don't do it before four o'clock, the mad devil will shoot another of our people tonight.'

When the general had gone, Manie sent for Mbali and told her the news.

'*Hayi,*' she whispered in disbelief and disappointment.

'*Ewe,*' said Nyathi and put his hand on her shoulder.

'Whether we like it or not, we are working against time,' said Manie. 'Benny, you'll have to fly up to Gauteng, I'll get Mavis to see how soon we can get you on a flight, but I think you'd better pack a bag in the meantime. I will talk to the DPCI in Johannesburg, so they can track Kotko down and watch him. Vaughn can coordinate this side, we need more ammunition when you interrogate him, those phone calls in December are not enough.'

'All right, Brigadier.'

'Mbali, everything points at the shooter knowing about John Afrika and Kotko's doings, that's our best chance to catch him. You and Vaughn must liaise closely, because the two cases are running together now. But begin at Table View station. Look at people who were there in September last year, who were dishonourably discharged, or under investigation.'

She nodded dutifully.

The brigadier checked his watch. 'We have to get a press release out about Kotko by two, half past two, so it can get on the radio and Internet. There won't be a policeman shot today.'

When Griessel had brought Cupido up to speed, he said: 'Vaughn, my cellphone doesn't have a speaker. Can you phone Hannes Pruis so we can both hear what he says?'

'No problem. Do you have the number?'

Griessel gave it to him.

Cupido phoned, turned the phone around and put it upside down on his desk. The ring was clearly audible.

'Will he be able to hear you talk?'

'Easy.'

'Hello?' the lawyer answered irritably, probably because it was just after seven in the morning.

'Mr Pruis, this is Benny Griessel of the Hawks . . .'

'Yes, Captain,' he said without enthusiasm.

'We are eager to hear more about Silberstein's connection with a Mr Makar Kotko of ZIC . . .'

The silence on the line confirmed Griessel's suspicions.

'Mr Pruis, you know who I am talking about?'

'I . . . the name sounds familiar . . .'

'Mr Pruis, you will have to come and explain to us why you withheld information about Kotko and his relationship with Hanneke Sloet.'

'I withheld nothing, Captain. How could I have known he was relevant?' But Pruis was on the defensive.

'With all your research, you must have known Kotko was involved in organised crime?'

Pruis did not answer.

'You have forty minutes to present yourself at our offices,' said Griessel. 'Or I will bring a warrant, and the entire team of the Hawks' Organised Crime group.'

Griessel and Cupido stood staring down at the upside-down cellphone. Pruis took some time to answer, 'What is your address?'

'We are in the book. Ask for Captain Vaughn Cupido when you arrive.' Then he indicated to Cupido to end the call.

Cupido grinned, picked up the phone and turned it off.

'You give him hell, Vaughn. He knew, from the beginning, and he didn't say a word.'

'I can't give him the Cupido treatment if Mbali is here, Benna.'

Griessel understood. 'Then only get her in after you've got the fucker to talk.'

43

At half past eight he drove to his flat to pack his bag. The traffic on the N1 to the city was dense and slow-moving.

He thought about John Afrika. He had felt sorry for him back in Manie's office. Afrika had only ever been good to him. Direct. Fair. Afrika had believed in him when the rest of the SAPS had written him off as a drunkard. Afrika and Mat Joubert. And Mat had left the Service.

The thing was, he didn't know if he could blame Afrika. What do you do if a member of parliament calls you up and says, 'Help out a little'? You are coloured, but still not black enough for affirmative action, you have a wife and children, a mortgage on your house. You are in your fifties, with maybe five, six years of service to go, you hope for one last promotion to give your pension a bit of a leg-up . . .

Afrika had tried to return the money. And the Russians' drunk-and-disorderly charge was a mere trifle.

What would he have done if someone had paid twenty-five thousand into his account, and it was one helluva administrative headache to get it paid back? While Carla's student fees, and Fritz's school fees, and Anna's maintenance, and his new expensive clothes all had to be paid for? How long and how hard would he keep on trying to reverse the payment?

Had Afrika told the whole truth? And what had Manie and Nyathi expected, as early as Saturday night, when the Giraffe came into his office and said, 'You find any monkey business anywhere, you come to us . . .'? On Sunday at Greenmarket Square, Mbali had asked him why they had put *her* on the shooter case. Everyone had had their suspicions, except him.

The Hawks was another world. And he still stood half in and half out of it.

What else were they going to dredge up? Who was the person on the ministerial committee that Afrika was protecting?

This was his first sample of big politics, his first taste of being caught in the crossfire.

This country wasn't simple.

Let him stick to his case. Henry van Eeden's words, 'Then I asked if everything was OK, and she said, yes, just an annoying Russian.'

And Sloet's friend, Sam Grobler, 'All men have a thing for Hanneke.' And Griessel could understand that, if you looked at the photos, the smouldering sensuality.

Makar Kotko had met Sloet somewhere. And he had

lusted for her, and he had phoned her. Over and over. But he was not what she wanted. She had said 'no'.

Or had she? If he thought about the vibrator, the pornographic movies, Roch telling him about her desires: if she knew about Kotko's links to organised crime, if she liked the risk . . .

No. If you compared the middle-aged Russian with his little teeth and the slicked-back hair with Egan Roch. It couldn't be.

If she said 'no' to Kotko, was that a motive for murder?

Would she have opened the door for him?

That was the big question.

Maybe. If he was of economic value to her. Or to Silberstein Lamarque.

In Roeland Street his reverie was interrupted when Nyathi phoned.

'Benny, we're sending Bones with you to Jo'burg.'

He understood immediately. It was better like that. In the circumstances, a black detective was much more politically correct.

His dress options were limited. He hadn't done laundry since last week, thanks to the investigation, and sleeping over at Alexa's. His entire life was in disarray. And for how many days should he pack?

He took out his battered case. He hated the thing, too many bad memories – it was the one he had carried when Anna had kicked him out of the house back then. It was distressing that he could fit his life into a suitcase so easily. It had been the darkest of times: the withdrawal symptoms after more than a decade of drinking. Homeless, rudderless, hopeless, alone.

But not irretrievably lost.

And look at him now. Still standing.

He packed all his clean clothes. Pulled on his new jacket, so that he wouldn't embarrass his Cape colleagues when he was in Gauteng.

Then he phoned Alexa to tell her.

'What's your problem?' Cupido asked Hannes Pruis.

They sat in the smallest DPCI office that Cupido could find, in battered chairs. Pruis sat with his back to the door, Cupido only half a metre away, his face as close as possible to the lawyer.

'My problem?' Pruis asked indignantly, but the arrogance of yesterday was gone. The man was tense.

'Yes. Your problem. Captain Griessel asked you about the communists. Yesterday I asked again, you and your lawyer buddies, but you knew nothing. Must have thought we're a bunch of fuckin' nitwit cops, who would never find out about Kotko.'

'It really isn't necessary to swear.'

'So now you decide what's necessary? You, who lie without blinking an eye, while it's one of your people who gets nailed with a *moerse* iron blade? Where's your morality? Where's your conscience? Or do you trade it in when you get your lawyering licence?'

'Kotko is not a communist.'

'That's your defence? The best you can do?'

Pruis moved his hands helplessly. 'But he *isn't*. He's a businessman. A capitalist . . .'

'You are pretty pathetic. Where did they meet, Kotko and Sloet?'

'In Johannesburg.'

'When?'

'Friday seventeenth December.'

'Go on.'

'Hanneke and I attended an Ingcebo meeting in

Johannesburg. There was a cocktail party afterwards, in the
Radisson Blu in Sandton.'

'That's a hotel?'

'Yes.'

'Who all was there?'

'People from all the parties involved. Ingcebo, Gariep, SA
Merchant Bank, the other legal firms . . .'

'And then?'

'Kotko was also there. With a few politicians.'

'Which politicians?'

'Youth League people. Edwin Baloyi. A few others.'

'And then?'

'Then Kotko saw Hanneke. He came and talked to her,
and—'

'Why?'

Pruis shrugged. 'Why do you think? Hanneke was an
attractive woman.'

'So he wanted to chat her up?'

'That's how it looked.'

'Where were you?'

'I was standing beside Hanneke.'

'And then?'

'When he heard what she did, he said he wanted to buy a
share in Gariep on behalf of a client, and whether we would
be interested in handling the contract.'

'And you obviously said: Yes, please.'

'It's what we do, Captain. We handle contracts.'

'Who was his client?'

'Magadan Zoloto. The Russian mining house.'

'When did you find out Kotko was Russian?'

'That evening.'

'In Johannesburg.'

'Sandton.'

'Now there's a difference?'

Pruis did not react.

'And when did you discover he's organised crime?'

'According to our due diligence ZIC was clean.'

'And Magadan?'

'The allegations against Mr Arseny Egorov are just that. Allegations.'

'Oh. So it's *mister* Egorov. When did you hear about the *allegations* about him.'

'On Monday.'

'What Monday?'

'The twentieth of December.'

'Did Hanneke Sloet tell you Kotko phoned her that Saturday?'

'Yes.'

'And on the Monday?'

'Yes.'

'What did he say to her?'

'He told her he was coming to Cape Town, he wanted to take her out to dinner.'

'And what did she say?'

'She said her schedule was full. She was packing. For the move. And for Christmas with her parents.'

'She told you all that?'

'Yes. She suspected Kotko's interest was . . . not necessarily business driven.'

'*Business driven*. Fuck sakes. And then?'

'Then we invited him to our offices. On Wednesday the twenty-second of December.'

'What time?'

'In the morning. Ten to twelve.'

'Despite the fact that you already knew about the organised crime connections?'

Pruis nodded slightly.

'And he came?'

'Yes.'

'What happened?'

'He gave us a brief to represent ZIC in obtaining a share in Gariep Minerals. We accepted the brief and discussed the cost structure.'

'And how much was in it for you?'

Pruis looked away.

'How much?'

'Fifteen.' Reluctant.

'Million?'

'Yes.'

'Sweet Jesus. Did you know he phoned her three times that afternoon and evening?'

'Yes.'

'The man was basically stalking her.'

'Yes.'

'And yet you never thought of telling us? Because you're still working on the Kotko contract, and that's fifteen million in your pockets, and you would rather let a murderer walk free than lose one fucking cent. You disgust me, you know that? Was Kotko in the Cape the day of Sloet's death? The eighteenth of January?'

Pruis's lips grew thin. He looked away.

Cupido knew what the answer would be.

44

Cupido closed the door of the small office behind him and phoned Griessel.

'Where you, Benna?'

'On the N1. I'll be there in ten minutes.'

'Kotko was in the Cape on the eighteenth, the day she died. He had a meeting with Silbersteins and Sloet, just before lunch. Cause they had to discuss his contract. But he had the hots for her, big time.'

'*Jissis*,' said Griessel.

'He's our man, Benna.'

'But what was his motive?'

'Again, I think it's rejection, Benna. She wouldn't *njaps* him.'

'What about the weapon that he put down on the floor? What did he want to take from her? Yesterday you asked, what did she have?'

'Maybe he just wanted to check if she was dead . . .'

'We're going to need more than that in the circumstances.'

'True. OK. Leave it to Beaver. Pop in when you get here.'

Cupido put the phone away and opened the door again. Pruis was standing with his cellphone, busy typing an SMS.

'What are you doing?'

'I'm letting my colleagues know where I am.'

'If I catch you letting slip one fucking word about this investigation, I'll fucking lock you up.'

'Do you want to read it?' He held the phone up so Cupido could see.

At the Hawks. Cancel everything for today.

'OK.'

Pruis sent the SMS.

Cupido said, 'Why did he kill her?'

'Why do you think it was *him*?'

'Because a lot of things fit. What did she have on him?'

'What do you mean?'

'You said you found out he was organised crime. Did you, like, use it as leverage? A bigger slice of the pie?'

'No. We don't do that.'

'*Ja*, sure.'

'We don't do that.'

'So why did he kill her?'

'I don't know.' But Cupido wasn't convinced.

'I'm telling you, I'm going to get a court order for that due diligence, and if I find something there that you haven't shared, I swear, we'll prosecute you for obstruction, I'll fucking destroy you.'

Pruis sat down, but the eyes flicked between table and wall. He said nothing.

Cupido took out his phone. 'OK. If that's the way you want to play it.'

He phoned.

'Wait,' said Pruis.

'What?'

'The due diligence didn't reveal much.'

'But?'

'We were . . . wary. So we asked Hanneke to investigate further.'

'And?'

'She hired a private company to look into Kotko, in January . . . Jack Fischer and Associates.'

'Those pricks? And then?'

'They found out he was KGB.'

'Kotko?'

'Yes.'

'Like in Russian Secret Service? That KGB?'

'Yes. He was head of the KGB's Africa bureau. In the eighties. Before the Wall came down.'

'*Jissis.*'

'That's how he got to know so many of our government people. And then he became Arseny Egorov's security. In the nineties.'

'His enforcer.'

'Something like that.'

'And that's it?'

'No.'

'So talk to me.'

'Apparently he liked to torture people. Back then.'

'Torture?'

'That's right. When he interrogated them.'

'How?'

'With a bayonet. In the anus.'

In Brigadier Manie's office Cupido brought them up to date with the latest information.

For the first time since the investigation had begun, Griessel felt the old stirring, his instinct kicking in. This was the one.

'The lawyer said Sloet knew about the KGB background,' said Cupido. 'He said Sloet did the investigation, she got the report from Jack Fischer and Associates. But he couldn't see why Sloet would want to blackmail Kotko with this. She was the kingpin of the whole contract, Kotko gave his business to Silbersteins because he fancied her so much.'

'In any case that is all circumstantial evidence,' said Manie. 'There is nothing that can be used in court.'

'Jack Fischer and Associates must have got the information about the bayonet from a source, Brigadier,' said Griessel. 'We will have to find out who that was.'

'Jack Fischer is not a friend of the SAPS any more,' said Manie dubiously.

'There are other ways too,' said Griessel. 'If Kotko likes blades, somewhere in Johannesburg there will be someone who knows. He will have a pattern.'

'You will have to put him through the grinder, Benny,' said Nyathi.

'Yes, sir.'

Manie was still sceptical. 'He was KGB. He won't be scared of questioning. And he has connections. We will have to place him at the murder scene. Forensically.'

They all knew they had nothing at the moment that would do that.

'Do we have enough for a search warrant?' Nyathi asked. 'For his house and his office?'

'Not yet,' said Manie. 'Let's see what happens in the next few hours. Which brings us to the shooter. Werner, how many people do you have available?'

'Half of the team is at Table View, Brigadier,' said du Preez.

'I have a feeling . . .' said Manie. 'There are a bunch of old detectives at Jack Fischer and Associates. Perhaps with a grudge against the SAPS. They investigated Kotko, they could have come across proof of the payment to John Afrika. Get a personnel list for Fischer's and give it to IMC, let them cross reference to triple-two rifle owners, Kia vans. Anything.'

'I want IMC to look at Fischer's Internet records. It would have logged if someone used an anonimail account. And I will go talk to Jack Fischer, after I've questioned Pruis,' said Mbali, the light of battle in her eyes.

'I think we should send Oom Skip Scheepers,' said Manie.

'Why, sir?' she asked indignantly.

'Because Jack Fischer is ex-SAPS. And he was Jack Fischer's commanding officer, years ago. We will have to use honey, Mbali. We're working against the clock, we don't have time for vinegar.'

She nodded, but she wasn't happy.

'Brigadier, I want to book Pruis. For obstruction,' said Cupido.

'Give him more rope,' said Manie. 'It's better to use it as leverage. For now.'

'We have to go, Brigadier,' said Griessel. 'Our flight is at ten o'clock.'

Manie nodded. 'I'll talk to the *manne* up there in the meantime, Benny, to get the timing of this thing right. It's going to take some fancy footwork. Hopefully we will have something on the table when you get there. But good luck. And good hunting.'

Mbali and du Preez asked Hannes Pruis to accompany them to the CATS interrogation room. It was cold as they walked down the corridors, but Pruis took his jacket off. There were sweat stains under his arms and down his back.

They sat down. Pruis asked for water. Mbali fetched a carafe and a glass. Pruis drank deeply, wiped the sweat from his brow and said he realised it looked as if he had been protecting Kotko. But he wanted to make it clear that before this morning, and Captain Griessel's phone call, he hadn't made the connection between Kotko and communism. It was twenty years since the end of communism in Russia. Twenty years. If they had asked him about a Russian it would have been a different matter . . . And he had never, but never, connected Kotko to Hanneke Sloet's murder. There was just no way, no motive, that made sense to him . . .

'But you knew about the bayonet?' Mbali asked in total disbelief.

'But Hanneke was never tortured . . . I swear, it never crossed my mind.'

'*Hayi*,' said Mbali, her disgust at the man obvious.

Du Preez pointed at the video camera beside the table. 'We are going to record the interview, Mr Pruis.'

The lawyer nodded.

Du Preez switched on the camera, and nodded at Mbali.

She asked, 'Did you know about Makar Kotko's ties to senior members of the South African Police Services?'

Pruis's eyes widened slightly. 'No.'

'Are you absolutely sure?'

'Yes. We knew he was connected to people in government. And the Youth League.'

'But no SAPS people?'

'No.'

'You had Sloet contract Jack Fischer and Associates to investigate Kotko?'

'Yes.'

'Do you have the Fischer report?'

'Yes. In my office.'

'Will you make it available to us?'

He hesitated for only a moment. 'Yes.'

'And there is nothing in the report about a SAPS member?'

'Not that I know of.'

'Did you do any other research, or have any other research done on Kotko?'

'We did due diligence on ZIC. His company.'

'And you found nothing about any SAPS members?'

'No.'

'Do you know about the trust Kotko controls?'

'What trust?'

'The Isando Friendship Trust.'

Pruis shook his head. 'I've never heard of it.'

'Are you absolutely sure?'

'Yes.'

'Who knew about Kotko's interest in Sloet?'

'How would I know how many people she told?'

'Who at your law firm knew about it?'

'The romantic interest?'

'Yes.'

'Just me. It's not the sort of thing Hanneke or I wanted to advertise.'

'On the eighteenth of January you and Sloet had a meeting with Kotko at your offices?'

'Yes.'

'Did you indicate to Kotko in any way that you knew about his KGB background?'

'No, of course not.'

'And his history with bayonets?'

'No.'

'Was there any way Kotko could have known about the Fischer investigation?'

'We pay them to be discreet.'

'Could he have known?'

'I don't really think so.'

'But it's not impossible?'

'Nothing is impossible. It's just very unlikely.'

'Mr Pruis,' said du Preez, 'if another member of the SAPS is shot today, and we find any evidence that you have not told us the whole truth, I will make it my personal number-one priority to criminally prosecute you. In any way I can think of. Do you understand?'

'Yes.'

'Is there anything else you would like to say to us?'

'I'm sorry. But I'm telling you, there is nothing else.'

Mbali stood up. 'We'd better share all of this with Benny,' she said.

45

After take-off, Bones looked at Griessel's hands, clamped tightly to the armrests. 'You OK, Benny?'

'I don't like flying.'

'It's safer than driving, *nè*.'

'They fall, Bones. Every now and then.'

Boshigo laughed.

Later, as they enjoyed the light meal with the gusto of detectives who'd had no time for breakfast, he said, 'You know I'm just window dressing on this trip? The black face to appease the gods . . .'

Griessel's mouth was full of food. He could only shrug.

'So, what do you say about all this stuff, Benny? The politics, the intimations of corruption . . .'

He finished chewing before answering, 'What can you say, Bones? That's how it is. And it's not new. When I was with Murder and Robbery, in the old days . . . The things we had to do. For politics. Cover-ups. Look the other way. Those days you never saw any of it in the papers. They got away with a lot more.'

'Nothing changes,' said Boshigo thoughtfully.

When the air hostess had removed their empty plates and plastic cutlery, Bones said, 'Last night, when you phoned, I was watching a movie. *In the Shadow of the Moon,* a documentary about the astronauts who went up there. And at the end of the movie one of the astronauts, when they were in the shadow of the moon, he looked at the earth and he said, it's so small and fragile. But everyone he knew was there, *nè*. And after they came back down, they went on this world tour, and in every land the people said to them, "We did it." Not, "You Americans did it." No. "We did it." I got all emotional, *nè*. I grew up in Fort Beaufort. When I was *this* tall, my father took me outside one night, he showed me the moon. He said Benedict, people have walked on that. Why? Because they dreamed, *nè*. He said, you must go into this world, *ukuphupha,* with a dream. And you must follow that dream, until you catch it. This morning when I heard about all the shenanigans, I thought, what is happening to us? Madiba had this dream, Benny. The Big Ukuphupha for South Africa. But we are losing that dream now. I sat there last night, missing my father, *nè*, he died in two thousand and five, and I thought, why can't we be "we" again? In this country. In the whole world. Because we are all on this one small planet.'

'According to Kotko's credit card, on the night of the eighteenth of January he paid for two rooms at the Southern Sun Cullinan Hotel in the Strand area,' said Captain Philip van Wyk.

'Two?' asked Manie.

'That's right, Brigadier. We're waiting to hear from the hotel who signed in. But there were two more payments on the card. One was for dinner, an amount of 1,232.45 rand at the Buena Vista Social Café in the Waterfront. The other one was for 3,000 rand to Midnite Moves.'

'The escort agency?' Cupido asked.

'Yes,' said van Wyk. 'His cellphone records show that he phoned Midnite Moves at 18.32 and 18.51. I thought you would want to know that.'

'Thanks, Philip,' said Manie.

'Sounds like a man setting up an alibi,' said Cupido.

'Exactly,' said Brigadier Manie. 'You'll have to go and find out, Vaughn.'

Griessel stared out at the expanse of the Karoo shifting past below them, and he wondered why he never thought about such things? Dreams for a country. And a planet that was *one*. Deep stuff.

Like Alexa and her 'people's dramatic images and conduits'. Trouble was, if he wasn't scurrying around with case files, he was thinking of his bank balance and his drinking problem and his divorce, about Carla's boyfriend and Fritz's tattoo. And how not to make a fool of himself. If he dreamed, it was about sex. With Alexa.

How did you get your head past all that and start worrying about the planet?

Mbali was on the point of walking out of the women's toilet on the second floor of the DPCI building when two Hawks detectives walked past.

'Now you know why Afrika got her to be JOC on the shooter,' she heard one say.

'Because of Amsterdam?' asked the other.

'That's right.'

It burned through her.

In her office her phone rang. She answered. It was a member of the Hawks' Crime Against the State group (CATS) saying there were no suspects who had worked in Table View station in September and had since been discharged. And the station commander assured them that he had not discussed General Afrika's phone call, about releasing the two Russian citizens, with a single soul.

She did what she always did when she was upset. She got up from behind her painfully neat desk, picked up her big black handbag and slung it over her shoulder. She closed the office door behind her, walked to the lift, and took it down to the ground floor. She walked out of the front door, up Market Street, to Voortrekker. At the traffic lights she waited until she could cross, and then turned left, past the entrance to Home Affairs, where passport photo salesmen and hawkers of pens and ID-book covers hustled. Past the Tote. Today she didn't look with repugnance at the good-for-nothings hanging about there. Past K's Hair Design and into Catch of the Day.

The little grey-haired woman greeted her. 'The usual?' she asked Mbali.

'Yes, please.'

She watched the woman scoop up the chips with a little steel shovel and slide them into the white paper bag until it was full, the salt and vinegar sprinkled over, the whole package wrapped up in a sheet of brown paper. She put it down beside the cash register.

'You should eet feesh.'

'Maybe next time.'

'One medium chips. One Coke. Twenty-six seventy-five.'

Mbali had the cash ready. She handed it over, took the chips and can of cold drink and put them carefully in her handbag. So her colleagues would not see them.

'Thank you.'

'See you tomorrow. Catch the bad people.'

'Bye.' She walked out. Only then, with her source of comfort safely in her handbag, did she think about the worry and the tension.

That was what everyone thought: John Afrika had requested that she lead the case because he thought he could manipulate her.

It was a triple blow. She wasn't making any progress. The allocation of the case hadn't been on merit. And Afrika had believed he could control her with his knowledge of the Amsterdam fiasco – the biggest, most horrible humiliation of her life. Which had only happened because she hadn't wanted to let her country down.

Her discomfort and the suspicions of Sunday were now confirmed.

What was she going to do?

Back in her office she shut the door, sat down, took out the Coke and chips and put them on the desk.

She unwrapped the paper. The aroma was strong.

She pulled the first chip out with her fingers, and put it in her mouth.

She would show John Afrika. And all the others, like Vaughn Cupido and his hangers-on, the ones who gossiped and sniggered and made insinuations about her fastidiousness, her figure, her sexual orientation. Musad Manie, who did not want to send her 'vinegar' to Jack Fischer. She would show them, she would catch this shooter. On her own. In her own slow, thorough, by-the-book way, which she knew irritated her colleagues immensely.

She ate all the chips, solemnly, one by one. Before they got cold. She crumpled up the bag and the wrapping and went and disposed of them in the rubbish bin in the women's toilet. Otherwise they left a smell in her office and they gossiped about that too.

She washed her hands.

She walked back, sat down at her laptop and opened a new Word file on the computer. She began to type.

- *The shooter knows about Kotko's payment to Afrika.*
- *Afrika's bank? (Where does the Isando Friendship Trust bank?)*
- *The shooter had to know Kotko is behind the Isando Friendship Trust.*
- *Who runs the trust?*
- *How does it work?*
- *The shooter knows that Kotko knew Sloet.*
- *Did Kotko tell a white, Afrikaans, middle-aged man? (Unlikely.)*
- *Who did Sloet tell? (Ask Benny.)*
- *The shooter must have known Sloet.*
- *The shooter cares so much about justice in the Sloet case that he is willing to shoot officers of the law. Why? Family? (Ask Benny.)*

She saved the document. Unlocked the drawer, and took out a chocolate bar.

At a quarter past twelve Captain Moses Zondi of the Hawks in Johannesburg was waiting for them in the arrivals hall. He was a big man with a short scar from a knife wound on his neck. He and Boshigo greeted each other like old friends.

Outside Benny lit up a cigarette.

'That stuff will kill you,' said the fit Boshigo.

As they walked to the car, Moses Zondi said, 'Kotko is at his office in Sandton. We have full surveillance, and the Task Team, standing by. If he moves, we will know. We have another team outside his house in Magaliesview, near Montecasino in Fourways. The moment we have the search warrant, we'll go in. Task team, Forensics, the works.'

'You have the right address this time, bro'?' Bones Boshigo asked. Nearly a year ago the Hawks in Gauteng had raided the wrong address when they had wanted to arrest the fugitive Radovan Krejcir for fraud. Since then they'd had to endure much mockery from their colleagues.

'Not funny,' said Zondi. Then he hit back, 'There's this rumour about the Slaapstad Hawks doing something really stupid in Amsterdam. What happened?'

'The boss isn't talking.'

'Which reminds me, you have to call your CO, right away.'

'Not me,' said Boshigo. 'Benny is running this one. I'm just the pretty black face, *nè*.'

Griessel drew deeply on his cigarette, held it between his lips and took out his cellphone. He phoned Manie.

'First the good news, Benny,' the brigadier said. 'Skip Scheepers got the name of Jack Fischer's source from them half an hour ago, the one who knew about Kotko and bayonets in his KGB days. The source is a member of the Executive Committee of COPE, the opposition party. In the nineties he was still with the ANC's Intelligence wing, he got to know Kotko in Lusaka. Colonel Nyathi talked to the source, and he is prepared to go on record. I think the source is playing politics, but now it's in our favour.

'The second thing is, Fischer and Associates' research says Kotko and his ZIC company made investments to launder money for his boss, Arseny Egorov. They say if we dig deep enough, there's enough evidence to prosecute him. And the third thing: Kotko was in Cape Town on the night of Sloet's murder. His credit card records confirm that. And we plotted his cellphone records for January. He made four calls, which all registered at the Dock Road tower at the Waterfront.'

That was only a few blocks away from Sloet's apartment building, and Griessel suppressed his '*jissis*'.

'Were any of the calls to Sloet, Brigadier?'

'No. But two were to an escort agency. We're finding out now how long the girls were with him. All that gives us enough for a search warrant, Benny. The guys in Gauteng put in the request, we should know within the next fifteen minutes. But now the bad news: if we want to get anything on the radio by four o'clock, we will have to make some big decisions by three . . .'

Very little time.

'First prize would be an announcement that we have arrested Kotko,' said Manie. 'But you will have to be absolutely certain that it's a watertight case. All hell is going to break loose, Benny. This guy has connections. We're talking about people in government, Ministerial Committee, the Youth League. We're talking about immense pressure, we're talking about weeks of media hysteria. All our jobs are on the line. Mine, yours, the commanding officer up there. Do you understand that?'

'Yes, Brigadier.' They had reached Moses Zondi's Hawks vehicle, a silver BMW 3-series sedan.

'Second prize is we leak that he is being detained for questioning. I don't know whether that would be enough to placate the shooter, but we will have to try. The same drama, the same political implications, so we will have to decide what the odds are.'

'Yes, Brigadier.' Zondi took Griessel's case, put it in the boot of the BMW, motioned him to get in. Griessel got in the back.

'The plan works like *this*,' said Manie over the phone. 'You go directly to Kotko's offices. As far as we know it is just him and a secretary. You begin questioning him straight away, the DPCI team will make sure the secretary does not phone anyone, or mess with her computer or any documentation.'

'Buckle up,' said Moses Zondi, and stuck a blue light on the front windscreen. Griessel pinched the cellphone against his ear and clipped on the seat belt.

'The minute the search warrant is issued,' said Manie, 'we'll send our teams to search his office and house. The team leaders will talk to Bones, so that you are not interrupted.'

'Right, Brigadier.'

Zondi pulled away, tyres squealing.

'Bones will inform you if they find anything that might influence your decision.'

'I'll tell him, Brigadier.'

'Phone me by ten to three, Benny. At the latest. And then tell me what we're going to do.'

They drove out of the O.R. Tambo airport building into the Gauteng summer sunshine, blindingly bright. Zondi put on a pair of dark glasses and turned on the siren.

46

Twenty-six minutes to one.

The traffic opened up to the wailing siren. Griessel had to talk loudly above the racket. He told Boshigo what Brigadier Manie had told him.

'It's like old times,' said Bones.

'When you worked with Vusi?' asked Zondi, and winked at Benny in the mirror.

'Exactly,' said Boshigo, deadly serious.

Cupido got three patrol vehicles from Caledon Square station to help. Because he didn't have a search warrant, he would have to rely on effect. And attitude.

They stopped with screeching tyres in front of the old white-washed one-storey building in Bree Street. Everyone jumped out, ran up to the black-painted security gate. Just to the right of it, on the wall, was an advertisement board, *Midnite Moves Private Club,* with the silhouette of a howling wolf's head outlined against a yellow full moon. Cupido rattled the steel bars of the door. It was locked. He looked into the gloom inside. Someone moved against a backdrop of booze bottles. 'SAPS,' he shouted. 'Open up.'

It took a moment before a buzzer sounded and the lock sprang open.

Cupido walked in alone.

Muted lighting, cheap red carpet and cream-coloured couches, a pine wood bar against the furthermost wall. Behind it stood a skinny, sallow man with a cigarette between his fingers, and a thin black moustache that he smoothed nervously with an index finger. His eyes flickered uneasily from Cupido to the uniforms outside.

Cupido took his identity card out of his pocket, smacked it down on the bar counter and said: 'Read it and weep.'

The man leaned forward warily and read.

'What's your name?' Cupido asked.

'Affonso?' he said with a peculiar doubtfulness, his narrow shoulders bowed.

'Affonso who?'

'Affonso Britos?'

'Are you asking me, or telling me?'

'I'm telling you?'

Cupido looked sharply at the man. He suspected it was nerves that were causing the question marks. 'Captain Vaughn Cupido. Do you know the Directorate of Priority Crimes Investigations, Affonso Britos?'

'Sorry. I'm not sure.' He sounded respectfully apologetic.

'The Hawks.'

'OK. I know the Hawks.'

'Great stuff, Affonso. What do you know about the Hawks?'

'They are scary?'

'That's the right answer. We are mean motherfuckers, Affonso. We can shut down your little whorehouse in five minutes flat, do you understand?'

'It's a private club?' said Britos with cautious objection.

'Now you're losing me. We don't want verbal gymnastics.'

'OK?'

'I can ask you for your liquor licence, Affonso. I can let those men out there come and check for fire safety violations. I can hit you with the whole Sexual Offences Act 23, if I had the inclination . . .'

'OK?'

'But we're not going to waste our time on trivialities, OK?'

'OK?'

'Cause *this* is a murder case.'

'Genuine?'

'Genuine. Serious stuff, so we're not going to fuck each other around. OK?'

'Who's dead?'

'Affonso, it works like this: I ask the questions, you give the answers. Understand?'

'OK?'

'So let's talk about the eighteenth of January. And Makar Kotko.'

'*Jirre*,' said Britos. 'Kotko. He's worse than the Hawks.'

'Bad answer. And let me tell you, he's yesterday's news. Today we will lock him up.'

'Genuine?'

Seventeen minutes to one.

He felt the pressure, tried to escape it by looking out of the window. He had last been here four years ago. Everything looked different – the airport, the freeways, the suburbs and the business districts. There was building work everywhere.

But this was Johannesburg. It always looked different. They never stopped building and moving. That was what he liked about this place. There was an energy here, you felt it, you saw it, you heard it. Everyone in a hurry, determined, still prospecting for gold.

Long green grass beside the roads, here and there red earth. So different from the Cape.

How do you interrogate a former officer of the KGB? Cunning, experienced, he would have seen everything, would know every technique in the book.

They were going to arrive there and Kotko would be sitting behind his desk, most likely with his face to the door, and with a bright window behind him. All the advantages on his side.

It wasn't going to work.

There was something about the tailored jacket in Kotko's photograph, and the hair that was so perfectly combed. The fact that he thought he had a chance with Hanneke Sloet. The buddy of government figures, a fat wallet. If Kotko were merely an envoy of the Russian Mafia-boss billionaire, his effectiveness ended with his unmasking. He would want to prevent that at all costs.

That was what he must use. Hit Kotko where it hurt most. Take everything away – his job security, his belief he was untouchable, his political safety net, his dignity, his machismo.

Play as rough as he could.

Fuck. If it didn't work, next week he would be doing a shop security patrol around Canal Walk with a radio on his hip.

He took a deep breath, took out his phone and called Brigadier Musad Manie.

'Benny?'

He told his commanding officer what he planned to do.

Manie was silent for a very long time. 'God, Benny. We are

going to take punishment if he's not guilty,' he said. 'OK, you'll have to work fast. I'll phone the commanding officer up there straight away.'

'Thank you, Brigadier.' He ended the call and shouted to Zondi, 'What's the nearest police station to Kotko's office?'

'Sandton, in Summit Road.'

'Do they have a very small interrogation room?'

'They have these really grotty holding cells . . .'

Mbali's telephone conversation with General Afrika was awkward.

She said she had to consider the bank as a potential place where someone might have established a connection between him and Kotko.

I don't have a connection with Kotko, Afrika said matter-of-factly.

But is it possible? she asked.

No. He banked at ABSA, and the Isando Friendship Trust account was with FNB. That was where his main problems began.

She thanked him and walked down to the Hawks' corporate crime group who were based in the southern corner of the ground floor.

The whole team was gathered in one office, busy analysing the financial statements of Kotko's ZIC consultancy group – which Oom Skip Scheepers had obtained from Jack Fischer and Associates – for money laundering.

She said she was sorry to interrupt them, but she had to ask if anyone could explain to her how you could look into payments from a trust.

There were a few alternatives, they said. The bank where the trust account was, the auditors who were responsible for the trust's statements, and the Receiver of Revenue, who had to check the statements.

She thanked them and walked back to her office. She would begin at FNB. And banks, she knew, were the slowest of all enterprises to respond.

Their names were Nika and Natalya. A matching pair, two platinum blondes. Accents heavy, clothing light, flaunting their bodies. They sat side-by-side on the cream-coloured couch in Midnite Moves, their long, bare legs ending in high, spiked heels. Cigarettes between the fingers.

'You are Russian?' asked Cupido in surprise, and motioned to the fascinated uniforms to move back from the doorway. He wasn't completely sure which one was Nika and which Natalya.

'Ukrainian,' said the one on the left. Perhaps Nika. 'But we speak Russian.'

'So, Makar asks for you both every time?'

'Yes.'

'Because he wants to speak Russian while he makes hanky panky?'

'Because we are good.'

'And he asked for you on the eighteenth?'

'Yes.'

'What time did you get there?'

'Long time ago. We cannot remember.'

Cupido consulted his notes. 'That night he called here twice, just before six.'

'Then it must have been about seven.'

'And you went to the Cullinan Hotel?'

'No. Restaurant first. Makar likes dinner.'

'Which restaurant?'

'Long time ago. Different one every time.'

'Was it the Buena Vista Social Café? In the Waterfront?'

'Maybe. Long time ago.'

'It's just over a month.'

'Month is a long time.'

'And then you went to the hotel?'

'Yes.'

'What time?'

'Maybe nine,' said the one on the right, shrugging.

Left said: 'Nine-thirty?'

They looked at each other, shrugged in unison, as though they didn't really care.

'What room?'

'Long time ago.'

'Was he alone?'

'Yes.'

'So what happened?'

'What do you think? Love happened.'

'With both of you?'

They did the shrug thing again, in unison. Cupido wondered whether it was a Ukrainian custom.

'What does that mean?'

'Threesome.'

'I see. When did you leave?'

'Next morning.'

'You were with him the whole night?'

'Yes.'

'Come on. He's in his fifties.'

'Makar likes cuddle. After love.'

'So you cuddled until the next morning?'

'Love. Cuddle. Sleep.'

'And he never left the room?'

'No.'

'The whole night?'

'Yes.'

'How much did he pay you?'

'One five,' said Left.

'Each,' said Right.

Cupido whistled through his teeth, impressed.

'Affonso take thirty per cent,' said Left.

'Bastard,' whispered Right.

'And how much did Makar pay you to give him an alibi?'

'Alibi? What is that?'

47

Nine minutes past one. They were on the sixth floor of the luxury office building on West Street in Sandton, outside the door of ZIC.

Griessel looked at the eight members of the task team, all kitted out in bullet-proof vests, helmets, boots, assault rifles. He knew they were cowboys, just like their Cape counterparts, fit and muscular, the overzealous gleam to carry out his wishes in their eyes.

Griessel nodded at the task team leader, who in his turn gave a hand signal to his man right in front, the one with the big, cylindrical sledgehammer. He swung the hammer back and slammed it violently into the closed office door of expensive Scandinavian wood.

It caved in, splintering thunderously.

The task team stormed through, with all the shouting and uproar that Griessel had asked for.

He walked in behind them, his service pistol in his hand.

He saw the secretary, a middle-aged woman who looked like someone's mother, caught halfway out of her chair behind the desk, her hands covering her mouth, eyes wide and frightened.

The hammer was swung back and the only other office door was broken open too.

Kotko sat far back in his chair, his mouth half agape, his hands pressed instinctively flat on the desk top in front of him.

He looked a little older than he had on the photo, in an expensive dark suit, a snow-white shirt and deep blue tie. The oiled hair was combed back.

The task team reached him, jerked him out of the chair, just as Griessel had asked. Pressed him down on the carpet, clamped the handcuffs around his wrists, then the jingling shackles around his ankles.

Griessel walked up to Kotko, bent down, pressed the barrel of the Z88 against the Russian's cheek. 'You are in very deep trouble, arsehole.'

'You cannot do this!' Kotko screamed, spraying saliva.

'Fuck you,' said Griessel. He rifled through the Russian's jacket pockets, found his cellphone and took it out.

'Take him,' he said to the task team leader. 'Quickly.'

Bones Boshigo walked in, wide-eyed at the action. 'The Giraffe phoned, Benny. We got the warrant.'

The pretty young coloured woman at the Southern Sun Cullinan Hotel in the Strand area told Cupido the second room paid for on the night of the eighteenth of January had been for two of his 'friends'. Fedor Vazov and Lev Grigoryev.

He recognised the names. The same pair that Afrika had got off the bar brawl charge.

'Thank you, sister,' he said, with regret that he did not have more time to devote some attention to her.

He asked for the head of security at the hotel. When the man arrived, an ex-policeman with a round beer belly, Cupido said, 'I see you have CCTV cameras everywhere. How long do you keep the videos?'

'Eight weeks,' said the security chief.

'Fucking excellent,' said Cupido.

The manager of Sandton's FNB branch phoned Mbali within twenty minutes after she had requested the information.

'Thank you for your prompt response,' said Mbali.

'Head office says it can save some police lives,' said the woman. 'All I can tell you is the Isando Friendship Trust is mostly an Internet account. There is no designated bank officer to take care of it. We have systems in place to alert us when the account gets overdrawn, or about POCA violations.'

'Do you have any white, Afrikaans, middle-aged men with access to the account details?'

'Yes. One or two.'

'Is it possible to see if they have looked at the account since last September?'

'Yes, but it's going to take a while.'

'How long?'

'About fifteen minutes.'

Twenty-one minutes past one.

Griessel sat in the back of the BMW, along with two burly task team members. They followed the speeding police van, both vehicles had their sirens on.

'So how are the wedding plans coming along?' Zondi shouted at Boshigo.

'*Eish*, brother, I'm still negotiating with her parents.'

'You getting married soon, Bones?' asked Griessel, who hadn't known about it.

'Yes, Benny. Maybe next year.'

'So, how much are you in for?' Zondi asked.

'Hundred thousand.'

'Jeez.'

'She'll have a degree in December.'

'Is that what your wedding is going to cost?' Griessel asked anxiously.

'No, Benny, that's the *lobola*, *nè*,' Bones shouted over his shoulder.

'You have to pay a hundred thousand so you can marry her?'

'*Yebo*. She's an educated woman.'

'Faux pas,' said Griessel.

'You've got a daughter, *nè*?'

'Yes.'

'That's what the reception will cost you. We guys all pay, one way or another.'

Twenty-seven minutes to two.

The Sandton police station was an ugly two-storey building of khaki brick, with steel shutters over the windows and a red zinc roof.

They had to wait at the portcullis, then drove to the back of the inner courtyard. The uniforms jumped out, unlocked the back of the police van. They followed Griessel's instructions, hauled Kotko out and marched him to the cell block at the rear.

He looked at Benny, hate written across his face as he made hurried little shuffling steps in the foot shackles. 'You are finished,' he said, his accent pronounced. 'Tomorrow you will have no job.'

Griessel grinned at him and followed on behind. The cell block stank of urine, vomit and disinfectant.

They dragged Kotko to the nearest cell, on the right, and shoved him into the single, battered plastic and steel chair that was positioned with its back to the door. Griessel and the two task team members followed. He motioned the uniforms to close the door. They slammed it shut with a loud metallic clang.

Griessel sat down on the bare mattress on the concrete bed. The task team members stood on either side of Benny, their assault rifles aimed at Kotko.

'You are in deep shit,' said Griessel.

'Fuck you,' said Kotko, and the grimace of fury bared his pointed teeth. With his hands cuffed behind him, he sat awkwardly bent forward, just as Griessel had hoped.

He took out Kotko's cellphone, held it in his hands. 'Who are you going to call now, Makar?' he asked with as much contempt as he could muster. 'You think you are this important person. You think if you pay people money, if you corrupt policemen and politicians, we can't touch you. But you're making a big mistake. Let me tell you what I'm going to do. I am going to have a press conference in exactly . . .' He looked at his watch. He saw it was nineteen minutes to two. '. . . forty-five minutes. And I'm going to tell the media I have arrested you. And then I'm going to tell them who you really are. This sick fuck who tortures people with a bayonet . . .'

He saw Kotko's eyes narrow momentarily in surprise.

'This cheap Russian gangster who is too disgusting to be liked by women, so he has to pay prostitutes . . .'

'Fuck you!' Kotko tried to leap off his chair at Griessel. The man's arms strained against the handcuffs and his face was blood red. The task team members pressed the barrels of their weapons against his chest, forcing him back roughly.

Griessel knew he was on the right track.

'You don't want people to know you are a loser. A pervert. I will tell the media you are a sad, middle-aged wacko who stalks women . . . who kept calling a woman because he hired her law firm. You know what she told her friends about you, Makar? That you are a pathetic Russian. That is what I will tell the media.'

Kotko spat at him. The spit landed on the lapel of Griessel's new jacket. He ignored it.

'And I will tell them that's why you killed her. Because your ego is so small that you could not take the rejection. I know what happened, Makar. You called an escort agency for a whore that night. And then you got all worked up, and decided you wanted the real thing. So you went to Hanneke Sloet's flat and you took out your little penis, and she laughed at you, because you couldn't get it up. Too old. Too pathetic. So you stabbed her. That's what I will tell the media, and then we will see how many political friends you have left, you sick fucking pervert.'

'I did not kill her!' screamed Kotko, out of control.

'Or was it something else, Makar? Did she blackmail you? For a bigger commission? Or cash? Did she say she'll talk to all your political friends about your bayonet days? Or to the media? Is that why you killed her?'

'I did not kill her,' he repeated, this time slightly calmer.

Griessel stood up, picked up the end of Kotko's tie and wiped the spit off his jacket lapel. 'You can tell that to the judge, you bastard.' He walked to the door and banged on it.

The uniforms opened it from outside. Griessel motioned to the task team members to go out. He followed them, slamming the door behind him, walked down the passage, past the rest of the task team, and the uniforms, and Bones Boshigo, who was standing near the exit, and out into the sun.

He took out his cigarettes, lit one. Noticed a slight tremor in his fingers. Jesus, what he would give for a Jack Daniels, neat, right now.

'How did it go?' asked Bones, deeply respectful.

'I think it went reasonably well.' He drew on the cigarette. 'Big ego. It helps.'

'What now?'

Griessel consulted his watch. A quarter to two. 'We'll give him five minutes. To take a good look at that cell.'

'Benny, you old fox,' said Boshigo.

'We'll see.'

'Mbali phoned,' said Bones. 'She said Table View's bad apples are all accounted for, and the Fischer private eyes look clean too. She said you must ask this guy who would have

known about the payment to John Afrika. And the Isando
Friendship Trust.'

'OK,' he said.

The FNB bank manager phoned Mbali back.

'Our two white Afrikaans employees did not access the
account of the Isando Friendship Trust in any way over the
past nine months,' she said.

'You absolutely sure?'

'Yes. As a matter of fact, none of our personnel accessed
the files since September. The log shows only routine system
maintenance.'

'OK,' said Mbali. 'Thank you very much.'

She sighed long and deeply when she put the phone down.
Then she positioned her small pudgy hands over the keyboard
of the laptop to Google the phone number of the South
African Revenue Services.

The security chief of the Cullinan Hotel played the videos
back on a computer monitor for Cupido. At twice the normal
speed, as they didn't have the time.

The first camera showed the front lobby of the hotel on
the night of the eighteenth of January. It showed how Makar
Kotko and two other men came out of the lifts, walked
through the lobby, and out through the door. The timeline
showed 19.02.

Cupido guessed they were his henchmen, Vazov and
Grigoryev.

He asked for the video to be fast-forwarded to 21.00. On
the time code 21.26, Kotko walked back in through the front
door. With Natalya and Nika on either side of him. With an
arm around each of them.

The henchmen were not with them.

48

Fourteen minutes to two. Griessel went back to the cell alone. Knowing that he still had one hand to play. And there was nothing in it. He was going to bluff. Big time.

He opened the door and said, 'You're under arrest for the murder of Hanneke Sloet. You're under arrest for money laundering, and for corruption. We're going to put you away for a long time, Makar.' Then he slammed the door shut behind him.

'You have to understand, I did not kill her,' said Kotko, his face turned towards Griessel. He had calmed down. There was pleading there now, as though he was depending on Griessel's sense of fairness.

Benny sat down slowly, shook his head. 'I know you did it. We have your cellphone records. They place you at her apartment that night. They show how you stalked her in December. You wiped the door handle, Makar. But we have stuff that can get latent prints from any surface. We have forensic evidence. Hair. We will match it to your hair. And you have a history of sticking blades into people. We have a witness for that. That's all we need to convict you.'

'No prints. No hair. Impossible.'

'Maybe I don't need that.'

'But I have an alibi. There were two girls. From the escort agency. You can call them now.'

'You paid two junkie prostitutes to say they were with you? That's your alibi?'

Kotko's face changed colour again. 'They are not junkies. I did not fucking kill her.'

'You can try your luck in court,' said Griessel, shrugging.

'Call the girls.' And then, with difficulty, 'Please.'

'I don't have time. The press conference is in twenty minutes.' He stood up. 'You will stay here for a few nights.'

'You cannot do this. I have the right to call my lawyer,' said Kotko.

'No, you have the right to legal representation. Section thirty-five-one D of the Constitution. It says I can detain you for forty-eight hours before I take you to court. You can call your lawyer tomorrow. Maybe.'

He walked towards the door. Kotko looked at him urgently. 'Please,' he said.

'See you tomorrow.' He opened the door, then stopped as though reconsidering.

'Please,' said Kotko again, a man who stood to lose everything.

'You're not giving me anything, Makar.'

'What can I give you? Money?' he asked hopefully.

'Are you trying to bribe me?'

'No, no, you said I must give you . . .'

'I was thinking about information.'

'What information?'

'Who knew about your payments to John Afrika?'

'Who's he?'

'The police general who got your two friends out of jail in Cape Town. You paid him twenty-five thousand rand.'

'I did not pay him a cent.'

'The Isando Friendship Trust did. We know all about it.'

Kotko swore in Russian. Then he asked, 'What do I get, if I tell you?'

'I'll postpone the press conference.'

Kotko thought it over. 'How long?'

'Depends on what you tell me?'

'I want to call a lawyer. And you must check my alibi first. Before talking to the media.'

'If you tell me the truth. About the Trust.'

Kotko bowed his head. He considered the offer, then looked up. 'No media talk today.' With finality.

'If you tell the truth.'

'OK.'

'So, who knew?'

'Just one man.'

When the man from SARS said his name was Gideon Cebekhulu, Mbali switched over to Zulu in relief and asked him where he was from. From there on it was easy.

He consulted his system while she held on. She waited five minutes before he said the auditors who had submitted and verified the statements of Isando Friendship Trust were De Vos and Partners. He gave her a post box address in Edgemead.

She said she needed a street address.

He said there wasn't one. But there was a cellphone and fax number.

She wrote it down.

'Freaky,' said Makar Kotko to Griessel.

'Who?'

'Freaky Deevoss.'

'You'll have to spell that for me.'

'F.R.I.K.K.I.E. is his name. D.E. V.O.S,' he spelled it out, slowly and carefully.

'Frikkie de Vos?'

'Yes.'

'Who is he?'

'My accountant.'

'Where can I find him?'

'You can't. He's dead.'

★ ★ ★

Mbali Googled 'De Vos and Partners'. She found a single web page, of amateurish design, offering accounting services at *Competitive prices!!!!!!!!*

She wondered why people felt they had to use more than one exclamation mark.

She noted the same cellphone and fax number that she had obtained from the friendly man at SARS. This time she had a name. Frikkie de Vos.

She called the cellphone number.

'The number you have dialled does not exist.'

She tried again. With the same result.

Luck was just not on her side. She got up. Corporate Crime would have to tell her how she could track down an accountant.

'You must phone the Camel urgently,' said Bones outside, in the blinding Sandton sunlight.

Griessel phoned at one minute past two.

Brigadier Manie's voice was urgent. 'Vaughn Cupido says it looks like Kotko didn't do it. The hotel video shows he was in his room with two escorts the whole night.'

'*Jissis*,' said Griessel. After all that trouble. And he had been so bloody certain.

'I know. But it doesn't mean he's completely innocent. Remember the two henchmen that John Afrika got off the assault charges at Table View?'

'Yes, Brigadier.'

'Vaughn says it could have been them. Fedor Vazov and Lev Grigoryev. They were in the same hotel as Kotko, and went out in the early evening with him, but only came back after twelve. Table View still had their address details on hand. The two are up there, not far from where you are. The task team has gone to get them. You'll have to tackle them too, Benny.'

'Right, Brigadier.' He hoped Manie wouldn't hear his faked enthusiasm.

'I'm sorry, Benny.'

'Brigadier, Kotko says there's only one man who knew about the payments from the Isando Trust. An accountant by the name of Frikkie de Vos. Trouble is de Vos blew his brains out with a shotgun on the fifteenth of January. Apparently he was a heavy gambler, and lost just about everything that Saturday night. Can we check the records to see if he's telling the truth?'

'I'll tell Mbali straight away.'

'What are we going to do about the media, Brigadier?'

'Benny, I wish I could tell you. I don't see any light yet. But we still have about forty minutes. Let's see where we stand then.'

Griessel went and had a smoke in the corner of the police station yard, on his own. So that the bottled-up cursing could be released. 'F-f-f-f-u-u-u-ck,' he said, the fricative stretched out and filled with emotion. Then he said it again and again, staccato swearing bubbling out with all his frustration.

His rage at the shooter was renewed, and fierce.

If Kotko had an alibi, if it wasn't him, why had the shooter sent the photo? Why was he messing with them? Why was he pushing them around?

For the fun of it. To see the police run around in circles, like headless chickens – what sort of sick bastard would do that? All the trouble to fly up here, all the suspense, all the rules broken to interrogate the Russian, all the risks taken by Manie and Nyathi and the Gauteng Hawks, and all for nothing?

Jissis, what sort of world was this?

And the craving for the bottle stirred in him. His defence mechanism for over a decade. When nothing made sense, drink. It didn't help to understand, but at least it made you feel less bad about all the shit.

He angrily flicked the cigarette butt through the high wire fence, and watched it land in a small explosion of sparks on the tarred road.

Then he turned and walked back to Bones.

The head of the Hawks' Corporate Crimes group put the financial statements of the ZIC consultants company in front of Brigadier Manie and said, 'He's a money launderer. There's no doubt about it. The procedure is the same every time: he buys shares in a South African mining company with dirty money, and channels the returns and dividends back to Arseny Egorov.'

'Did you talk to a prosecutor?'

'There wasn't time.'

'Is there enough, Willie? To get a conviction?'

'It seems like this guy thought no one would look too closely, Brigadier. Very careless, probably because of all his political clout. We've got the goods on him, there's no doubt.'

'With his connections and all?'

'Once we put the evidence on the table, his connections will evaporate like mist in the sunshine.'

Mbali had a premonition.

She walked into the IMC at the Hawks, found a weary Fanie Fick behind his computer and put a note down in front of him. 'You should get some sleep,' she said.

'I'm just happy to be part of a big case again,' he said, looking at her with his hangdog eyes, and smiling.

'I want to see if Hanneke Sloet dialled this number.'

'One second,' said Fick, and typed the number into the database. Mbali felt sorry for him. She had followed the Steyn case in detail when she was still at the Bellville detective branch. She knew she could easily have made the same mistakes.

The progress bar ran across the screen.

A comment appeared.

'Yes,' said Fick, somewhat surprised. 'On Wednesday the twelfth January.'

'Six days before she was killed,' said Mbali. And she knew why IMC hadn't followed up on it. De Vos was an accountant. They thought it was merely a work-related call to a company that was connected to the empowerment transaction.

'Whose number is it?' Fick asked.

'An accountant,' she said. 'Frikkie de Vos. The problem is, he's dead.'

Before he could ask why that was a problem, she had walked out.

49

At a quarter past two the task team brought in Fedor Vazov and Lev Grigoryev – two men in their forties. Griessel noted the tough leanness, the physical self-confidence, the lack of anxiety, the stoic patience. Old soldiers, he suspected.

They had identical tattoos in the angle between thumb and index finger. It looked like a C and a six.

He questioned them in a small office in the police station proper, because there were no more cells available. Displaying no emotion, with quiet, calm voices and broken English they answered his questions. They were the bodyguards of 'Mister' Kotko. Mister Kotko needed bodyguards because this was a very dangerous country. No, they didn't accompany Mister Kotko to his office every day because it was safe there. It was only when he went to other places.

Yes, they remembered the visit to Cape Town on the eighteenth of January. They stayed in the same hotel as Mister Kotko. They spent the day in the reception room of a legal firm, while Mister Kotko was in meetings. That evening they had dinner at a restaurant with Mister Kotko and his two lady friends. Then Mister Kotko and the friends went back to the hotel. And they went to the Jack of Diamonds, the strip joint. They couldn't remember what street it was in, but it was about two blocks from the hotel. About nine o'clock. They couldn't remember the exact time when they went back to the hotel.

'So Cape Town is not such a dangerous place?'

'What do you mean?'

'You let Mister Kotko go back to the hotel on his own.'

'He said we can go.'

They didn't know whether anyone would remember them at the Jack of Diamonds. Maybe the girl who had entertained them to a lap dance in a private room. Cathy. Or Cindy. Or something. Maybe the barman, because they had ordered quite a lot. And left a big tip.

No, they wouldn't object to having photos taken of them to show to the people at the Jack of Diamonds. They had nothing to hide.

No, they didn't know the name Hanneke Sloet.

At twenty to three Griessel knew he would get nothing more out of them.

Even worse was his suspicion that they were telling the truth.

For the first time Musad Manie sounded angry. 'Why, Benny? If it wasn't Kotko, and it wasn't his henchmen, why is the shooter bothered with them?'

'Brigadier, I may be wrong. But even if it were these two, we have nothing to connect them to the case. And I strongly doubt that Hanneke Sloet would have opened the door to them.'

'Hell, Benny, I can't understand this one. I just don't understand it. We're not a bunch of palookas. Someone is messing with our heads, and I don't know who it is any more. Vaughn says there are video cameras in the hotel lifts, at the stairs, in the lobby, and the exit. There's no way Kotko could have left his room without being recorded. And we don't have anything else.'

'No, Brigadier,' he assented.

Manie sighed. 'Here's what we're going to do, Benny. Cloete is here with me. We're going to tell the media that Kotko and his two pals were arrested today for money laundering. And that we are also investigating him for corruption, and organised crime activities, and possible involvement in the murder of Hanneke Sloet. Maybe the shooter will swallow that. Then I'll phone the National Commissioner, and we'll wait for the bombs to drop.'

'Yes, Brigadier.'

'So go and arrest the lot of them, and tell our Gauteng colleagues to keep them behind lock and key until we are sure. Then you and Bones come home. As soon as you can get on a flight. So we can look at this thing all over again.'

The sniper directed his web browser to News24.com for the eleventh time since three o'clock.

At the top he saw the headline: *Russian arrested for money laundering – questioned about Sloet case.*

His heart rate increased.

He clicked on the report, and read.

Johannesburg. The Hawks are questioning a Russian business-man, Makar Kotko (53), about his alleged ties to the slain Cape Town lawyer Hanneke Sloet, after arresting him on charges of money laundering and corruption in Sandton this afternoon.

The Sloet case, which has baffled police for more than a month, took a sensational turn this past week, when a lone gunman began shooting members of the SAPS, claiming in emails to the media that authorities know who the murderer is.

According to Gauteng Hawks spokesperson Sipho Ngwema, Mr Kotko is the managing director of ZIC, a Russian investment consulting service with offices in Sandton.

The sniper checked the right-hand lower corner of his computer screen. He saw it was two minutes past four.

He thought he would feel relief. Happiness. They hadn't arrested him for the Sloet murder. They had missed the cut-off time, hadn't kept their part of the ultimatum.

That meant they were protecting Kotko. The whole corrupt gang. He was right. Captain Benny Griessel was working for John Afrika. They were all in it together.

But all he felt was renewed tension.

He would have to finish what he had begun.

Tonight he would wait for Benny Griessel.

At a quarter past four, after she had received the information about the suicide from the Bothasig station, Captain Mbali drove to the house of the late auditor Frikkie de Vos.

It was a large, neglected place in the quiet Trafford Close.

There was a Pam Golding Properties *For Sale* sign on the front lawn next to the driveway.

She rang the doorbell.

Silence at first, then footsteps. Someone peered through the spyhole. 'I don't want to buy anything.' A woman's voice.

'South Africa Police Services. I need to talk to you about Mr Frikkie de Vos.'

'I don't speak English much.'

'My Afrikaans is bad. I am police. I have to talk to you about Frederik de Vos.'

'Show me your card.'

Mbali held the card up to the spyhole.

The door opened.

'Frikkie is dead,' the woman said. 'You people should know that.'

She wasn't a pretty woman. And she was crying.

They sat in the sitting room, a fussy space with too many little tables and wall hangings. 'If the house doesn't sell within six months, the bank will take it back. Then I lose everything. And do you know how many offers there have been? Not one. Not a single one. The market is dead. And look at this place. How do I fix it up? There's no money in the bank... there's no pension, no savings, nothing. Frikkie gambled. Casinos, horses, dogs, rugby, everything. If he *could* bet, he *did*.' She smelled faintly of alcohol, her hair was thinning and unkempt, her mouth small and grim. There were food stains on the faded, light blue short-sleeved sweater. Her lower lip quivered, she wiped her nose with a tissue and said, 'The worst of all is, I miss him so much.'

'I am sorry for your loss,' said Mbali.

'Thank you.' The tears flowed.

'Mrs de Vos, where do I find your husband's associates?'

'Associates? What associates?'

'He is De Vos *and Partners*.'

'No, *liewe Vader*, I don't know, it's been ten years ...'

'How do you mean?'

'It's been ten years since he started using the firm's money for gambling. That's when the partners left.'

'But he still called himself De Vos and Partners?'

'On the sign, yes. But it was only him. No right-thinking

auditor would come within a mile of him. Why are you looking for them?'

'I need to look at his client list. Do you know where the records are?'

She wiped the tears away with the back of her hand and asked in surprise, 'But don't you know about the break-in?'

'What break-in?'

'At Frikkie's office.'

'No.'

'Someone got in. The week after his death. Walked off with the computer and the back-up. Must have read in the paper that Frikkie was dead, knew there was no one there.'

'All the records were on the computer?' Her heart sank.

'That's right.'

'And he only worked alone?'

'Are you from the Bothasig station?' Mrs de Vos asked.

'No. I am from the Hawks.'

'Because Bothasig knows all *those* things.'

'They only have the file on the suicide. It doesn't say anything about Mr de Vos's work.'

The woman shook her head. 'They asked all the questions after the break-in, and I told them.'

'What did you tell them?'

She took out a fresh tissue, blew her nose at length, pushed the tissue under the sleeve of the blue sweater and said, 'Let me tell you about Frikkie. When he took the money ten years ago, everyone left. Partners, clients, friends, everyone. He was very lucky not to lose his registration, I think it was because the partners knew it wouldn't make much difference. Frikkie wasn't one for work. Gambling, yes. But not work. So they thought he would go under quietly. But Frikkie was no fool. He got other people to do the work. Sort of stray dogs, if you know what I mean. The business is full of them. The drinkers, the lazy, the stupid, the ones who've been fired. Accountants who couldn't get work anywhere else any more. Frikkie would say: Come and work with me. They would come, and go. One after the other. And let me tell you straight, the only clients Frikkie could get were people who wanted to cook the books. Or who were skimming off the top. That sort of thing. That's why his employees never stayed. They were scared. Of being caught. And if you ask me, it was one of his crooked clients who stole the records. That's what I think.'

'Can you remember their names?'

'I kept my nose out of it, I don't know who his clients were.'

'No, I mean, the people who worked for him.'

'Not a cooking clue.'

'And the bank statements? Where are they?'

'They aren't going to help you.'

'Why?'

'Because Frikkie wasn't a fool. His crooked clients paid him cash. And he paid his lame duck people cash. And he gambled with cash. And he never paid a cent of tax on the whole lot.'

50

The Jack of Diamonds in Prestwich Street had a playing cards theme. There were neon examples outside, a massive framed one on the rough, varnished brick wall inside. Playing cards for beer mats and menus and the drinks list at the bar. Playing cards on the barman's shirt.

Cupido sat down on a bar stool. 'Hi, Jack,' he said.

'You think you're the first to try that one?' said the barman, not amused.

'Still clever,' said Cupido.

'You're a cop,' said the barman. He had a hand-rolled cigarette behind his ear. A laconic expression.

'A Hawk, pappie. Your worst nightmare.' He shoved his identity card across the counter.

'You still have to pay for your drinks.'

'Are you a comedian, Jack? Who do you think is going to have the last laugh?'

'I'm just putting all my cards on the table here.'

'You *are* a comedian.' Cupido took the two photos out of his jacket pocket, and put them down in front of the barman. 'Play this hand, wise-ass.'

The barman took the cigarette from behind his ear, lit it slowly, and studied the pictures. Eventually he said. 'Yep, they've been here. Last time was about a month ago.'

'So they are regulars?'

'About every month or two.'

'Evening of Tuesday, eighteenth of January?'

'Maybe. Thereabouts.'

'What can you remember?'

'They took Sandy for a private lap dance in the Queen of Hearts . . .'

'Where's that?'

'There.' He pointed to a curtained doorway, behind him. There were playing cards on the curtain.

'Don't you think the playing card theme is a little overdone?'

'So you're an interior decorator now?'

'I'll redecorate your face if you don't lose the attitude. How come you remember about Sandy?'

'Because she complained.'

'Why?'

'About those two. They wanted blow jobs.'

'And now you're going to tell me you don't do that kind of thing in this posh establishment.'

'Sorry, I don't do it personally, but you can ask one of the girls.'

'One more crack and I'll fucking arrest you.'

'Cool it. They didn't want to pay. Blow job is extra.'

'And then?'

'I asked them nicely.'

'And then?'

'Then they paid.'

'What time did they leave here?'

'Late.'

'What is "late"?'

'Twelve. One. Thereabouts. Drank a lot. Left a big tip.'

Mbali knew the Bothasig Police Station was one of the best in the Peninsula. That's why she was puzzled as to why they had said nothing about the break-in at Frikkie de Vos's office when she enquired about the suicide case file.

Until she drove there and asked the investigating officer.

He was a young Xhosa sergeant, full of respect for her Hawks status and rank, and he told her it wasn't a break-in.

'There was no sign of illegal entry, Captain. And there was no purchase record of the computer or the back-up drives. I mean, she reported the burglary almost a *week* after she says it happened. She kept saying how she was completely broke, and kept asking me for the case number to file an insurance claim. And there was a safe in that office, and it's still there, nobody touched it.'

'So you didn't open a file?'

'I did. Just to give her the number. I mean, she'd just lost her husband, who'd gambled away all their savings. But there was no burglary. That's why we didn't tell you about it.'

'OK. Now, tell me from the beginning. When did she report the burglary?'

'On the twenty-first of January. Six days after the suicide.'

'She came in here?'

'No, she called the station. A vehicle with two uniforms went out to the office . . .'

'Where is the office?'

'At the back of the Panorama Shopping Centre in Sonnendal. Hendrik Verwoerd Drive.'

'Hendrik Verwoerd Drive?'

'That's right.'

'This DA municipality. They have money to build bicycle lanes for the rich, but they don't have money to change a street name like *that*?'

'Viva, ANC, viva,' said the sergeant. '*Amandla.*'

'*Ngawethu,*' said Mbali, the response to the Struggle cry an instant reflex. 'And then?'

'I was called out. So I saw right away there was no forced entry. Two locks on the door, these small, high windows, but there was nothing. And inside too. Everything was fine. No mess, everything in order. But missis de Vos said there was a computer there, and two back-up hard drives. But you know how, when you pick up a computer, you can see the clean square where it stood?'

'*Ewe.*'

'Nothing like that. And then I asked for the purchase receipt for the computer, and she said her husband didn't keep receipts. He just worked in cash. So then I asked about the safe. Big as a fridge, standing right there. With a combination lock. And she said there was nothing taken from the safe. I mean, Captain, why would they not take the safe? If they wanted to steal stuff.'

'How did she know there was nothing taken from the safe?'

'I don't know. Maybe she opened it.'

Griessel leaned back in the seat of the plane and shut his eyes for a moment. He was exhausted. His head felt thick, as if the extent of the case had grown too big. There wasn't enough room for everything any more.

'We are not palookas,' the Camel had said.

Manie was wrong. Benny Griessel was a palooka. His instincts had told him it was Kotko. He had been so sure. Everything fitted. *Jissis.* What was the matter with him? Was he losing his touch? Even in his drunken years he never made such horrible errors of judgement. Maybe that was the fucking problem, this sobriety. Maybe he should get the attention of the air hostess and order a Jack and Coke, because what difference had being sober made?

At that moment it was such an immediate, seductive escape that he had raised his hand halfway before he came to his senses.

What was the matter with him?

It was the weariness. The frustration.

He needed to rest. He had to think. He wanted to close his flat door behind him and pick up his bass guitar and just sit there, his brain in neutral, his fingers strolling along the neck, the notes vibrating in his belly. He wanted to go to sleep in the knowledge that tomorrow would be a relaxing day. He wanted lie down beside Alexa Barnard on her bed, behind her back, slip his hand around to her soft breast.

He opened his eyes, not liking the direction his thoughts were taking him. He sighed, glanced at Bones beside him, staring into space.

'Let's take it from the beginning,' said Griessel.

'Sure,' said Boshigo, but without enthusiasm.

Methodically, Griessel laid everything out for him: by coincidence Makar Kotko was at a reception in December with the people of Gariep Minerals, when he noticed Hanneke Sloet. His lust for the sensual Sloet was immediately obvious. His strategy was to offer Silberstein Lamarque the opportunity to draw up the Gariep share contract, in the belief and hope that it would persuade Sloet to have sex with him.

Kotko kept on phoning Sloet and inviting her to dinner, but she constantly said no. Perhaps because Silbersteins quickly learned that Kotko might be organised crime. Or maybe just because she genuinely didn't have time between the move to Cape Town and a visit to her parents over Christmas. But most likely because she wasn't sexually interested in Kotko at all.

After the twenty-second of December, Kotko stopped phoning her.

Why?

Sloet moved into the new flat, and early in January she was ordered to investigate Kotko thoroughly. The report from Jack Fischer and Associates revealed his KGB history, and the fact that he liked to torture people with a bayonet. In spite of this, Silbersteins continued to do contract work for ZIC.

That gave Kotko two possible motives to murder her – both flimsy: he was a sick bastard, and didn't like being rejected. Or Sloet let him know somehow that she had information about his past and would make it known. Or use it to her professional or financial advantage. Perhaps she had a document, that evening, or a memory stick, of the sort Fritz used to store music. And that was why Kotko sent someone. Someone who put a sharp weapon down on the floor to take the document out of her hand.

On the morning of the eighteenth of January Kotko and Sloet met at a Silbersteins conference. That night Kotko and his hangers-on were sleeping only four blocks away from Sloet's apartment. Kotko hired two sex workers and spent the night with them, and his henchmen were at a strip joint till after twelve. Well established alibis.

But nothing prevented him from hiring a fourth person to murder Sloet. It was unlikely, because she would hardly have opened the door for a stranger. But Kotko might have known enough about her by then to get someone she knew. The alternative was that she was on her way out at ten o'clock that night. The attacker could have waited by the door, and surprised her when she opened it. But she wasn't wearing underwear, and in general was not dressed to go out. So, also unlikely.

'What am I missing?' he asked after Bones had listened attentively to everything.

'Beats me, Benny. When I was studying in the States, they always said: You must cover all the bases. Baseball term. Well, you've covered all the bases.' After a moment of thought he said, 'Do you remember what the Lamborghini man said?'

'Henry van Eeden?'

'*Yebo*. He said Sloet had her priorities straight, *nè*. The report from Fischer and Associates must also have informed her that Kotko was very well connected politically. In the BEE world you just don't fuck with a guy like that.'

'That's true.'

'And the rejection theory. I don't know, Benny. You establish alibis for yourself and your muscle, you hire a man who might get into her flat, maybe not . . . It's a lot of trouble, a lot of risks, just to massage your ego.'

'OK,' said Griessel.

'You're not convinced?'

'We're missing something, Bones. That Silbersteins meeting on the eighteenth . . . I don't know.'

The air hostess put a meal tray in front of each of them.

'What a sad life we lead,' said Bones Boshigo, 'when the only balanced meal we get is airline food.'

Griessel didn't hear. His brain was busy with the tangled web of the case. 'Why?' he asked.

'Because this is all we've had to eat today.'

'No, Bones. I mean, why would the shooter lie to us? About

Kotko? His whole story is about the police protecting the communist. That's his entire justification.'

51

Mbali drove to the Panorama Shopping Centre first, and clicked her tongue when she saw the Hendrik Verwoerd road sign. She parked, got out, went in search of the little office, as the Xhosa sergeant from Bothasig had directed her.

It was hidden away around at the back. It looked almost like a service entrance, just the usual sun-bleached brown wooden door, with a keyhole below the handle, and an additional outside bolt from which hung a big shiny new Yale padlock.

She walked around the corner to the main entrance of the shopping centre. She found a security official, showed him her identification card, and explained what she wanted. He was eager to help. He called a colleague over his radio, asked her to wait, and came back after a few minutes with the colleague. Both were carrying plastic milk crates.

She went with them back to the office. They stacked the crates under the window and carefully helped her to climb up. She had to stand on tiptoe to see through the window.

There was nothing inside, what she could see of the room was completely empty.

She climbed down, thanked the men, and walked back to her car. She climbed in, switched on the engine. Switched it off again. She took her cellphone out of her capacious black handbag, and typed a number in. It rang for a long time.

'Hello,' said Fick, out of breath.

'Fanie, it's Mbali. Are you very busy?'

'No, I'm sorry, I was on my way home. The new shift is still in the parade room.'

'Could you ask them to get the cellular records for the de Vos cellphone number? The one I told you about?'

'I'll do it,' said Fick. 'Before I go.'

She knew he must be very tired, but he was so eager to help. 'I appreciate it,' she said.

There was a moment, just before he turned off the R27 onto the N1, that the red-painted Chana skipped and stuttered, and the sniper clamped his fists tighter around the steering wheel.

But then the engine ran smoothly again.

What if he broke down on the freeway, this time of the afternoon? So terribly exposed. Traffic police would stop . . .

He glanced back quickly. Just the toolboxes. Even if they opened them, they first had to lift the top tray to see the rifle.

And he wasn't wearing the wig today. A new green Springbok cap. Dark glasses.

He just had to stay calm, not look guilty. But the Chana had to last. Just until tomorrow.

He listened attentively to the engine, the city ahead of him.

He kept left, in the slow lane, for the Oswald Pirow off-ramp, on the way to Griessel's flat.

Just after six the bombs began exploding.

Manie sat waiting for the call to say yet another policeman had been shot. He tried to steel himself for it, but he knew it would still be the final blow.

The telephone rang. He answered.

It was the National Commissioner. He was furious. He said he hadn't believed the mess with the shooter and the Sloet case could get any worse. But it had. He said the media had gone crazy. They were calling him, the Minister of Police, and the President of the ANC Youth League. Hundreds of calls, he said. Far-fetched allegations. About Kotko, about the

Youth League, about the very strong possibility that the shooter was entirely correct, the government and the SAPS were protecting a murderer.

Manie, worn out by the pressure and suspense of the long day and little sleep, allowed the commissioner to scold and shout and blame. There was nothing else he could do. He knew he had made this bed for himself. It had been the right thing to do. And now he had to sleep on it. Unfortunately it was figurative sleep only.

For twenty-seven long minutes he listened to the tirade.

Then he put the receiver down softly on the cradle.

It rang again immediately.

Here it comes now, he thought. The shooter's next victim.

He wiped his hand across his brow, and picked up.

It was the National Director of the Hawks, in Pretoria.

He wasn't happy either.

For the second time Mbali sat in the fussily over-decorated sitting room, with the widow of Frederik de Vos. 'There was cash in that safe,' she said to the woman.

The widow cast her eyes down to the brandy glass on the table beside the easy chair. She picked it up and took a sip. The ice tinkled in the room's silence. She put the glass down again carefully.

Mbali suspected the action was a kind of admission. 'The day after your husband died, you went to his office. To get the money. Because you knew it was all there was. You saw that the computer was gone, and you suspected that someone else had a key. So you went and bought a new lock for the office door. Is that right?'

The widow looked away.

'Mrs de Vos, you have not committed any crime, as far as I know. You can tell me.'

Again the woman picked up the glass and swallowed.

'I give you my word. You are not in trouble.'

Mrs de Vos breathed slowly in. She said, 'It was only on the Monday. On Sunday I was too crushed.'

'You had the combination of the safe?'

'It was his lucky number. Double four, double seven, double four. That's all he ever used. But I never had a key to the door lock. But the hospital gave me this plastic bag . . .' Her face crumpled, her eyes grew moist. 'This little bag of his things. His cigarettes, his Zippo . . .' She sobbed, picked up the glass again.

'And the keys.'

The widow nodded, and sipped at the brandy again.

'And you went in on the Monday. To get the cash.'

A nod.

'And you saw the computer and the drives were missing.'

A shake of the head.

'No?'

She took a tissue from the sleeve of the blue jersey, blew her nose. 'The computer things were still there, on the Monday. In the other office. The one his people always used. When I went back on the Friday, they were gone.'

'When did you go in on the Friday?'

'I took the *afslaer*'s evaluator.'

'What is an *afslaer*?'

It took a moment for Mrs de Vos to find the English word. 'They sell you stuff. You know . . . when people can make a *bod* . . . a bid.'

'Auctioneers?'

'*Ja*. I had to sell the stuff.'

'And then you bought a new lock?'

'*Ja.*'

'Where is the furniture now? The furniture from the office?'

'At the auctioneers.'

Mbali sighed. That probably meant the furniture was forensically contaminated. But she would have to make sure. 'What else was in the safe?'

'Nothing. Just the money.'

'How much cash?'

The lower lip trembled again. 'I think there was a lot. Frikkie said, a week before he died, there was a decent pay day coming, *this* Friday. And then he took it and went and played roulette at GrandWest and he lost every cent and he went and blew himself away in a park. In a little park . . .'

She waited for Mrs de Vos to calm down. Then she asked, 'How much was left?'

'Four thousand two hundred. That's all. That's my inheritance. That's what Frikkie left me.'

'I'm sorry.'

'That was Frikkie . . .'

'I have to know who had a key to that office.'

'His people.'

'Are you sure?'

'Frikkie was never at the office. That was the only way they could get in. He gave them the key.'

'How many people were there?'

'I don't know.'

'And you really don't know who they were?'

The widow shook her head and picked up the glass.

'I need a photograph of your husband,' said Mbali. 'And the details of the auctioneer. And the keys to the office.'

The sniper parked in the spot he had identified the evening before – just around the corner of Vriende Street, in Schoonder, with the nose of the Chana pointing at the Gardens Centre.

From here he would have an unimpeded view of the automatic steel gate of Nelson's Mansions, the old 1950s block of flats. And he would be safe – the streets in the area were densely parked with cars, flat and town house dwellers who probably didn't have garages. Another vehicle would not attract attention.

The night before he had sat here in the Audi for over an hour. He saw how every occupant of Nelson's Mansions stopped at the gate, fiddled with a remote. He had used his watch to see that it took an average of twenty-two seconds for the gate to open completely. He would have nearly thirty seconds, from the moment that the detective stopped and pressed the button until he drove in.

Thirty seconds, to shoot the tyres of both wheels on this side. And then, the driver.

That was what he had practised, in the veld beside the R304 and the Little Salt River this afternoon. Three shots. Maybe four. Front, back, driver.

Until he had only ten bullets left.

Yesterday he saw there was a street light, about halfway between this parking place and the driveway of the flats. Over the distance of about forty metres he could see, clearly enough, the face of everyone who stopped ... Without a scope. He had studied Griessel's photos carefully on the Internet and in the newspapers. The over-long, unkempt hair, the peculiar Slavic eyes, the careworn face.

He would recognise him.

He made sure the Chana's doors were locked. He waited, since there were quite a few pedestrians, on their way home.

When it was quiet, he climbed quickly over to the back, and pulled the screen down.

He took off the cap and dark glasses, put the strap of the torch around his head, and switched it on, at the lowest setting. Opened the tool chest, lifted out the tray, and put it aside.

He took out the rifle.

52

At twenty past seven Mbali finally traced the cellphone number of the auctioneer.

She identified herself and said, 'I need access to the furniture of Frikkie de Vos.'

'Who?'

She gave him all the details she had.

'Come and see me tomorrow,' the auctioneer said.

'No. I need access now. It is related to this mad dog who shoots the police. A matter of life and death.'

'Shit,' said the auctioneer.

'Profanity is the common crutch of the conversational cripple.'

'What?'

'Please tell me, how do you load and transport furniture for auction?'

'Just like everybody else.'

'Which is how?'

'We wrap it, and then we ship it . . .'

'What do you wrap it with?'

'Plastic.'

'When do you wrap it?'

'Before we load it, for crying out loud.'

'Good. I will meet you at your warehouse in half an hour.'

'I live in Somerset West. It's going to take me an hour.'

'Then you had better leave right now.'

Then she phoned the head of the PCSI, the elite Provincial Crime Scene Investigation unit.

Griessel phoned Alexa while they were driving back from the airport.

She didn't answer.

He phoned Ella. Her phone went to voice mail. He tried to remember what Alexa had said this morning before he left for Johannesburg. The big rehearsal tonight. Or was it tomorrow night? He had only been half listening.

He hoped there wasn't any more trouble. Please not tonight.

Beyond Tygerberg Hospital his phone rang. He answered in a hurry, hoping it was Alexa.

'Benny,' said Colonel Nyathi, 'where are you?'

Griessel said they were ten minutes away from the DPCI offices.

'We're having a meeting when you're back.' In a funereal voice.

The sniper was uncomfortable and frustrated. So many times when cars stopped at the gate he had looked through the scope. And so many times he had to relax his trigger finger. It was nearly eight, and the policeman still hadn't made his appearance.

Then another vehicle turned in, at the T-junction of Vriende and Buitenkant Streets, and he saw the blue lights on the van's roof and the SAPS colours and emblem.

He froze. It drove slowly in his direction.

He could hear his heart hammering.

He felt an irresistible urge to slam the sliding gap in the side panel shut – at that moment it seemed gigantic, a gaping wound.

The patrol vehicle moved beyond his field of vision. He listened, turning his head to hear better. The sound of an engine, the hiss of tyres on the tar.

Behind the Chana.

Were they stopping?

Seconds ticked by.

The engine sound seemed quieter, and he thought they must have stopped.

Until he realised they had driven on. West.

His hands were clammy on the rifle.

The meeting began on a sombre note.

Nyathi said they had called Brigadier Musad Manie to Pretoria. 'To go and explain what the National Director called "this fiasco in Cape Town".'

A flurry of growling indignation and anger passed through the room. Nyathi hushed them. 'The brigadier asked me to tell you this summons in no way reflects on your hard work and exceptional efforts. He had to make some big decisions today, he made them on his own, and he knew there were certain risks involved—'

More cries from the floor. Nyathi held up his hand for calm. 'Please, let me finish. He knew about the risks, and he's confident that top management will understand when he explains the circumstances. He asked you to continue with the same dedication and vigour you have shown under very difficult circumstances, and he wants you to know that he absolutely believes in our ability to crack these cases. I am in complete agreement. Now, let's see where we are. Benny?'

Griessel stood up slowly, the guilt bearing down heavily on him. Manie had to take the brunt of the fact that he had not achieved anything. With Kotko. With everything. And what could he tell them now, when he himself had no idea what to do?

He stood beside Nyathi. 'I'm sorry, Colonel,' he said.

'Not your fault, Benny.'

A chorus of assent.

He stood there, searching for words, searching for an approach that would not make him look like a fool, aware of the fact that his view might not be correct, that he could make an even bigger mess.

He cleared his throat. He said, 'We will have to take another look at Kotko, because we're missing something. He's in the middle of something. Something to do with the shooter, with Sloet, with . . .' He nearly mentioned John Afrika by name, and then realised it was probably not common knowledge. '. . . to do with the allegations against the SAPS, with the deals, the lawyers. And I don't think it's just coincidence.'

Supportive murmurs. They bolstered his courage.

'I want to look at the Fischer report again, Colonel. I want us to go through Kotko's cellphone records from the beginning again, every person that he talked to in December and January. Look at all the hotel videos again. Go and stand in that hotel room to see if there's any way to slip out. See if any of the city's street cameras can tell us anything. We'll have to show photos of Kotko and his men around Sloet's apartment block. We'll have to talk to Silbersteins again, about their meeting with Kotko on the eighteenth. I was not present at Pruis's interrogation . . .'

'We must throw the book at him, Benny, he's a sly *bliksem*,' Cupido called.

'I felt that way too. The thing is, there are just too many coincidences. Sloet's death on the day of that meeting. Kotko's background. His calls. The photo that the shooter sent. The involvement of . . . a SAPS member. And not one of us believes in coincidences.'

Heads nodded, calls of 'yes' and 'that's right'.

He couldn't think of anything else. 'That's all I have, Colonel.'

'Thank you, Benny. People, our biggest enemy at the moment is fatigue. We have been under tremendous pressure, most of you have not slept much in the last forty-eight hours, and now I can see how tired you are. None of us is thinking clearly any more. The brigadier and I discussed this at length, and we both came to the conclusion that there is not much we can do tonight. We suggest that you all spend an hour or two with your families, and then get some rest. Let's come back here early tomorrow morning, let's say six o'clock, and take a new, fresh look at things. We have a skeleton staff on the night shift, if there is another shooting victim tonight, we will unfortunately have to call in the CATS team . . . Where is Mbali . . . ?'

'In Amsterdam,' someone whispered.

They laughed, more from a release of tension than spite.

'She's asleep already,' someone else added.

'That's what we should all be doing,' said Nyathi. 'People . . .' He took a few steps forward and his voice softened, 'get some rest. If we can break this case tomorrow, we'll go a long way towards strengthening our commanding officer's hand. Let's do it for him. Please.' The last word was an undisguised plea.

Silence descended on the room.

Mbali sat at a little table in the corner of the big warehouse.

She watched the PCSI, the elite forensic team, busy inspecting Frikkie de Vos's furniture. To one side, with his hands on his hips, stood the frustrated owner of the auctioneers company.

Mbali looked down at the notes she was busy making. It was a timeline, in her small, neat handwriting.

Wednesday, 12 January: Sloet calls de Vos on his cellphone, because he is Kotko's bookkeeper.
Saturday, 15 January: de Vos commits suicide.
Monday, 17 January: Mrs de Vos takes cash from safe. Computer/ drives in office.
Tuesday, 18 January: Hanneke Sloet killed.
Friday, 21 January: Mrs de Vos discovers theft of computer/drives.
Monday, 24 January: Shooter sends first email.

She read it again, making a tick after each one. Then she wrote:

Suicide? Check pathologist report.
   Kotko killed de Vos? Why?
   Isando Friendship Trust fin. Statements tie Kotko to police corruption.
   Theft of computer/drives on 19 or 20 Feb?

And right at the bottom, her strongest intuition, the key to tracing the shooter. She underlined it. Three times.

Only at half past ten did the PCSI team leader walk over to her. 'There is no doubt,' he said. 'Someone wiped all the furniture very carefully. There's absolutely nothing.'

'I thought so,' she said.

There was a missed call on his cellphone, after the meeting. ALEXA the screen had said.

He phoned back, got her voicemail and left a message. 'Hello, Alexa, I hope everything is fine,' then immediately thought it was an idiotic thing to say. He pressed on with: 'I . . . My cellphone will be on for the rest of the night . . .' He wanted to say he missed her, or something. But his courage failed. 'OK. Bye.'

He went to fetch his laptop from IMC and walked to his office to get the Fischer report to read at home.

On the desk, positioned so that he couldn't miss it, lay a printout. Cellphone records. With a note from Fick.

Benny
Here are Calla Etzebeth's records. Hope it helps.
Fanie

He looked at them. The Neanderthal rugby player with the low brow and close-together-eyes had phoned Carla in the past three weeks at least six times a day, and sent fifteen, twenty messages.

That was not a random photo from Rag. This was his daughter's boyfriend.

Jissis.

53

A quarter to eleven.

The sniper's limbs were stiff, his backside numb, and his back sore from sitting awkwardly. The adrenaline had come and gone, the tension ebbed and flowed. He had considered leaving many times in the past hour, his head telling him Griessel wasn't going to come, something had happened. His imagination had nearly made him shoot twice, two dark-haired men who looked vaguely like the detective. He was in too much of a hurry, wanted to swing the scope to the front wheel too quickly. He only just stopped himself in time.

He would wait till midnight. No later.

Then he heard the car coming, in his blind spot, from east to west down Vriende Street.

He quickly rubbed his right eye, gripped the rifle, and looked through the scope.

A white BMW drove right past him, out of focus, too close.

Brake lights lighting up, in time for Nelson's Mansions.

Flicker light.

The car turned in. The BMW stopped. He focused the cross hairs of the scope on the driver. Saw the hair. The right eye.

It was Griessel.

He felt the shock of the adrenaline surge. He had to make sure. He had enough time, nearly thirty seconds. He forced himself to look again. Was he sure, completely sure?

It was Griessel.

He swung the telescope towards the right front wheel.

Griessel dug the remote out of his jacket pocket, automatically, his head was dull. He found it, pointed it at the gate. It began to move, reluctantly.

He heard the smack, felt the light shock through the steering wheel.

He swore, a half-formed thought – the front tyre, he must have driven over a nail. An unwillingness to accept the implications, he didn't want to change a tyre at *this* time of the night.

Another smacking sound. Only then did everything come into focus – someone was shooting at him. The window right beside him exploded.

The sniper fired the last shot, ripped off the hiking pole strap, tossed the rifle quickly down in the tray.

He jerked up the screen between loading bed and driver's cab and jumped over into the seat.

He looked at the BMW, forty metres away, the glass glittering on the tar. Griessel was sitting there, head bowed.

Christ. He'd shot him dead.

He turned the key. The engine groaned and choked. It wouldn't take.

He thought his heart would stop.

He tramped on the accelerator, turned again.

A whining sound, without success.

A movement out of the corner of his eye, his head whipping to the right.

Griessel opening the door of the BMW, leaping out.

He turned the key again. His whole body leaning forward in urgency and fear.

Griessel running towards him, his right hand under his jacket.

The engine took.

A gun in the detective's hand.

Panic, like a serpent in his head.

He slammed the Chana into gear, the revs high.

A booming shot, the bullet's crack, his window shattering, head jerking in fright, glass spraying on his face. He pulled away, tyres screeching along with the engine, desperately wrenching at the steering wheel to get out of the parking place, but not fast enough.

Griessel right beside the Chana, fist slamming against the panel, the detective screaming something, the sniper racing out of the parking spot. Another shot. A burning pain exploding in his hand. As he raced down Schoonder Street, in the side mirror he saw Griessel running, jacket flapping, pistol aimed at the Chana. He ducked instinctively, as another shot smacked into the panel van.

The corner with Myrtle Street too close, going too fast, braking too late. The tyres squealing he jerked the steering wheel, the rear end of the Chana swinging too far, the right side thumping dully against a vehicle, metal scraping on metal. Accelerator to the floor, the engine stuttering, the panel van juddering, shuddering.

Fear overwhelmed him so that he screamed, shrill, in mortal fear. Another shot cracked, further back, but he didn't hear it hit.

Then the engine was strong again suddenly and he pulled away down Myrtle, looked down at the pain in his hand.

His little finger was gone, only the bloodied stump remained.

Day 6
Thursday

54

It was just after one in the morning. The roadblocks, the feverish hunt for a red Chana with a broken window and multiple bullet holes, had produced no results.

In Vriende Street the curious, the hordes of uniforms and SAPS vehicles, and Colonel Nyathi, his brow furrowed with worry, had finally left. Only the night sounds of the city and the single patrol vehicle in front of Griessel's flat remained. Nyathi had insisted on that, against all his objections. 'They'll look after you tonight. Tomorrow we'll bring in the VIP Protection Unit.'

He walked to the vehicle. He told the two sergeants that he wanted to stand on the corner one last time.

They looked at him wide-eyed, full of respect for 'the one who had survived the shooter'. The JOC leader of the Sloet investigation.

He paced off the distance again, and looked back at the gate.

It was close.

Two tyres shot out, one after the other. And then, the shot that had missed him, because at that instant, when he'd realised he was being fired at, he'd jerked back his head.

He suppressed his rage at the shooter until he was back in his flat. Only then did he let out a single fierce four-letter word.

He showered and went to sit at the kitchen counter with the report on Makar Kotko from Jack Fischer and Associates. He knew he'd never be able to sleep now.

Towards the end of it he had to read some paragraphs and whole pages over again, his concentration flagging.

When he finally went to bed, close to three o'clock, it was with a reluctant respect for the Russian. A man who had to make his career in the backwaters of Africa, hellholes of civil war, poor infrastructure, corruption, poverty, disease and wretchedness.

A man who had to make do with the flotsam and jetsam of KGB personnel who weren't good enough for the espionage hot-spots of the First World. Who had to tread on eggshells, walk a tightrope between the minor and major tribal and national conflicts, foreign ideologies, who had to use some fancy footwork to navigate between the conceit and greed and power-hunger of the despots of the Dark Continent, who constantly came and went, and always played the West and East off against each other.

Kotko had made a success of it all. And after the fall of communism he had used his experience, his knowledge and contacts and unique talents, with skill and purpose, to carve out a new career: his retirement vocation as a Southern African envoy of organised crime, with enough money for expensive German cars, a luxurious house, lavish parties, and paid sex.

Reluctant respect, because Kotko was sick: he took pleasure in the pain of others. Traitors, opponents, suspects, were never eliminated with a gun. Always slowly and sadistically with his favourite cutting-and-stabbing instrument, the longer, coarser blade of the INSAS bayonet for the AK-47 from Indonesia, slowly inserted and twisted in the anus of the victim.

He lay on the bed and thought that it could have been the weapon that was used to murder Hanncke Sloet. But with a single swift stab in the torso. That last fact, in his world, made a big difference.

This time, Kotko hadn't done his own dirty work.

* * *

When the eastern horizon began to change colour, in the veld beside the old Atlantis railway line, the sniper lifted the mountain bike out of the Chana.

Pain shot through his hand. The pills, meant for headaches, were of little help. The wound had begun bleeding under the bandage again. The long, traumatic night had taken its toll. But he had to finish the job.

He propped the bicycle against a Port Jackson tree, came back, opened the cans of petrol one by one, and poured the fluid over the panel van – the engine, the cab, the interior. Difficult work with the injured hand.

He tossed the cans in the back. Walked away with the bottle of fuel, a scrap of cloth hanging from it. He lit the rag and tossed the bottle like a *jukskei*, underarm, for greater accuracy.

He stood and watched the flames bloom, hesitating a moment and then enveloping the whole vehicle with a dull pop.

He walked quickly to the bicycle, put on the cycling helmet, pushed it through the sand to the dirt track, mounted, and began pedalling furiously.

He was already on the tarmac of the R304 when the petrol tank of the Chana exploded. He looked back over his shoulder, and saw the flames and smoke cloud blossom above the trees.

At ten to five, when Griessel emerged from the flat, they were waiting for him: the VIP Protection Unit – four broad-shouldered policemen in black suits and white shirts with dark grey ties.

He sighed, and got into one of the black BMW X5s. He wanted to quip: 'Work, James,' but he just couldn't muster the energy.

On the way to work he prepared for the six o'clock meeting.

He would have to delegate tasks. Give the priorities to IMC. His greatest hope was that they would mine gold from the ore of Kotko's cellphone calls. If he had been dumb enough to use his usual number to negotiate a murder with a hireling.

Then he saw the newspaper billboards: HAWK IS NEXT, SAYS SHOOTER.

That woke him up.

There must have been another email.

Nyathi was waiting for him, and handed him the printouts.

He realised the colonel had not slept.

He read the first one.

762a89z012@anonimail.com
Sent: Wednesday 2 March. 23.39
To: b.griessel@dpmo.saps.gov.za
Re:
Today I will shoot you dead.

Only those six words.

Rage pierced his fatigue and he looked up at Nyathi, searching for words to express it.

'Read the other one.'

762a89z012@anonimail.com
Sent: Wednesday 2 March. 23.39
To: jannie.erlank@dieburger.com
CC: j.afrika@saps.gov.za; b.griessel@dpmo.saps.gov.za
Re: Mercy
'You shall take no satisfaction for the life of a murderer, which is guilty of death: but he shall be surely put to death.' Numbers 35:31
'Thine eye shall not pity him, but thou shalt put away the guilt of innocent blood from Israel, that it may go well with

thee.' Deuteronomy 19:13

They took bribes. The media should go and look at the evidence in black and white the directorate of prority crimes is corrupt they are protectiing the generals that they work for. I have to wipe out those who shed inoncent blood.

It is war now. Today I will shoot a Hawk.

Solomon

Before he could take pleasure in the knowledge that stress must be to blame for those spelling mistakes, before he could say anything to express his contempt, Nyathi laid a hand on his shoulder.

'We have secured the building. But I think you should stay in the office today.'

He argued vigorously, but to no avail. He pleaded, offered alternatives, suggested solutions.

Nyathi listened to it all as they walked to the big parade room. Then he just shook his head.

'No.'

There was rebellion in the room. It was borne on the aggressive voices of nearly thirty detectives, the undertone of controlled rage at the shooter, his emails, his attack on a colleague. And the DPCI's lack of action. 'Where is Mbali?' came the accusing question.

Nyathi struggled to silence them. He sketched the safety precautions, cautioned them to be careful.

Griessel stood up. First, they insisted on hearing from his own lips about the night before. His account drew out a rumble of indignation.

'Where is Mbali? The big Kia hunter.'

'Probably still sleeping.'

A chorus of accusation and dislike.

The ever-friendly, ever-restrained Nyathi stood up, so obviously upset that silence was immediate and overwhelming.

'Is this what we do? When we are shot at by madmen, and the media, and the top brass? Is this what we do? When our commanding officer is fighting for his career in Pretoria? You should be ashamed of yourselves. While you were sleeping, Captain Kaleni worked. Straight through the night. She has followed leads the rest of us missed. She is hunting down this dog who is shooting us, and I think she just might catch the bastard before this day is out. So shut up. And show some respect.'

When Griessel began to talk again, he had their full attention.

55

The day's work began with renewed energy, activated by Nyathi's words, and a female detective who had put them all to shame.

The day's work began with so much promise when the SAPS station at Melkbosstrand informed them that they had found the burned-out Chana.

At half past six they phoned in the engine number, and Nyathi, Mbali and Griessel sat watching the IMC screens as they searched for the name of the owner on the vehicle registry system.

Neville Alistair Webb. Fifty-five years old. Langley Road in Wynberg.

They sent the task force to bring him in, acutely aware of the urgent need to make progress.

At 8.12 they shoved the short, dismayed and protesting Webb into Mbali's office. 'I didn't do anything, I didn't do anything,' he said, red in the face.

Griessel sat and listened. She asked the questions.

'You own a 2007 Chana panel van, Mr Webb.'

'Shit. I knew it.'

'Please do not swear, Mr Webb. What did you know?'

'That he was a crook.'

'Who?'

'The guy who bought it.'

'You are saying you sold the Chana?'

'Of course I sold it. How do you think I paid off my creditors? I sold the van, I sold the shop, I sold the stock, I sold my car . . .'

'When did you sell it?'

'Almost too bloody late . . .'

'When?'

'Last week of January.'

'To whom?'

'I don't know.'

'You don't know?'

'No, I don't know. And you know what, I don't care. I really don't care. Because he paid me cash, and I paid my debts, and what he did with the bloody van is his problem, not mine.'

'You had better start caring, Mr Webb. The vehicle was used in the shooting of several police officers, one of whom was killed.'

'Jesus.'

'May I ask you to refrain from profanity, Mr—'

'No, you may not. You break down my door like barbarians, you assault me in my house like a criminal, in front of my wife, you drag me here, and you're trying to blame me for making a perfectly legal sale of my legally owned property? And then you expect me to speak in a civilised manner? Bullshit. If I could still afford a lawyer, I would have called him, and sued your arses. So here's what I'm going to do. I'm going to tell you what happened, and then I'm walking out of here. And if you don't like that, you can shoot me. Because I really don't care any more. You hear me? I don't care.'

'What happened, Mr Webb?'

'The Internet happened, that's what. Amazon and Kindles and iPads happened. You know how long I ran my bookshop? Twenty years. Put two kids through university. And then? E-books. Boom. Recession. Boom. Savings. Boom. No more Book Webb. Just one big financial mess.'

'What happened with the sale of the Chana?'

'I advertised it in the *Argus*, on *Auto Trader*, on *Gumtree*. The market is swamped, everybody's in trouble. Nobody wanted to buy it. Nobody. After almost six months, I'm on my way to insolvency, and finally this guy calls me, last week of January, and he says he'll pay cash, he's in Jo'burg, he's busy, he'll have someone fly down and pick it up, I must just leave the keys and the registration papers under the driver's seat carpet and park the van at the airport. So I think it's a bit weird, but the next day he calls and says I must check my account. And the money is there. So I did what he asked. And when he called again, I gave him the number of the airport parking spot, and that's the last time I heard from him.'

'But the vehicle is still registered to you.'

'And that's my fault?'

'Can you prove that you sold the van?'

'How the hell am I going to do that?'

'You tell us.'

'Look at my bank statement, for God's sake. Twenty-two thousand, in cash, last week of January.'

'Where were you last night at eleven o'clock?'

'At home. With my wife.'

'Just the two of you?'

'No. We had a party. Elvis was there. And Frank Sinatra. Great guy.'

'Just you and your wife.'

'I'm leaving now.'

'Mr Webb, please sit down.'

'I have nothing more to say.'

'Mister Webb—'

'Shoot me.'

That was the highlight of the morning.

Xandra nt hapi. Bad reh ystdy. X w u. B warnd.

He was still trying to decipher Ella's SMS – it was worse than Fritz's – when his phone rang.

ALEXA.

'Where are you, Benny?' Her voice was cold and stiff.

'At work. How are—'

'Here in the Cape?'

'Yes . . .'

'I thought you were in Johannesburg, Benny?'

'I was there yesterday, I—'

'You couldn't have let me know that you were back?'

He had phoned her back. When was it, last night some time. Had he left a message? Too many things had happened, too little sleep. 'I think I left a message.'

'You didn't say you were back. When did you get here?'

'Yesterday afternoon. Alexa, I—'

'Did you prefer to be alone, Benny?'

'No. We worked till very late, I'm sorry, it was a bit crazy.'

'Is today a bit crazy too? Or can we see each other?'

Jissis, what could he say? With the bodyguards and the fact that he was penned in here. 'Alexa, I want to see you, the trouble is just—'

'I understand.' She cut the call, and he stood there with the phone to his ear and the words on his tongue and the power-lessness paralysing him. He called Ella's number, because he at least wanted to find out what *Bad reh* meant.

She didn't answer, but sent another SMS.

Xandra X. Tlk ltr.

He was trapped in the building. With too much time to think while they waited for the Kotko and de Vos cellphone reports, for the feedback from the teams that had gone out to the hotel, the city CCTV centre, to Silbersteins.

He thought about his inability to sustain any relationship. With his children, his ex, with Alexa. Was it the job, or was he the problem?

It had to be him, because there were lots of policemen whose marriages lasted.

He thought about his inability to comprehend the Sloet case. And how Mbali Kaleni, so much younger, with much less experience, through all the chaff of Kotko and the transactions and the Trust, had seen the grain. He thought about Bones Boshigo's words yesterday. 'You're an old fox.' The only truth in that was the 'old'. He never made the connections, he never thought the whole thing through like Mbali. He was too busy playing the strong man in that cell with Kotko, too focused on his conviction that it was the Russian himself who had killed Sloet.

He had lost his touch, somewhere in the months that he was doing training and mentoring work for Afrika. And just could not shake off that rust, it was inside him, encrusted with the damage of thirteen years of drunkenness. Maybe that was why Afrika had recommended him to the Hawks. So he could rid himself of Griessel-the-toothless-jackal.

Had he ever had a worse week in his life?

Fuck knew, he would have to pull his finger out. He would have to catch a wake-up and shake off this paralysis, never mind how far behind he was with sleep.

But the day kept dealing out the knocks.

Rumours that the Cape Hawks were a topic of debate in parliament were confirmed. The opposition talked about 'this nest of vipers' that needed cleaning out. A man said on a phone-in radio programme: 'Leave this guy alone, let him shoot the whole corrupt gang, so we can begin afresh.' So-called law enforcement experts used words like 'turning point' and 'low point' and 'crisis' in interviews. The flood of media calls began to include foreign journalists, and everything was reinforced with reporters and photographers who set up camp outside the DPCI building. Bellville uniforms had to come and maintain order, direct traffic.

The fragile, bespectacled Dr Tiffany October sat down with Griessel and Mbali and methodically explained the pathology report of the suicide of Frikkie de Vos. If you took into account the blood spatter against the head rest of the Toyota Fortuner, the precise entry and exit wounds of the shotgun, the gunpowder residue on de Vos's hands and in the back of his throat, the size of the vehicle cab, and the total absence of any other bruises, grazes or wounds, she said, there could only be one explanation: the man had committed suicide.

Later, in the afternoon, all their other theories toppled one by one, like dominoes.

It was Griessel who took the calls, who had to pass on the news. From Silbersteins, the Cullinan Hotel, and the city CCTV control centre, that the teams were coming back empty handed. Every time his heart sank further, and the desperate fatigue seeped deeper into his bones.

He was there when the spider's web of de Vos's cellphone calls – blown-up and projected onto the IMC wall – brought more disappointment. When Mbali, now practically walking in her sleep, called the widow in search of an explanation, and had to hear that 'Frikkie's crooked clients only emailed, they were too scared of cellphones'. And she didn't know which email address de Vos used, it must be on the computer somewhere.

Mbali sat in the IMC centre with her head bowed, her back turned to them, and Griessel saw her shoulders shudder at the onslaught of tears, but she did not look up.

And then the mortal blow.

It came some time during the drowsy depression between three and four o'clock. The long corridors were quiet, the telephones had stopped ringing, and only Fick was still busy at his computer, the irregular click of his mouse the only sound in the room.

They heard the footsteps approaching on the tiled floor, measured and weary. Nyathi, always so proud and erect, leaned against the doorjamb, his body crumpled like that of an old man, his voice barely above a whisper. 'The brigadier has just come out of the National Commissioner's office. He called to tell me that he will be facing a formal disciplinary hearing tomorrow morning at nine. He's their scapegoat. They want to suspend him.'

In the shocked silence that followed, in a hopeful tone that was completely out of place, Fanie 'Fucked' Fick said: 'Now *that's* very weird . . .'

56

Fick saw the expressions on the faces that turned towards him, the reproach and disgust.

'No, really,' he said, and pointed at the screen.

'What, Fanie?' asked his immediate boss, Captain Philip van Wyk, crossly.

'This Frikkie de Vos,' said Fick. 'We only looked at his cellphone up to the day of his death. Because that was the last day that he *made* calls.'

'So?'

'But I looked at calls received. I . . . there was nothing else to do . . .'

'What is it, Fanie?'

'*After* he died, on the nineteenth of January, he was phoned four times from the same number. There were voice messages left twice. On the twentieth, another two calls. What's so peculiar to me – they are from the police station in Victoria West.'

'Victoria West?' said Griessel, dumbfounded, because that didn't fit any scenario.

'Give me the number,' said Mbali, and pulled the phone on the desk closer.

He read it out to her. She phoned.

'Put it on speaker phone,' said Nyathi.

She pressed the button. They all listened to it ringing.

'South African Police Service, Victoria West,' a woman's voice answered.

'This is Captain Mbali Kaleni, Directorate of Priority Crime Investigations in Cape Town. I would like to speak to your station commander, please.'

'Please hold.'

They all sat irritably listening to tinny electronic music.

'Captain Kaptein.'

'May I speak to the station commander?' Mbali asked sternly, suspecting a practical joker.

'That's me.'

'What is your name, Captain?'

'Leonard Kaptein.'

'They are going to *have* to promote him,' one of the IMC people whispered, because '*kaptein*' was the Afrikaans for captain.

'This is Captain Mbali Kaleni, Directorate of Priority Crime Investigations in Cape Town. I am investigating the shooting of several police officers this past week . . .'

'Solomon?' asked Captain Kaptein.

'Yes,' said Mbali. 'So I don't have to tell you how urgent this is.'

'*Blikslater*. But what can we do?' the station commander asked in his distinctive Northern Cape accent.

'Someone from your station called the cellphone number of a Mr Frederik 'Frikkie' de Vos on the nineteenth and twentieth of January, and left voicemail messages. Mr de Vos owned an accounting firm in Edgemead in Cape Town, and is involved in this case. I need to know who it is that called, and why.'

'*Blikslater.*'

'Can I give you the de Vos number?'

'Yes.'

She read the number slowly, every word formed with care, as if she was talking to a child.

'Can I call you back?'

'No, Captain. I will hold the line.'

In the room of the Hawks Information Management Centre in Bellville, they could hear Captain Leonard Kaptein, five hundred kilometres to the north-east as the crow flies, shout loudly and excitedly: '*Julle!*' Followed by the sound of his government issue chair being knocked over and clattering to the floor.

'*Julle!*' the cry came again, but quieter, as he must have gone out of the door. 'I want everybody. Now! It's about Solomon. Get everyone on the radio . . .' Then he was beyond the receiving distance of the telephone, only the cooing of a dove in Victoria West sounding calmly down the line.

Nobody spoke.

They waited.

Nine long minutes. Too scared to hope.

A train rattled past on the far side of Tienie Meyer Street, on the way to Bellville station.

They heard voices and rapid footsteps. '. . . you sure, Wingnut?'

'*Ja,* Captain.'

'Hello?' said Leonard Kaptein.

'I'm here,' said Mbali.

'I'm putting on Sergeant Sollie Barends. Tell the woman, Wingnut.'

'Hello, this is Sergeant Sollie.' It was a younger voice, uncertain, as though finding the occasion quite overwhelming.

'This is Captain Kaleni.'

'Captain, my English is not so good.'

'Hold on.' Mbali turned to Griessel. 'Can you talk to him?'

He nodded, shifted his chair quickly up to the table and said in Afrikaans, 'Sollie this is Captain Benny Griessel. What do you know about the call?'

'OK. Captain, it was me who called that de Vos.'

'Why?'

'About the little rifle, Captain.'

'What rifle?'

'The triple-two, Captain.' Something happened in the IMC centre, intangible and inaudible, a subtle electric charge.

'Sollie, explain to me carefully, from the beginning.'

'OK.' They heard the rustle of pages. 'It's all here in the case file, Captain,' said Sollie Barends. 'That Monday, that's the seventeenth of January, Aunty Jacky Delport phoned – that's Mrs Jaqueline Johanna Delport of the farm Syferfontein this side of Vosburg – and she said the little rifle was missing. That's her late husband's triple-two. Because on Sunday she began clearing out and cleaning up and she noticed the rifle was gone, and she swore it was the *mannetjie* from the bookkeepers, that's the *mannetjie* who came to do the books for the estate. Then I drove out there, to investigate—'

'Sollie, just hang on a minute. Where is Vosburg?'

'A hundred kilometres from us here. Little place. But the farm is only seventy.'

'Do you know who the *mannetjie* is?'

'He's a Samuel. From the Cape.'

'Is that his surname?'

'No, Captain, the aunty thinks it's his name.'

'She thinks?'

'Captain, Aunty Jacky is eighty-seven, the old brain is not so *lekker* any more.'

'When was this Samuel there?'

'Here at the end of November, Captain.'

'It took her two months to realise the rifle was missing?'

'That's what I asked her too, Captain. She said she didn't need the rifle. And she didn't have the heart to clean up the Oom's workroom.'

'Why did she get someone from the Cape to do the books?'

'That's what Oom Henning told her to do. In the letter.'

'What letter?'

'That would be the letter he left. Along with his will.'

'What did he say in the letter?'

'He said she can get married again, but just not to Willem Potgieter. Potgieter is the neighbour there. A bachelor. He and Oom Henning had a big fight . . .'

'Sollie, what did the letter say about de Vos?'

'Only Frikkie de Vos was allowed to come and do the books.'

'Why so?'

'It looks like de Vos had been doing Oom Henning's books for the last eight years. The aunty said it's because of the *klippies* and the gambling.'

'What do you mean?'

'Oom Henning . . . Captain, everyone in the district knew Oom Henning was smuggling diamonds. Before my time already, I believe the diamond branch came here to try to catch him out, but he was too clever. He went up to Sun City about twice a year, or down there to your side, then he would come back and tell everyone how he had won. But really it was diamond money. The aunty said Oom Henning met de Vos in a gambling den, one time. Ever since then, he had to do the books, to hide the money from the diamonds from *Jan Taks*, the taxman. Everything got sent down to Cape Town, at the end of the financial year. But when Oom Henning died, she said she wasn't sending anything away, de Vos could come to the farm himself and do the books, under her four eyes. But then he sent that *mannetjie*. Samuel.'

'And Samuel stole the rifle?'

'She said it could only be him, the rest of the time the Oom's workroom was locked. So I phoned de Vos, but he never answered his phone. I sent letters too.'

'You're absolutely sure this Oom Henning owned a triple-two?'

'Yes, Captain. A Sako, three years old. Receipt is on the farm, the licence, everything.'

'Sollie, we think this Samuel could be the shooter. Solomon.'

'*Grote Griet*, Captain.'

'So you must tell me everything you know about him.'

'But I really don't know anything,' said Sollie nervously, the anxiety that he might let them down almost audible on the line.

57

'Aunty Jacky didn't like the *mannetjie*. She said he was too skinny, you couldn't trust such a skinny little man. And he drove a shiny car.'

'A shiny car?'

'That's all she could tell me, Captain.'

'Does she live all alone on the farm?'

'No, Captain, there are farm people too. The aunty is still farming.'

'How long was Samuel there?'

'Two days, Captain.'

'Where did he sleep?'

'On the farm, Captain.'

'Sollie, thank you very much. You're a good detective . . .'

'*Jissie*, Captain . . .'

'But now I must talk to your SC.'

'He's standing right here, Captain. Thank you, Captain.'

'Hello?' said the station commander.

'This is Benny Griessel, Leonard. We need your help badly now.'

'Just say.'

'How good are you people with fingerprints?'

'We're OK.'

'The first thing is, send Sollie and your best fingerprint man back to Aunty Jacky. To the room the man slept in. Tell them to work very carefully, tell them we want every last print. And then they must race back and send them to us.'

'We'll do it.'

'But while they are there, get Sollie to talk to everyone on the farm. Every single one. Everything they can remember about the man. Everything. Anything. His surname, his appearance, his clothes, his car. And send all the other people you can spare to Vosburg. House-to-house, anyone who might have seen the man. Maybe he filled up with petrol there, or had a meal, or something.'

'We'll do it.'

'Leonard, our problem is time. You'll have to be thorough, but you'll have to be fast.'

'We *can* be fast.'

★   ★   ★

They had to wait.

The word spread through the Hawks' building like wildfire – there was hope, there might be a breakthrough – so that the IMC room was soon overflowing, and Colonel Nyathi had to ask everyone to please go and wait in the parade room, he would personally let them know if there was any news.

But Cupido made himself at home at Griessel's side, as though he belonged there. And Bones Boshigo said, 'Colonel, you might need someone who understands the art of book-keeping,' and planted himself, leaning against the wall.

Half past four came and went, without a word.

By five o'clock the IMC night shift arrived. The day shift did not want to leave. Van Wyk didn't have the heart to force them, but Nyathi put his foot down, 'We need you to be fully rested tomorrow, we don't know if this will bear any fruit. Please.'

They dawdled, wasting time. It was twenty past five before the last one went home.

It was the hate that drove him now.

The sniper put the late Oom Henning Delport's triple-two Sako rifle in the boot of the Audi, closed it carefully with his left hand and walked around to the driver's door.

He was dressed in black – he might have to stand in the dark shadows of the trees beside the railway line, if it got late. If he couldn't get a clean shot from the car.

He got into the silver car. The pain in his right hand was constant and sharp, especially when he didn't keep the hand raised. He had gulped down a handful of headache pills at ten – he didn't dare walk into a pharmacy with this wound and ask for anything stronger. He didn't know whether Griessel knew that he'd been injured. He had lain down, between eleven and three, slept maybe forty minutes, waking often, panicked, bathed in sweat. No more painkillers. He had to be alert now.

For vengeance.

He switched the engine on, pressed the remote.

The garage door slid open.

Sergeant Sollie Barends, detective of the SAPS at Victoria West, went by the nickname of 'Wingnut', because of his very prominent ears.

But the eighty-seven-year-old Mrs Jaqueline Johanna Delport called him '*seunie*' or my boy. She sat at the big kitchen table, busy peeling figs. 'No, *seunie*, I told you: he was bad-tempered and he was skinny.'

'Aunty, the police are looking for him down in the Cape. For terrible things. I'm asking Aunty please to think nicely about then.'

'The old head isn't so strong any more, *seunie*.'

'Can Aunty remember what colour hair he had?'

'Sort of mousy.'

'Mousy brown or mousy blonde?'

'Yes. Something like that.'

'Mousy blonde?'

'Something like that.'

'Was he tall or was he short?'

'Not *too* tall.'

'But tall.'

'Not too much.'

'Taller than me?'

'Stand up so I can see ... *Ja*. You're *darem* not too tall either.'

'Did he have a moustache or a beard?'

'No.'

'Did he wear glasses?'

'Rita,' she called to one of the ageing maids standing at the stove, stirring a big pot full of boiling fig jam. 'Did he wear glasses?'

'No, *mies*, not that I can remember.'

'No,' said Jacky Delport, 'he didn't wear glasses.'

Sergeant Sollie sighed. 'Aunty, his car . . .'

'I don't know.'

'Aunty said it was shiny . . .'

'*Ja.*'

'Like in shiny silver?'

'Rita, was it shiny silver?'

'*Ja, mies*, like shiny-shiny.'

'Like shiny-shiny,' Jacky Delport repeated. 'A flat one.'

'A sports car?'

'No, I wouldn't say a sports car. But, you know, flattish.'

'*Diets*,' said Rita.

'*Diets*, you say?' asked Mrs Delport.

'*Ja, mies, Diets.*'

'Is that *Deutsch*?' asked Sergeant Sollie hopefully.

'*Ja*,' said Rita.

'A BMW?'

'Is a BMW *Diets*?'

'*Ja.*'

'Then it could have been a BMW.'

'Anything else, Aunty? Please.'

She thought for a long time before she asked, 'What did the *mannetjie* do down there in the Cape?'

'He shot policemen. Didn't Aunty see that on the TV? The Solomon shooter . . .'

'Does it look like there's a TV here?'

'No, Aunty, I'm just saying . . .'

'There's no signal here. Then Oom Henning said he wants to get a satellite dish. Six hundred rand a month. So we can sit and watch naked people swearing. Six hundred. I put my foot down.'

'I understand, Aunty.'

She tossed another peeled fig into the big white enamel

dish. As though it had suddenly occurred to her. 'Shot policemen?'

'*Ja*, Aunty. Shot one dead. Injured a whole lot of them too.'

'What for?'

'We don't know.'

'That's not right, *seunie*.'

'I know, Aunty.'

'That's not right. Policemen. Just making a living like everyone.'

'Yes, Aunty.'

'Rita . . .'

'*Ja, mies*?'

'Can you leave the jam for a little bit?'

'It's got to be *stirred* now, *mies*.'

'Aunty . . .' said Sollie Barends, the urgency of the case pressing on him.

'Shush now, *seunie*,' said Jacky Delport, and stood up with difficulty. 'Rita is going out for a bit, I will stir the pot.'

'*Ja, mies*.'

'Shut the door.'

'*Ja, mies*.'

'And don't you stand at the door and listen.'

'No, *mies*.'

Mrs Delport went over to the stove, and stirred the boiling jam. 'Come closer, *seunie*,' she whispered, conspiratorially.

The sergeant crossed over to her side.

'Lift your hand.'

'Aunty?'

'Lift your right hand, *seunie*.'

He raised his right hand. 'Now say after me: I swear on my mother's life . . .'

'I swear on my mother's life . . .'

'What I am going to hear now, I will never repeat.'

* * *

The cellphone signal came and went. They heard the hiss of a vehicle, and Sergeant Sollie Barends's voice over the loudspeaker.

'The aunty said . . . swear on my mother's . . . with Potgieter. For years . . . who it is—'

'Sollie,' said Griessel, and got no response. 'Sollie, can you hear me?'

'—kan.'

'Sollie, stop. If you can hear, stop where there is signal.'

Seconds ticked past. Only the hiss.

'He's gone,' said Mbali, deflated.

'Captain, can you hear me now?'

'Yes,' said Griessel. 'We couldn't make out what you were saying.'

'Oh. The aunty said . . . Are you still there?'

'Yes, we can hear you.'

'Captain, the aunty made me swear on my mother's life I wouldn't tell. But my mother will understand, it's a matter of life and death.'

'What did she say, Sollie?'

'She said she and Oom Willem Potgieter from the farm next door have shared a love for years, that's how she describes it. And when the *mannetjie* was here about the books, that night, Oom Pottie came to check, out of jealousy, she says. Scared she would cheat on him. With a young man. Are you still there?'

'We're here. We're listening.'

'And so he peeped in the window at the *mannetjie* who was still sitting and working. And he told her he knew the man. But she thought he was talking nonsense. But he said, no, not personally, but he knew him, and he was trouble.'

'And?'

'Now I'm driving over to the Oom.'

'He didn't tell her who the man is?'

'No, Captain . . .'

'Or how he knew him?'

'No, Captain, she said she told him he was lying, he was just jealous, she didn't want to hear.'

Sounds of frustration through the IMC room.

'Sollie, you'd better get moving then,' said Griessel. 'As quickly as you can.'

58

The sniper parked under the tree, against the fence along the railway line.

The branches hung low over the Audi, the foliage dense and green.

He surveyed the area. The station was only twenty metres away, but the path led people to Ford Street. Nobody would see him.

He got out, walked around to the boot. Looked around again.

No eyes or attention on him. He opened the boot, took out the plastic bucket, snapped open the lid. He bent, scooped the mud out with his hand and smeared it over the number plate. Walked around to the front number plate, repeated the process. Put the bucket away in the boot. Made sure once again that there were no people around.

He wiped his hands clean on the cloth, picked the rifle up with his left hand, pressed the boot shut. The pain in his hand was agonising. He walked back, climbed quickly into the car. Pressed the barrel of the gun down into the foot well of the passenger seat.

Only then did he look up, at the entrance to the building.

Clean shot.

Not the Chana. Not what he had planned. The risk was

higher. But it would only take one shot. And he knew the maze-like escape route off by heart.

The clock on the IMC wall ticked past six o'clock.

The team members sat ready at their computers. On the various screens, the databases waited for input: the national population register, the SAPS record centre interface, the vehicle registration system.

Cupido was talking. He was the only one. He was going on about how it would be someone from Silbersteins. He listed the reasons. They were the spider, right in the middle of this web. They connected Kotko and Sloet and Afrika and the shooter. They were in minerals and stuff. He was sure they did business up there in Vosburg too, what with the oil in the Karoo.

Nobody was listening to him.

Quarter past six.

The telephone remained silent.

Griessel dashed out to go and relieve himself. He knew the telephones would ring as soon as he left the room.

When he hurried back, at nineteen minutes past six, still nothing had happened.

At twenty-one minutes past six the phone rang in the stifling silence. '*Hayi*,' Mbali said, jumping.

Griessel pressed the button.

'Griessel.'

'Captain, this is Sollie, Captain.' Despite the static on the line they could hear the tone of his voice, the note of apology, as though he was conscious he was about to disappoint them all.

'What have you got, Sollie?'

'Captain, I don't know if the Oom is so *lekker* in the head.'

'How so, Sollie?'

'Captain, he's seventy-six, his glasses are as thick as the

bottom of a Coke bottle . . . I think he must have seen wrong, it can't be right.'

'Please,' whispered Mbali.

'What does he say, Sollie?'

'He says it's that *ou* who got off in the Chev case.'

'The Chev case?'

'No, the Chev case. The cook. The woman who cooked food.'

'The chef?' asked Cupido loudly, he couldn't help it.

'That's right. The cheffff,' the sergeant over-corrected. 'What was her name?'

'The Steyn case?' asked Griessel. 'Estelle Steyn?'

'That's him, Captain. The Oom says it's that *mannetjie*.'

Griessel's mind wanted to discount what he'd just heard, it didn't make any sense.

'No, man,' said Cupido disappointed. 'It can't be. He was a consultant. At KPMG.'

'KPMG are CAs,' said Bones. 'Chartered accountants.'

'Bookkeepers,' said Mbali, and the hope and excitement penetrated her voice. 'Auditors. What was his name?'

'Brecht,' said Griessel.

'His first name?'

'I'll Google it quickly,' said an IMC member.

'He hates the police,' said Mbali. 'Very much.'

'He was Eric or something,' said Cupido, still sceptical.

'He hates . . .' said Griessel and looked at the spot where Fanie Fick usually sat. Fick the investigating officer in the Steyn case. Fick, with his hangdog tail-between-the-legs-bloodhound-eyes who was a daily reminder of the massive errors of that case.

'Erik Brecht,' said the one who had been Googling. 'Erik *Samuel* Brecht.'

'Where's Fanie?' asked Mbali.

'At the Drunken Duck,' said Griessel. Where Fick went

every afternoon after work. Benny knew the place. In the past he had frequently drowned his own sorrows there.

And then he remembered the shooter's email. *Today I will shoot a Hawk.* And it all fell into place. '*Jissis!*' He sprang up and ran to the door, then realised he had no car, he had no idea where the flat-tyre BMW was. He stopped in his tracks. 'Vaughn, *he's* the Hawk who's going to be shot. Come!'

Fick drank another Klipdrift and Coke. One last one.

They hadn't even said thank you.

He was the one who had thought further, who had looked at de Vos's records from after his death. Noticed the calls. Looked up the number. *He'd* thought of all that.

But no 'thank you', no 'good work, Fickie', no 'of course you must stay until we find out what's going on'. No, just pack it up, stack it up, and bugger off. Go to bed, see you in the morning.

Because he was Fanie 'Fucked' Fick. No one really wanted to know him.

He hoped they didn't find anything.

Erik Samuel Brecht checked his watch.

Just a few more minutes.

Captain Fanie Fick, the man he hated most in all the world, came out of *that* door at half past six, like clockwork. Every weekday. Half drunk. On his way home.

He pulled the rifle up with his good hand.

The pain didn't bother him now.

He shoved the barrel out of the window.

Clean shot.

Sixty metres.

Then it would all be over.

Then he could get on with this meaningless life.

★ ★ ★

Cupido raced like a madman down Voortrekker Street, siren wailing, lights flashing. The traffic was mercifully light.

'He missed me on purpose!' yelled Griessel.

'What?'

'Last night. He missed me on purpose. So he could send the email. To me. But he didn't mention my name to the media.'

'Benny, I don't know what you're talking about.'

'He had a plan, Vaughn. From the beginning. He had a *fokken* plan.'

He took out his Z88, held it in his hand.

Fick put his empty glass down solemnly.

Time to go home. To his wife. And his two daughters.

And the disappointment in their eyes.

Because he drank. Because he had gone rotten. Given up.

They never would understand. This albatross that was hung around his neck. He would never get rid of it as long as he was in the police. For the rest of his life, he would be the one who had fucked up the Steyn case. Put an innocent man through hell. Nobody remembered the inhuman pressure from Estelle Steyn's parents, top management, and the media, nobody remembered the support and encouragement of the commanding officers, the forensic unit, the public prosecutors.

Get him, Fanie, get him.

And he had.

He stood up, said goodbye to the barman. Walked to the door.

He was the scapegoat, sacrificed on the altar of the SAPS.

Just as they wanted to do with Manie now. That's why he had felt no sympathy there in the IMC room. That's the way this miserable system worked.

Someone had to go down in flames, take the blame.

★ ★ ★

The barrel of the Sako triple-two protruded from the window, the home-made silencer extended, visible. His eye was against the scope. The ugly railed entrance to the Drunken Duck was in his sights, then the hanging sign. *OPEN. Pool. Darts. Pub. Grill.* The white neon light shone ever more brightly from inside, as the sun sank low.

Erik Brecht heard the sirens approaching.

Logic told him it couldn't be for *him*.

The entrance darkened.

Captain Fanie Fick. With his stiff upright walk, the concentrated attempt to hide his intoxication.

He aimed the sights on Fick's heart.

The sirens were high-pitched and shrill, just behind, where Voortrekker became Strand Weg.

It would mask the shot better.

He breathed out, pulled the trigger, his body flooding with a sense of immense relief. The rifle bucked in his hands and Fanie Fick fell.

Tyres screeched around the corner.

Griessel saw the body lying on the concrete seam between Keast Street and the parking area, and he cursed. Cupido saw the movement, a glimpse of something beyond Francis Road, between the trees, a car behind dark foliage, on the station side. He raced over the island, the police car slamming against the kerb, bouncing and sliding across the sand and the meagre grass. He shouted, 'There's the fucker!'

A surreal sound, a cellphone ringing, and Griessel realised it was his. Alexa, he swore it was Alexa, fate's crazy timing.

A flash of faster movement behind the trees, Cupido spun the steering wheel, he would have to cut him off. The back of the car skidded in the sand, the wheels losing traction, then he was on the tar, squealing tyres, shooting forward into Loumar Road. He hit the Audi, bonnet angled to bonnet, airbags exploding. They jerked forward against the seat belts, the crash echoing in their ears, tearing metal, shattering glass.

Griessel's cellphone rang again. He tried to get out, but the airbag was pressing him tightly. He was winded, blinded. The bastard was going to get away, he had to get out. He lifted the Z88, shot a hole in the airbag, fumbled for the handle, wrenched the door open, leaped out. The Audi was right next to him. He saw Brecht still behind the wheel, his face grim. The right hand, white bandage wound around it, reached for something.

The cellphone kept ringing.

Griessel aimed his pistol. 'Pick up the gun!' he screamed, because he wanted to shoot the fucker. 'Pick up the gun!'

Brecht sat transfixed.

Cupido was out, came running around the car.

'Radio for an ambulance!' shouted Griessel. 'And go and help Fanie!'

The cellphone was quiet.

A train rumbled past, undisturbed.

59

The news of Fanie Fick's death added a ruthlessness to the interrogation.

Mbali spoke, and Griessel sat and stared at Brecht. The cold, emotionless eyes, the brooding silence, the distance that said he had only scorn for them. That reserve, as though he carried secrets with him, even now, here, undeniably guilty. Griessel could understand why Fanie Fick had been so sure of his case back then.

Mbali laid out the evidence against him in a relentless voice. She said they knew he had stolen the rifle from a farm near Vosburg. They knew he had bought the Chana. They would investigate his computer forensically, they would connect him to everything. They would prove that the whole thing, from the moment he sent the first email to John Afrika, was part of a strategy to avoid the investigative spotlight when he shot Captain Fanie Fick. His Bible quotes and right-wing rhetoric were deliberately misleading, part of his big lie. They knew now why he had played the game with the police and the press, why he had been so careful in relaying the information about 'the communist'. Because he was unsure whether de Vos's widow knew about his and her husband's contracts. Everything made sense now. She said, 'I am going to do my best to remove you from society for as long as possible, because you are a premeditating, cold-blooded murderer.'

Not even a hint of reaction.

'Now we know Captain Fanie Fick was right. You killed Estelle Steyn too,' she said, because that was what forensic psychologist, Captain Ilse Brody, had suggested over the phone half an hour ago.

And she was right.

Brecht straightened up, and abhorrence washed over his face. 'No!' he shouted. 'No. Estelle's murderer is out there somewhere, and what are you doing? What? You take money, you look the other way. You break people. You destroy lives, *that's* what you do.' And to Griessel's surprise the eyes brimmed with tears as well as fury. 'Fick destroyed my life. He took my future, he stole it. *He* murdered *me.*'

'How can you say that?'

'How can I say that? The court found me not guilty. But the world doesn't work like that. I walk into the office, and I see how they look at me. I walk down the street, I sit in a restaurant, I phone a girl, I look into the eyes of Estelle's mother, and I see that I am guilty. You think I'm afraid to go to jail? I'm in jail already. I've lost everything already. I had to get away, from everything. I sit in my house. I work for scum like de Vos. Nobody wants to hear from me. *That* is my prison. And Fanie Fick? You promote him, to the Hawks. *That's* justice. *That's* how your system works.'

The cuffs jangled as he gestured. 'I'm glad I shot him. I'm glad he's dead. The next time you accuse an innocent person, you'll think twice.'

Griessel saw the gap. 'But you did that,' he said. 'You accused Makar Kotko. You found him guilty of murder, and it wasn't him.'

'You know it was him. Did you also get paid, when you worked with Afrika?'

'Can I call a journalist? So you can give him your proof?'

'You wouldn't.'

'I will. But you can't. Because you don't have proof.'

'I have,' he said, quite desperate. 'Hanneke Sloet came to me. She knew how he tortured people. She knew about the Trust. I showed her the payments, to the politicians, to the police. Payments that I had to cook. She said it's a disgrace what happened to me. She said someone ought to tell the media about Kotko, so that a guilty person could be arrested for a change. He killed her because he didn't want it to come out.'

'Someone *ought* to tell the media? Did you think she would have done it? While her firm stood to make fifteen million out of his contract?'

'He killed her.'

'What's your proof?'

'That's proof enough.'

'Did you give her the original statements of the Trust?'

'No.'

'Did you tell her, if she went to the media, that you would make the statements available?'

'No.'

'Did you see payments that Kotko might have made to a professional hit man?'

'No.'

'You made a mistake, Samuel. Tell me, why did you give your second name to the old woman on the farm? Did you know there were guns on the estate?'

No reaction.

'Where is your proof? Because Kotko has an alibi. His two henchmen have an alibi. Where is your proof?'

No response.

Griessel walked to the parade room. His JOC team was waiting for news.

They sat talking, voices subdued. Fanie Fick's death hung like a shadow over the whole unit. They fell silent when he entered, looked at him expectantly.

'Nothing,' he said. 'Sloet did go to him, she did see the statements of the Trust. She said the media *ought* to know. So he believed it was Kotko.'

'*Bliksem*,' someone said.

'Tomorrow we'll start from the beginning again,' said Griessel. All he could think of now, was his bed. And the sweet bliss of sleep.

They all stood up. 'Is it true that you shot the airbag?' one asked.

He nodded. 'I was afraid he would get away.'

They smiled, shaking their heads.

'While his cellphone was ringing the whole time,' said Cupido. 'Benna, I have to know, who phoned?'

He had forgotten about the call. 'I don't know.'

His colleagues grinned. He took out his phone, saw the SMS that said there was voicemail. He called it up.

It was Nxesi, the Green Point detective: 'Captain, I am sorry to bother you, I know you are busy. But the people from the wireless keep phoning – they want access to the building. No rush, thank you very much.'

'It was Tommy Nxesi,' he said.

'Go figure,' said Cupido. 'What did he want?'

'People who want to get into Sloet's apartment, to test the Wi-Fi signal.'

'Oh.'

They walked down the passage. And Cupido stopped. 'To test the Wi-Fi signal?'

'That's right.'

'Was it broken?'

Griessel tried to remember. 'I think they are installing it.'

'Can't be,' said Cupido.

'I suppose it could be out of order.'

'For how long?'

'Why do you ask?'

''Cause . . . Can we phone Tommy Nxesi?'

He noted Cupido's focus. He sighed, said, 'OK,' and tapped on his cell, made the call.

When he had finished: 'The Wi-Fi was only installed at the end of January, Tommy says. They have to test it in every apartment now.'

'That's strange.'

'What is it, Vaughn?'

'Let me check the photos first.'

'What photos?'

'Crime scene, of her bedroom.'

'They're in my office.'

They walked together, Cupido's hand on the back of his neck, his head bowed. The Wandering Thinker. Griessel followed him reluctantly, hardly able to keep his eyes open. Interrogating Brecht had sapped the last of his energy.

They opened the thick case file, slid the photos out. Cupido arranged them on the desk. 'Check this,' he said, pointing a finger at one photo. It showed the table top in Sloet's bedroom. Her laptop, a few files, a fountain pen, a glass of red wine, nearly empty, an Apple iPhone. Close to it was the brown high-backed chair and the brown standard lamp, switched on.

He didn't understand. 'What am I looking at, Vaughn?'

'She sent the email, to that big deal maker, just before ten?'

'That's right. To van Eeden.'

'But how, Benna? No cellular dongle, no wireless. And it's an old iPhone that, they can't do Wi-Fi hotspots.'

He hadn't the faintest idea what his colleague was talking about, as Cupido could see. '*Jissis*, Benna, there was no connectivity. How could she have sent the mail?'

'Are you saying van Eeden was lying?'

'No, Lithpel Davids' report confirmed it. The mail was sent.'

'I don't understand, Vaughn.'

'Benna, I think this laptop has a built-in 3G modem.'

'What does that mean?'

'It's like a built-in cellphone, but it connects with the Internet on the cellular network. If you take the SIM card out and put it in a phone, and you put money on it, you can make voice calls too.'

'Ah,' said Griessel, beginning to understand.

'She could have made calls that we don't know about. Or received them, from Mr Fucking Kotko. Lithpel missed a trick, canny coloured, that bro', but nobody's perfect. Let me give him a call.'

It was after eleven when Lithpel phoned back. He said of course Sloet's Dell Latitude D630 had a built-in 3G HSPDA 3.66GHz Tri-band Embedded Mobile Broadband card in it. But Tommy Nxesi's original request was just that he should look at emails sent, websites visited, documents created – and any of the aforementioned that might have been deleted. And that is what he had done. He assumed that the detective knew about the card, and 'it's not my job to do on-site training'.

Could he see if there was a call history on the card?

Yes, he could see, but there was nothing. Someone could have deleted it.

Could he see what the number on the SIM card was?

Of course he could. And he gave them the number, which they duly handed over to the IMC night shift, to start their well-oiled procedure to acquire a two-oh-five subpoena. And then beg their contact at Vodacom to give them rapid, urgent access to call records this one last time.

Which all only came through at twenty past twelve, when the exhaustion was greater than the anticipation, and Griessel lay sleeping, his head on his hands.

Cupido woke him. 'No calls, but a whole lot of SMSes to one particular number,' he said. 'All the time, for months. And also on the night of the murder.'

'Fuck,' said Griessel, and tried to rub the sleep from his eyes.

They sat watching the operator trying to match the number with all the suspects they had on the system. And found nothing.

'Let's look at RICA,' the operator said, because the new Regulation of Interception Act should have all the details of owners of SIM cards.

Seven minutes of waiting. The name and address appeared on the screen.

'Can you believe it?' Cupido asked.

Griessel couldn't. It made no sense at all.

60

They stopped in front of the big wrought-iron gates in Hohenhort Avenue, Constantia.

Cupido was in the driver's seat, and nudged Griessel, 'Benna, are you awake?'

'I am.' But not entirely.

'Is this the place?'

'Yes.'

Cupido pressed the button of the intercom repeatedly, each jab punctuated with a 'Hello? Hello?'

It took nearly ten minutes to elicit a response. Henry van Eeden's voice, sleepy and irritable. 'What is it?'

'This is the SAPS. Open up.'

'You'll have to show me some identification.'

Griessel leaned across so the video eye could see him. 'Mr van Eeden, this is Benny Griessel, I was here just the other day.'

'It's half past one at night.'

'We are aware of that.'

A hesitation. Then, 'Come in.'

The gate rolled open. Cupido drove in. He whistled as the night vista of the estate opened up to them. 'How rich *are* they?'

'Very.'

The exterior lights of the house lit up as they approached. The paved parking area was empty, the Lamborghini probably cosily tucked away in the garage.

They got out, Griessel walked in front, along the path, up the steps. The catnaps he had taken in the office and the car had only made him feel even more dull. He shook his head, as if to shake the cobwebs out.

Van Eeden opened the door. He was dressed in a white

dressing gown with a burgundy Oriental dragon motif. Barefoot. 'Captain, what's going on?'

'Can we talk, Mr van Eeden?'

'Of course.'

'This is Captain Vaughn Cupido.'

Van Eeden put out his hand. Cupido ignored it. The man frowned, led the way to a sitting room, switched on lights. Modern and in good taste. 'Please sit down. Can I put coffee on?'

'No, thank you, Mr van Eeden.'

Van Eeden sat down, leaning forward, elbows on knees. 'I take it this couldn't have waited till morning.'

'Mr van Eeden, I will ask you again, where were you on the evening of the eighteenth of January?' Griessel asked.

'I told you I was in Somerset West. I gave a speech. In front of three hundred people. Didn't you talk to the congress people?'

He hadn't. That was one of the things that had escaped him, in the hurly-burly of the investigation. Griessel took out his notebook, paged through it until he found the SIM card number. 'Does this number look familiar?' He read it to van Eeden.

Van Eeden deliberated for a moment. 'No,' he said, shaking his head innocently from side to side.

A light went on in the passage outside the door, and then someone appeared in the doorway. Griessel recognised her, van Eeden's wife, the lovely, serene woman who reminded him of Alexa. He couldn't recall her name.

'What's going on?' she asked.

'This is Captain Griessel, Annemarie. I'm not sure what's going on.'

She looked at Griessel.

'Evening, ma'am.'

'Good evening. Shall I make some coffee?'

'Please,' said van Eeden.

She hesitated for a moment. Then she turned around and walked out.

'It's a cellphone number registered in your name,' said Griessel.

'In my name?'

'On the RICA database,' said Cupido, aggressively, now spoiling for a fight. 'Which means you presented your ID. In person.'

'Captain, you have my cellphone number. You know this is not mine.'

'Then why is it registered in your name?'

'I don't know. It must be a mistake.'

'You have only one phone?' Cupido asked.

'Just the one cellphone. There are quite a few land lines.'

'Do you have a cellular modem? For your laptop?' asked Cupido.

'I have.'

'What is the number?'

'I don't know. Do they have numbers?'

'They do. Can you fetch the modem, along with your laptop?'

'Just a minute.' He stood up and walked out through one of the doors.

Cupido looked at the art on the walls. 'And they call this art,' he said. 'My six-year-old cousin could do better.'

Griessel looked. Abstract. Vaguely familiar. He stood up, went closer.

In the right-hand corner, in square brush strokes, was the artist's name. *Aalbers.*

Van Eeden came walking back. He carried the laptop carefully. The black modem, with a yellow MTN logo, was protruding from the side.

'Turn it on,' said Cupido.

Van Eeden put the laptop down on the coffee table, pressed a button. 'I didn't know they had numbers,' he said.

'Of course not,' said Cupido sarcastically.

They waited in uncomfortable silence for the computer to start up.

'Open the modem application,' said Cupido.

Van Eeden slid a finger over the mouse panel, and tapped.

'Now read out that number,' said Cupido.

Van Eeden got halfway, then he looked up at Griessel. 'I didn't realise . . .'

'Read the full number, please.'

The man read.

'You will agree that it is the same number as the one that we read out to you.'

'Yes. But I really didn't know . . .'

'Mr van Eeden, is this your laptop?' Griessel asked.

'Yes . . .'

'Which only you use?'

'Yes.'

'Where was the laptop on the night of the eighteenth of January?'

'With me.'

'In Somerset West?'

'That's right. My notes for the speech were on it.'

'And the modem?' Cupido asked.

'The modem was there too. I always put it in the case along with the laptop.'

'So the laptop and the modem and you were in Somerset West?'

'That's right.'

'From what time?'

'I can't remember precisely . . .'

'More or less?'

'Well, the dinner was from seven o'clock. I must have been at the hotel from just before seven.'

'And then?'

'Then I ate with the congress chairman.'

'And then?'

'Then I gave my presentation, nine o'clock. Nine to ten. But there were a lot of questions, I only got away at half past ten.'

'And the laptop and the modem were with you the whole time?'

'Yes.'

'You are absolutely sure of that?'

'Yes. Absolutely.'

Cupido laughed, a laugh of delight. Hehehehe. 'Genuine?' he said.

'Yes.'

'Now, that modem, on the same night, all on its own, as if by magic, out of the case, sent forty-seven SMSes to Hanneke Sloet. Between six-twenty-one and nine-nineteen.'

'How on earth?'

'Maybe not on earth. Maybe divine intervention.' Griessel could hear Cupido was firing on all cylinders now. He must have known his colleague would relish interrogating a super-rich white man who was lying through his teeth. 'Cause the mystery deepens,' said Cupido. 'In the past three months, that innocent little modem sent Hanneke Sloet an average of seventeen text messages a day. And on the night of the murder, lo and behold, they were not only sent, but they all registered on the cellular tower here, near your house. Constantia. How do you explain that?'

61

Henry van Eeden could not explain it. 'Someone must have cloned the number or . . . what do you call it when they take over control?'

'Hacked it?' Cupido asked.

'That's right. That's what must have happened.'

'Wait, let me get this straight: you say you have never in your life sent Sloet an SMS with that SIM card?' Cupido asked.

'Captain, that's quite a broad statement. Miss Sloet and I communicated often, in various ways . . .'

Now it was Miss Sloet, Griessel noted. When he and Bones were here, van Eeden had talked of Hanneke.

'So you have SMSed her from your little laptop after all?' asked Cupido.

'I may have . . .'

'May have. To the tune of seventeen a day. But not that evening?'

'Definitely not that evening.'

'Somebody hacked your card?'

'Yes.'

'While your laptop was switched off? In its bag? In Somerset West?'

'That's right.'

'This mystery hacker goes to all that trouble, to have an SMS conversation with someone you know personally?'

'It looks like it.'

'And she likes it so much that she sends a whole bunch of SMSes back to the hacker?'

'That I wouldn't know.'

'That's your story, and you're sticking to it?' Disbelieving.

'Captain, you can believe whatever you want.'

Then Annemarie van Eeden came in with a tray. 'Henry, what's going on?' she asked.

'It's a misunderstanding,' her husband said, uncomfortably, rising to take the tray from her.

'What sort of misunderstanding?'

'Please, let me sort it out.'

She looked at van Eeden. Griessel saw the expression, fleeting, as though just for a second she saw a future without the peace of mind that this wealth, this massive estate, the beautiful house, afforded. That's the problem with having money, you never stop worrying about losing it.

Then she brushed her husband's cheek with her fingertips, a tender touch, full of love. 'I am sure you will,' she said, and left the room with her usual grace.

Van Eeden put the tray down on the table. 'Help yourself,' he said.

Benny needed it. He poured out all three cups.

Cupido solemnly took out his cellphone, the HTC Desire HD of which he was so proud, and put it down on the table. 'Do you see this phone?'

Van Eeden didn't want to answer. 'Yes . . .'

'If it rings, then you're nailed.'

'Captain, I have been patient up till now . . .'

'And we humble policemen are duly grateful, my lord.'

'I must object. You are twisting my meaning.'

'Whatever. It won't help. You are going to do time. And let me tell you why. If we at the Hawks want access to cellphone call records, then we gotta apply for a section two-oh-five subpoena, in accordance with article two-oh-five of the Criminal Procedure Act. It's not too hard, the courts say it's only a relatively mild invasion of privacy. We just have to connect you to the case. Then we can see who you phoned or texted. But to see *what* you texted, *daais 'n ander storie*. Big invasion of privacy. Same article two-oh-five subpoena, but the judge schemes it a bit differently. Now we got to *uithaal en wys*, show that you're a proper suspect. Got it?'

He got only a vague nod.

'We didn't just drive up to your magnificent gates for some social chitchat. We are the Hawks, pappie. We've got our ducks in a row. Captain Benna, wily old veteran that he is, remembered you were scared Hanneke Sloet would steal your job . . .'

Van Eeden grimaced in protest, but Cupido silenced him with a wave of the hand. 'Captain Benna also reckons that you're the kingpin, the main man, the big dog deal maker, the Big Mac of the whole BEE place, you're the one who stands to score the sweetest if it goes through, but you're also the biggest loser when it all goes south. If the Russian Mafia involvement and pension fund fraud and all that ugly stuff gets into the media. But the thing I think will make up the judge's mind, the critical factor, as they say in the classics, is the fact that you purposely, knowingly and wilfully withheld information pertinent to a murder investigation. That's what's gonna nail you.'

Van Eeden shook his head, slowly and with righteous indignation.

'I know what you're thinking,' said Cupido, still with obvious delight. 'You're thinking, but I deleted all those SMSes. You think, if you take them off your laptop, then they're gone, baby, gone. Big mistake, pappie. Big mistake. Let me educate you about the cellular industry. They have servers. Every SMS that you send logs on those servers. Time, date, sender, recipient. And the SMS itself. The *content*. The actual text. All sitting there. On that server. For a year, pappie. The *outjies* there by IMC, the Information Management Centre, that's the Hawks' genius squad, our *competitive* advantage, that you'll understand as a business-man, *nè*, those *outjies* they say to me it's because the SMS takes up so little space on the server, just a few bytes, so they can keep it a long time. *That* you didn't know, hey?'

Van Eeden was poker-faced, only his pallor betrayed him.

'Now, if my HTC Desire HD smartphone, running on Google Android two point two Froyo, powered by the cellular giant Vodacom, if this phone rings, it means the judge said, open up those servers. Let the light of truth and justice shine upon the rich man's messages. Then, pappie, you're going to need more than divine intervention. Like, maybe, a very good lawyer.'

Van Eeden stared at the phone.

'Oh, and did I forget to mention, along with the article two-oh-five, we applied for a search warrant too. So things are going to be a little busy around here pretty soon.'

Van Eeden's gaze flicked from the phone to Griessel.

'Is there something you want, Mr van Eeden?' he asked.

Van Eeden bit his lower lip.

Cupido's phone rang, loud and shrill.

Van Eeden's whole body shuddered. With a sweeping gesture Cupido picked up the HTC, swiped the screen, held it to his ear. 'This is your captain speaking,' he answered.

'Mr van Eeden,' Griessel prodded.

The millionaire suddenly leaped to his feet. 'I had an affair with Hanneke,' he said.

'Hold your horses,' said Cupido over the phone. 'The rich man's coming clean.'

62

He walked as he talked, pacing back and forth across the spacious room. The words came with difficulty, as though he had forgotten where he had hidden them. There were silences, when he looked in the direction where his wife had disappeared from the room.

It began in December 2009, only a week after he and Hanneke Sloet had met for the first time at a work-related meeting. He said it was 'inevitable', a 'whirlwind', they were 'soulmates'. And, after a long pause, it was a hugely physical attraction that bowled them both over.

He said after the first time, in the Cape Grace, in a room that he'd booked at the last minute, they met in hotels, in Johannesburg, in Cape Town. A few times in her apartment in Stellenbosch, but it was tense, they were never sure whether her friend, Roch, might turn up. They were careful. Discreet. He often left his cellphone lying around in this house, he was too afraid to use it for SMS communication, sure that he would forget to delete something some time. Hanneke's phone was often left with her personal assistant when she was in Silberstein meetings. That's why they had decided on the computer SMSes.

A year ago, in February 2010, she decided to break off her relationship with Roch. Van Eeden was opposed to this, because despite the intensity of the affair he had no long-term plans. But she was honest. She wanted him. She insisted on more time with him, she was unhappy about the fact that they could never be seen in public together, she upped the pressure on him to get a divorce. He thought he could handle it, that it would burn itself out, would blow over. Until she had her breasts enlarged. All because one afternoon after 'a session' he confessed that he liked large breasts. That was when he realised she was more determined than he had thought. And then she gave him the photographs. That she had had taken for him. He didn't know what to do with them. He locked them in his office safe, and two days after her death he cut them up and burned them. He kept one. Only one. Which they would find in his safe.

And in January she had moved to the city, so that they could see each other more easily and more often. She had a key to her front door made for him. And then she began to pressurise him. They had been together a year already, they were sure they were in love with each other. It was time for him to get a divorce. It was time for them, without shame, to be together for ever.

Then he had to tell her he wasn't prepared to do that.

On the evening of the eighteenth she informed him by SMS that she was going to see Annemarie, his wife. She was going to tell her everything. If he didn't have the courage to end his marriage, then she would do it for him.

She left him no choice.

'What did you use to stab her?' Griessel asked.

He stood up. 'Come and see.' He led them to his study, a magnificent room of bookshelves and glass display cases with true-to-life models of old wooden ships. And a sword, antique and worn, fashioned from dull greyish-brown copper. 'It's a Jian,' he said. 'Two thousand years old. The Chinese gave it to me. To say thank you.'

'Why did you use it?' asked Griessel.

'It was what I had.'

Griessel asked him to return to the sitting room. He asked him to describe exactly what happened that night in Hanneke Sloet's apartment.

Van Eeden said he SMSed her to tell her he was on his way. From Somerset West. He went in through the parking garage, so that no one could see he was carrying the sword. He unlocked the door. Hanneke must have heard him, because she was standing there. And then he stabbed her. It was a dreadful moment. But he had to protect his world.

Then he put the sword down and went up to her bedroom, to delete the SMSes on her laptop. And then he wiped the floor and the door and the sink clean with a cloth he found in the kitchen.

On the way home he threw the cloth out of the car window.

'What time did you arrive at her apartment?'

'About half past eleven.'

'Are you sure?'

'Round about then.'

'You drove through from Somerset West?'

'Yes.'

'After you had given a speech to 300 people?'

'Yes.'

'Mr van Eeden, that doesn't make sense. How do you explain the SMSes that were sent from your laptop? From here in Constantia?'

'You have your confession, Captain. What more do you need?'

'The problem,' said Griessel, 'is that you phoned Hanneke Sloet twice, that evening. At 22.48, a call that registered on the cell tower at Somerset West, and again at 23.01, registered on the Nyanga tower.'

'Yes, I did.'

'But she didn't answer.'

He shrugged. 'She must have been in the bath.'

'But why did you phone her? If you were on your way there to murder her? If you wanted to surprise her?'

'I wanted to make sure she was at home.'

'You're lying,' said Cupido. 'Because she didn't answer. So how would you know?'

'The pathologist's report says she died closer to ten o'clock,' said Griessel. 'And he's reasonably sure, because we know exactly when she ordered a take-away and ate it that night, we know what she ate, he could track the digestion of the food accurately.'

'*Reasonably* sure. What does reasonably sure mean?' asked van Eeden.

'How could the SMSes have been sent from here if you and your laptop were in Somerset West?'

'It doesn't matter.'

'Mr van Eeden, within the hour we will know what was written in those SMSes.'

He jumped up, waving his arms, almost shouting now. 'What does it matter? What does it matter? I'm telling you *that* is what happened. I killed her. She wanted everything. My work, my money, my life. She was like a bloodsucker, a parasite, she wanted to suck me dry, she just wanted *more* and *more*. She swallowed me whole. I know I should never have jumped into bed with her, I *know*, but it was too late by then. I made a mistake, one massive mistake, but I'll pay for it now – isn't that enough for you?'

'Why are you lying?' Cupido asked.

'Who are you protecting?' asked Griessel.

'I am not protecting anyone.' He walked up to them, his wrists held close together. 'Take me. Lock me up. You have everything that you want.'

'He's protecting me,' said Annemarie van Eeden from the doorway.

'Don't listen to her. Annemarie, go away.'

'I am the one who killed that woman.'

'Annemarie, please . . .'

'Henry,' she said soothingly, 'you didn't handle it very well. Sooner or later they would have realised.'

'Annemarie . . .' he said helplessly, knowing everything was lost.

63

She came in and sat down with them, with an immense inner calm.

She said she only found out about the affair early in December last year, but she had suspected it for months. There were so many telltale signs for a wife to spot.

In December, alone at home, she had walked into Henry's study, and saw the laptop unattended. And it was on. Henry, who always carefully turned off his laptop, protected it with a password, had apparently forgotten. Or maybe he had wanted her to see. Maybe he had wanted her to do something about it.

And she had begun searching deliberately, because the suspicion, the doubt was too great. She came across the SMSes. She saw how intense it was. She saw a side of Henry that she hadn't been aware of. Her husband, the dirty talker. Her husband, the sex addict.

She wrote down all the cell modem's details. She hired a private detective, who found someone to intercept the SMSes.

She received them all. For a month and a half, a flood of vulgar sex messages, like a banal bodice-ripper paperback.

And the increasing demands of 'that woman'. And Henry's reluctance to end the affair. Then she knew she was going to lose everything.

She didn't know what to do.

She could deduce from the messages between the woman and her husband that he had a key to her door. She went looking for it and found it in Henry's jacket pocket. She had a duplicate made, quickly one afternoon between Christmas and New Year. She knew the woman was visiting her parents, and Henry wouldn't miss it. It was without premeditation, a way of hitting back, a small triumph.

And then that Tuesday night.

'Annemarie, please,' van Eeden warned again.

She gave him a serene smile and said, 'Henry, the courts are much more lenient to the wronged wife.'

On that Tuesday night of the eighteenth of January, Henry left just after six, a little late, for Somerset West. He wasn't telling the truth when he said his notes were on the laptop.

Henry never spoke from notes, he talked off the cuff. He was such a smooth talker. Usually.

Shortly after his departure she heard a telephone ringing, and went into Henry's office to answer it, it was the nearest room at the time. The call was insignificant, one of the garden staff was sick.

She dealt with the phone call. Then she noticed that the computer was on, with a screen that read: *Shut down. Log off. Restart.* She realised Henry had been in too much of a hurry for the last command. She sat down, without a plan. And she saw the little block that signalled a new SMS.

It was from 'that woman'.

It asked: *Are you there?*

So she answered: *Yes.*

And so the conversation began.

The rest just happened, while she was perpetuating the fraud. Because later, the woman asked: *Why don't you come around quickly?*

Quickly for a quickie? she answered, in the language she had been familiar with for over a month.

A cum-quickly quickie.

You'll have to make it worth my while.

Shall I wait for you without panties?

I want more.

What exactly are you thinking, Mister Kinky?

She looked up, and saw the sword in the glass case. A moment's hesitation, then everything fell into place. In her mind's eye she could see how it might unfold.

A blindfold.

That's new. I like that.

At the door.

On the carpet?

No. At the door. Ten o'clock. Sharp.

She left at about twenty to nine, with the sword on the seat beside her.

At ten o'clock she unlocked the door with her duplicate.

The woman was standing there, wearing the blindfold.

She lifted the sword, and with a sense of incredible relief and immense violence, she stabbed it into the woman's heart, and pulled it out. The woman fell, silent, the only sound the crack of her head hitting the floor.

She put the sword down. Because she knew the police would find it, along with the SMSes on the laptop. They would accuse Henry.

That was what she wanted. That he should be punished for the pain. She had already lost her man, it was the rest she wanted to protect.

'Would you like to continue the story, Henry?'

He shook his head.

'Correct me if I get something wrong. Apparently she had sent Henry another SMS, to his phone. Something like: *I'm not going to stand at the door blindfolded and without panties the whole night you know.* Because she assumed he was on his way to her already, and not at his computer. Dear Henry only received it after his speech, and he knew something was wrong. So he phoned her, but she didn't answer. Then he drove to her apartment. I can't deny it, it gives me pleasure to imagine what he must have thought when he saw his sword lying there, beside his soulmate. Then he saw the SMSes on her laptop. He tried so hard to clean up, to protect himself and me. But it didn't work, did it, Henry?'

Day 7

Friday

64

His cellphone woke him.

He mumbled, '*Jissis*,' grabbed it and said, 'yes?'

That's when he saw that it was already nine o'clock.

'Benny,' said Colonel Nyathi, 'I know you were probably sleeping, but I just wanted you to know the brigadier is flying back this morning. The hearing was cancelled.'

'That's good, sir,' he said in a voice croaky with sleep.

'He asked me to thank you, Benny. He will do it personally when he gets back.'

'But it wasn't me, sir. It was Vaughn who cracked it.'

'That's not what Vaughn is saying. Oh, and we're waiting for you before we start the meeting.'

'What meeting, sir?'

'The celebratory one.'

'Sir, my car is at work . . .' Cupido had dropped him off at four this morning.

Nyathi laughed. 'I'll send someone.'

He stood waiting at the gate to his block of flats for a detective from the Violent Crimes group to pick him up. He looked at the opposite corner where Brecht had sat in wait for him. He thought how he had got it all wrong.

Mbali Kaleni and Fanie Fick had caught the shooter.

Vaughn Cupido, who had wangled the timely phone call last night with a program on his cellphone. 'It's an Android app, Benna. Fake-Call Me.' And he still didn't know how it worked. Cupido had caught the van Eedens, and now he was giving Griessel the credit – his respect for his colleague had risen to new heights.

But it was only one of the many things that he had read incorrectly. Cupido, the shooter, the Sloet case. He had to accept that he didn't have the head for the deals, the companies, the trusts. He didn't have the knowledge of computers and cellphone modems and iPhones that couldn't 'hotspot'.

He wasn't worth a Hawk's arse.

Old fox. *Wily old veteran.* Fool. Alexa Barnard didn't even want to talk to him. It was her concert tonight, and she wouldn't want him there to share her great moment.

Because he was a fuck-up.

Mbali shook her head when the gathering applauded her. She waddled to the front, and then said, 'Some of you thought that I was appointed because John Afrika could manipulate me.'

A murmur rippled through the room.

'I heard the gossip,' she said. 'I know I am not popular. I know I can be difficult to work with. I know it is not easy to have a woman around. But I want you to know nobody will manipulate me. So, let me tell you what happened in Amsterdam, so that it can be out in the open.'

Dead silence.

'Our hosts, the Amsterdam police, thought it would be a treat to take us on a bicycle tour of the city. And I was too proud to tell them that I cannot ride a bicycle. I did not want them to think that South Africans are backward. So I tried. And I lost my balance, and I lost my way, and I rode into a canal. They had to rescue me from that filthy water. With a boat. It must have been pretty funny. But for me it was a very big embarrassment. And then my pride kept me from laughing at myself, and I wanted to keep it a secret. But I have now learned that secrets have consequences. Next time it will be different. Thank you.'

And she sat down, in the midst of them.

Griessel made another mistake.

Nyathi said, 'Go, Benny, take the rest of the day off, you deserve it,' and he instinctively drove to Stellenbosch, to someone who cared for him, someone who said with pride: 'My father is doing the Sloet case.' To look for comfort there.

He phoned Carla when he arrived on the campus, and said he was there to take her to lunch. She was uncomfortable and said, 'We're in the Neelsie . . .' She hesitated before she invited him to join them.

He found her there, with the Neanderthal, a giant. He towered over Griessel and over Carla, as she introduced him, 'Pa, this is Calla; Calla this is my pa.'

The Neanderthal crushed his hand, pumping it enthusiastically: 'Oom, it's a privilege, Oom.'

They sat down, Carla and the Neanderthal close together, his muscular arm around her. Carla's little hand was on the tree trunk of a leg.

'Calla is my friend, Pa.'

'I'll look after your daughter very well,' he said.

He can actually talk, Griessel thought.

'You'd better,' said Carla, and gazed at her rugby player with love and admiration. 'My pa is a Hawk.'

'With a gun,' said Griessel. He wanted to say it light-heartedly, but the threat was still there.

They didn't hear him. They kissed. Right there in front of him.

He drove to his flat, collected his dirty laundry and took it to the Gardens Centre.

He sorted it in pathetic little piles in front of the washing machine. The sum total of his wardrobe.

He thought of searching Henry van Eeden's walk-in wardrobe, the row upon row of shirts and trousers, brand new and fashionable, that had been hanging there. He thought of Makar Kotko's expensive suit and shirt.

Life wasn't fair.

He hung the clothes up on the washing line at the block of flats. He must buy underpants, there were too many with holes. And more new shirts. Some time or other, when his credit card recovered.

In his sitting room he took out his bass guitar and sat down on the couch. He found no solace in it. It reminded him of the concert tonight, and that he wouldn't be going.

He lay down on his bed, his head filled with self-pity.

The ringing of his cellphone woke him.

This is no life, every fucking day the same thing, he thought.

He answered.

'Benny, Alexa has gone,' said Ella, shrill and anxious. 'And she has to sing at eight.'

'What's the time now?'

'It's nearly half past six.'

'What happened?'

'We were here at her house. She was terribly nervous, since yesterday, after the bad rehearsal. She hardly slept at all. She was so stubborn, I practically had to beg her to get ready. I was in the bath, and when I came out, she was gone.'

'How long ago was that?'

'About fifteen minutes.'

'OK,' he said.

'What are we going to do?'

'I'll go and fetch her.'

* * *

He found her sitting in the Mount Nelson's Planet Bar, at
one of the little tables, alone. There was a bottle of gin on the
table, a glass in her hand.

He first walked to the barman, unnoticed. He asked for a
bottle of Jack Daniel's.

'I'll have to open it, sir.'

'That's fine.'

He paid, got a glass, and walked over to her. Pulled out a
chair and sat down.

She looked at him in surprise.

He picked up the bottle of Jack, and poured a full glass.

'What are you doing?' she said in a frightened voice.

'I'm drinking with you.'

'Benny . . .'

'Alexa, be quiet. I'm drinking.'

She put her glass down. 'You've been clean for two
hundred and twenty days.'

'Two hundred and thirty three.' He lifted the glass to his
mouth, his whole being ready for the heavenly taste.

She grabbed his arm. The liquor spilled on the table.
'Benny, you can't do it.'

'Alexa, please let go of my arm.'

'You can't do it.'

'Why not? At least I have an excuse. I'm a fuck-up. What
do *you* have?'

'What happened, Benny?' she asked, but she didn't let go
of his arm.

'What does it matter?'

'Benny, please. What happened?'

'Everything happened. Fanie Fick was shot dead, because I
am a moron. My colleagues had to solve the Sloet case, because
I'm not a detective's arse. I can't read people any more. I have
lost Carla, the only person . . . the only woman who still wanted
anything to do with me. She's in love with the Missing Link. My

son wants to have "Parow Arrow" tattooed on his arm, and I have no way to stop him, because I need to ask him to give me lessons about Wi-Fi hotspots and Twitter and Facebook and cellphone modems, so that I don't make more of a fool of myself than I already have. Like Saturday night, when I humiliated the woman I am half in love with, in front of her friends. And drove her back to drink. And now she won't answer me when I call. That's my reason to drink, Alexa, not the pile of crap you have deluded yourself about. Let go of my arm.'

She clung to him even more tightly. 'Benny, why did you never say you were half in love with me?'

'Because you are Xandra Barnard, and I am just a stupid policeman.'

'Why only half in love? Because I drink?'

'I am totally in love with you, Alexa.'

'So why don't you ever touch me?'

'Because I'm afraid you won't want me to touch you.'

'Do you want to?'

'Yes.'

'Why?'

'Because to me you are so beautiful. And sexy, and smart. And deep. And arty-farty. When you're sober.'

'Really?'

'Alexa, are we going to drink, or are we going to coo?'

She looked at him with a deep tenderness, then she put her glass down and beckoned a waiter closer. 'Can you take all this away?'

She turned to Griessel and she said, 'We are going to coo,' and tried to wrest the Jack Daniel's from his grip.

'And then will you go and sing?'

'Yes,' she said.

'And then?'

'Then you are going to touch me.'

He let go of the glass.

Acknowledgements

One of the greatest challenges of the writing process is to do justice – and express the extent of my gratitude – to the people whose valuable time, help, advice, knowledge, insight, goodwill, support, and encouragement made the book possible. Whatever is credible in *7 Days* is due to them. The leaps of fiction and errors are my own. I would like to express my deepest appreciation of:

- Theo Winter of the institutional investment firm Sortino (and a BMW motorbike man), who explained to me and Benny the complex secrets of BEE transactions and contracts, pension funds, and the financial world in general with so much patience and trouble, and, in addition, helped to identify sources of conflict and potential mischief. And thereafter checked the manuscript to make sure we didn't make total fools of ourselves.
- Captain Elmarie Myburgh, criminal behaviour analyst of the SAPS Investigative Psychology Section. Once again she answered countless questions, made suggestions, shared knowledge and contacts, and helped to read the final manuscript under great pressure.
- Colonel Renier du Preez of the Directorate of Priority Crime Investigations, for the day that I could spend with the Cape Hawks. His and his team's professionalism, dedication, approachability, generosity, and patience made a strong impression on me, and left me with much greater

insight (and respect for their incredible work). Thank you also to Assistant Commissioner Angie Bhuda, Colonel Giep Joubert, and Colonel Johan Schnetler of the DPCI in Pretoria for their time and trouble.

- Gavin Smith of Villiersdorp, gunsmith and master craftsman of silencers.
- The hospitable friendship of Daniel Cathiard of Château Smith Haut Lafitte, and the estate's cooper, Jean-Luc Itey.
- My wife, Anita, who makes everything possible with her love, tolerance, support, and sacrifice.
- My editor, Dr Etienne Bloemhof, and agent, Isobel Dixon, for their immeasurable loyalty, wisdom and insight, and Hester Carstens for her input and eagle eyes.
- Colonel Patrick Jacobs of the Bothasig SAPS station, Peet van Biljon, John Serfontein, and Sunell Lotter.
- I am pleased to give credit to the following sources:
- *Investigating the Russian Mafia*, Joseph D. Serio, Carolina Academic Press, Durham, 2008
- *McMafia, Seriously Organised Crime*, Misha Glenny, Vintage Books, London, 2009
- *From Fear to Fraternity*, Patricia Rawlinson, Pluto Press, New York, 2010
- *Illicit*, Moisés Naím, William Heinemann, London, 2006
- *How sharp is sharp? Towards quantification of the sharpness and penetration ability of kitchen knives used in stabbings*, S.V. Hainsworth, R.J. Delaney, G.N. Rutty, *International Journal of Legal Medicine*, 2008
- *Forensic Pathology: Principles and Practice*, David Dolinak, Evan W. Matshes, Emma O. Lew, Academic Press, 2005
- *Silencer 101*, Cameron Hopkins, *Guns Magazine*, July 2000
- *Media 24's chronological newspaper archives of Die Burger, Beeld, Volksblad, Mail & Guardian*
- www.Fin24.com

- www.sake24.com
- www.saps.gov.za
- www.marketwatch.com
- www.beretta.com
- www.defenceweb.co.za
- www.islamfortoday.com
- chemistry.about.com
- www.authorstream.com
- www.detectpoint.com
- www.cellucity.co.za
- www.sako.fi
- www.sakosuomi.fi
- www.wikipedia.org
- www.ableammo.com
- www.science.howstuffworks.com
- www.chana-sa.co.za
- www.allexperts.com
- www.cienciaforense.com
- www.library.med.utah.edu
- www.myarmoury.com
- www.enotes.com/forensic-science/hair-analysis
- www.arkivmusic.com
- www.old-smithy/bayoncts/ak47_and_related_bayonets.htm
- www.pamgolding.com
- www.deonmeyer.com/afrikaans/indeks.html

Glossary

Afslaer: Afrikaans for 'auctioneer'.

Ag: Very similar to 'ai': ah!, oh!; alas, pooh!, mostly used with resignation.

Ai: Ah, oh; ow, ouch, mostly used a little despairingly.

Amandla: A rallying cry in the days of resistance against Apartheid, used by the African National Congress and its allies. It is a Xhosa and Zulu word meaning 'power'. (Also see 'Ngawethu' below.)

Anton L'Amour: A legendary rock guitar virtuoso in South Africa.

Assegai: Originally from Berber za ya 'spear', Old French 'azagaie' and Spanish 'azagaya') is a pole weapon used for throwing or hurling, usually a light spear or javelin made of wood and pointed with iron. (Source: http://en.wikipedia.org)

Befok: Afrikaans expletive with wide application. Can mean 'very angry' (He is befok) or 'really great' (The experience was befok.)

Bergie: Cape Flats Afrikaans for a homeless person, often a vagrant, living on the side of Table Mountain (berg = mountain). (Cape Flats slang refers to the Afrikaans spoken on the Cape Flats, a vast area east of Cape Town, where the majority of 'Cape Coloured' people reside. 'Coloured people' refer to the descendants of Malaysian slaves in South Africa (forced migration by the Dutch East India Company), who intermarried with white farmers and local Khoi people – as opposed to Blacks (descendants of the Bantu people) and Whites (descendants of European settlers).

Bliksem: Mild profanity, used as an exclamation or adjective ('Damn!' or 'damned'), a verb (I will 'bliksem' you = I will hit you hard).

Blikslater: Milder form of 'bliksem' (see above).

Chana van: Chana is a Chinese automotive company. Various vehicles are imported to South Africa, including the 'Chana Panel Van', a light delivery vehicle (http://www. chanab4.co.za/models/panel-van)

Coloured: See 'bergie' above.

Cooldrink: South African English, referring to most fizzy drinks.

CATS: The 'Crimes Against the State' group, a subdivision of the DPCI – the Directorate for Priority Crime Investigations of the South African Police Service.

Dagga: Afrikaans word for Cannabis (marijuana).

Daais 'n anderstorie: Afrikaans for 'that's another story'.

Darem: Afrikaans for 'at least'.

DPCI: The Directorate for Priority Crime Investigations of the South African Police Service, popularly known as 'The Hawks'.

Eish: Originally from Xhosa, now widely used as an expression of exasperation or disbelief.

Ewe: Originally from Xhosa and other Nguni languages in South Africa, now widely used as an expression of agreement.

Fok, Fokken, Fokkol: 'fuck', 'fucking', and 'fuck all'. (Afrikaans.)

Fokkof: 'fuck off'. (Afrikaans.)

Fokkofpoliesiekar: Name of a former popular Afrikaans rock group. Literal translation: 'Fuck off, police car'. (Afrikaans.)

Grote Griet: 'Good Grief!' (Afrikaans.)

Hayi: IsiZulu for 'No!'

Hendrik Verwoerd: Dutch born Hendrik Frensch Verwoerd (8 September 1901 – 6 September 1966), Prime Minister of South Africa from 1958 until his assassination in 1966. He is (not fondly) remembered as the 'architect of Apartheid'.

Icilikishe: 'Lizard' (Xhosa.)

IMC: Information Management Centre, the technology support group of the Directorate for Priority Crime Investigations of the South African Police Service.

Ja: 'Yes'. (Afrikaans, widely used.)

Jirre: 'God'. (Exclamation, Cape Flats Afrikaans.)

Jis: 'Yes', mostly used in greeting. (Afrikaans, Cape Flats Afrikaans, widely used.)

Jissie: Mild Afrikaans expletive, similar to English 'jeez'.

Jissis: 'Jesus'. (Afrikaans expletive.)

JOC: Joint Operational Centre – group heads and detectives of the various Directorate for Priority Crime Investigations units, organised under one operational leader to investigate a case.

Jukskei: A sport unique to South Africa. Jukskei is believed to have originated around 1743 in the Cape, South Africa, developed by 'transport riders' who travelled with ox-drawn wagons. They used the wooden pins of the yokes (Afrikaans: Skei) of the oxen to throw at a stick that was planted into the ground. (Source: http://en.wikipedia.org/wiki/Jukskei)

Julle: 'You guys', plural form of 'you' (Afrikaans.)

Kak: 'Shit'. (Afrikaans, but used by all 11 official South African languages.)

Klippies: 'Small stones' (Afrikaans), often used to refer to diamonds.

Kouevuur: 'Cold fire', the title of an achingly beautiful

Afrikaans song composed by the late Koos du Plessis, reinterpreted by singer/songwriter Theuns Jordaan recently.

Laaitie: Afrikaans slang, used to refer to a boy, or a son. Sometimes used as 'lighty'. ('He is still a laaitie' – he is still a boy. 'He's my laaitie' – he is my son.)

Lekker: Very versatile Afrikaans word (but widely used in South Africa) meaning luscious, or tasty. Often used in reference to good food, but also any pleasurable experience.

Liewe Vader: 'Dear Father', a milder form of 'Dear God'.

Lize Beekman: South African (Afrikaans) singer/songwriter: http://lizebeekman.co.za or watch on YouTube: http://www.youtube.com/watch?v=Yer2pGae-rA

Lobolo: (Or Lobola, a Zulu, Xhosa and Ndebele word, sometimes translated as bride price.) A traditional Southern African custom whereby the man pays the family of his fiancée for her hand in marriage. The custom is aimed at bringing the two families together, fostering mutual respect, and indicating that the man is capable of supporting his wife financially and emotionally. (Source: http://en.wikipedia.org/wiki/Lobolo)

Madiba: The nickname of Mr Nelson Mandela, derived from his Xhosa clan name.

Manne: 'Guys'. (Afrikaans.)

Mannetjie: Diminutive of 'guy'. (Afrikaans.)

Maties: Refers to the University of Stellenbosch, students of this institution, or its rugby team. ('I study at Maties' or 'My son is a Matie' or 'The Shimlas beat the Maties in a rugby match'.)

Mies: 'Ma'am' or 'madam', a relic of apartheid, when black and coloured people were expected to call their female white employers by this 'respectful' title. Now strongly discouraged, but still in use.

Moered: 'Moer' is a wonderful, mildly vulgar Afrikaans expletive, and could be used in any conceivable way. Its origins lie in the Dutch word 'Moeder', meaning 'Mother'. 'Moer in' means 'to be very angry', but you can also 'moer someone' (hit somebody: 'I moered him'), use it as an angry exclamation ('Moer!', which approximates 'Damn!'), call something or someone 'moerse' (approximates 'great' or 'cool'), or use it as an adjective: I have a 'moerse' headache – I have a huge headache.

Moffie: Derogative term referring to a gay man. Similar to 'faggot'.

Molo: 'Hello!' Xhosa greeting to one person. ('Molweni!' to more than one person.)

Ngawethu: 'To us', Xhosa word, widely used in response to the rallying cry 'Amandla' (see above). (Amandla! (Power!). Ngawthu! (To us!))

Nooit: 'Never!' (Afrikaans.)

Nè: 'Yes.' (Afrikaans.)

Njaps: Cape flats Afrikaans slang for 'having sex', similar to 'bonk'

Oke: 'Guy'. (South African English.)

Oom: Respectful Afrikaans form of address to a male ten or more years older than yourself. Means 'uncle'.

Ou: 'Old'. (Afrikaans.)

Outjies: Diminutive form of 'guys'.

Parow: Northern, middle class suburb of Cape Town. (Also the surname of 'Jack Parow', the stage name of Afrikaans rapper Zander Tyler (born in 1982 in Bellville, adjacent suburb).)

Rag: Originally, a student-run charitable fundraising organisation at most South African (and UK) universities, the word has come to represent the colourful annual student festival held to raise funds.

Rand: (R) The South African currency. The value is more or less $8 or €10 or £12.

PCSI: The Provincial Crime Scene Investigation unit, an elite forensic science team of the South African Police Service.

RICA: The Regulation of Interception of Communication Act is a recent South African government law, making it compulsory for all citizens to register all new and existing mobile phone numbers.

SARS: The South African Revenue Service – the tax authority.

Seunie: 'Sonny'. (Afrikaans.)

Shici: 'Nothing'. (Xhosa.)

Theuns Jordaan: Popular Afrikaans singer/songwriter, and actor. (www.theunsjordaan.co.za) or watch on YouTube: http://www.youtube.com/watch?v=R_vurV79pHk

TOMS: The Tactical Operational Management Service, a subdivision of the DPCI – the Directorate for Priority Crime Investigations of the South African Police Service.

Uithaal en wys: 'Deliver the goods', an Afrikaans expression.

Ukuphupha: 'Dream'. (Xhosa.)

Unjani: 'How are you?' (Xhosa.)

Uxolo: 'Sorry!' (Xhosa.)

Uyesu: 'Jesus!' (Xhosa.)

Vrot: 'Rotten'. (Afrikaans.)

Yebo: 'Yes!' South African slang, widely used by all language groups.

TRACKERS

Shortlisted for the CWA International Dagger for
the best translated crime fiction novel of 2011

Out now in Hodder paperback
and also available as an eBook

'How fulfilling the rewards are for those seeking
crime fiction with real texture and intelligence
. . . His key achievement is the astutely drawn trio:
the conflicted bodyguard, streetwise but falling
for a major deception; the young woman fleeing
a desperately unhappy marriage and discovering
something that changes her perception of herself;
and the ex-cop, finding that the incendiary
reserves of violence in his personality are nearer
to the surface than he thought. TRACKERS
is **a sprawling, invigorating and socially
committed crime novel**.'
Independent

HODDER

THIRTEEN HOURS

Shortlisted for the CWA International Dagger for
the best translated crime fiction novel of 2010

Out now in Hodder paperback
and also available as an eBook

'What makes this novel so **outstanding** is its
setting and Meyer's superlative talent for suspense
...This is **a vigorous, exciting novel** that
combines memorable characters and plot with
edge-of-the-seat suspense.'
The Sunday Times

HODDER

Award-winning crime fiction with South African soul

Deon Meyer pulls the reader into the 'melée of modern South Africa' and 'captures the criminal kaleidoscope of a nation'
The Times Literary Supplement

Don't miss Deon Meyer's earlier novels
out now in Hodder paperback
and also available as eBooks

HODDER

In the best books, the ending often comes as a shock.
Not just because of that one last twist in the tale,
but because you have been so absorbed in their world,
that coming back to the harsh light of reality is a jolt.

If that describes you now, then perhaps you should track down
some new leads, and find new suspense in other worlds.

Join us at www.hodder.co.uk, or follow us on
Twitter @hodderbooks, and you can tap in to a
community of fellow thrill-seekers.

Whether you want to find out more about this book,
or a particular author, watch trailers and interviews, have
the chance to win early limited editions, or simply browse
our expert readers' selection of the very best books,
we think you'll find what you're looking for.

And if you don't, that's the place to tell us what's missing.

We love what we do, and we'd love you to be part of it.

www.hodder.co.uk

@hodderbooks

HodderBooks

HodderBooks